SHADOWS OF THE PAST

MAGGIE COBBETT

Published by GuyRichardson

Dedicated to the memory of my

old friend Jean-Claude Quehan

Acknowledgements

Thanks are due to Jerry Anderson, Linda Bradshaw, Nick David, Sarah Dixon, Carol Mayer and John Walford for their editorial input and especially to my son, Richard Cobbett, without whose help this project would never have come to fruition.

"She'd never seen anyone killed before. However well deserved, it was butchery. He caught her eye as he went down and the last thing she saw was the glint of the blade as the axe was raised again..."

Prologue

1937

Seventeen year old Thérèse Gaudet née Morcel, shivering a little in her flimsy nightgown, leaned out of the landing window to gaze up the road that led out of the village towards Paris. The smell of beeswax from the dark wooden floorboards polished by generations of Gaudet women was irritating her nostrils. Might the addition of a little lavender oil improve it? No. That would remind her of Sunday Mass and make it even harder for her to relax in the high old fashioned bed only recently vacated by Luc's waspish old widowed mother. The flowers on her grave had scarcely had time to fade before he set about finding a bride. Thérèse blushed at the thought of Madame Joubier, the village laundress and a friend of her late mother-in-law, thumbing through the sheets and telling everyone that the marriage seemed to be going well. There was something to be said for doing your own washing, even if it did leave your hands sore and cracked, but taking care of her new home and helping Luc to run the café left no time for that.

Only time would tell if marrying him had been the right thing to do. Her mother, once just as blonde and pretty, had drummed into her time and time again that being the belle of the village had its drawbacks. Madame Morcel had been obliged at fifteen to make a hasty marriage to the gardener's boy from the château and was terrified that her eldest daughter might fall into the same trap.

"Would you rather I became a nun than had a boyfriend?" Thérèse had raged, until the look on her mother's face convinced her not to pursue the subject. Taking the veil might indeed have its attractions for a woman struggling to feed and clothe the six sons and daughters she already had and haunted by the fear of doubling their number before her childbearing years were over. Contraception was, of course, an invention of the Devil; abstinence not a subject to be broached with a husband still, in his own opinion at least, in the full flower of his manhood. He had been delighted when approached by his daughter's suitor, saw no problem with the age gap and even guffawed that experience was a good thing in a bridegroom. Luc, eager to claim the rights bestowed on him by church and state, had certainly shown no lack of confidence on their wedding night. Although he had been both patient and gentle, Thérèse had bled onto the crisp new bed linen, a fact relayed to her credit on the local grapevine.

Her thoughts turned once again to the boy she might have married. The sky was beginning to lighten now and she could just about make out the roof of the forge in the distance. Soon Alain Binard would be loading coal into its hearth and lighting the fire ready for his father to heat iron into the incandescent red, orange, yellow and white needed for their different tasks. Shy with girls, Alain had only ever been on the fringe of her admirers. Well, it was too late now and her parents were not sorry. Blacksmithing was a trade in decline and the garage the Binard family ran on the side had yet to prove itself. The Gaudets' café, now called *Chez Luc*, offered a much more certain future for Thérèse and also solved the problem of what to do with the runt of their litter. How she hated that phrase, common though it was amongst the rural community!

Had the thought of her unfortunate brother conjured up the figure limping down the road towards her? No, that was impossible. Valentin was fast asleep in Luc's old bedroom, surrounded by his favourite books and unlikely to stir until she woke him up to start the day's chores.

Shaking herself, Thérèse closed the window and clambered back into bed. Luc grunted sleepily and rolled over towards her. The dawn chorus was striking up as she snuggled up to him and placed her icy feet against his warm ones. Marriage did offer some compensations and, whoever the stranger making his painful way into the village might be, he was no concern of hers.

Part One

1987

Chapter 1

The day that her decree absolute came through, Laura Fitzgerald bought herself a second hand Triumph Spitfire. It was bright red and caused quite a stir when she parked it next to more sedate vehicles outside Tamara's salon, recently renamed *Fringe Benefits*. Having her hair done was always a treat and relaxed her no matter what mood she was in.

Leaning over the backwash and closing her eyes, she said, "It wasn't just the price or the colour I fell for, you know. The folding hood's permanently attached."

Tamara smiled at her enthusiasm. It made a pleasant change from the air of gloom that her favourite client had worn over the last year. "Aren't they always?"

"No. When we first got together, my husband – sorry, ex-husband – had one with a kind of DIY arrangement."

"However did that work?"

"Oh, sticks that slotted in and a canvas cover. Of course," she added wryly, "when you're in love you don't care about cold water trickling down the back of your neck."

"No, I suppose not."

"The salesman tried to convince me to buy a later and more expensive model with a hard top, but it didn't appeal half as much to my spirit of adventure."

"Good for you!"

"Thank you. If hitting the road in style is good enough for my ex, then it's good enough for me. He's up in Scotland with his girlfriend and some of their born again biker friends, celebrating his sixtieth birthday and our divorce. Would you believe that he's put the dogs into kennels, after all the promises he made when I agreed to let him have them both?" Laura couldn't help a note of bitterness creeping into her voice.

Tamara, sensitive as always to the moods of her clients, said, "Sit up now, Mrs Fitzgerald, and we'll get you dried off. That car will certainly turn a few heads. Just pop on a scarf and some big sunglasses and you'll look like a film star. Where are you planning to go?"

"France, to begin with."

"*Vous parlez français?*"

"*Mais oui.*"

In truth, Laura hadn't been at all sure where to go, but one Monday morning a few weeks later she found herself enjoying a leisurely breakfast in Giverny. The croissants were fresh, the coffee was milky and the sun was shining. What more was there to wish for on such a beautiful morning? Well, apart from a couple of soft pillows on the next bed she slept in rather than the unforgiving bolster favoured by the French.

She chuckled as she remembered the young second hand car salesman's initial reaction to her choice. She hadn't told Tamara the half of it. His well practised sales patter had plainly been at war with his reservations about a Spitfire's suitability for a lady of her mature years and yet she'd driven it safely all the way from York to northern France without adding a single scratch to its shiny bodywork.

The feeling of accomplishment and a good night's sleep, despite the hardness of the bolster, had combined to make Laura feel much more positive about her future than she had for a very long time. The greater part of the summer stretched out in front of her and the divorce settlement had left her without any immediate money worries. She wasn't just going to drive around aimlessly either. As she bit into another croissant, her thoughts turned to the Gustave Caillebotte print that had inspired her choice of itinerary.

She might so easily have missed *Fruit displayed on a stand* at the auction, included as it was in a mixed lot of bric-a-brac, but a shaft of light from one of the high windows of the dingy old chapel had caught its glowing colours just in time. Food, she knew, was a favourite subject for many of the Impressionists and she had no doubt that they enjoyed eating it as much as committing it to canvas. Putting the other items aside for the Oxfam shop, she'd hung the print over her dining table as a talisman. Surrounded by maps, guidebooks and biographies, she'd smiled up at it frequently while planning her route. French art and French cuisine! What better combination could there be for a newly single woman with a keen interest in both?

Having chosen a little hotel within easy walking distance of her first objective, Laura was at the front of the queue to visit Claude Monet's beautifully restored house and garden. That man certainly loved colour! Pink walls and green shutters were only a start. The bright blue and white tiles of the kitchen shone in the sunshine pouring in from the garden and as for the yellow dining room... She could not restrain herself.

"The Monets must all have been dazzled!" she exclaimed. "I couldn't sit down to eat in here without my sun glasses."

The guide frowned at the interruption and continued stiffly, "Take a look at the beautifully laid table, ladies and gentlemen. The family always ate well, basing their cooking on what they could grow themselves or obtain from the nearby farms. They also copied dishes created by some of the great restaurants they'd been to and used recipes given to them by friends. They got *bouillabaisse* from Paul Cézanne, for example."

"Fish stew," muttered Laura, scribbling the details into her new notebook. Easier to write quickly, it sounded far less appetising in English.

"Another recipe, they got from the Tatin sisters themselves. Did you know that *Tarte Tatin* was invented by accident? The story goes that one of the sisters was cooking some apples in butter and sugar but left them too long in the pan. As an experiment, she put a pastry base on top of the fruit and baked the whole thing in the oven. When it was turned over, the guests all loved it and it became the signature dish of the Hôtel Tatin."

The guided tour allowed Laura sufficient time to soothe her eyes in the cool greens of the kitchen garden and by the lily pond before moving on to her next goal. It was a real pleasure to drive with the soft top down and follow the meanderings of the Seine through the verdant plateau of the Vexin. The pale blue of the sky was broken only by a few tiny white clouds and the poplars lining the road shimmered in true picture book style. Someone to share it with would have been a bonus, but why dwell on that?

The next stop on her route was Auvers-sur-Oise, the village where Vincent van Gogh had spent the last few weeks of his life. Laura particularly wanted to visit the artist's old lodgings and the little Gothic church that his painting had made famous all over the world. Although hungry by the time she arrived at the Auberge Ravoux and very tempted by the delicious smells coming out of the kitchen, she paid the small sum required and made her way straight upstairs. Lit only by a skylight and with bare walls and floorboards, the little attic where the tragic Dutchman had survived a mere two days after shooting himself looked comfortless indeed. What bitter irony, she thought sadly, that someone whose paintings now changed hands for millions of pounds should have died convinced of his failure both as an artist and as a man. In a place so charged with memories and emotions it seemed almost disrespectful to think of food, but her stomach had started to growl and she succumbed to the temptations of a rustic terrine followed by chocolate mousse. So far, so good!

Leaving behind the cheerful crowd in the dining room, she walked past the church and up the hill to visit the cemetery where Vincent and his younger brother Theo lay side by side at the back. Their headstones were disappointingly plain and only ivy covered their graves. Bearing in mind a letter to their sister in which Vincent had written, 'The uglier, older, meaner, iller, poorer I get, the more I wish to take my revenge by doing brilliant colour, well arranged,' this seemed all wrong to Laura and she almost ran back down into the village to buy a suitable tribute. Before she left Auvers-sur-Oise, a jaunty bunch of sunflowers in a jug of water stood between the brothers' resting places. She could do no more.

Four miles down the road in Pontoise, the Camille Pissarro Museum had already closed by the time she arrived and Laura wasn't really sorry. She'd phoned ahead to book a room in Louveciennes, reckoned by some to be the birthplace of Impressionism, and was looking forward to a hot meal, bath and an early night. It wasn't far and there was more than enough petrol in the tank to get her there. The sun had gone in and she was sure that she'd heard a rumble of thunder in the distance.

Black clouds had completely taken over the sky by the time Margot Binard returned to her cosy kitchen and made herself a cup of tea. The break in the weather hadn't been unexpected. She smiled as she patted Mac's silky head and replayed the events of the day in her own.

The morning had been a sunny one and she'd bustled around as usual, happily aware that two hungry men, drawn in by the heady perfume of baking, were watching her every move. Little Mac, already fed, was snoozing in his basket under the table.

"Breakfast won't be long," she'd called over her shoulder, stooping to take a tray of rolls out of the brightly polished oven.

"No hurry, sweetheart. Here, let me help. Ouch!"

"Jean-Claude! How many times have I told you to use a cloth? Here, put your hand under the cold tap."

He turned round to nuzzle her cheek, laughing at her mock reaction to his early morning bristles. "Well, if you were only warming them up …"

"Warming them up! The very idea! These are freshly made, my love."

"And you've got the burnt fingers to prove it, lad," chuckled Alain as they all settled down to breakfast. "Any of your wild strawberry jam left, Margot?"

"Oh yes. I know it's your favourite, so I made plenty."

Was it her imagination, or did a shadow really fall across the kitchen when her husband said, "I'm afraid that I've got to drive into Paris for some parts later on. Would you like me to get you anything while I'm there?"

"No. Not today."

"Don't look so doubtful, darling. I'd get it right this time. No more oily finger marks on your list, I promise."

"I should hope not! Have you any idea how long it takes to get through five *kilos* of hundreds and thousands?"

There was a loud snort from across the table as Alain reached for another roll. "It wouldn't have taken very long when he was young, Margot. He used to dog the footsteps of his grandmother and the aunts, as though I never fed him at home, and they always fell for it!"

"Well, I know you did your best, old man, but it wasn't the same."

"What did you expect? I was born to be a blacksmith, not a cook! Left on my own like that and with you to bring up!"

Strong emotions were always near the surface with Alain and Margot hastened to refill his cup. "You did a great job, Papa. That's why there's never been anyone else for me but Jean-Claude. Not since..." Her voice trailed off as the shadows beckoned. Shaking herself, she poured out more tea, aware of her father-in-law's disapproving gaze.

"I don't know how you can drink that stuff in the morning."

They were on safer ground now and Margot rallied. "To each his own, I suppose. Now then, Papa, will you be in for lunch? Or are you going to the café to see what's on the menu today?"

"To see his girlfriend, you mean," teased Jean-Claude.

"Don't start that again! You know perfectly well that there's never been anything like that between Thérèse and me."

"I know that she's always had a *tendresse* for you."

Alain flushed. "Well, that's as may be, but she missed her chance when she married Luc Gaudet." Turning to Margot, he said, "As you're going to be on your own, my dear, I'll come in and have lunch with you. Make as much as you usually do and I'll have Jean-Claude's share as well as my own."

"One of these days you'll explode!" laughed his son. "Now, Papa, I want you to promise me that you'll redirect anyone who rings up for the breakdown service."

"You think I'm really over the hill, don't you!"

"And halfway down the other side. See you later."

Margot followed her husband outside and threw her arms around him. Cold beads of sweat were breaking out on her forehead and he frowned as he bent to kiss her goodbye.

"Same old dream? I thought so. Well, I'll be as quick as I can. You know I hate leaving you. Keep an eye on Papa and don't let him do anything silly. He still thinks he's a teenager, you know."

She bit her bottom lip to stop it trembling and tried to put on a brave smile. "I'll try, but please hurry back. I only feel truly safe when you're near me."

"I know." Pausing to glance up at the sky, he added, "Why don't you and Papa treat Mac to a walk in the forest this afternoon while the weather holds? Take your basket along and do some foraging. There's a storm forecast for later on, but you should be all right for the next few hours."

"I might just do that, but don't be long. I'll be counting the minutes."

Keeping herself busy would be the only way to combat the spectres that hovered still on the edge of her consciousness.

Chapter 2

Darkness was already falling when a mud spattered Triumph Spitfire splashed slowly through deep puddles into the main square of Saint-André-la-Forêt. The rain had stopped at last, but the only witness to the car's arrival was a gaunt figure silhouetted in the doorway of a brightly lit café. Her eyes narrowed to a cold stare as the car came to a halt beside her and Laura wound down the window.

"*Pardon, Madame. Une station-service, s'il vous plait?*" She was completely floored when the woman not only gave a contemptuous shrug but went back inside and slammed the door behind her. Laura could only marvel that the frosted glass panel bearing the café's name hadn't cracked. She'd phrased her enquiry politely enough, hadn't she, so what was the problem? Surely it wasn't the sight of her car's GB plates? Would someone else in *Chez Thérèse* be prepared to help her or would they all feel the same? Laura hadn't met such a hostile reaction since her suggestion during a school exchange to Rouen that the French themselves had been partly responsible for the burning of Joan of Arc.

Disconcerted, she sagged back into her seat. It was getting very late and the café seemed to be the only place still open. Why did the whole of France have to go on holiday at the same time? How on earth did local people, let alone visitors, manage to buy what they needed to survive August? If the owners of all the closed petrol stations she'd passed during the last couple of hours died of sunstroke in Berck-sur-Mer or the Riviera, it would be no more than they deserved!

Laura had got herself hopelessly lost shortly after reaching the outskirts of Saint-Germain-en-Laye. Being caught with the hood down when the sky turned black was bad enough, but peering through wipers defeated by the torrents of water hitting the windscreen only to flow horizontally along the side windows was worse. It was no wonder that she'd missed the turn off for Le Port Marly and found herself faced with a maze of roads too minor to be worthy of the name. Reaching a service station on the A13 was her last hope, but it would be touch and go whether she made it before her tank ran dry.

Nervous for the first time since leaving home, she fumbled in the darkness for a torch and tried to make some sense out of the map that she'd brought with her from England. No good! The scale wasn't up to showing every village in the back of beyond. Tired and hungry, Laura ruled out staying put until daylight. A more practical choice of car might have given her the option of curling up on the back seat for a few hours, but sleep was very unlikely in the cramped and now thoroughly damp conditions inside the Spitfire. The only other option was to set off again and hope for the best. Nothing could be gained by retracing her route, so she'd have to take pot luck and drive as slowly as she could to conserve fuel.

Just after she passed the barred sign at the edge of the village, the storm renewed its onslaught. The rain was coming down harder than ever and only the occasional flash of lightning revealed a forest on one side of the road and dark fields on the other. To make matters even worse, the windscreen was starting to steam up. Disaster struck when she leaned forward to wipe it. A large vehicle with headlights blazing loomed up on her right and forced her to slam on the brakes.

The accident victim, wrapped in an old tartan rug stained with oil, was drifting in and out of consciousness when strong arms carried her through the back door of the café and into the kitchen. Startled, Valentin wiped his hands on his apron and hobbled across to help.

"Don't worry, I can manage," said the other man. "The poor lady doesn't weigh much, but I need somewhere to lay her down."

"You'd better take her up the back stairs to my sister's room. It's first on the right. I'll let her know." Leaving a trail of muddy footprints behind him, the man obeyed.

The scowl on Thérèse's face when she came down some time later to relieve Valentin at the bar didn't bode well, but she had customers to serve and waved him back into the kitchen. A lifetime's experience had taught him that she'd say nothing until she was ready, so he sighed and got out a mop.

He was collecting the ash trays from the tables and piling them up on the bar ready for washing when Thérèse slid home the bolts on the door leading onto the square and turned to him, hands on hips.

"Alain won't get away with this. Now we've got another fine mess to clear up. If only I could just..."

Valentin was alarmed by the wild look in her eyes, one that he knew only too well. "Don't even think about it. For heaven's sake! Those days are well and truly over."

"Are they really, little brother? Are you sure?"

"Of course I am. You'd have to be quite mad to think otherwise."

"Well, maybe I am. After all I suffered, could you blame me? But I'm not as touched as..."

"Won't you calm down, both of you! How about one of your camomile tisanes, Madame Thérèse? You look as though you could do with one, although you'd be better off with a proper drink for once."

"You're still here, Charlot?"

Of course he was, thought Valentin. After his latest divorce, Charlot was back at his mother's and in no hurry to leave. Better just resign themselves to his nightly presence at the bar after all the other customers had gone home.

"I suppose that you'll take a glass? Cognac?"

"Of course. A large one." Charlot frowned as he shifted the cigarette to the other side of his mouth. "I've heard that the old fool was just the same as a boy. Blasting through the village in a cloud of dust and scattering all the chickens."

"Less of the 'old fool', if you don't mind!" snapped Thérèse. "He *was* like that, of course. There's no denying it. But at least he could see where he was going in those days."

"I know. My mother's had a go at him about it, but what can she do if even his own son can't convince him that he needs glasses? Where is Jean-Claude, by the way?"

"Oh, he slipped out again after he'd dumped the Englishwoman onto my bed and asked me to get her into some dry clothes before she caught her death. She was a dead weight and it was very awkward. I could have done with a hand to undress her, but you know what he's like. He went crimson when I suggested it, as if he hadn't been a married man for more than twenty years, and said that he had to get straight back to Margot."

Charlot smirked. "You should have called on the expert. I'd have been glad to help."

"I'll just bet you would!"

"And where are he and Alain now?"

"Stuffing their faces, I expect. Whatever their precious Margot was keeping warm for them, they'd both eat the pattern off the plate. I can't for the life of me think why. It's not as though she can really cook, is it? Do you remember that weird dessert she made the last time I allowed myself to be persuaded to eat round there? Call that a *tarte aux pommes*? There was more crust than apple, no proper layers, no glaze..."

"Oh don't start that again, sister! Just be thankful that her recipes are the only things that she remembers from before. God help us all if the rest ever came back to her!"

"Well I wish that she'd forgotten the recipes as well."

The tin ashtrays rattled as Charlot banged his fist on the bar. "We'd all be better off if she and her bloody friends had never come here, but let's stick to the point, shall we? For once, Margot's not the problem. Even if this other woman's lost her memory too, she'll get it back fast enough when she sees the damage to her car. How bad is it?"

"Apparently it's going to need a lot of work. If she'd skidded into the trees instead of a field, it would have been a complete write off and so would she, which would have made things a lot easier to handle.

Whoever she is, she's going to make a devil of a fuss about it when she comes round. The first thing she'll insist on is calling the police."

Charlot steepled his fingers and thought for a moment. "Not if we can frighten her into believing that it was her own fault."

"What do you mean?"

"Easy. Tell her that she ignored my poor uncle's right of way. Or, even better, say that several witnesses will swear that she was driving too fast for the weather conditions and he didn't stand a chance."

"What witnesses?" asked Valentin. "There wasn't a soul around when it happened." The others rounded on him.

"Oh, for heaven's sake!"

"You've always been too honest for your own good! Go on, Charlot. You seem to have it all worked out."

"Well, we can say that the driver of the other vehicle is in a critical condition in hospital. Not expected to live, maybe. She won't want to hang around here and risk being locked up."

"But what if we can't make her understand?" objected Thérèse. "We can't put Alain through a police investigation. Not after all he's been through. God, I hate Englishwomen! They've never brought us anything but trouble in the end."

"This one spoke to you in French, didn't she?" asked Valentin.

"Only a few words. I expect she got them from a phrase book she bought on the ferry."

"Well, if you'd been more helpful we wouldn't be in this situation. One of us could have got her a can of petrol and she'd have been well away from here by now."

Thérèse set her cup down with a thud and glared at him. "Do you think I don't realise that? She caught me off guard and I just wanted to see the back of her."

"Don't worry about it," said Charlot, holding out his glass for a refill. "The less French she speaks, the easier it should be to pull the wool over her eyes."

"I wouldn't be so sure of that, Monsieur!" Clutching the banister with both hands, Laura Fitzgerald was making her way down the polished wooden stairs into the café.

Chapter 3

Coming round in a high double bed in a strange room hadn't been too much of a shock at first, even though Laura had no idea of its location. Touring could be like that, she mused, not really caring. What was the name of that film about travellers racing through seven European countries in eighteen days? *If it's Tuesday, this must be Belgium*, wasn't it? In the soft glow of the bedside lamp, the heavy oak furniture and dark yellow wallpaper with its rash of tiny roses failed to provide any clues. Remaining awake only long enough to thump the hard bolster, she drifted off again, a kaleidoscope of images from the last few days whirling round and round in her dreams; the choppy grey waters of the English Channel, the bustling ferry port of Le Havre, the Japanese bridge in Monet's garden, bright yellow sunflowers and dull grey headstones... Drowsy and confused, she had a vague feeling that something was wrong but drifted off again.

The next time she woke, it was with a start and she sat bolt upright. Her situation really did matter to her now. Where on earth was she and what had happened to her own clothes? The nightwear she'd packed for the journey was of a kind to raise no eyebrows if the fire alarm went off in the early hours, so whose was this fine lawn creation? Trimmed with lace and ribbons, it could have come straight out of a young bride's trousseau.

Pain was radiating out of a cut on her forehead and an egg sized swelling above her nose, although the nose itself didn't seem to be broken. If it had been, she reasoned, there would have been lots of blood and her nostrils weren't even sticky. Further reassurance was to hand when she found that her shoulder bag, its contents seemingly intact, had been placed on the chair by the bed. She hadn't been mugged, then.

All the same, Laura's head swam as she kicked her legs free of the warm covers, stood for a few seconds on the bedside rug and then tottered across bare floorboards to the door. Was she locked in? No. The handle was stiff, but it only took a hard tug for her to be out of the room and into a dimly lit corridor. Two other doors led off it and a narrow strip of carpet linked the half landings at each end. The one to her left was in darkness. The other owed its light to whatever was below. From the same source came the sound of a heated dispute and the pungent smell of dark tobacco. Well, at least it would appear that she was still in France! The hissing and spluttering of a coffee machine was making it hard to hear what the argument was about, so Laura crept closer to listen.

The sudden appearance of a stranger clad only in a flimsy nightdress had rendered two of the trio speechless and it was left to the grim looking woman to state the obvious.

"Madame speaks French."

"I get by."

The woman glared at her for a moment and then began to flick non-existent dust off the zinc top of the bar. Nothing could have been less relevant to Laura's plight, but she was struck by the contrast between the pale blue eyes, now lowered, and the lashes clumped with black mascara. The heavily pencilled brows peeping out from beneath a thick black fringe were equally dark and the whole look might have been designed to be as unflattering as possible.

Laura was wondering what to say next when a friendlier voice invited her to take a seat. It belonged to a foxy-faced man with thinning hair faded to a dull red. He was feasting his eyes on Laura's unfettered breasts, all too obvious through her skimpy attire. The cool breeze blowing across from an open window was adding to his enjoyment as much as it was giving her goose pimples.

"No thank you. I prefer to stand." Scrambling up onto a bar stool would only expose more flesh for him to leer at. Feeling very vulnerable,

Laura wondered how to convince these people that ganging up on her wasn't going to work.

"How about some coffee then? Or tea? Isn't that what English people generally prefer? And something to eat, perhaps?" The other man, his black waistcoat and long apron tying him to the café, was taking down one of the neatly stacked chairs from a nearby table. "Please, do come and sit down, Madame." Unlike Foxy, he was studying Laura's face. His own was full of anxiety, although she had no means of telling whether that was for her or for the man they all seemed determined to protect. Either way, feeling herself starting to sway on her feet, she gave in.

"Thérèse, maybe you could close that window and find something extra for this lady to put on? It's getting quite cold in here." The black eyebrows shot up, but she nodded.

Slightly built with fine grey hair and a gentle voice, the waiter seemed the least intimidating of the three. Laura threw him a grateful look and he held out a thin hand for her to shake.

"My name is Valentin Morcel. Madame Gaudet here is my sister and this young man is Charles Legoux, but we call him Charlot. Like Chaplin, you know."

Young man? Foxy couldn't be far off forty, but that put him a generation behind the other two and not much less behind Laura herself. He raised his eyes at last to her face and grinned knowingly as she told them her name. They'd probably been through her documents, she thought, unless they assumed that every driver with GB plates must be English. That was quite possible, of course. In her experience, most French people did.

Introductions over and with a crocheted woollen shawl around her shoulders, Laura felt more in control. Raising her chin, she addressed them all in a tone that brooked no contradiction. "Now look here! I was driven off the road by someone you all know and I've got every intention of reporting the incident to the police. He could kill the next person he runs into. Just look at my face! I'm stiff and sore all over as well. Ouch!"

"You need some ice on that," said Charlot, withdrawing a stubby finger. "As for the rest, well, it doesn't sound too serious and there's certainly no need to involve the police. My cousin's a mechanic and he can fix anything. It may take a day or two, but you need to rest and he'll get your car back to you as soon as it's ready. You'll be staying here, of course."

"Here? I can't. I'm expected in Louveciennes and then..."

Her protests were interrupted by the arrival of a cup of hot water with a muslin tea bag dangling in it and a whole buttered baguette filled with thinly sliced ham.

"*Bon appétit, Madame,*" said Charlot, raising his glass to her and draining it. With a sigh, Thérèse topped it up again.

Eating in front of an audience wasn't something that Laura normally cared to do, but she was too hungry to refuse.

"Would you like something else?" asked Valentin, as she wiped the crumbs from her mouth. "Some cheese or a slice of apricot tart?"

"Don't be silly," snapped his sister. "Madame needs to go back to bed now that everything's settled."

Settled? Tired as she was, that was the last straw for Laura and she prepared to do battle. Getting her insurance company to pay for the Spitfire to be transported back to England for repair would annihilate her no claims bonus, but she was damned if she'd let a man used only to farm vehicles and tinny old 2CVs get his hands on it. "It may be settled in your mind, Madame, but it certainly isn't in mine! I'm expected in Louveciennes and I'd like to use your telephone to speak to the police. Now, if you please."

"That won't be possible," was the smooth reply. "The storm has brought down the telephone lines, you see. In any case you're in no fit state to do that. Young Dr Simmonet has promised to come round and take a look at you. Just as a precaution, you understand. After all, you did lose consciousness for quite a while."

"Did I?" Somewhere at the back of Laura's mind was a vague memory of being scooped out of her car and put to bed, but something must have happened in between. All she knew for certain was that she didn't want to stay with these people, particularly the woman. This sudden concern for her welfare was even more unsettling than her previous hostility. "Look, if it isn't possible to ring from here, I'll pay one of you to drive me to Louveciennes."

Charlot's eyebrows shot up as he looked her over again. "Dressed like that?"

"No, of course not. Please let me have my own clothes, Madame. I assume that you have them."

Thérèse folded her arms tightly across her chest and shook her head. "They're too wet to put on. The village laundry was already closed when you were brought here and I don't have an electric dryer, so I hung them up over the stove in the kitchen. You'll just have to wait, I'm afraid."

"Well, how about the things in my suitcase? They should be all right."

"Maybe, but your suitcase was left behind in your car and it's been taken to the garage. We couldn't get you to Louveciennes tonight anyway. It's not far, but my brother and I don't have any transport of our own."

"My foot doesn't really allow for driving, you see." Valentin raised his leg slightly and pointed at his built up shoe.

"And you've had too much to drink, haven't you, Charlot?"

"Definitely."

Eyes bright with anger and frustration, Laura had to accept that she would be going nowhere that night. Maybe it was just as well. Her head throbbed and she was bone weary. Determined to renew her demands as soon as it was daylight, she retreated upstairs.

Instead of the young doctor she'd expected, a man who looked well into his sixties if not older was ushered into the room and apologised for keeping her waiting. "You won't need any stitches in that cut," he said, "but I'd better give you a shot of penicillin just in case."

"Is that really necessary?" Laura hated injections.

"It's merely a precaution." Too weary to resist, she held out an arm for the needle. "You've certainly been shaken up, but it could have been a great deal worse, you know. What you need now is a nice long sleep. Madame Thérèse here will keep an eye on you through the night. To be on the safe side, you understand."

The Frenchwoman's face was a mask. "Oh yes, Doctor, you can be confident of that. My brother will be moving up to the attic, so I'll be just next door in his room. I'll hear if Madame stirs from her bed."

Did an odd look pass between them? Laura's eyelids were so heavy that she couldn't be sure. As they closed, she heard two sets of footsteps moving out into the corridor.

"It's all right. She's asleep now. So how long will these repairs take, do you think?"

"I wouldn't hold your breath. Jean-Claude may be good at what he does, but he can't perform miracles."

"Neither can I. That's Father Ferdinand's domain."

"And a fat lot of good he's been at times, I must say. If it hadn't been for his bending the rules, the wedding would never have taken place and..."

"Yes, yes, I know all that, but..."

The rest of their conversation was lost to Laura, who fell into a dreamless sleep.

Valentin could see that Jean-Claude was furious. It was bad enough that his father had defied all common sense and taken out the breakdown lorry on his own, nearly killing an innocent tourist, but even worse that the poor woman was being held a virtual prisoner only a few hundred yards from his home.

"Well what do you suggest, Mr High and Mighty?" asked Thérèse. "Do you want this stranger staying here while you repair her car? Writing about us all in her diary? And it wouldn't be just about my cooking either!"

"How do you know that she keeps a diary?" His eyes tightened at the corners. "Oh, I see."

"Naturally I went through her handbag. What else could I do? I found the number of the hotel she'd booked and phoned through to Louveciennes to say that she'd had a change of plan. She might still insist on going there as soon as she wakes up, though. We can't pretend for ever that the phone lines are down. Do you really want the police coming to your place and asking questions about the accident?"

"No, of course not. But it wouldn't be right to keep her knocked out any longer, whatever you've arranged with the good doctor. I remember when Margot... Well, never mind about that. This lady needs to be safely occupied in some way until I've finished the repairs and then she can be on her way without any harm done."

"You're too soft for your own good, lad, just like my brother. If you'd only let me..."

"No!" Jean-Claude's mouth was set in a stubborn line. "Let me talk to her. I've got an idea how she can be kept busy well away from here. My cousin can help."

"Victor? He'd be far too busy."

"Not Victor. Charlot. He's at a loose end at the moment."

"Charlot? Are you out of your mind? You know what he's like with women!"

"I'll tell him to keep his hands to himself or he'll have me to answer to. Under different circumstances, I'd have asked my father, but..."

"I hardly think so!"

Chapter 4

Laura awoke to the smell of coffee. Her limbs felt heavy, but she made her way to the window and opened the heavy shutters onto bright sunshine and a denim blue sky. Although it was still very early, the bakery across the square was doing a brisk trade and Valentin was on his way back with a loaded tray.

A tap on the door announced the arrival of his sister with fresh towels and a pile of neatly ironed clothes. She acknowledged Laura's thanks with a brusque nod. "Would Madame like to eat in her room?"

"No, thank you. I'd rather come down." Despite a fuzzy head and an arm more tender than it should be from a single injection, Laura was determined to take control of the situation and waste no more time. Immediately after breakfast, she would demand to be taken to her car, inspect the damage and then contact the nearest police station. She felt badly in need of a shower, but the little bathroom at the end of the corridor only offered an old fashioned tub that would take a long time to fill, so a quick splash in the washbasin would have to do.

Mr Fix It, flanked by Valentin and Charlot, didn't approach Laura until she'd put down her empty coffee bowl. The bright blue overalls worn all over France by men who worked with their hands were exactly what she'd expected to see, but not on Alain Delon, often billed as the French James Dean.

"Alain?" Hastening to wipe away her milky moustache, Laura blinked and accepted the large hand being held out to her. It was rough to the touch but very clean. Freshly scrubbed in her honour, perhaps?

"No, Madame. That's my father. Let me introduce myself. My name

is Jean-Claude Binard. These other gentlemen you already know. May
I join you?"

Feeling very foolish, although his resemblance to the film star was
a striking one, Laura waved him to the seat beside her. It was a warm
morning and his sleeves were rolled up, revealing strong arms that seemed
strangely familiar.

"I hope you're well rested," Jean-Claude was saying.

"Yes. Thank you."

"And I deeply regret the pain and inconvenience that my father
has caused you."

"Thank you, but..."

"Anyway, we both hope that you're feeling much better today. If
Papa weren't so upset about it all, he'd be here to tell you so himself.
Please let me explain what happened. I'm afraid that he went to deal
with a breakdown whilst I was away from the garage and on his way
back... Well, he was brought up with the idea of *priorité à droite* and still
thinks that it should apply everywhere. Foolish, I know, but he's too old
to change his ways." Charlot, who had sat down at the table uninvited,
nodded his agreement.

Had the young salesman thought the same of her, Laura wondered,
when she traded in her old Ford Escort for the car of her dreams? She
might not be much younger than Binard *père*. The man in front of her,
his handsome face creased with anxiety, would be forty at the most and
if she and Marcus had had children...

"Not that he'd admit it, of course, any more than he'll accept that
his eyesight isn't what it was. I've really laid down the law this time and
he won't be driving again until he's seen an optician. Madame? Are you
following me, or am I speaking too quickly for you? I'm afraid that I
don't speak much English."

Laura pulled herself together. What did it matter how old his father
was? She was never likely to meet him and didn't want to. "I'm following
you perfectly, Monsieur, and yes, I'm feeling a little better now, thank
you. I just hope that the phone lines aren't still down or that you or

someone else will be able to offer me a lift. I need to make some urgent arrangements about my car."

He smiled. "Oh, you don't need to worry about that. The repairs are well in hand and will be free of charge, of course."

"What? But they can't be well in hand. Not already. The accident only happened last night."

"No, no. You're confused. Today is Thursday, you know. Look!" He pointed to the big calendar behind the bar. Supplied by the local fire department and depicting a traffic accident involving an overturned truck, it confirmed the date.

"But that isn't possible. I can't have slept for so long. Can I?"

"Evidently you have and it can only have been for the best. Anyway, I only need another day or two and your car will be as good as new."

"But my insurance company should have authorised the repairs from a registered garage. They won't accept a fait accompli."

"If the job is good enough, and it will be, why should they ever know? In the meantime, I'll be more than happy to pay Madame Thérèse for your food and accommodation."

"Well, I don't know..."

"Please, Madame. You'd save us a great deal of trouble and you can trust me."

She'd probably kick herself later for being won over so easily, but his deep set eyes, the colour of builders' tea, shone with sincerity.

"All right then, but..."

"You're wondering how to amuse yourself in this little backwater. We all agree that there's nothing for you to see in the village, but my cousin has agreed to drive you around the area."

Charlot appeared to be in his Sunday best, but his glib compliments on her own hastily thrown on outfit didn't appeal to Laura at all.

"That's a very kind offer," she said, "but I'd be just as happy pottering around the village, or maybe taking a gentle walk in the forest. I love to cook and France is famous for wild mushrooms, isn't it?" Looking at Valentin, she said, "Maybe *you* could show me where to find some."

Surprise and alarm crossed his face and he spread out his hands in a gesture of regret. "I'm afraid that I shall have to decline, Madame. It's too early for wild mushrooms and in any case it's many years since I walked in the forest. No, I am sure that you will have a much more interesting time with young Charlot."

Foxy, who had been looking rather hurt, brightened and turned an expectant face to Laura. "In any case, you wouldn't want to ruin those pretty nails grubbing around in dirt and leaves, Madame."

As an alternative to spending the day with him? Yes, she would, but she hadn't yet given up on Valentin. "Oh, that's so disappointing. I thought the season started round about now." Wondering if the best spots for gathering edible fungi might be a closely guarded secret, she added hastily, "I wouldn't want to keep them, you know. I'd give any we found to your sister to use in the café. Maybe Madame Gaudet could be persuaded to share a recipe or two?"

"I really don't think so."

"Even if I tell her that I'm thinking of writing a book when I get back to England." That caught his interest.

"Really? What would be your theme?"

"The importance of food in painting. How the way to an Impressionist's heart was through his stomach." Maybe the joke had lost something in translation? No one laughed and Jean-Claude had begun to tap his fingers on the table.

"Valentin has his work to do here, Madame, and I must get back to mine. Please go with Charlot. He'll find you plenty to write about and I guarantee that you won't regret it. Eh, Charlot?" He gave his cousin a glance that looked very much like a warning.

Laura made one last desperate attempt to get out of the arrangement. "Is your wife interested in cooking, Monsieur? Instead of putting your cousin to such trouble, maybe she and I…"

A chill descended on the company as Jean-Claude shook his head without hearing her out. His departure was so abrupt that Laura turned to the other men for an explanation.

"Did I say something wrong?"

"No, no. Of course not. You weren't to know that Margot rarely sees anyone outside the family. She wouldn't be of any help to you anyway. To be quite honest, she's a little *gaga*, but don't tell Jean-Claude that I said so." To make sure that Laura understood, Charlot tapped the side of his head and pulled a hideous face. "So you'll come out with me today, will you?"

What other choice did she have? Valentin, his expression unreadable, had already started to clear the table of her breakfast things and she was growing tired of being an object of curiosity for the men clustered around the bar. Some of them were already drinking wine and she wondered what state they'd be in by the end of the day. At least Charlot's breath didn't smell of alcohol.

"Where are you thinking of taking me?"

"I thought we might start with Louveciennes."

"All right. That's not a bad idea. I'll be able to pop into the hotel I booked and apologise for not showing up the other night."

"There's no need for that. As soon as the phones came back on, Madame Thérèse did it for you."

"But how did she know which one to ring?"

"You must have told her, I suppose. Anyway, it's done and they sent their best wishes for your speedy recovery. I must repeat," he added in a silky voice, "that you're looking very lovely this morning."

"I doubt that, Monsieur," she snapped. Laura appreciated a genuine compliment as much as the next woman, but this was ridiculous. Although the cut on her forehead was starting to heal and the swelling above her nose had gone down a lot, her unwashed hair felt lank and she knew that she was looking very far from her best. "I'll just need to go up to my room for a moment. Will you wait for me here?"

"It will be my pleasure, Madame."

As they were about to set off, Valentin came towards them with a big book tucked under his arm. It was a well illustrated guide to mushrooms and toadstools in France.

"I've brought this for you to read later on," he said. "You might find some information useful for your own book. I'll ask Thérèse to put it into your room when she goes up to make the bed."

"Thank you very much. Now then, on the subject of the bed, perhaps you could help me?" Even on such short acquaintance, she felt more confident approaching Valentin than his dour sister and explained about the bolster. "Would it be possible to have a couple of extra pillows?"

"I'll see to it myself," he replied with a shy smile.

Jingling his keys, Charlot led her to a blue Citroën DS that had seen better days but was at least clean and polished. Opening the passenger door with a flourish, he asked, "Do you know why you should worship my car?"

"No," replied Laura wearily. She'd heard that particular pun several times before, but the fact that her own attempt at humour had fallen flat earlier on was no reason to ruin his.

"Because DS sounds like *déesse* which is our word for a goddess." He roared with laughter, she smiled politely and off they went.

It only took them a few minutes to reach Louveciennes, park and pick up some leaflets from the tourist office. As they strolled along, however, it became increasingly apparent that Charlot had little interest in the Impressionists. He kept turning the conversation to Anaïs Nin and offered to show Laura the house she rented for a while in rue Montbuisson.

"Renoir used to live just round the corner," he said by way of encouragement, "although not at the same time."

"Obviously not," said Laura crisply, "given that he died just after the Great War and she was only in Louveciennes for four years during the 1930s."

Charlot smirked at her. "You're very well informed. Does that mean that you have an interest in erotic writing?"

"Not at all," she said hastily.

They arrived in Moret-sur-Loing in time for a late lunch. Laura was enchanted by the medieval town and almost forgot her irritation with Charlot. They ate pancakes at a tiny waterside restaurant and cruised down the river on a barge, spotting the bridge and magnificent church of Notre-Dame de Moret, already familiar from Alfred Sisley's paintings. It was disappointing though that the house where he'd lived and worked wasn't open to visitors. Even worse, they found his grave surrounded by a party of English schoolboys with clipboards.

"Dealers were fighting over Sisley's works only three months after he died," their teacher was saying. "*Flood at Port Marly* sold for well over 40,000 francs in 1900 and we'll be able to see it in the Musée d'Orsay when we go back to Paris."

"Cool! Can we go and see that barley sugar place now, sir?"

"You mean the Musée du Sucre d'Orge?"

"If you say so, sir. That's quite a mouthful"

"And you want to learn how the nuns of Moret used a secret recipe dating back to the 1600s?"

"Yes, sir. Especially if they're giving away free samples."

The teacher laughed. "Sorry. I don't think it's open today, but I know a shop where you can buy some of the sweets."

"Even better," chorused his charges.

"Follow me, then!"

Laura wasn't far behind them and crunched all the way back to the car. Charlot, who'd been quite restrained until then, declined to share what she'd bought. He'd saved the drive back to the village to boast about his many conquests. There was nothing, it seemed, that anyone could tell him about the fair sex. More than once she had to dissuade him from draping his arm round her shoulders as though they were teenagers or even squeezing her knee as he changed gear. Worse was to come. On the outskirts of Saint-André-la-Forêt, he pulled up at the side of the road and made such a crude pass that Laura nearly swallowed her latest piece of barley sugar. Did he really think that a woman her age would be flattered by his advances? Be grateful, even? The sleazy, slimy...

"*N'insistez pas, Monsieur!*" Prising his hot freckled hand from her thigh, she was very tempted to use stronger language or even slap his face but wouldn't have put it past him to retaliate in kind. With no wish to add to her injuries, she wrenched open the door and stalked off.

He made no attempt to pursue her but shouted, "I might have known that you'd be frigid. You Englishwomen are all the same!"

How many of her fellow countrywomen had Charlot known, wondered Laura, more irritated than frightened, and how had he met them?

As she approached *Chez Thérèse*, she noticed that the war memorial, only seen before from her bedroom window, was stained a deep red by the setting sun. At first glance, she thought that the shadowy figure placing flowers on the top step was Jean-Claude Binard. It was only revealed as a much older man when he straightened up to study the inscriptions. His broad shoulders were hunched as if he too had been having a bad day.

"You idiot! I knew this would happen. Jean-Claude will kill you when he finds out. Now what are we supposed to do?"

"It wasn't my fault. She led me on."

"I'll just bet she did! You always say that." Valentin had locked the door behind the last customer. Now he was sweeping the cigarette ends and sugar wrappers into a neat pile by the bar, where Charlot sat slumped over his glass. "You never learn! Haven't three divorces taught you anything?"

"What would you know about it? No woman ever set her cap at you, as far as I'm aware."

No woman I ever wanted, thought Valentin, but he wasn't going to admit that to the younger man. "Stop trying to change the subject. You were supposed to be taking Madame Fitzgerald into Paris tomorrow."

"Well you'll have to go instead. Or Thérèse can take her."

Valentin sighed and admitted defeat. Much as he loved his sister, he couldn't see her giving any Englishwoman a pleasant day out. Thérèse wore her scars, most of them anyway, on the inside but was far from adept at hiding her bitterness. "Oh, very well. If I really have to go, then I will."

Chapter 5

"Is there any chance of getting my car back today, do you think?"

Valentin pulled an apologetic face. "Not a hope, I'm afraid. Jean-Claude phoned earlier to say that he's still waiting for a part to be delivered."

"Damn! Oh well, it looks as though it's going to be a long day. I'll just potter around then. There must be something to see in the village."

"Wouldn't you rather go to Paris?"

"With that gentleman? I don't think so."

"Then with me, perhaps?"

"With you? But aren't you too busy."

"It's all right. My sister can manage without me for once. We can take the bus to Saint-Germain-en-Laye and then the RER into Paris. It's only a short journey. I'm not really up to coping with all the steps in the Métro, so we'll take a taxi to the Louvre or the Musée d'Orsay. Which would you prefer?"

Laura's eyes were glowing. "The Musée d'Orsay, please. I'm so glad that the old station wasn't demolished after all. The building is a work of art in itself and so many of my favourite paintings are gathered there now. I never managed to see them when they were in the Jeu de Paûme. Just give me time to get my things together."

By the time they reached *Le Déjeuner sur l'Herbe*, the bread and fruit that Manet had provided for his naked lady and her fully clothed male companions reminded a rapturous Laura that it had been a long time since breakfast.

"May I treat you to lunch?" she asked Valentin, whose forehead was beaded with perspiration from the effort of tramping round the long galleries.

"Stopping for lunch is a wonderful idea, Madame, but no true Frenchman would allow a lady to pay. It will be my pleasure."

Laura would have been happy to settle for a quick snack but realised that he needed more time to rest, so she allowed him to lead her to the museum's elegant restaurant with its chandeliers and 1900 style décor. The set menu wasn't too expensive and offered plenty of choice.

"This must be a nice change for you," she joked as they waited to be served.

"Yes indeed."

"Do you and your sister both cook?"

"Good Lord no! She tried to teach me when I was a boy, but I had no talent for it and even less enthusiasm. Our regulars would soon vote with their feet if I ever took over the kitchen. There's plenty of other work to do though, and I help Thérèse as much as I can. Her husband died shortly after the war, you see, and it's just been the two of us ever since."

"Was Monsieur Gaudet injured in the fighting?"

"No, but his health was broken by years of forced labour. A lot of the local men who survived the war were never the same again. Some were luckier, like young Dr Simmonet whose skills were put to good use to help the other prisoners, but many of them died far too young. That's why so many businesses in the village are owned by widows."

"Just out of interest, why do you call him 'young' Dr Simmonet? I'm sure he's older than I am."

Valentin laughed. "That's because he took over the family practice from his father, who'd brought half the village into the world. You're right about his age. Jean-Pierre Simmonet was at school with my sister and Jean-Claude's father."

Over coffee, he watched Laura scribbling in her notebook and enquired what in particular had caught her interest.

"Oh, I'm just writing down a few snatches of conversation I heard on our way round."

"Like what?"

"Well, one man was remarking to his friend that he'd like to take some clippers to the model for Courbet's *L'origine du monde* and he wasn't surprised that John Ruskin had found his bride's pubic hair so off putting. I'm not convinced by that story myself, but... Oh dear, I hope I'm not embarrassing you?"

"Not at all," he said, but two bright flags of colour had risen on his cheekbones. Laura chose her next example with more care.

"Well, one woman said to her friend, 'Do you realise, my dear, that Vincent was a Post-Impressionist, not an Impressionist?' Her friend wasn't going to be outdone and said, 'Of course, my dear. You only have to look at that frantic brushwork.' How pretentious can you get!"

"And what were those Americans by *The Birth of Venus* arguing about? I could tell you were amused."

"I didn't catch it all, but the man said, 'Cabanel? You can't really like those sugary cupids!' His wife got onto her high horse and yelled, 'Don't you tell me what I'm allowed to like, Robert Spangler!' He backed down then, of course."

"Spangler? I've never heard that name before."

"Nor I. There can't be many Spanglers in my part of England."

"How about Fitzgeralds?"

"Not many of those either."

Valentin pursued the matter no further. Although very drawn to Laura, he didn't want to sink to Charlot's level in her estimation by asking questions that she might consider too personal. That fear had also ruled out any compliments on her appearance. His sister's snooping had revealed the fact that the Englishwoman was a good ten years older than he'd thought, but the smart outfit she'd chosen to wear for their day in Paris suited her slim figure to perfection. Only the high heeled shoes might have been a mistake. Women, he knew, would put themselves through any amount of torment to look good. During the dark years of the

Occupation, some had risked their lives for a piece of parachute silk and his poor sister had always been keen to make the most of what she had, until... Well, this was no time to dwell on the past.

The afternoon saw the pair on the river and Valentin, keen to impart information, soon found that his companion could identify more of the landmarks than he could. "Are you sure that you've never visited Paris before, Madame?"

She dimpled. "Only in my dreams, Monsieur, but I've got a good guidebook and an even better memory." A sharp eye for detail too, he noted and, much as he admired that, it worried him.

By the time they returned to the village, they had dispensed with all formality.

"I hope you're not too tired from all the walking we've done, Valentin."

"Not at all, Laura. I've had a wonderful time." It was true but, as they shook hands and parted company, Valentin knew that he would pay for it the following day.

Laura overslept and found only Thérèse serving in the café when she came down. Her polite enquiry about Valentin was met with ill concealed disapproval.

"Still in bed. He's worn out."

"I'm very sorry to hear that. He was an excellent guide."

"Hmmph! From what he told me, you seem to know more about Paris than he does. Not surprising, I suppose. He very rarely leaves the village."

"Really? With all those theatres and galleries so close by? If I lived in Saint-André-la-Forêt, I'd be up there every week."

"None of that interests either of us," was the sharp reply. "We're quite content to stay where we belong."

Her attempt to make polite conversation having failed, Laura turned to a more pressing subject. "Do you know if my car's ready yet?"

"No, and I'm very sorry about that. Believe me, no one is more anxious than I to see you on your way."

"Time for a look around the village then."

"No! There's nothing at all to interest you here. Look, you could catch the bus into Saint-Germain-en-Laye again. There's a lot to see there and I can recommend a good restaurant for lunch."

Laura was tempted. After all, one of her favourite Sisley paintings featured a panorama of the Seine valley with the château heights in the distance, but her feet were quite sore. She could always go there later, once she had her car back.

"No, I don't think I'll bother, thank you. I'll just amble round here. Maybe buy a newspaper and find somewhere to sit in the sun. Have a coffee. Find someone to chat to. I might even get a few ideas for my book."

"That's most unlikely, I'm afraid."

"Oh, I might not come across anyone willing to discuss painting, but I did plenty of that in Paris yesterday with your brother. Everyone is interested in food, don't you think? I'll ask them about the kind of things available in the forest and the dishes they make from them. If all else fails, I'll walk up there and take a look for myself."

"That's really not a good idea," hissed Thérèse. "After all the heavy rain we've had lately, the ground will be muddy and treacherous. The forest can be dangerous at the best of times and it's very easy to get lost. There are no signposts and a lot of the old paths are overgrown."

"Maybe Valentin could help."

Thérèse tightened her lips even further. "My poor brother is no longer capable of such exertion."

"No, Madame. You misunderstand me. I just thought that maybe he could advise me on the best direction to take."

"He would advise you not to go into the forest at all. If you fell and broke your leg, no one would find you. You might even be attacked by a wild boar. Footprints have appeared recently and holes too where one of the beasts has been poking its snout. And then there are the hunters. Some of them shoot at anything that moves."

Laura was losing patience. "Look, I probably won't even go out of sight of the main road. Just wander a little way in to see what I can find. Wild mushrooms, for example, like the ones in the book your brother has been kind enough to lend me."

"Mushrooms? He lent you that book so that you wouldn't need to go anywhere near the forest."

"Well, I'd like to anyway. Nothing beats seeing a place for myself and I've got a new film in my camera."

"You won't find a thing. Valentin told you, didn't he, that it's too early for mushrooms. Anyway, most of them are poisonous."

"But I wasn't planning to put them straight into my mouth."

"Well, something else you should know is that parts of the forest are said to be haunted."

"By the ghosts of reckless mushroom hunters?"

Laura's sarcasm was wasted on Thérèse, whose face contorted with anger. "A lot of bad things have happened up there. That's all I'm going to say, Madame. You've been warned."

Laura could feel the Frenchwoman's hostile eyes boring into her back as she left the café and couldn't for the life of her think why. After all, she'd agreed not to cause any trouble for the man whose recklessness had stranded her in the village. She hadn't been a difficult guest. Quite the reverse, in fact. She'd gone out of her way to thank Madame Gaudet for taking care of her after the accident and for giving up her own room. Furthermore, she'd made a particular point of praising her cooking. To be fair, that wasn't hard to do. The previous evening she'd enjoyed a delicious *carbonnade* of braised beef so much that she'd ventured to ask for the recipe. As they discussed the flavouring of the beer sauce with onions and spices, the woman had almost cracked a smile. There must be one buried in her somewhere, but how far it was from the surface was impossible to guess.

The village proved to be as lacking in interest as she'd been told and Laura's attempts to strike up a conversation fell on stony ground.

By eleven o'clock, she'd bought a fancy notebook, a folding umbrella, a roll of sticking plaster and a pair of gaily striped espadrilles, all without exchanging more than a dozen words with anyone. There was no museum, but the old bell tower visible above the roofs at the far side of the square looked vaguely familiar and she decided to take a look.

The heavy door creaked as she entered the church. An angular woman in black was arranging flowers around the lace trimmed altar. Another woman, very like the first except that one side of her face was distorted as if she'd suffered a stroke, was leaning awkwardly out of her wheelchair in an attempt to dust one of the pews. The lavender fragrance of the polish and the sunshine streaming through a stained glass roundel onto the stone flags of the aisle should have given the building a welcoming air. Instead, the chill seeping through the thin soles of Laura's new espadrilles was nothing to the icy glare from the elderly sisters. She was about to leave when she saw the tall figure of a priest coming in through the side door. His halo of silver hair and general air of benevolence were surely not those of a man who would rebuff a stranger.

"Excuse me, Father. Perhaps you can help me. I was wondering if any of the Impressionists had ever painted your bell tower." From his startled expression, Laura assumed that the little church received few visitors.

"The Impressionists? That would be long before my time, but I'm not aware that any of them ever came here."

"Well, do you think you could show me round? You have some beautiful stained glass and I'd be happy to make a donation."

The priest shook his head and said, "You must excuse me, Madame. There's nothing out of the ordinary for you to see and I'm very busy this morning. Good day to you." Pausing only to genuflect, he swept past her and disappeared into the confessional.

Having run out of ideas, Laura decided to see for herself what progress had been made on the Spitfire. The bus taking her and Valentin to Saint-Germain- en- Laye had passed the Garage de la Forge and she knew that it was only a short walk from the square. A Citroën Dyane with its roof rolled back was parked on the forecourt, but there was no one about. It was lunch time, of course, sacred to the French. How could she have forgotten! Not yet hungry herself after her late breakfast, she headed across the main road and through the old stone archway, neglected and crumbling, that led into the forest.

The track on the other side was wide enough for motor vehicles, but there were no tyre marks in the rich, damp soil. A succession of narrow paths to left and right, some almost completely overgrown with grass and ferns, looked much more interesting. Laura chose one at random, resolving not to go too far in case she really did get lost. She had a sneaking suspicion that Madame Gaudet wouldn't bother to send out a search party if she failed to return.

It was wonderful to be walking through a natural forest with its random collection of trees rather than the prim rows of carefully managed conifers she'd seen in so many English woods. There were fallen branches, thickly knotted tree roots and a few rabbit holes to trip up the unwary, but no rusting fridges, broken televisions or old sofas. Only a couple of discarded shotgun cartridges showed that hunters did indeed sometimes come this way.

As Laura walked on, a loud cawing from high up in the trees caught her attention. If you see one rook, it's a crow. If you see lots of crows, they're rooks, she mused. Or was it the other way round? Marcus would have known, but Marcus wasn't here. He would also have been able to identify the bird making the tapping sound and sharp chack-chack-chack in that old beech tree. Heard but not seen, the opposite of the ideal Victorian child. A flash of red in the corner of her eye had her whipping round just in time to see the back end of a squirrel disappearing upwards and she wondered how many other wild creatures were taking advantage of the camouflage offered by the thick foliage. Peering up into the branches, she longed for the binoculars she kept in the Spitfire. The path seemed to be coming to a dead end anyway and she was tired of brushing the overhanging branches aside to protect her face.

There was still no one around when she arrived back at the garage, but the side door of the workshop was slightly ajar and she could see her car inside. With hair full of leaves and twigs, she wasn't anxious to draw attention to herself and it wasn't as though she needed anyone's permission to retrieve her own property. She just hoped that no one had beaten her to it. This remote spot hardly struck her as a hotbed of crime, but any Pierre, Paul or Jacques could be passing by on his way to Paris.

The door creaked and she was just reaching for the binoculars when she heard an eager yapping and sharp teeth sank into her flesh. As Laura cried out in surprise and pain, Jean-Claude rushed in, a large napkin tucked into the bib of his overalls. He didn't look at all amused to see a bedraggled Englishwoman sitting on the concrete floor, blood dripping from her ankle onto her espadrilles and a triumphant Scottie dog bouncing up and down beside her.

"Lost my balance," was all he got by way of explanation. His lips were a rigid line as he dumped his pet onto the back seat of the Dyane and returned to pull Laura to her feet.

"What the hell do you think you were doing? Why didn't you get Valentin to phone me if you wanted something from your car? There was no need for you to come here and help yourself."

Should Laura apologise for disturbing his lunch? No! Damned if she would! She was the injured party after all. "Now look here, young man, don't you dare to wag your finger at me. That's a dangerous animal you have there."

"Dangerous animal?" He halted in mid-rant and Laura thought that she detected a flicker of amusement. Certainly his tone was milder as he continued, "I'm sorry that Mac hurt you, but it's his job to chase off any strangers he finds hanging around our workshop. The tools and other equipment here are very valuable, you know."

"As is my car."

"As is your car, of course. Come on now. I'll take you back to the café and Madame Thérèse will see to your ankle for you or ask Dr Simmonet to take a look at it. You mustn't worry. Our little Mac doesn't have rabies."

Laura was being firmly led towards the Dyane when a voice called out from the house that adjoined the garage. Constructed from rough stone, its features were outlined in brick and each window was protected by grey wooden shutters. Left like that, it would have looked very drab, but the downstairs sills boasted colourful window boxes and tubs of bright flowers flanked the front door.

"Jean-Claude! Bring the lady inside." He hesitated and then, with the utmost reluctance, turned towards the slight figure in the doorway.

"My wife," he muttered, as he obeyed.

Margot was smoothing down her old fashioned floral apron. Despite a few strands of grey in her chestnut hair and the dark circles under her big green eyes, the way in which she greeted Laura had something of the eagerness of a child.

"I'm so pleased to meet you," she said. "Do come in. You're with my husband, so that's all right. My name is Margot and this is Papa, my father-in-law." The man Laura had seen placing flowers on the war memorial reached across the big table to shake her hand. An older, mus-tachioed version of his son and still capable of breaking a few hearts, she thought, although his expression belied the polite words.

"Delighted, Madame."

Tutting sympathetically, Margot filled a plastic bowl with warm water and gave the afflicted ankle a thorough wash, patting it dry with a fluffy towel before dabbing on some antiseptic cream. An expertly applied bandage finished the job and she sat back on her heels and beamed with satisfaction.

Laura smiled back. "I think you must have been a Girl Guide like me, Madame. That's how I learned first aid."

"Maybe I was. I don't know." She lowered her eyes and started to pick nervously at her cuticles.

Jean-Claude took one look at his wife's urgent fingers and moved round to stroke her hair. "It was a long time ago," he said quietly, "so what does it matter?" The sudden sadness in the room was unsettling and it didn't look as though any explanation would be forthcoming.

To break the silence, Laura turned to Mac, liberated from the Dyane and eyeing her suspiciously from the doorway. "How old is your little dog?"

Margot's smile returned at once. "We don't know exactly. Quite young, though. We found him in the forest last winter and now he's devoted to us."

"Belonged to a Parisian, I expect," growled her father-in-law. "They think it's smart to parade around with a pet until they get bored. The poor little creature was still wearing his tartan jacket when we found him. I don't suppose that sort of thing happens in England. Aren't you supposed to be a nation of animal lovers?"

"Not all of us, I'm afraid. My own pets have always come from rescue centres."

"How many do you have?"

"None at all now. My ex-husband took the dogs. He suggested keeping one each, but I didn't think it was fair to split them up after all the years they'd been together. I kept the cat, but she was already seventeen and only lived for a few months after he and I parted company. I wouldn't have been here otherwise. I couldn't have left her."

"I'm very glad to hear that." The smile transformed his face and Laura felt that she might have made up for her earlier faux pas in disturbing the family's lunch. According to Valentin, he was the same age as Thérèse Gaudet. Could they be old flames? Was that why she was so keen to protect him?

A determined voice broke in upon her musings. "Now, Madame, we should be on our way. Lean on me if your ankle troubles you." Jean-Claude's tone was polite, but the way in which he whisked her out of the house left Laura in no doubt that she had outstayed her welcome.

Chapter 6

Satisfaction was written all over Thérèse's face when she spotted the bandage. "Has Madame had a little accident?"

"Nothing to worry about," snapped Laura's escort. "Margot took care of it for her."

"Margot did?" The woman couldn't have sounded more surprised if the injury had been treated by Marie Antoinette, but a frown from Jean-Claude prompted her to change the subject. "Would you like something to eat?"

"Please, if it wouldn't put you out too much." It was three o'clock and all the lunchtime customers had gone. From the kitchen came the clatter of plates being washed and stacked ready for the evening.

"Not at all. It's no trouble. Please sit down and rest your ankle."

Valentin was surprised to see the hard working Jean-Claude in the café at that time of day and even more so to learn the reason for his arrival. "I suppose you didn't really have a choice," he concluded.

"None at all. I just wanted to get her right away from my house, but Margot insisted."

"And you couldn't say no?" Thérèse looked as though she'd like to spit into the creamy Vichyssoise that she was ladling out for Laura. Piling the bowl high with watercress, she added, "Stupid question, I suppose. When did you ever say no to your wife?"

"When did your husband ever say no to you?" he retaliated. "It was hardly my fault that she turned up at the garage looking for her blasted binoculars. You were all supposed to be keeping her busy while I fixed the car."

Thérèse sniffed. "How could I know that she'd walk Valentin off his feet yesterday? Just look at him now! He can hardly stand at the sink. He was in a terrible state when he got back from Paris. As for Charlot, well!"

"Don't talk to me about that idiot. If he'd known how to treat females with more respect twenty years ago we might not be in this mess."

"You can't blame it all on him. That girl was trouble from the word go and everyone knew it."

Valentin had heard enough. "Can we please all stick to the point? Don't worry, Jean-Claude. I've got an idea to keep Madame Fitzgerald well away from Margot."

"I wish I could believe that."

"She's interested in French food, isn't she, so why not get Victor to help. I'm sure she'd love to see what goes on behind the scenes at the bakery. Victor won't say anything out of place and he can talk for hours about his different breads. Maybe he could even teach her to make something. Do you remember how your aunt used to let you all play with the dough when you were children?"

Jean-Claude laughed, his usual good humour restored. "Yes, of course I do. I'll go across and see him now."

Unaware of the invitation coming her way, Laura had decided to go out in search of a replacement for her ruined espadrilles and spotted Alain Binard seated by the war memorial. He was leaning back, eyes closed, to absorb the strong sunshine. The little Scottie was dozing in the shade beneath the bench but opened his eyes at Laura's approach and barked.

"What? Oh, it's you, Madame. I didn't expect to see you again so soon." His expression suggested that the surprise wasn't a pleasant one.

"Just taking a little walk. I don't have anything else to do."

"No. I gather that your day out with my nephew wasn't a great success."

"To put it mildly. No wonder all his wives left him!"

Alain gave a rueful smile. "Well, he's always had a roving eye, I'm afraid."

"Unlike your son? Oh, I'm sorry. That's really none of my business." The smile had gone and Laura could have kicked herself.

"No, it isn't. But, since you ask, Jean-Claude hasn't so much as looked at another woman since he met Margot. She's his life and he'd do anything to protect her. So would I." An awkward silence followed.

"It's very hot today," Laura said eventually. "I'll bet Mac would enjoy a swim."

"Yes indeed. He's looking forward to a dip in the river. Margot doesn't want us under her feet while she's baking."

"That sounds delightful. Could you show me the best way down there, do you think? I'd love to..."

The words died on her lips as Alain sprang to his feet and said, "Oh, we're not going just yet, I'm afraid. Other things to do first. Good day to you." He hastily untied Mac's lead from the bench and strode off, the dog's short stumpy legs barely managing to keep up.

Laura, who knew a snub when she heard one, flushed angrily. It was the last straw. Bitten by his pet, admitted only grudgingly into his home and then shown the door without so much as the offer of a glass of water on such a hot day, she felt a childish desire to hurl insults after Alain Binard's retreating back. She could do it too. All those years spent with the volatile Marcus had given her an extensive vocabulary. On the other hand, the lady of the house had taken a great deal of trouble over Laura's ankle and had received no proper thanks for it. Maybe now would be a good time for putting that right. Decision made, she headed back to the garage. A teenager who looked a little like Valentin was manning the pumps and stared at her curiously as she walked past him to the house.

Margot, hair scraped back and with flour on her eyebrows and lashes, gazed at her uncertainly. "My husband is not at home now."

"I know and I'm sorry to disturb you, Madame. Your father in law did tell me that you were baking, but I don't know how much longer I'll be in the area and I wanted to thank you for your kindness this morning."

"Oh, it was nothing, I assure you." She looked down at the shiny palette knife she was clutching and moved it to the other hand.

Laura found herself repeating, "It's very hot today." Talk about stating the obvious! No wonder the British had a reputation for being obsessed with the weather.

Margot drew the back of her free hand across her forehead and gave her a tentative smile. "Yes, it is. Would you like to come in for a cup of tea?"

Laura's surprise at the offer was nothing to the one that awaited her in the kitchen. Not since thumbing through her mother's Be-Ro recipe book had she seen such perfectly made scones, maids of honour, Shrewsbury biscuits, walnut bread and other teatime treats. They all lay on cooling trays and a sponge cake that looked feather light was waiting to be sliced and filled.

"What a beautiful selection!"

"Thank you. Please choose whatever you like. I bake every week, but we never get through it all. What's left goes out for the birds."

A few minutes later, fortified by an excellent cup of tea and a ground rice tart oozing with raspberry jam, Laura said, "That's just what I needed."

"Of course. You must have been thirsty walking up here from the village."

"Yes, but that's not the only reason. This is the best tea I've had since I left home."

"Just normal, don't you think?"

"Not in my experience." For fear of being thought tactless, Laura decided not to recount the times she had been disappointed by 'English' tea in France. Stewed, tepid, so weak as to have no taste or even served with condensed milk. "I believe in one teaspoonful for each person and one for the pot."

"I beg your pardon?"

"Oh, that's just a little saying that we have in England. Is that where you learned to make such good tea?"

"I don't think so, Madame."

"From English friends in France then, or maybe from one of your schoolbooks? I remember learning a lot about French customs and traditions from mine."

"I don't know. That is, I can't remember."

One look at Margot's stricken face warned Laura to change the subject before the younger woman's cuticles came under attack again. "Would you like to hear about the book I'm planning to write?"

Margot's smile returned. "You're a writer, Madame?"

"Trying to be. Maybe you could help me."

"I could help you? How?"

"Well, I'm an art lover who also loves to cook, so it's going to be about my twin passions; the wonderful paintings and the great food I find on my wanderings through France."

"I'm afraid I don't know much about painting."

"Maybe not, but you're certainly an artist in the kitchen. Perhaps we could go through some of your recipe books together."

"I'm sorry. That won't be possible."

"Oh well, it doesn't matter." Laura stood up to leave, but a hand shot out to detain her.

"No! You don't understand. I don't have any recipe books. I just make whatever comes into my head."

"All these?"

"Oh yes. Lots of other things too. Cooking is my greatest passion. Well, after Jean-Claude, of course." She blushed and her eyes shone as she said his name. "He's so kind, you know. He has to go to Paris sometimes and he finds me ingredients that aren't stocked in the village shops."

"Don't you go with him?"

"No."

"Never?"

"No, I'm a homebody and that's the way I like it. Tell me now, what would you serve with roast pork in England? That's what I'm planning to cook this evening."

"Apple sauce, I should think."

"How strange. That's what I thought too."

They were halfway through their third pot of tea when Alain walked in. Making no attempt to hide his displeasure at seeing Laura there, he sent his daughter-in-law outside with a bowl of water for Mac.

"Why did you come back here?" he demanded as soon as Margot was out of earshot.

Laura bridled at his rudeness, although it was what she'd come to expect. "I came to thank Madame Binard for her kindness to me earlier on today. Your son didn't give me the chance."

"I told you that she was busy this afternoon."

"So you did, but I only intended to take up a few minutes of her time."

"A few minutes indeed! You've been here much longer than that."

"And how would you know, Monsieur?"

"Because we've all... Well, never mind how I know." He looked bleakly at the crumbs falling from her lap when Laura stood up.

Chapter 7

The first thing Laura saw when she got out of bed the next morning was a white envelope pushed under her door. Even without the oily thumb print, she would have guessed who had written the note inside. Jean-Claude Binard was asking her in no uncertain terms not to call on his wife again. Margot was *fragile* and easily upset around strangers.

"Of course I'll respect his wishes," she said to Valentin as he served her breakfast. "I don't understand it, though. She seemed perfectly happy to chat to me yesterday afternoon. Well, except for one awkward moment. Why are her husband and father-in-law so anxious to keep me away from her?"

"If you really want to know," said Thérèse, who was listening to their conversation from behind the bar, "Margot isn't quite right in the head. I wouldn't say that she's actually dangerous, but..."

For a moment, Laura's imagination went into overdrive. Charlot had told her much the same thing. Was the handsome Jean-Claude shackled to a mad wife like the one in *Jane Eyre*? And she, Laura, had just spent an hour or so alone with her in a kitchen full of sharp knives!

"No, that's not fair. Margot's just highly strung and very forgetful. That's why she says such odd things at times. Jean-Claude's a little over protective. That's all. She's his anchor."

"More like a millstone, if you ask me," snapped his sister.

Laura studied Valentin's anxious face, wondering whether he really believed what he'd told her. "I'm sure you'd feel exactly the same in his position," she said doubtfully.

"Probably," he admitted. "Marriage was never on the cards for me,

I'm afraid. Not from lack of inclination, but because of this." He pointed once again at his built up shoe. "And I didn't even have one of these when I was young. My parents weren't well off to begin with and nothing was available during the war and the Occupation."

What a shame it was, thought Laura, that no young woman had seen through Valentin's disability to the kind, intelligent man that he was. His pale blue eyes, very like his sister's, had taken on such a haunted look that she wanted to give him a hug. Instead, she said, "That must have been a terrible time for you all. Did your family suffer a great deal under the Germans?"

Glancing towards the bar, Valentin replied, "Not as much as some and we've done our best to put all that behind us. Please don't think me rude, but I'd rather not talk about those days." Seizing the moment, he said, "It's not really any of my business, Laura, but I've been wondering about Mr Fitzgerald. Jean-Claude told me that you're divorced."

Instead of taking affront, she gave him a rueful smile. "Yes. I don't expect to see him again."

"Oh, that's a pity."

"Not really. We hadn't been getting on well for a long time."

"What line of work was he in?"

"Interpreter. We met in Geneva when I was teaching in an international school."

"So that's why your French is so good."

"I'm glad you think so. It isn't as fluent as it was in those days, I'm afraid. Use it or lose it!"

"Well, you certainly haven't lost it. Would it be impertinent of me to ask if you miss your husband?"

"No. Not as much as I thought I would, anyway. I'm quite enjoying my independence. Now then, I'd like more coffee, please, and then I'm going bird watching. I heard some interesting calls during my walk in the forest."

"As long as you're not planning to include any of our local songbirds in your recipes, I'd be happy to lend you another of my books. The illustrations are in colour and it's the ideal size to carry around."

"That would be very kind."

"I'll go and get it."

As he disappeared up the stairs, Laura chalked up another point in his favour. The idea of capturing tiny birds such as the rare and delicate ortolan for the table appalled her too.

When Valentin handed her the book, he said shyly, "I've got some free time this afternoon and I know a spot where we might see a king-fisher."

"Thank you. I'd enjoy that."

"As for this morning, if you turn right along the main road, you'll see a footpath you can follow. That way, you stand no risk of getting lost or..."

"I know! Going anywhere near the Garage de la Forge. Don't worry. Pushing my nose in where it's not wanted has never been my style."

Nor was it but, as luck would have it, she hadn't walked far before she saw Margot Binard a few yards ahead of her with Mac. His sharp little ears pricked up and he came bounding towards her growling. Oh no! It was too late to turn back and pretend that she hadn't seen them. Margot, though, looked more startled than displeased. She put down the wicker basket she was carrying over one arm and patted the Scottie's head. As she clicked her tongue and whispered into his ear, he stopped growling and offered Laura a polite paw. She saw no harm in accepting it, regardless of the way she'd been discouraged from seeking further contact with his mistress.

Margot, however, seemed quite unaware of that and laughed as Laura let go. "Mac will let you shake hands with me now." Her grip was firm and her expression friendly as she continued, "We're on a hunting expedition today."

"Not for wild boar, I presume?"

"Indeed not. The season hasn't begun yet and I think Mac would be out of his league there anyway, don't you? We're looking for berries to make into jam. My father-in-law knows this forest like the back of his hand and usually comes with me, but there was an emergency call in the early hours and he's still asleep."

"I thought he wasn't going to drive the breakdown lorry again after my accident."

"Your accident? I know Mac bit you, but..."

"No, I mean the accident with my car. The red sports car that your husband has ramped up in his workshop."

"Oh, is that yours? I didn't know. Only that Papa is desperate to try it out before it's returned to its owner. You're right about the lorry, though. He just goes along for the ride now and in case an extra pair of hands is needed."

Margot's lack of knowledge or curiosity about the circumstances of the crash struck Laura as very odd, but she didn't pursue the matter. She was more concerned that Jean-Claude might pop up from behind a tree and start haranguing her.

"Is your husband also having a lie in this morning?" she enquired.

"No. He never does." Margot's cheeks reddened and she went on, "Well, sometimes with me on a Sunday, if you know what I mean." Laura smiled as they exchanged a woman to woman look. "He's gone to Paris. Your car is nearly ready, but he's been held up waiting for a small part that should have been delivered a couple of days ago. He's so cross with the supplier that he rang him this morning and said that he'd pick it up himself."

No prizes for guessing why Jean-Claude had run out of patience, thought Laura, but a walk in the forest with Margot might provide some material for her book. "What sort of jam are you going to make?"

"That all depends on what I can find. During the summer, I usually pick enough wild strawberries, raspberries and blackberries to keep us going all year round. Later on, of course, there are sweet chestnuts and sloes."

"Oh, I love sloe gin. I make my own every year and elderberry liqueur as well."

"So you're interested in foraging too?"

"Yes, very, and I'd love to hear more about yours. I set off today, though, with the intention of bird watching."

"Hence the binoculars?"

"Yes, and I've got this book too. Valentin at the café lent it to me. He's been very kind."

"That's typical of Valentin. He's a dear man, so gentle and unobtrusive, but a very good friend to all of us. He even helps out on the pumps occasionally when none of his nephews is available at short notice. I just wish that his eldest sister didn't unnerve me so."

"Unnerve you? Why?"

"Thérèse doesn't like me, although I can't imagine what I've done to deserve it. You should see the way she looks at me when they visit and she always finds fault with my cooking." Margot had dropped the basket, empty except for a small knife, and started to fidget with her fingers.

"Could you help me to identify some of your local birds?" asked Laura in an attempt to distract her. It worked.

"Oh yes! Papa has taught me all about them."

"Well, I heard one tapping away at a tree in the forest yesterday and making a sort of chack-chack-chack noise. I wasn't able to see it, unfortunately."

"That sounds like a great spotted woodpecker," said Margot without hesitation. She took the book and flicked through to find a picture of a big black and white bird perching on a branch. "Do you see that red patch on the back of its head? That shows you that it's a male."

"Do all woodpeckers sound much the same?"

"Far from it. The green woodpecker laughs and the tiny lesser spotted one goes cheek-cheek-cheek. I'll bet some of them are keeping an eye on us now to make sure that we don't take all the berries."

"I thought they'd prefer insects."

"They do. Any kind of insect, in fact. The green woodpecker loves ants. But they'll all eat berries if they can't find enough insects. Nuts too."

"Mushrooms?"

Margot took Laura's joke seriously and hesitated for a moment. "No, not mushrooms. The birds don't mind how many of those I take."

"I've been told that most wild mushrooms are deadly."

"Some of them are, but others are wonderful. Ceps, chanterelles, parasols, giant puffballs, to name but a few."

"I read somewhere that you can go to any French pharmacy to find out if the mushrooms you've gathered are safe to eat. Do you ever do that?"

"I have no need to go to the pharmacy," Margot replied simply, her face shining with evident satisfaction. "Papa knows them all and he's taught me. We spent a lot of time together in the forest when I first..."

The pounding of feet along the path behind them cut her words short. Alain Binard's moustache was positively bristling with anger and concern as he glared at Laura. "You again!" Yet his tone softened when he addressed his daughter-in-law. "Margot. When I woke up you'd gone. Why didn't you wait for me?"

"I'm fine, Papa, really. There's nothing for you to get upset about. I haven't found any berries yet, but this lady and I have been having a nice chat."

There was a wary set to his face as he turned to Laura. "A chat about what, might I ask?"

"Birds. Berries. Mushrooms. I gather that you're a mine of information about the forest, Monsieur."

"Some might say that. Come home now, Margot. We'll get the berries tomorrow." Without a word of farewell to Laura, she meekly took the hand he held out to her and they disappeared back down the path with Mac trotting between them.

The kingfisher proved elusive, but her afternoon by the river with Valentin was balm to Laura's hurt feelings. Here was a man who, without in any way trying to take advantage of their isolated surroundings, seemed very happy to be with her. They were able to share their delight in the birds they spotted but also to stroll along in companionable silence for several minutes at a time. Only when Valentin stumbled over a tree root and struggled to regain his balance, did the subject of his disability crop up again.

"I was born with a club foot, just like my grandfather's, and it was never treated properly. Dr Simmonet said that there was an operation I could have, but my mother wouldn't hear of it. She'd been told by the priest's housekeeper that gangrene and amputation were bound to follow."

"Had she been reading *Madame Bovary*?"

"Maybe, although she'd never admit to it. It's considered to be a classic now, of course, but it was banned at one time. Madame Dupré claimed to have read about it in *La Croix* and insisted that no Catholic paper would print inaccurate information. Dr Simmonet told my mother that things had come on a lot since Flaubert's day, but she wouldn't be convinced to let him try anything more radical than splints and plaster. Neither did any good, I'm afraid."

"But when you were older and left the village, surely then…"

"That never happened. Oh, I wanted to, of course. I couldn't run around with the other boys, so I spent all my spare time reading and I was usually top of the class." He blushed modestly and added, "Not that the general standard was very high. Most of my contemporaries couldn't wait to leave. French literature and history were my best subjects and the schoolmaster used to lend me some of his own books to read. Monsieur Kahn was the kindest, most patient man that I've ever known and such an inspiring teacher that I used to dream of following in his footsteps. He pleaded with my parents to let me continue my studies, but my father said that no one was going to tell him what was right and wrong for his son. In any case, the Morcels had never attended school a day longer than they were obliged to. Always too many mouths to feed, you see, and not enough money to go round." His eyes grew misty as he went on, "So I left, but I didn't earn a sou until Luc Gaudet offered to take me on if Thérèse married him."

"And you've been working in the café ever since?"

"Yes. The war broke out not long afterwards and my brother-in-law was called up. Needless to say, I wasn't fit enough to be a soldier and

Thérèse really needed me then."

"Were you in the Resistance?"

"Wasn't everyone?" he asked with a wry smile. "Come on now. I think it's time we were turning back."

Good news awaited Laura at the café. She would have the Spitfire, fully restored to its former glory and with a full tank of petrol, by twelve o'clock the following day at the very latest. A final lunch at the café and it would be farewell for ever to Saint-André-la-Forêt and its strange inhabitants!

Chapter 8

Laura's packing only took a few minutes and there was an element of defiance in her decision to take a last look at the forest. This wouldn't be the morning to get lost or caught up in a thicket, so she decided to stroll up the main track and see where it led.

After about half an hour, the thick wall of trees on each side gave way to an arched avenue of beeches. Behind them could be glimpsed a series of large grassy mounds too regular in shape to be natural, although some had mature trees growing out of the top. Others were dotted with the jagged foundations of old stone walls, partially covered by creepers. Drawn to take a closer look, Laura soon thought better of it. Here and there were holes much too deep even for badgers to have made and she feared disappearing into one of them.

A pile of moss covered boulders marked the end of the track, which had led into a large clearing with an eerie feeling of desolation about it. At the far side, improbable though it seemed, Laura was convinced that she could see the arched entrance to a railway tunnel. Gravel crunched underfoot as she made her way towards it through the long grass, only to find that it was much smaller than she'd first thought and completely blocked up. Finding no clues as to its former purpose, she soon lost interest and moved on.

A narrow path, dark and barely discernible, led back into the trees. Laura decided to see where it went, but she hadn't gone far before loud rustlings in the undergrowth made her uneasy. She froze, half expecting to see malevolent little piggy eyes staring at her. What a triumph that would be for Thérèse Gaudet! To her relief, it was only a rabbit that bounded past and so she kept going until the path ended in a pretty sunlit glade. It seemed the ideal spot to pause for a while and gather her thoughts before heading back to the village.

More rabbits were at work there. They'd shot back underground at her approach but, as Laura remained quiet and motionless, they ventured out again one by one to resume their labours. She watched with fascination as they tunnelled into a long green platform. Were they extending their warren? It certainly looked like it. Roots, soil and stones were being dislodged by their strong hind legs, some landing right at Laura's feet. Then something else caught her eye and she picked it up. Taking a travel tissue from her pocket, she spat on it and started to rub away the dirt.

It was a small badge bearing the instantly recognisable symbol of the CND. A rusty pin attached it to a piece of rotten leather. Wondering which young protestor had dropped it and if there was anything else of interest hidden alongside, she edged closer to get a better look at the rabbits' excavations.

For a moment, she thought that the scattered bones might belong to the discarded pet of a bored Parisian or some poor creature injured and left to die by hunters. Then she caught sight of the unmistakeably human skull and started to retch.

Saint-André-la-Forêt was shimmering in the midday heat as Laura, her heart pounding from the effort of running most of the way back, went in search of the village policeman.

A delicious smell wafted out towards her when the door was wrenched open by a highly irritated elderly man.

"Yes?"

Laura recognised him by the prominent port-wine stain on his left cheek as one of Thérèse Gaudet's customers. If he knew who she was, which seemed highly likely in such a small community, he wasn't giving anything away. Looking down his nose at her tangled hair and torn trousers, he made her feel like an escapee from an institution.

"Even if the remains you've found are human, Madame, which I very much doubt, I see no need to disturb my son's lunch. The bones will have been there for many years. Since the last war, perhaps, or even the one before. This area has seen a great deal of fighting."

"But they can't be as old as that!" argued Laura. "There was a CND badge lying alongside them and the movement didn't start until the late 1950s."

"The CND?"

"The Committee for Nuclear Disarmament. Have you never heard of the Aldermaston March? No, I don't suppose you would have, but a lot of British people were involved."

His expression became even colder, if that were possible, and he took a step backwards into the building. "Leave it to me," he said. "I'll ask my son to look into the matter when he can. In the meantime, I advise you to leave well alone. Good day."

Still clutching the badge, Laura was fuming as the door closed in her face. Whether Jean-Claude and his father liked it or not, she was going to pick up her car straight away, collect her belongings from the café and put as much distance as possible between herself and Saint-André-la-Forêt.

The Spitfire was waiting on the forecourt. It had been washed and polished and looked fine, but gratitude was the last thing on Laura's mind. If the keys had been in the ignition, she'd have driven off without so much as a by-your-leave.

The front door of the Binards' house stood open, so she gave a cursory knock and marched in, ignoring Mac's offer of a paw.

Margot, who was just spreading a green and white oilcloth over the kitchen table, looked quite relieved to see her. "Jean-Claude and Papa have gone off to a breakdown and won't be back for ages, but Charlot promised to take your car round to the café for you. He hasn't turned up yet and I can't think what's keeping him."

"It really doesn't matter. I'm here now. Give me my keys, please, and I won't disturb you any longer."

"Oh, it's really no trouble, Madame. I'm glad of your company. I hope you'll stay for some lunch before you set off?"

"No thank you. I only want my keys."

"A cup of tea, perhaps? I've just made a pot for myself."

Laura, in no mood to be sociable, shook her head, but Margot looked so disappointed that she felt guilty and sat down. "Just ten minutes and then I must be off. Oh, by the way, perhaps this could be passed on to your local policeman some time. It might assist his enquiries, if he ever gets round to making any."

Nothing could have prepared Laura for Margot's reaction to the sight of the little badge. Colour flamed in her cheeks as she let go of the tea pot, seized Laura by the shoulders and started to question her in a strange mishmash of French and English. So the woman really was unbalanced! Anxious as she was to be on her way, Laura didn't feel that she could leave her alone in such an agitated state. In any case, Margot was standing squarely between her and the outside door.

Extricating herself with difficulty, she said, "Sit down, Madame, and please calm yourself. It's nothing out of the ordinary, you know. Everyone had one of these badges years ago." This was definitely not the time to go into details about the circumstances of the discovery.

"Everyone?"

"Well, not everyone, but thousands of us did in the UK."

"And in France?"

"I really couldn't say."

"Tell me where you found it. Please!" The look in the green eyes was so wild that Laura started to doubt her ability to cope with Margot alone. She'd even have been happy to see Charlot swaggering into the kitchen.

"Up in the forest. Past the big clearing. Why? Do you think you know who lost it there?"

"Lost it? Yes, perhaps she did. That is, I think I remember, but I'm not sure. Something terrible must have happened." She buried her head in her hands as the babbling gave way to choking sobs. All Laura could do was put an arm round her shaking shoulders and wait for the storm to pass.

After a while, Margot raised a red and tear stained face towards her and said, "I'm so sorry, Madame. The memories come and go, you see. Just fragments sometimes. It's always been the same."

"Always?"

"Since I woke up here all those years ago with no idea of who I was. I'm sorry. You want to go and I shouldn't be burdening you with all this." The brave words didn't ring true. How could Laura possibly leave her alone now, even if she hadn't been so intrigued?

"That's fine," she said. "You obviously need to talk and I've always been a good listener." Margot's look of gratitude convinced her that she was doing the right thing.

"Well, Jean-Claude and his father found me lying unconscious in the forest one day and took me in. Just like Mac, I suppose. Another stray. It was over twenty years ago, or so they tell me, and I can't remember anything at all before that. I came round with no idea where I was. Even trying to remember my name was like looking through swirling fog in a long dark tunnel."

"Didn't they call a doctor?"

"Yes. The cuts on my hands needed stitches. I've still got the scars. Look!"

"Did they notify the police?"

"I suppose so, but I was never identified. I had no papers, you see, nothing at all. No memories. Just such terrible dreams."

"Dreams about what?"

"The same thing, night after night. Sometimes even when I thought I was awake. Shadows, awful shadows on the bedroom walls. A huge man looming over me. A woman with an axe. A baby. I knew somehow that the baby was dead, but it was still moving round and round with the others. I used to sit up and scream, but I couldn't explain the dream to anyone. All my words had gone. They had to teach me to speak again, just as though I were a child."

"But you did remember your name eventually. Margot."

"No, not even that. They had to call me something, so Jean-Claude suggested Marguerite after his favourite flower. The garden behind the house is full of them in the summer, you know. I'm Margot for short."

"I can only imagine how frightening all that must have been for you, not even to know your own name."

"Yes indeed. Jean-Claude had given up his bedroom for me, but every time I called out he ran upstairs and held me in his arms until I went back to sleep." She gave a watery smile and ran a hand across her forehead, as if soothing away a bad headache. "He could always comfort me, but he never tried to take advantage, if you know what I mean."

Laura did know and her opinion of Margot's husband had gone up immeasurably. How lucky she had been to fall into his gentle hands rather than the clutches of his lecherous cousin!

"Much later on, when I felt better, we started to kiss a lot and then... Well, I wanted to as much as he did and he said that's how babies were made and we'd better get married first. Apart from the time he had to do his National Service, when Papa looked after me, we've never been apart for a single night." The tears had stopped and her voice was full of pride. "Jean-Claude said that he would love and protect me for the rest of my life."

"Protect you from what?"

The furrow between Margot's eyebrows deepened as she thought about it. "I don't really know. He said that there were bad people out there, but he and his Papa, who would be my Papa now, wouldn't ever let them hurt me."

It was time to change the subject again, although Laura's choice was an unfortunate one. "And your children? I suppose they've grown up and left home now."

A great sadness came over Margot's face and Laura thought that she was going to cry again. "We never had a baby after all and now we've given up hope. Please, I really need to see where you found the badge. Will you take me there?"

"That really isn't a good idea. I haven't told you the whole story, you see, and I don't want you to get upset again."

"What could be worse than never getting my memory back?"

Getting it back, perhaps, thought Laura. Why else would the two men have gone to such elaborate lengths to protect her? Did she, Laura, have the right to open Pandora's box? "What about your husband?" she asked in desperation. "Your father-in-law? Shouldn't we wait for them?"

"No. I wouldn't go up there alone, but there's something about you, Madame. I don't know what it is, but I trust you to keep me safe." The hope in her eyes would have melted a far harder heart.

"All right, but you must call me Laura."

There were areas of deep shadow in the forest as Laura led the way along the now familiar track and into the big clearing.

Margot stood stock still and gazed around, bewildered. "There's nothing here."

"Did you expect there to be? Surely you've been this way before?"

"No. It's supposed to be haunted and yet..."

"Have you remembered something?" Laura was sure that she'd seen a flash of recognition.

"I thought so for a moment, but it's gone again."

"Do you know what that blocked up entrance might be?"

As she spoke, a cloud crossed the sun and Margot shivered. "I don't know, but this place gives me a very bad feeling and I wish we hadn't come. Mac hates it too. I can tell."

It was true. The little Scottie had lost all his normal exuberance and started to whimper. Had he picked up on his mistress's mood or was there really something sinister in the atmosphere? In any event, Margot's grip on Laura's hand had tightened and she spoke with renewed urgency.

"Hurry up, please, and show me where you found the badge. Then take me home. I don't like this part of the forest at all."

"Neither do I. Let's forget the whole thing. You'll only get more distressed than you already are if we go on."

"How do you know that?"

It was a reasonable question and one that Laura felt obliged to answer. "Because of what I found with it."

"What did you find? I insist on knowing. I'm not a child."

Oh dear! She wasn't, of course, but Laura had grave doubts about Margot's psychological maturity. It was too late now, though. They were quite alone and she could only hope that the sight of the bones wouldn't tip her companion over the edge.

Rabbits scattered at their approach and Mac, still whimpering, showed no interest in chasing them. Their work had progressed well during Laura's absence and the pitiful remains she'd found before had been partially covered with soil. Without saying a word, she found a stick and wiped them clear.

Margot gasped and then, kneeling to place the little badge next to the skull, looked up at Laura with tear drenched eyes. "Oh, God," she said, "I know who this must be. Everything has started to come back to me and I really wish it hadn't."

Laura knelt down beside her and took the trembling hands in her own. There was only one thing for it. "Let's go back to your house and make a nice cup of tea," she said gently. "Then you can tell me all about it."

Charlot was standing by the front door, tapping his foot impatiently and looking at his watch. "What time do you call this?" he said sharply.

"I might ask you the same question," retorted Laura. "You were supposed to deliver my car by twelve, weren't you?"

"Yes, well I was delayed and I've been hanging around here for the best part of an hour when I've got much better things to do with my time." His attention switched to Margot, who was unlocking the door. "What's the matter with her, anyway? She looks as though she's been crying. Have you done something to upset her?"

"No. Of course not."

"Well I'll be off then. I won't wish you bon voyage and I hope never to see you again."

"The feeling is quite mutual, Monsieur, I assure you."

As he turned on his heel to leave, a tremulous voice called out in English. "Are you coming, Laura?" Engulfed by wave after wave of memories, Margot needed all the support that her new friend could give her.

Charlot hesitated, shook himself and set off for the village as fast as his legs could carry him.

Part Two

1965

Chapter 1

Daisy sighed, sure that her rucksack and rolled up sleeping bag had doubled in weight since they left the village behind them. It was dry underfoot, but having to pick her way between the ruts made by heavy tyres made the going slow.

"How much further can it be?" asked Kate. She didn't really expect an answer, but Ronnie snapped,

"How the hell should we know? That funny looking woman in the café said about twenty minutes, but we've been walking for at least half an hour. Do you think she sent us the wrong way on purpose because we didn't buy anything?"

"I shouldn't think so. We found the garage and the archway and this looks like the main track into the forest. I'm sick to death of carrying these cases, though."

The other girls ignored the complaint. Who but Kate would bring a whole matching set of luggage to a work camp in the middle of nowhere? They still hadn't got over the fact that she'd actually decided to come.

"It didn't look far on that sketch map they sent us," she continued.

"You mean the one that showed Paris six inches away?" scoffed Ronnie. "We sat for hours on that smelly bus."

"No we didn't, although it took us long enough to find it. The driver really did remind me a bit of Jean-Paul Belmondo."

"Jean-Paul who?"

"The actor in that poster for French New Wave cinema that someone put up in the common room."

"Oh, him! He looks as though the fag in his mouth is only held on with spit."

Kate flinched. "Do you have to be so crude, Ronnie?"

"Well, the driver should have been looking where he was going instead of drooling over you. I'm sick of it. You're only carrying your own luggage now because there weren't any boys hanging around when we got off the bus. Oh, don't smirk like that!"

"Well, it's not my fault you frighten them all off. Is it Daisy?"

"I just wish that you'd both stop bickering," she replied, already tired of having to act as a buffer between Beauty and the Beast. It wasn't as though they were really friends; just the only three from their 'A' level French class to respond to the advertisement that had been doing the rounds at school.

Kate Fairbairn was a haughty blonde with rarely a hair out of place. A summer baby and not quite seventeen yet, she was the youngest girl in their year but one of the most sophisticated. Ronnie Tanner, dark-haired, dumpy and on the plain side, never missed an opportunity to antagonise her.

The trio struggled on, tired, grubby and cross after a journey that seemed never ending. It had begun the night before at Leeds City Station, where their parents saw them onto the milk train and bombarded them with last minute instructions. Kate's father gave each girl one of his business cards with orders to phone him immediately if they had any trouble with the 'Frogs'. The Tanners, who were going on holiday themselves, kept reminding Ronnie not lose their contact details. Daisy's widowed mother, looking sideways to make sure that the men weren't listening, slipped a little package into her hand and said it would help with 'those days'.

Bleary eyed when they reached King's Cross, they fought their way through the morning rush hour to Victoria Coach station. The Skyways flight across the Channel from Lympne to Beauvais was Daisy's first time in the air and she was relieved not to need a sick bag. A coach ride followed and they were able to breathe fresh air for a few minutes in the Place de la République before plunging down into the stuffy tunnels of the Métro.

The first snag on French soil was finding no sign of the bus they'd been told to catch when they emerged. None of the people rushing by would pause long enough to make sense of Daisy's polite attempts to make enquiries, so an exasperated Kate took the travel instructions from her and stopped a middle-aged businessman in his tracks.

"I deeply regret, Mademoiselle," he said, as though apologising for the inadequacies of the entire Parisian transport system, "that you have been inconvenienced. See here where the print is smudged. The bus you seek does not go from here, the Pont de Saint Cloud, but from the Porte de Saint-Cloud. That is Line 9, direction Pont de Sèvres. Please allow me to escort you."

"No, thank you."

"Then allow me to give you my telephone number. Maybe we could..."

He stared despondently after Kate as Daisy and Ronnie followed her back down into the Métro. They had to pass through nearly twenty more stations, but at least the route was a direct one.

The crowd waiting at the bus stop eyed the girls with undisguised curiosity and only Daisy ventured a polite *"Bonjour, messieurs-dames."* Everyone nodded back and a dark haired boy in bright blue overalls gave her a friendly grin. He was clutching a large newspaper wrapped parcel.

Oil from whatever was inside had leaked onto his hands and there was even a smear on his forehead. Daisy was just plucking up the courage to offer him a tissue when a blue and white single decker arrived.

The three English girls, taken aback by the free for all, were the last to board and just managed to squeeze themselves and their belongings into seats towards the rear. The boy who had grinned at Daisy stood smoking and chatting to the driver. She couldn't help staring at the way his hair curled over the nape of a deeply tanned neck, but she kept her thoughts to herself. Kate, although unlikely to be interested in anyone in overalls, might see it as a challenge and she would never hear the end of it from Ronnie. When the combination of tobacco smoke, petrol fumes and the sour smell of overheated bodies started to make her feel queasy, she tore her eyes away from the boy to concentrate on the scenery.

It was a welcome diversion when the driver's radio started to play the only French pop song that she knew well, introduced by a student teacher who was a fan of Françoise Hardy. It was such a rare departure from their usual diet of grammar and translation that the whole class had seized the opportunity to learn the plaintive lyrics of *Tous les garçons et les filles* by heart. Now she and Ronnie and even Kate were actually singing along with it in France to the amusement of some of their fellow passengers. The boy at the front was watching them with a broad smile on his handsome face. Oh, how she'd like to find love like the girl in the song and walk along hand in hand with someone just like him. Her mother would approve, she was sure.

"Go out and enjoy yourself, darling," she was always saying. "Don't worry about me. I'll be fine." Daisy did worry though and had taken a lot of persuading to set off for France. It wasn't just her mother's health that concerned her. Money was tight too and she hoped that her fluency would improve sufficiently to justify the expense of the journey.

Once out of Paris, they passed farms, market gardens, orchards and huge fields of wheat. The afternoon sun flickering through the dark poplars that lined the road had made Daisy quite drowsy by the time the cultivated areas gave way to the forest marked on their map. It looked shady and inviting and she was almost sorry when the sign for Saint-André-la-Forêt appeared and they turned off the main road. Kate stood up and stretched like a sleek exotic cat, nearly causing the driver to swallow his latest cigarette.

The bus had drawn up in exactly the sort of little square that Daisy had imagined, even to the bright yellow box outside the post office, the white marble war memorial in the centre and the group of elderly men in shirtsleeves playing *boules* on a patch of gravel nearby.

A few other passengers were leaving the bus there too, the boy with the oily parcel amongst them, and he'd disappeared by the time the girls struggled to the front. The driver leapt off to help Kate with her cases and it was only after he'd set off for the next village that she noticed something missing.

"Damn! I haven't got my sleeping bag." She got no sympathy from Ronnie and it was up to Daisy as usual to defuse the situation.

"Don't worry, Kate. We'll ask someone at the *chantier* to ring up the bus company. Now then, where do we go from here? According to that blue and white sign, we're in the Place des Martyrs, but the one carved into the wall above says Place de Verdun. Why would they change it?"

"Who cares? Look, I'll ask those old men."

"Don't! Your shorts would probably give them a heart attack. Let's try in this café. Whoever Thérèse is, she's bound to know."

"It seems ages since we left the main road," moaned Kate, putting down her cases and flexing her slender arms. "And don't you think it was a queer place to build an archway like that? With a few odd bits of wall but nothing to stop people just walking round them."

"I suppose it belonged to an aristocratic family at one time. Didn't you notice the coat of arms?"

"Can't say that I did. I wonder what happened to them."

Ronnie was bored. "Got the chop during the French Revolution, probably. Now can we please move! I'd kill for a drink and the chance to sit down."

Their trek was nearly over. As they emerged from the trees, they were greeted by a cheerful row of international flags on white poles. No one was about, but there was a plume of smoke from the stone chimney of a long single storey wooden building at the far side of the clearing. Two vehicles were parked in a fenced off space immediately behind it and they could scarcely have been more different. One was a shiny white Alfa Romeo sports car with red upholstered seats; the other a grey Citroën van whose corrugated bodywork reminded Daisy of her late father's roll top desk. The only way into their enclosure was barred by a gate, heavily padlocked and sporting a sign saying *PRIVÉ*.

"I wouldn't need telling twice that it's private," said Kate. "Just look at those dogs!" Two mangy Alsatians had barked at their approach and were now snarling and straining at their chains.

Daisy flinched. "Poor things! They look as though they could do with a bath and a good meal."

"So could we," said Kate. "Get your priorities straight!"

"Do you think this is the right place?"

"It must be. Who else would go to the trouble of hanging up all those flags?"

"Even though ours is upside down," sniffed Ronnie. "Any Girl Guide could tell them that. Weren't you a patrol leader, Daisy? I'm surprised you didn't notice?"

"I did, but wasn't it a kind thought to make us feel welcome?"

"I suppose so."

"Where is everyone?" asked Kate. "Oh, crikey! Forget Belmondo! Look at *him!*" A young man with thick wavy hair as blond as hers had appeared in the main doorway of the building. Their eyes locked as he strolled towards them and said,

"Kathryn Fairbairn, Veronica Tanner and Daisy Dobson?"

Kate gave him the full benefit of her baby blue eyes, even Ronnie smiled hopefully and Daisy thought how much more attractive their names sounded in a French accent. A torrent of words followed, from which all she made out was that his name was Raoul Favrin and they had been expected hours ago. Her own hand and Ronnie's received only the briefest of shakes, but Raoul held on to Kate's as she enlisted his help to recover her sleeping bag. Then, directing the girls to leave their luggage outside, he ushered them into the building.

It took a while for their eyes to become accustomed to the gloom of the main room. It was crammed with long wooden tables and benches and the only light came from two grimy windows. The floor hadn't been swept either and Daisy, who'd occasionally stayed in a British youth hostel, started to wonder just what kind of work camp this was. Would an irate bearded warden in shorts and sandals appear at any moment to launch a tirade?

Instead, a small fair haired man with a tired face limped out of the adjacent kitchen, wiping his hands on his greasy apron.

"This is Valentin Morcel, our chef," said Raoul.

"He's not my idea of a Valentine," sniggered Ronnie. Whether he understood the words or not, Daisy couldn't tell, but the tone was clear enough. She stepped forward and shook his hand warmly to make up for Ronnie's lack of tact.

"I'm very pleased to meet you."

He gave her a shy smile. "Likewise, Mademoiselle. I hope you will enjoy your stay with us."

Raoul, his mouth twitching at the corners, invited them to sit down and they collapsed gratefully round the nearest table. "Valentin has something for you." Instead of the refreshments they'd hoped for, it was an old copy of a sports newspaper, a selection of vegetables with half the field clinging to them and three sharp knives.

"These must be prepared straight away."

"But we're shattered," exploded Ronnie in English.

"Shattered? Sorry, I speak a little of your language but..."

"Tired. Hungry. Thirsty. Is that good enough for you?" Raoul gave her what Daisy's mother would have called an old fashioned look.

"It's not Valentin's fault that you weren't here when you should have been. Your names are on the kitchen rota and I expect you to do the job I've given you. The others will soon be back for their evening meal. If you've any objections, take it up with the *patron* when he returns."

Whoever the *patron* might be, Valentin hurried back into his kitchen and started to rattle pots around as though his life depended on it.

Daisy settled down without complaint to get on with a task she was well used to. Ronnie slashed viciously at a few unfortunate potatoes and Kate gave Raoul her most winning smile. As soon as he'd gone, she put down her knife with a look of distaste and went outside to rummage through her luggage in search of hand cream.

Chapter 2

It wasn't long before a noisy group of young people burst in and took their places at the tables. There was a variety of accents and yet, to Daisy's surprise and disappointment, all the conversations seemed to be taking place in English.

She didn't much like the look of the scruffy boy who sat down next to her without a word of greeting but was prepared to give him the benefit of the doubt. He'd just put a big carton of milk onto the table and was filling his own glass, so she held out hers.

"No chance, gel! That's mine. If you want some, you'll have to get your own." She flushed, staggered by the rudeness. The crude *LOVE* and *HATE* tattoos on his knuckles did nothing to improve her opinion of him.

A neatly dressed young man sitting opposite looked reproachful and said in careful English, "You only have to ask Valentin. He keeps a large supply."

Daisy smiled at him uncertainly and said, "Some water from the kitchen will be fine."

He caught her arm as she stood up, nearly knocking off the round spectacles that gave him an owlish look. "Not from the tap. It's supposed to be safe to drink, but the taste is bad. Please, share my mineral water. I have a large bottle here and your friends may have some too. My name is Jaap, by the way. I'm from Rotterdam in the Netherlands."

"Yap?" spluttered Ronnie.

Daisy shot her a warning glance. "Pleased to meet you, Jaap. We're from Leeds in England. These are Kate and Ronnie and my name is

Daisy. It's very good of you to offer to share, but it wouldn't be fair. We'll buy our own drinks. I just hope that they're not too expensive."

"Oh, no, you misunderstand me. Valentin will let you have whatever you like and there is no charge."

"Really?"

"Yes. I was surprised too, given that we pay such a small amount to be here, but it's very nice for us."

"I'll have champagne," laughed Ronnie. "Or would that be asking too much?"

"Just a little, perhaps."

Wine and beer were also on offer, but the girls settled for Orangina. With his milk no longer in danger, the surly boy tossed back his long greasy hair and introduced himself as Doug Rothery from 'The Smoke'.

"Which part of London?" Ronnie was only making conversation, something she rarely did, but he snapped back,

"Does it matter?"

"There's no need to jump down my throat, pal! I was only wondering where you went to charm school."

Ignoring her, Doug turned to Kate. "How's your French, darlin'?"

"In need of practice, although I don't know how that's going to happen here with all the happy campers speaking English."

"Not quite," said Jaap. "Hans-Peter and his sisters are at this moment having a big argument in German, but I know what you mean. I too was disappointed to find no native French speakers staying here. There was a Swedish girl when I first arrived and some Belgians from the Flemish speaking part of their country. The Italians over there speak better French than they do English, but they're leaving tomorrow morning."

"Did you reply to the same advertisement as we did?" asked Daisy. "I'm looking forward to the 'friendly contact with local people' it offered." *Especially if it included the boy from the bus,* she added to herself.

Doug leered. "Oh, you won't have to wait long, especially when the lads from the village see your mate. Unless Raoul gets in there first, of course." There was no need to ask which girl he meant. Kate preened, accepting the compliment as no more than her due, and Ronnie gave him a dirty look. "Water off a duck's back, darlin'," was all he had to say about that as he wandered off to another table.

"I saw the advertisement in a Dutch newspaper," said Jaap, "but Doug didn't apply like the rest of us. He just turned up in the village one day and asked around for a cheap place to stay. His grammar isn't very good and yet he must have been in France a long time to speak as fluently as he does. Rather different from the rest of us, I suppose, who have learnt French at school but are more proficient on paper."

"So you don't think he's a student?"

"He told me that he'd 'dropped out', whatever that means. Expelled, perhaps? When I asked him what he did for a living now, he just said, 'this and that' and changed the subject."

"How about you?"

"I am studying Modern European History and Politics. One day, I hope to be a diplomat."

"I'm sure you'll be very good at it."

"Thank you."

"What are you saying to make Jaap blush?" asked Doug, returning to his seat.

"Just a little compliment," replied the Dutch boy.

"Oh, yes. What's she after?"

"Nothing," protested Daisy.

"I'll believe you, gel, but thousands wouldn't!"

After all that Daisy had heard about French food, her first experience of it was a big disappointment. The grated carrot salad wasn't bad, although it could have done with more seasoning, but the *ragoût de bœuf* and the accompanying vegetables that she'd mostly peeled herself were almost inedible. Chewing on a piece of tough beef, Daisy wondered how anyone could ruin such a simple dish. She was struck by a wave of homesickness as she recalled the flavoursome stews that her mother had taught her to make from cheap cuts. Cooked very slowly over a low heat, the meat was always tender.

Seeing her expression, Jaap suggested filling up on bread and cheese. "The Camembert is quite reliable," he smiled.

"No dessert?"

"Yes, but that comes last and it's only likely to be a bowl of peaches from one of the farms or a yogurt. I don't think Victor brought anything extra this evening."

"Victor?"

"He's still at school, but he delivers the bread and sometimes helps Valentin in the kitchen. His mother runs the village bakery and sends up something special a couple of times a week."

"I don't know what you're grousin' about," said Doug, who'd hardly raise his eyes from his plate. "I'll finish yours if you don't want it."

Whatever Daisy might have said was cut off by the abrupt opening of the outside door. Raoul stood there with Kate's sleeping bag under his arm.

"I met your bus driver," he explained. "He'd finished his shift and was very much hoping to deliver this to you himself, but I told him that I'd save him the trouble."

"Thank you very much." A titter ran round the table as Raoul left and everyone pictured the disappointed driver.

Kate yawned. "Now that I've got this, I'd really like to see our dormitory. A shower and a comfy bed are all I need now."

"I hate to remind you of something," said Doug with obvious satisfaction. "You're still on kitchen duty. The de luxe accommodation will have to wait."

There was no escape. As the dining room emptied, Raoul reappeared and gave them their orders. Handing Kate a little brush to sweep the crumbs off the tables, he said to the other girls, "You two can do the washing up. *Allez-oop!*"

"Right up!" growled Ronnie, not caring if he understood. Once again, Daisy did most of the work.

Valentin didn't come in to check. He had his feet up outside, a heavy black boot on one and a green espadrille on the other. When the girls emerged from the building, he held up his book for them to see. It was *Le Grand Meaulnes*, one of their 'A' level set texts. Daisy was keen to tell him so and stammered something about its being an interesting story.

"I'm glad you think so," he smiled. "It's one of my favourites."

"Big Moan? It's the most boring thing I've ever read," said Ronnie. "What do you think, Kate?"

"I was just thinking that he'd be better off reading a few cookery books." She'd spoken in English and Daisy prayed that Valentin hadn't understood. There was no time for recrimination. Raoul was back, already shouldering Kate's luggage.

"This way to the dormitories, ladies."

They trotted after him and stared in disbelief. About a hundred yards from the building where they'd had dinner, was the gaping mouth of a tunnel. A broken light fitting and what looked like an old fire bell were just visible through the overhanging foliage. Inside, a stone staircase led down into complete darkness. Raoul reached for something on the wall and the dim light barely lasted long enough for him and Kate to descend safely. Daisy and Ronnie were left to stumble blindly down the last few steps.

"God, it's blacker than the Styx!"

"And what's that horrible smell?"

"Drains, I should think. Or sewers?"

"We'd better catch up. I wouldn't want to get lost down here."

Raoul had switched on another light and he and Kate were disappearing down a stone passageway to the right. They stopped at the second of two doorways. Access to a third was blocked by an iron gate shaped like a portcullis and nothing could be seen beyond.

"Surely we can't be expected to sleep down here," said Ronnie. "It smells damp and I've seen more cheerful dungeons."

Raoul had shown them into a long, narrow chamber with a curved ceiling so low that they could almost reach up and touch it. The only natural light came from a small arched window at the far end. It looked out into the forest, but its double row of thick iron bars had failed to protect the glass. At right angles to the two long walls stood a dozen bedsteads, most of them piled high with the possessions of girls who had arrived before them. The three unclaimed beds near the window each held only a thin mattress, rough grey blanket and hard sausage shaped bolster. Also provided were a deeply scored wooden table, a few rickety looking chairs and a rusty stove, cold and thick with dust.

Before the girls could take it all in, Raoul had set down Kate's cases and was on his way back down the passageway.

"Make yourselves at home," he called over his shoulder. "I'll see you at breakfast."

It was Daisy who broke the appalled silence. "Well, at least there are plenty of lights in here."

"Correction," barked Ronnie. "There are plenty of light fittings, but someone's swiped most of the bulbs. What a dump!" No one disagreed.

Kate was staring up at a line of iron hooks that ran the full length of the highest part of the ceiling. "I really need to hang up some clothes. They'll be creased enough already."

"You mean you're actually planning to stay down here?"

She tossed her head. "Of course not. This is ridiculous, but we don't have any choice tonight, do we? It's getting quite dark already. I just want something decent to leave in tomorrow." She picked up her vanity case. "I wonder where the bathrooms are."

"I've got a horrible feeling that they're down the other end of the passageway," said Daisy.

"You mean where that awful smell was coming from?"

"I'm afraid so. We'd better take a look." Groping along the wall, she managed to locate a light switch.

The first thing the girls came across after passing the bottom of the steps was a row of stone sinks built into the wall. A little further on, a set of wooden cubicles spanned the width of the passageway, blocking access to anything beyond.

Ronnie opened one of the doors with her fingertips and recoiled. "Ugh, what a stink! There's just a big hole with places to put your feet.

I wonder what this handle does."

"Don't pull it!" Daisy and Kate had spoken in unison, but it was too late and Ronnie's shoes were engulfed by a puddle of unspeakable filth. If it hadn't been for Daisy catching her elbow, she'd have skidded on the slimy floor and landed in it.

"It's disgusting."

"Well, there's nothing else, unless you want to go back up to the main building."

"Maybe the others are better? They can't all be blocked."

"They're not, but has anyone got any tissues?"

Tired and miserable, the girls made the best of a bad job and returned to the dormitory to settle down. Sleep seemed to come quickly to her companions, but Daisy was regretting ever having set foot in France. Once she got back to England, she'd never leave it again!

Chapter 3

A jolly hockey sticks sort of voice broke into Daisy's dream of bright blue overalls and dark wavy hair. "Come on, now. It's time you three were up. Everyone else has gone to breakfast." The owner of the voice saved them the trouble of groping for their watches. "It's nearly eight o'clock and it's going to be a nice warm day. You'll be all right in shorts."

Ronnie sat up and sleepily wiped the crust from her eyes. "How can you tell? It's so dark down here."

"Oh, that's easy. We take it in turns to go up and do a recce. I'm Caroline, by the way, but my friends just call me Caro."

"And I'm Lucinda," said the girl standing beside her.

"Daisy."

"Ronnie."

"Kate. Look, you two, I'd kill for a shower. There must be one somewhere, surely."

"No. I don't think even the staff have one. Don't worry, though. You'll be able to use the public showers in the village this afternoon. They're attached to the laundry and free to us due to some kind of special arrangement with the woman who owns them. She'd do our washing as well, but we find it just as easy to do it ourselves. It's not as though we've brought much."

"What about loos? Is that foul hole in the ground arrangement all we've got down here?"

"Yes. Ghastly, isn't it? It's called a *toilette à la turque*."

"Well remind me never to go to Turkey!"

Caro glanced at her watch. "Look, you'd better get a move on. You don't want to get on the wrong side of B.B. on your first morning." She'd pronounced the letters in the French way and Daisy was confused.

"*Bé Bé*. Baby?"

"The big boss. The *patron*, as the staff call him. His name is Bertrand Baltzinger, but B.B. is what we call him. Not to his face, of course."

"No sense of humour?"

"Yes, when he's in a good mood, but he's very unpredictable. One moment he can be as nice as pie and the next he's what Doug calls a real *pisse-vinaigre*. I'm sure you can work out what that means. Doug told me that he gave Valentin a black eye a few weeks ago for burning his steak."

"Steak?"

"Oh, yes. He doesn't generally eat with us and the poor chap's up till all hours catering to his requirements. I'm in his bad books myself at the moment."

"Valentin's?"

"No, B.B.'s, but I'm sure he wouldn't dare to get rough with any of us."

"She had a go at him about the way he treats his dogs," explained Lucinda. "There's no wonder they're vicious. No one understands why he needs them, because there's nothing up here worth stealing."

"He told me to mind my own business and called me a *petite salope*, a little slut. Do you know that expression? No? Neither did we. It's certainly not school textbook French, but it was one to add to the list."

Daisy was curious. "What list?"

"Over there, pinned onto the back of the door." Caroline pointed to a long sheet of paper that had been neatly divided into columns. "Doug knows all the rude words and translates them for us. Jaap and Hans-Peter know most of them too, I expect, but they're too gentlemanly to use them in mixed company." She glanced at her watch. "There'll be a few more words to add if you don't get yourselves over to breakfast soon."

"Why didn't we meet this B.B. last night?"

"Oh, he spends more time in Paris than he does here. Got a lady friend, I expect."

"He's not married, then?"

"Not that I've ever heard."

Rummaging around in the gloom for clean underwear, jeans and T-shirts was a nuisance for Daisy and Ronnie, but Kate was in despair.

"This is ridiculous," she said. "It's bad enough not being able to have a wash or do my hair properly, but I don't like leaving all my nice stuff down here. Anyone could walk in."

"True. But unless you want to carry it all up to breakfast with you, you'll just have to chance it like everyone else."

"Thanks, Ronnie! If I did decide to stay, I'd find somewhere to hide the important things. And I'm going to hang my suitcase key round my neck."

Daisy was surprised. "So you might stay after all?"

"Very unlikely, but I'll see what happens this morning."

"By which you mean how you get on with that Raoul character, I suppose."

"Oh, shut up, Ronnie!"

Kate, who despised jeans and was wearing a new pair of tailored shorts, led the way up the steps and out into sunshine so bright that it made them blink.

As they went into the dining room, Valentin smiled at Daisy and held out his hand for her to shake. The others ignored him but were agreeably surprised by the attractive breakfast laid out for them. There were big bowls of milky coffee and baskets full of fresh rolls. Light, crusty and slightly chewy they were delicious with either butter or jam and most people were helping themselves to both.

"Even Valentin can't ruin breakfast," Doug informed them. "Mind you, we do find the occasional dead cockroach that's got into the flour."

"You seem to have survived," commented Daisy, as fastidious Kate started to pull her roll to pieces. "How long have you been in France?"

"Oh, quite a while." He was wearing the same outfit as on the previous evening and she wondered if he might just be hard up rather than mean. His grubby jeans and baggy grey shirt both looked as though they'd seen better days.

"Well, I'll probably be leaving today," said Kate. "I didn't come all the way to France to be a skivvy and sleep down a rabbit hole."

"Skivvy! You hardly lifted a finger last night!"

"Look, Daisy, your mother might let you ruin your hands peeling potatoes, but mine certainly doesn't."

"And the washing up?"

"Without a decent pair of Marigolds? Not likely!" Daisy, whose mother's budget didn't run to the purchase of rubber gloves, was lost for words.

Jaap broke the awkward silence. "It's not so bad here, you know. Raoul's job is to organise the work, but he's... What's the word, Doug?"

"Lazy. Bone idle. He calls himself the foreman and he's in day to day charge, but he doesn't care what we do most of the time. As for his *patron*, he's an original all right. When he shows up, we never know whether he's going to give us all a pat on the back or bite our heads off. Organise an expensive day out or complain about someone leaving a tap runnin' or wastin' electricity."

"Is that why Daisy and I were left in the dark when Raoul showed us the way down to the dorm? The light snapped off when we were only halfway down the steps."

"Yes. You'll just have to learn where the *minuteries* are located and time yourselves between them. Sometimes the lights fail altogether, though. There's no mains electricity up here, of course, and the generator ain't very reliable."

"Great! We should have brought torches as well as sleeping bags!"

Some Germans were on the kitchen rota, but Valentin approached Daisy's table and said nervously, "I'm sorry, but you must wait inside until the *patron* comes to speak to you."

After all the build up, the girls might have been expected to be nervous too. Daisy was, but Ronnie yawned and Kate started to inspect her finger nails.

"Two broken already!" she complained. "I'll have to file them all to the same length."

"You've brought a manicure set to a work camp in the middle of a forest?"

"Certainly I have." She glanced at Ronnie's badly chewed nails and nicotine stained fingers and added, "I have my standards." It was true. Kate rarely smoked, but when she did it was through an elegant little holder that she kept in her handbag.

A shadow fell over the room as Bertrand Baltzinger appeared in the doorway and stood looking at them through mirrored sunglasses. He was a big man in his mid-forties, tall, broad, and with the bull neck of a rugby player. The rolled up sleeves of his checked shirt exposed brawny forearms covered in tattoos. Gold teeth flashed as he greeted each girl in turn and asked her name. There were no tattoos on the hand he offered and even Kate couldn't find fault with his clean, well trimmed nails, but the effect was spoilt by a whole knuckleduster of heavy rings. All were gold and the one on the little finger of his left hand sported a ruby.

"A thousand apologies, young ladies, for not being here to greet you yesterday, but I trust that my staff has taken care of you?" Without waiting for an answer, he continued, "I don't know what you've been expecting, but your stay here won't be all work, you know. I'm already finalising details for the next cultural excursion."

He's just a big teddy bear, thought Daisy, as Kate smiled sweetly and even Ronnie assumed an air of polite interest. Had the other young people been trying to pull their legs about him? If so, Valentin must have been in on the joke as well, although his apprehension had looked quite genuine. Wait, though. The tone had become more serious.

"We don't have many rules and those we do have are for your own safety. We're quite isolated here, you see, but not far from Paris and its criminal element. Do you understand me, by the way, or am I speaking too fast for you?"

"A little perhaps," admitted Daisy, who was finding him more difficult to follow than Valentin.

"Very well," he continued with exaggerated slowness. "That's why it's essential that no one stays behind when we have a day out and why my dogs are turned loose then and also at eleven o'clock every night. You wouldn't wish to be outside while they're on patrol, I assure you."

"But what if someone's ill?" asked Ronnie.

The gold teeth flashed again. "In an emergency, Mademoiselle, ring the bell at the top of the steps and wait there for one of us to come."

"And the dogs?"

"Are trained never to cross the threshold. The only other rule, by the way, is that the staff quarters are out of bounds to you. We respect your privacy and expect you to respect ours. Is that clear?" They all nodded and he looked pleased. "Very well, then. My deputy will explain everything else to you, but just remember what I've said. I wouldn't want your stay with us to be spoilt by any... unpleasantness. I'll see you later on. Have a nice day."

"Was that a threat?" whispered Kate as they walked across to join the group gathered around Raoul.

"No. Of course not. It's his job to look after us, isn't it? I expect he's just got our best interests at heart."

"Good old Daisy! You'd have given Hitler the benefit of the doubt. If this B.B. cared about us so much, he'd get someone in to fix the plumbing."

At their approach, Raoul broke off what he'd been saying to the other young people and turned to greet them. "Has everything been explained to you? Do you have any questions?"

"Just one," quipped Ronnie. "Can we ring the bell for room service?"

"Do I look like a waiter?" Everyone laughed, including Raoul himself.

Daisy nudged Kate. "I think Ronnie's planning to stay. Have you decided yet?"

Kate was looking at Raoul. "I might, if he isn't too much of a slave driver." Right on cue, he winked at her and she blushed prettily.

"OK, everyone. Jobs for this morning. First of all, I want all the mattresses brought up to air. After that, gentlemen, I'd like you to collect any rubbish you can find and then get on with the painting. Ladies, please gather up the spare blankets and hang them on the washing lines over there to get some sun on them. Divide the rest of the work between you, whatever you think is needed. Oh, Kate, I need some help in the office. Would you mind?"

"Would she mind!" glowered Ronnie.

Caro agreed. "It's all right for some."

"You're lucky not to get that disgusting loo again," said Lucinda. Perhaps B.B.'s forgiven you."

"I don't care whether he has or not. I shan't do it. When he told me to clean it out last time, I just threw a bucket of water at it from the doorway. Did he really expect me to get down on my hands and knees with that old scrubbing brush he gave me?"

"Yes, I think he did. You're lucky he didn't go down there and check."

"What could he have done?"

"Nothing really, I suppose, except teach you a few more choice expressions."

"I'll bet our French teacher doesn't know most of them."

"Ours certainly wouldn't," agreed Daisy. "She'd have a fit. All the same, I suppose it's only fair that we all take it in turns to do the mucky jobs."

"You just wait and see," was the reply. "The boys are never told to do them. I don't think B.B. likes girls very much."

Chapter 4

Ronnie whistled through her teeth. "Look at the state of these mattresses! I don't even want to imagine what caused some of the stains. I'm glad we brought our own sleeping bags."

Daisy was panting and wiping her brow. "It's just as well that they're so thin though. I don't think I could have carried a heavier one up all those steps."

Soon all the blankets were hanging on a line suspended between two tall trees. A second line was filled with an assortment of dripping socks and underwear, washed in a bucket of cold water from an outdoor tap. There was a lot of laughter and horseplay. Of the boys, only Jaap and a big blond German student called Hans-Peter were taking their work seriously. They were rolling some of the boulders that had already been painted white by the others to the top of the track and embedding them in the soft earth.

"B.B. wants it lined all the way down to the main road," Jaap explained when Daisy went to see what they were up to.

"What's the point?"

"He says it's to make it safer for vehicles coming up here at night. Deliveries from the village always arrive in daylight, so I suppose he just means his and Raoul's cars. Valentin can't drive."

"Poor fellow," said Hans-Peter. "It's a hard life for him, coping with his disability and being at the beck and call of the other two? I don't know what's going on there."

"Neither do I, but I wish his cooking were as good as your English."

"Thank you, Daisy. My French is more basic, I'm afraid."

"Mine too. I came here to improve it and I've hardly spoken a word of the language since we landed in Beauvais."

"You will do, I'm sure. We get plenty of free time and the locals don't speak much English."

Doug had been right about Raoul. When he'd run out of things for Kate to do in the office, he set up a deckchair. As long as someone walked past him occasionally with a wheelbarrow or a paintbrush, he was quite content to sun himself, roll cigarettes and read his newspaper.

"He's so handsome, isn't he?" sighed Kate. "Just look at those muscles! I'll bet *he* eats his spinach."

"Like Popeye? He's all right, I suppose. Too old for you, though." All the same, Daisy couldn't deny that Raoul's appearance was striking. His tight navy T-shirt showed off bulging biceps and a flat stomach. Spotless white trousers and navy espadrilles completed the outfit.

"Very French," continued Kate. "An Englishman would have insisted on ruining the look with socks. What do you think of him, Ronnie?"

"Daisy's right. He's much too old for you, if that's what you mean. He must be at least twenty-five."

"You're only jealous. He wouldn't look twice at you."

Sensing that he was under scrutiny, Raoul glanced up from his newspaper and waved, jewellery flashing in the sunlight. He wore fewer rings than his boss but sported a heavy gold identity bracelet.

"Good grief! You can't be serious, Kate!"

The warm mattresses, grubby as they were, made perfect sun loungers and Daisy stretched out on one after lunch, feeling that she was finally on holiday. An English boy called Geoff was sketching Hans-Peter's twin sisters, whose hair and eyebrows were so fair that they were almost white.

"They're begging for it," mouthed his friend, "but their big brother won't let them off the leash. I'm Danny, by the way."

"And I'm Maureen," said a girl busy painting her toe nails. "This is me friend Siobhan."

"From Dublin."

"Begorrah! You'd never guess!"

"That's enough from you, Mr Art Student, unless you want an Irish kiss." She pretended to head butt him.

"No thanks. I'd just like you to sit still."

"Oh, go up the river on a bicycle!"

Danny, his own dark hair tied back with a leather thong, had been inspired by their freshly bleached bouffants to draw them as a pair of very brassy looking sunflowers.

Very little work was demanded of anyone that afternoon. Raoul set up a second deckchair and beckoned for Kate to join him. She strolled across looking as cool and detached as usual and returned half an hour later all pink and giggly.

"What did lover boy want?" asked Danny.

"Oh, just to chat, I think. When I leaned over for him to light the cigarette he'd rolled for me, he saw what I was wearing round my neck and asked if it was the key to my heart."

"God! How cheesy can you get!"

She ignored the comment. "I said no. Just to my suitcase. Then he wanted to know if I'd got a boyfriend."

"What a surprise!"Everyone laughed except Maureen.

"I'd be watching yourself with that one."

"Why? Have you been out with him?"

"Feck, no! I just didn't like the way he got over Lena so quickly. She was crazy about him, but the minute she'd gone he started chatting up Astrid and Renate."

"Both twins at once?"

"The randy eejit probably couldn't tell them apart. Anyway, Hans-Peter wouldn't let either of them go out with him unless he went along as well, so that was the end of that."

"Was this Lena German too?" asked Daisy.

"No, Swedish. You'd have liked her. We all did."

"We never got the chance to say goodbye," added Siobhan. "Sure and it was all so sudden, you see. A message arrived while the rest of us were down in the village and Raoul took her straight to the airport."

"Why all the rush?"

"He told us when he got back that her brother had been in a car crash and wasn't expected to live. Anyway, that was the last we ever saw of her."

Geoff looked up from his watch, his freckly face wreathed in smiles. "Only an hour until knocking off time."

"What happens then?"

"Everyone disappears down to the village. There's nothing much to do around here. When you've seen one tree, you've seen them all."

"What time do we have to be back?"

He sighed. "That rather depends on whether you can afford to skip one of Valentin's gourmet meals."

"I certainly can't. Isn't that against the rules, anyway?"

"You mean like the eleven o'clock curfew? No, and even that isn't always enforced. It just depends on B.B.'s mood."

The last task of the day was to take the mattresses and blankets back down to the dormitories.

"Showers!" rejoiced Kate, who hadn't carried any of them. "Come on, you two."

They were heading for the row of flagpoles when Doug caught up and said, "Hey, come with me, if you like. I'll show you a short cut through the casemates, but you'll have to watch your step." He led them down through a clump of trees towards the blind back of a ruined building.

Daisy caught Kate's arm. "I don't like the look of this. Let's go the way we know."

Doug heard her and whipped round. "It's quite safe. There are lots of places like that round here, although some are so overgrown that you can't get into them. This one's all right. You're not scared of the dark, are you?"

Ronnie, full of bravado as usual, pushed past him. "Of course not."

Little light penetrated the cheerless vault, unfurnished apart a few grubby old mattresses pushed up against the wall. The straw on the floor around them was littered with cigarette packets and beer bottles.

"Nice place for a party, I don't think!"

Doug kicked a bottle aside. "I've seen far worse. This is where some of the local kids come to get away from their parents."

A huge hearth at one end showed no sign of recent use, but the drain tunnel opposite stank of urine. It ran the full length of the wall and disappeared into a hole protected by an iron grid. A pair of heavy wooden doors hanging off rusty hinges at the far end revealed the forest beyond.

"What was this place used for?" asked Daisy, not liking to admit that she couldn't wait to get out of it.

"It was part of some fortifications. One of the village lads told me that a whole ring of them was built around a century ago to defend Paris. There are supposed to be tunnels that run for miles. Even all the way into Paris, accordin' to some stories. He called it a labyrinth and the open area up top was the parade ground."

"When were the soldiers last here?"

"During the war, I think. It's a very touchy subject and the older people won't talk about it at all. Kids like Victor will tell you that their fathers all fought for the Resistance. According to Raoul, though, the *patron* is the only one with a medal. You must have seen it in the office, Kate?" She nodded. The frame had been hard to miss. "He likes to show it off when he has his friends round for meals. Not the stuff we get, of course. You wouldn't catch *them* eating horse meat."

"You wouldn't catch me eating it either!" Daisy couldn't read *Black Beauty* without bursting into tears.

"What do you think you had for lunch?"

"You're kidding!"

"You think so?"

Doug deliberately led them past the *boucherie chevaline* with the horse's head sign outside and scoffed at Daisy's cry of revulsion. She was glad to see the back of him when he left them at the entrance to the showers. At least they were the first to arrive, thanks to his short cut. The price was clearly marked outside and the girls wondered whether they were expected to pay after all, but the white haired owner refused to take their money. Instead, she handed them each a couple of towels and ushered them through to a row of spotless cubicles. The water was piping hot and the joy of washing away the grime of the last couple of days soon raised Daisy's spirits. She thanked the sad eyed younger woman waiting to mop out her cubicle for the next customer and joined Ronnie outside to wait for Kate.

"Have you ever seen anyone with such an ugly nose?"

"Shush, Ronnie. She might hear you."

"Well, it's definitely been broken at some time and badly. I wonder if her husband did it."

Their interest was short lived. When Kate came out, grumbling about the lack of a hair dryer, they turned their attention to exploring the village.

Daisy was thrilled. "Oh, look!" she said. "There's a *boucherie-charcuterie* and a *bar-tabac* and a *pharmacie...*"

Ronnie groaned. "What are we? First formers?"

Kate dug an elbow into her ribs. "Don't be mean. She's never been to France before."

Daisy was unperturbed. Her mother had been too ill to do without her when most of her classmates had taken part in the Yorkshire-Lille exchange and she was determined to make the most of this opportunity.

"That must be the *mairie* over there with the French flag outside it. The mayor of a village like this has to marry couples to make it official, you know, even if they have a church wedding."

"Well I'm sure that isn't going to affect any of us, Daisy, unless you want to marry a country bumpkin."

Ronnie was the first to spot a mouth watering display of cakes in the window of the shop adjoining the bakery. It also sold sweets, big bars of Suchard chocolate in their distinctive purple wrappers and a variety of ice creams. Service came with a smile from the plump lady behind the counter and each girl's purchase was put into an individual cardboard box.

Kate and Ronnie had been unable to resist the chocolate eclairs, but Daisy had a chewy meringue with a chestnut cream topping and whipped cream on top. It was going to be messy to eat with her fingers, she was sure, but well worth it.

"Let's go and sit over there," said Ronnie, leading them towards a bench by the war memorial. Resting her feet on the white chain link fence, she started to eat her eclair. Kate followed suit, but Daisy was uncomfortable.

"Don't you think that's rather disrespectful?" The others, mouths full of cake, shook their heads. Daisy remained standing to eat her meringue and study the inscriptions. Soldiers from both world wars were listed and there was an extra brass plaque in memory of civilians martyred by the Germans during the Occupation. "That's odd," she said. "There are two people listed with no surnames. Just Fleur and Paul. I wonder who they were."

"Who cares?" said Ronnie, wiping her sticky fingers on her jeans. "Hey, wasn't he on our bus yesterday?"

Daisy whipped round to see a figure in bright blue disappearing across the square. "I don't suppose he was impressed with you two," she said quietly.

"If you fancy him," retorted Ronnie, "it's just as well that he didn't stop. Your face is plastered with cream and sugar."

Daisy looked so crestfallen that Kate took pity on her. "Oh, cheer up! Why should we care what someone we don't even know thinks of us? Look, I'll tell you what. Let's go over to the café for a drink before we go back."

"We mustn't make a habit of it, though." Daisy had come to France with far less than the £50 limit imposed on travellers by the UK government the year before and needed to make it last.

"I can't imagine that a cup of coffee will break the bank. Come on, you two. It's on me."

"Have you noticed her roots?" remarked Kate, as the owner of *Chez Thérèse* busied herself behind the bar. "They're blond, so why would she dye her hair black? It must take a lot of effort to keep up to. I'd never dream of changing mine. And those eyebrows!"She wet a finger to smooth her own fine brows and then casually swept back her long silky locks.

"Stop it, Kate," hissed Daisy. "She's watching you through the mirror over the bar. I'm sure she knows we're talking about her."

"What if she does? No one forces her to dye her hair. She probably thinks it suits her."

Ronnie grinned. "Well I don't. Do you remember that film we saw in English of *A Tale of Two Cities*?"

"Oh, yes. The whole class swooned over Dirk Bogarde."

"Well, it's as though Lucy Manette has changed into Madame Defarge. What a coincidence that she owned a wine shop and her name was also Thérèse! I wonder if this old hag keeps her knitting under the bar. From the look on her face, Kate, you'll be first for the chop if she does!" Still laughing, the girls drained their cups, paid what they owed and left the café.

Chapter 5

The showers and cakes had put new life into Daisy and her companions and they sat down on the steps outside the dining room to enjoy the late afternoon sunshine. Maureen and Siobhan joined them, pink sponge rollers only partially concealed under their chiffon scarves, and Victor came out of the kitchen to try out his English. It seemed to consist mainly of parroted obscenities, which failed to impress the girls but seemed to amuse Raoul, who was leaning out of the office window. He beckoned to Kate to come across and two minutes later she came back in triumph.

"Guess what! I've got a date tonight."

"With Raoul?"

"Of course with Raoul. Who else round here is worth going out with?"

"Where's he taking you?"

"Oh, don't look so suspicious, Daisy. Somewhere in Paris for dinner, I think. I couldn't understand everything he said."

"Are you going in that horrible old van?"

"God! I hope not. It's probably filthy inside."

"The van belongs to B.B. anyway," said Siobhan. "He's just had a new part fitted, but it's still not running properly. The Alfa Romeo is Raoul's car."

"It would be! How appropriate!" sneered Ronnie, but Kate was too busy planning what to wear to react to the sarcasm. It would take her long enough to apply her make-up well enough to achieve a 'natural' look. She came back up from the dormitory in a pink Biba shift dress and white sling backs with kitten heels.

Raoul pursed his lips in a silent whistle as she teetered across the gravel to join him. "You look just like B.B."

A look of horror crossed her face. "What?"

"B.B. Brigitte Bardot."

"Thank heavens for that!" snorted Ronnie.

Raoul had changed into a white jacket, open necked black shirt, black trousers and white leather loafers. The aftershave wafting across to the group on the steps completely overpowered any perfume Kate might have been wearing, but the general effect was impressive and it was hard not to be envious. At the very least, Kate would have something to boast about to her friends back in England.

Once the Alfa Romeo had roared off down the forest track, Daisy turned to Ronnie and said, "Do you think we should have brought dresses too?"

"Why? Would you want to go out with Raoul?"

"No, of course not."

"It might have been nice to be asked, I suppose, if only to wipe the smug look off Kate's face."

"He wouldn't have invited either of you anyway," said Maureen. "The gentleman prefers blondes right enough."

"Natural blondes, that is," added Siobhan. "Unlike his precious Brigitte Bardot. Or Marilyn Monroe, come to think of it. He hasn't given Maureen and me a second glance. Don't worry, though, Daisy. Raoul isn't the only decent looking chap around here. Just you wait until after dinner!"

A glimmer of hope made Daisy rummage through her rucksack for something pretty to wear. Her denim A-line skirt wasn't too badly creased and she added a white broderie anglaise blouse with short puffed sleeves.

"You look very pretty tonight, Daisy," said Valentin, as he brought out the dish of the day, overcooked pasta in a watery cheese sauce.

"Looks like Hopalong's linin' you up for a date!"

Daisy glowered at Doug. "Don't be silly. He's just being kind. In any case, he's probably older than my mother."

"Well, I've seen him watchin' you. I'll bet he's glad you didn't go off with Mr Smooth."

It wasn't long after the tables had been cleared that a group of teenagers appeared through the trees. As they dismounted from their motorbikes and mopeds, a lot of vigorous handshaking and cheek kissing went on between those already acquainted and Daisy and Ronnie felt rather out of it. That was before Victor headed towards them with a couple of strange boys in tow.

"I'll bet the little squirt's going to try and pair us off," said Ronnie. "Which one do you want? Pug Face or the ginger one? He wouldn't be bad if he did something with his hair. It looks like a bog brush."

"I don't want either of them," said Daisy, who'd spotted another boy coming up behind them, tool bag in hand. Her heart started to race, but he walked straight past, just pausing long enough to ruffle Victor's hair.

"Where's your friend this evening?" asked Bog Brush. "The blonde, I mean."

"Why?"

"Oh, Victor told me that she's very pretty and I thought she might let me buy her a drink in the village."

"You're too late, chum. She's gone out with Raoul."

"Raoul? *Merde!* Well, would you like to come instead?" It wasn't a flattering invitation, but Ronnie clambered onto the back of his bike before he could change his mind.

"What about my other friend?"

"Thanks for the afterthought," muttered Daisy under her breath.

"Oh, she can ride down with Gérard."

Pug leered and Daisy felt that she was left with little choice after the others set off. Why, oh why, had she changed into a skirt, though? The French boy's hot eyes were fixed upon her legs as she tried to preserve some modesty.

She had to grip hard with her knees to avoid the need to hold onto him as they raced over the uneven ground and took side turnings far too narrow for comfort. Not only was Pug showing off, but it wasn't long before her other misgivings were justified. Steering with one hand as they bumped along through the trees, he reached round with the other and groped as high up her skirt as he could reach. A shocked Daisy pushed his hand away at once and shouted at him to stop. She scrambled off the bike as soon as he pulled up, but so did he. During the half hearted wrestling match that followed, she failed to persuade him that she wasn't 'that sort of girl' and it was only when she employed a colourful phrase learnt that very day from the list on the dormitory door that he got the message. No apology followed. With a Gallic gesture of indifference, Pug climbed back onto his bike and rode off without her.

Starting to feel like Mole in the Wild Wood but determined not to panic, Daisy wasn't sure what to do for the best. Should she stay put and hope that Ronnie would insist on coming back to look for her or should she try to find her own way down to the village? She'd only been alone with Pug for a few minutes, so he couldn't have stranded her far from the main track. On the other hand, a wrong turning might take her further into the forest. Would Ronnie even notice that she was missing, though? She might be getting on too well with Bog Brush to give anyone else a thought for hours.

Daisy was still thinking the matter through when she heard the sound of a more powerful engine than Pug's and saw a single light bobbing through the trees. Without hesitation, she rushed headlong towards it and flagged down the rider.

A puzzled voice enquired, "What are you doing here all by yourself?"

Daisy had never been as glad to see anyone in her life. "Please could you take me down to the village?" she stammered.

"I'd be happy to, but I've been working under a van and you wouldn't want to get oil on your pretty blouse."

"It really doesn't matter." Before he could raise any further objection, Daisy was seated behind him with her arms clasped around his waist.

The first stars were coming out when they pulled up outside *Chez*

Thérèse. Most of the tables outside were occupied by cheerful young people. Ronnie, with Bog Brush draped over the back of her chair, was in the thick of it and barely glanced at Daisy and her new companion. The two art students were doing their best to impress some pretty French girls and Caroline and Lucinda were sharing a golden pyramid of thin, crisp chips with Doug and Jaap. Daisy's mouth watered and her rescuer laughed.

"I don't think Valentin feeds you very well. Shall we have some *frites* too?" Very happy to be included in the 'we', Daisy nodded. He saw her seated at a table for two by the open door and disappeared inside.

"Hey, look who's here at last!" called Doug. "What have you done with Gérard?"

"Gérard?"

"Don't try and look so innocent. You disappeared with him fast enough after Victor introduced you."

Daisy shuddered. "That little creep? I've no idea where he is, but I hope I never see him again."

"Got a bit frisky, did he? Well, what did you expect?"

"He *is* French," giggled Caroline. "He probably thought you'd be insulted if he didn't make a pass."

Jaap leaned across. "Don't worry about him, Daisy. He doesn't come in here much. His parents own the *bar-tabac* across the square."

"Where that loud music's coming from?"

"Yes," answered Lucinda. "That's where you'll find Maureen and Siobhan most evenings. We only went there once and didn't like it."

"They just enjoy mixing with the bad boys," added Caroline.

Doug was unimpressed. "The *blousons noirs*? A few country hicks who think they look tough in their leather jackets. They'd run a mile if they ever met real hard men like the Krays."

"I expect there are people just as bad as that in Paris."

"But not out here in the sticks, whatever B.B. might say to keep us in line."

"The only other reason that place is popular is because it's got table football and a jukebox," said Jaap. "There'd be plenty of room for those here if Madame Thérèse got rid of her old piano. It's not as though it's ever played. She keeps it locked all the time."

"Why does she hang onto it then? You'd think she'd be glad of the extra money."

"I don't know. I wouldn't dare to ask her and Valentin will only say that she has her own reasons for keeping it."

Doug wasn't listening. "Just look over there now! I see trouble brewin'."

Several of the boys milling around outside the rival establishment were staring across at the German twins, despite the presence of their formidable elder brother, but Daisy didn't care. Her conversation with the young mechanic was stilted at times and yet the harder each strained to understand what the other was saying, the more they laughed about it.

"I only asked what that was called," she protested, as he placed a bright green drink in front of her.

"Sorry," he grinned. "I thought you wanted to try one. It's called a *diabolo menthe*, made from mint syrup and lemonade."

Daisy was too polite to say that it tasted like mouthwash, but she couldn't help pulling a face and he offered her a sip of his beer to take the taste away. Sharing a glass brought them even closer together and they laughed off the snide comments from other tables about the oil stains on her blouse. At least they weren't in the shape of handprints, she thought, although better his than Pug's if they had been.

"Do you mind if I smoke, Day-zee?"

"Not at all." He produced a battered packet of Gauloises from the top pocket of his overalls and offered her one.

"Thank you." The cigarette was untipped and the strength of the dark tobacco nearly took her breath away. Eyes streaming, she reached out for the *diabolo menthe* and took a grateful swig. "I don't really smoke."

"You don't say! That's good, though. I smoke too much. My father thinks..."

Whatever it was that his father thought would have to wait. There was a crash as a table went over and pandemonium broke out. Two of the leather jacketed boys had come across to chat up the twins and one of them was lying flat on his back.

"Fight, fight, fight!"

Both establishments emptied rapidly as their young customers squared up to each other, but it was Thérèse Gaudet's intervention that startled everyone. Elbowing the crowd out of her way, she flew at Hans-Peter, shook her fist in his face and started to screech at him. Daisy couldn't understand most of it and had to have it explained to her later that *Boche* was a rude word to call a German. It seemed that they still weren't welcome in the village as far as the café owner was concerned. The strange woman ranted at the startled boy until her fury was spent and then rushed back inside, hiding her face in her apron. The door slammed, and the blind came down.

Everyone was embarrassed by the outburst, even Antoine, the boy Hans-Peter had punched. He muttered an apology to the young German, who handed him a couple of paper serviettes to mop up the blood from his cut lip. People started to drift away in twos and threes, some towards the *bar-tabac* and others homeward. A rumble of thunder in the distance made those on foot quicken their step to reach cover before the rain came down.

Daisy, who was walking with the group that included Hans-Peter and his sisters, wanted to know if he was all right.

"A bit shaken," he confessed. "I wasn't expecting anything like that to happen to me in France so long after the war. You wouldn't think that such a shrew could be Valentin's sister, would you? He's so harmless."

"I certainly wouldn't! I hope she doesn't bully him."

Hans-Peter hesitated for a moment and then said, "Do you want to know the irony of what happened this evening? My mother was French, or so I've been told."

"Oh, dear. I'll bet Madame Thérèse would feel awful if she knew that."

"Perhaps she would, although my having a German father might be enough for her to hate me."

"You were born during the war, weren't you? That must have been very difficult for your parents, with their countries being on different sides."

"You'd think so, but the truth is that I never knew either of them. I was adopted, you see. *Mutti* only told me that one day when we'd had a row and she was very sorry about it afterwards. I'd never have known otherwise."

"Are your sisters adopted as well?"

"No. We look quite alike, don't we, but we're not blood relatives. The twins were born to my adoptive parents after they'd given up hope of having children of their own. I had to take something of a back seat after that but was expected to look after them just the same. As you've seen, I still do."

"Would you like to find your real parents?"

"Of course, but so many records have been lost that it's very unlikely."

Jaap shook his head sadly. "You might not like the truth if you found it," he said. "Terrible things happened in all the occupied countries, as I'm sure you know."

There was no sign of Kate in the girls' dormitory and Daisy was getting ready for bed by the time Ronnie appeared, her neck covered in red marks.

"Love bites from Bog Brush?"

"Don't call him that any more. His name is Charlot and I'm meeting him again tomorrow night. Anyway, you're a fine one to talk. How come you turned up with that boy from the bus? I see he'd had his oily hands all over you before you even got to the café."

"He certainly had not!"

"Well how did your blouse get into that state?"

"He'd been fixing B.B.'s van before he picked me up on his bike. Pug Face abandoned me in the middle of the forest because I wouldn't let him maul me."

Ronnie didn't sound unduly concerned. "Oh, is that what happened? Well, did you hit it off with your knight in shining overalls?"

"I thought so, but he just said goodnight, shook my hand and left me to walk back up here with the others."

"Would you go out with him if he asked you?"

"Might do, I suppose."

"What's his name, by the way?"

"Jean-Claude."

Chapter 6

The sky was a leaden grey as everyone splashed across for breakfast the next morning. The tables were already laid and Raoul was making the coffee.

"Where's Valentin?"

Raoul shook his hand at Ronnie as though he had burnt his fingers. "That's none of your business."

"Charming!"

"But you can all have the morning off. It's too wet to do any work outside."

As soon as the office door closed behind Raoul, Doug said, "He won't tell you, but I got it out of Victor when he brought the bread. One of the dogs bit Valentin last night. He'd taken some extra scraps out for them and got too close. The boss was furious."

"With the dog?"

"No, with Valentin. The dogs are half starved to keep them keen. He called him a *minus*, a moron, and said that he'd got better things to do than waste time taking him to see the doctor. Then he shoved him into the van anyway and off they went."

"I'd tell Baltzinger where to stick his job," was Danny's opinion.

"I don't think Valentin can," said Jaap thoughtfully. "You must have noticed how he only stammers when he's around him. Victor always looks nervous too. He's got some kind of hold over them, I'm sure, but I can't figure out what it is."

Doug had lost interest. "Oh, what does it matter? Anyone fancy a game of cards? I've got a couple of packs down in the dorm."

"Can't you bring them over here?"

"If you think I'm gettin' soaked twice..."

Kate wrinkled her nose. "Why ever did we agree to this?"

"Because we'd nothing else to do?" Daisy was right. The dining room boasted only a few old copies of Paris Match and a solitary table tennis set. That had been commandeered by Hans-Peter in an attempt to keep his sisters out of trouble. He'd pushed a couple of tables together and Jaap, who apparently posed no threat, had been invited to join them in a game of mixed doubles. Danny and Geoff had their sketchpads out as usual, Maureen was teasing the lacquered mass of Siobhan's hair into a new style and Caroline and Lucinda were writing postcards home. There was a rack of them in the office, but Daisy had been disappointed to find none at all showing the *chantier* or even the village. It was a shame, because there was a box on B.B.'s desk for outgoing mail and he even allowed the young people to help themselves to stamps.

Apart from the changing room smell, the boys' dormitory differed from the girls' only in that it had bunk beds and unbroken glass in the barred window.

"At least your lights work," remarked Ronnie.

"That's because we've pinched your bulbs. Push all that washin' off the table and we'll make a start. How about Strip Poker? Don't look so shocked, Daisy. Have you never heard of the Swingin' Sixties?"

"I don't think they swing as much in Leeds as they do in London."

"So you Yorkshire girls are too prudish to play?"

"No, but it's freezing down here." Kate had a point. The rain lashing against the barred window made the stone chamber feel very bleak.

"Anyway, what would we get out of it if *you* lost?" asked Ronnie. "You're hardly Charles Atlas."

Doug shrugged off the insult. "How about riskin' a few bob on ordinary Poker, then, or Pontoon?"

"You must be kidding!"

"Not even a tanner, Ronnie?"

"Is that supposed to be a joke?"

"I'd let one of you hold the bank?"

"Definitely not."

"I might as well put the cards away, then."

"I didn't want to play anyway," yawned Kate. "Did you, Daisy?"

"Not really. We're all supposed to be over here to practise our French, instead of which we've only got each other to talk to."

"You were practisin' your French all right last night, Ronnie. That lad Charlot had his tongue half way down your throat when I saw you."

"Saw us where?"

"Propped up against that big tree behind the café."

"Oh, shut up, Doug. You're only jealous."

"Don't flatter yourself. Anyway, get out of here, the lot of you, if you don't want to play. You're not supposed to be in our dormitory anyway."

"So why did you invite us in?"

"It was worth a try."

Moving next door gave the other girls the chance to huddle in their sleeping bags and pump Kate about her date with Raoul.

"Did he try it on?" was all that Ronnie wanted to know.

"Certainly not!"

"Well there's a surprise!"

"So where did you go?"

"Right into Paris, Daisy. We had a *steak-frites* and then walked along the Seine. Some of the buildings were floodlit and the reflections in the water were beautiful."

Ronnie burst into song. "Under ze breedges of Paris..."

Kate smiled. "I must admit, Ronnie, that I did think of that and there were couples snogging all over the place, but Raoul just wanted to talk."

"About himself, I suppose."

"No, not at all. He wanted to know all about me and even asked if I dyed my hair."

"Cheeky monkey! Did you ask him if he'd got all his own teeth?"

"No, of course not. Actually, he was so interested in me that I didn't get the chance to ask him much at all. It made a nice change from boys who just want to talk about themselves or football."

"Well, he's hardly a boy, is he?"

"He's only twenty-five."

"And the rest!"

To stop Ronnie goading Kate any further, Daisy said, "I know it's early days yet, but you look really smitten. Do you think there's any chance that Raoul might be THE ONE?"

Kate bit her bottom lip and nodded. "Maybe. I like him a lot, but we'll see how it goes. I don't know how my parents would feel about my marrying a foreigner."

"Aren't you rather jumping the gun?"

"I suppose so, but it's going to be marriage or nothing for me. I've got no intention of ending up like some I could mention. Do you remember that Third former last year?"

Daisy shuddered. "I can't imagine anything worse than having to give up your baby."

"I can't imagine anything worse than having to keep one and look after it," countered Ronnie.

"Or trying to get your figure back after the birth!" said Kate with feeling.

By lunchtime, the rain had all but stopped and Valentin was back, very subdued and with a large bandage around his right hand. There was also a black bruise along the left side of his jawline.

"At least he got away with a few stitches and a shot of penicillin," said Hans-Peter.

"Maybe they should have given the dog a jab too." Daisy tutted at Doug and went over to ask Valentin if he was in any pain.

"My hand is sore," he said with a watery smile. "It could have been much worse, I suppose. The poor dogs are vicious, but at least they don't have rabies."

"And your face?"

He flinched. "Oh, that doesn't matter. Give this a stir for me, will you?" The liquid in the big pan looked even less appetising than usual and had probably come out of a tin, unlike the nourishing soups that Daisy's mother had taught her to make from scratch.

She hadn't really believed the horror stories about the bread until there was a shriek from Lucinda.

"Oh, God, look! I've just found a dead cockroach."

"I also have one," shuddered Astrid, pushing aside her plate with a dramatic flourish.

Kate had turned quite pale. "I've got half. I must have swallowed the rest."

"No," squeaked Renate. "I think I have it."

More and more dead cockroaches were found and bread started to fly through the air as the young people expressed their disgust. One piece even hit B.B. as he came in from the office to find out what all the noise was about. To everyone's relief, he roared with laughter and threw it at Valentin, who ducked just in time. Then, squeezing his large frame in between Doug and Jaap, he demanded a bowl of soup for himself. After the first mouthful, he clicked his teeth in disapproval and laid aside his spoon.

"Les Halles in Paris! That's the place for good soup," he said, wagging a meaty finger at his table companions. Maybe I'll take you there one day." With a broad smile, he gave Jaap a thump on the back that nearly knocked his face into his bowl and left them to their meal.

The rumour went round that afternoon that Valentin was suffering from delayed shock and dinner was likely to be even worse than lunch.

"Poor little bloke!" exclaimed Ronnie in a rare moment of sympathy. "I'd be in shock too if the Hound of the Baskervilles had sunk its teeth into me. Still, it's going to be a miserable evening if Charlot doesn't turn up."

"Oh, it might not be too bad. At least the weather's better now."

"There's our Daisy! Ever the optimist!"

Fortune was indeed on her side. Around five o'clock, Victor delivered a note from Charlot to Ronnie. He wanted her to go to the cinema with him and bring Daisy along too.

"Why would I want to play gooseberry?"

"You won't have to, you idiot. Your Jean-Claude asked him to invite you. Charlot said that the four of us will all get something to eat at *Chez Thérèse* afterwards. I just hope that Madame Defarge is in a better mood than she was last night!"

Kate looked on sourly as they bustled around getting ready, but they knew better than to take her along. Being the odd girl out really wouldn't be Kate's style and she'd win hands down in any competition for male attention.

Daisy's date looked quite different without his overalls. Freshly shaved and with hair still slightly damp, he was wearing a pair of well pressed jeans and a white open necked shirt. The pale blue sweater draped around his shoulders, sleeves casually knotted in front, made him look very French, she thought. Their arms bumped together occasionally as they walked along, but he made no attempt to hold her hand as he might have done Kate's.

Cinéma Garnier stood on its own in a narrow side street and was of more recent construction than the neighbouring buildings. Its brick walls were covered in posters, pasted one over the other, and the film to be shown was *Compartiment des Tueurs*, starring Yves Montand and Simone Signoret.

"Compartment of killers? I wonder what that's all about," mused Daisy.

"Does it matter? I don't suppose we'll be seeing much of it."

"Ronnie!"

The boys only had to pay for their own tickets, as there was no charge for the young foreigners from the *chantier*.

"Thanks to B.B., I suppose that makes us cheap dates," sniggered

Ronnie.

"Speak for yourself!"

Monsieur Garnier, who seemed to run the cinema entirely on his own, disappeared into the projection box as soon as everyone was settled. It was the second evening in a row that Daisy regretted wearing a skirt. The seats were covered in a red fabric that was as hard and itchy as horse-hair and it was difficult not to fidget. She tried to focus on the screen, where the occupants of a sleeping car were being picked off one by one as their train rattled along. With little idea of who they were or why they were being murdered, she soon lost interest. There were no subtitles, of course, and the dialogue was far too rapid for her to follow. Charlot, who had led the rush for the back row, had been all over Ronnie from the moment the lights went down. She heard him curse as he caught his hand on the pin of the little badge she wore with every outfit, even her school blazer. Jean-Claude, on the other hand, was concentrating on the film. He glanced sideways at Daisy occasionally and smiled when their eyes met, but he made no move to touch her.

The interval came as a relief. Rummaging for their cigarettes, the audience surged towards the door and soon the little street echoed with sighs of satisfaction.

"In England, you can smoke inside the cinema," remarked Daisy.

"Really? What about the fire risk?"

"It doesn't seem to be a problem. There's an ashtray on the back of each seat for the people behind to use. We've got them in the theatre too."

"What a great idea! That would be against the law in France."

As soon as he'd ground out his cigarette on the pavement, Charlot strolled a few yards up the street to relieve himself against a handy wall. A few other young men did likewise, although not Jean-Claude.

"At least they had the decency to turn their backs," said Ronnie. "Charlie Boy needn't think he's touching me again, though, until he's washed his hands!"

Daisy had turned away, scarlet with embarrassment, even though Jean-Claude whispered that *le pipi rustique* was quite usual in France.

"Well it certainly isn't in England! They'd all be arrested."

Her cheeks were still burning when they went back inside for the second half of the film, but it wasn't long before an arm went round her shoulders and nothing else mattered after that. Having staked his claim, Jean-Claude held her hand on the way to the café. His palm was calloused and there were traces of oil under his nails, but Daisy had to fight the temptation to burst into song as they walked along together.

"A *diabolo menthe* for you?" he joked, handing her the menu. "After all, it is the colour of your eyes."

"In that case, you should be having cream sherry."

"*Touché!* I think I'll stick to beer, though."

Despite setting out as a foursome, the couples were at different tables, so this was starting to feel like a real date. When Jean-Claude asked about her family, Daisy opened her handbag and showed him the little folding frame that held her two most precious photographs.

"My parents had these taken during the war," she explained. "My father died a few years ago and I don't have any brothers or sisters, so Mum and I are very close."

"She looks a lot like you," he said. "Papa was widowed when I was very young, so I never really knew my mother. Like you, I'm an only one, so it's just the two of us at the garage now."

"The Garage de la Forge on the main road?" Daisy knew perfectly well that it was, having asked Valentin if there was more than one garage in the village, but she wasn't going to admit it and waited for him to nod. "Why is it called that? You're not a blacksmith as well as a mechanic, are you?"

"No, but my grandfather was. Even my father for a while, until cars started to take over from horses."

"Poor horses!" Daisy hoped that they hadn't all ended up on a slab in the *boucherie chevaline* but didn't like to ask.

The contrast between Valentin's cooking and that of his sister could hardly have been sharper. Daisy's beautifully soft *omelette paysanne* was loaded with potatoes and smoky bacon, sprinkled with chives and served with a big green salad and a basket of crusty bread. She had no room left for cheese or dessert, although Jean-Claude had both.

Charlot and Ronnie had already disappeared by the time he said, "It's getting late. I'll walk you back." Daisy smiled and nodded. The forest held no terrors with him by her side and she was happily anticipating their first kiss.

It wasn't to be. They were halfway up the track when an impatient horn sounded behind them and a long black car with tinted windows swept past.

"Do you know who that could be at this time of night?"

Jean-Claude shook his head, but she felt the muscles in his hand tighten and he looked very uneasy.

"Come on. We'd better hurry."

Standing by the car were two strange men, deep in conversation with Raoul and his boss. The taller man was dark skinned and had a beautifully cut white suit. The other, his head shaven, was dressed from head to toe in black. A gold ring like a pirate's twinkled in one ear.

All four looked annoyed to see the young couple approaching and Jean-Claude wasn't slow to take the hint. He escorted Daisy to the top of the steps leading down to the dormitories, gave her an awkward peck on both cheeks and melted away into the night.

It wasn't even eleven o'clock and the dogs were still chained up, but the underground area was already crowded with resentful young people. Daisy found Kate sulking on her bed.

"I was sitting outside with Raoul and a few of the others when his friends arrived. At least, I suppose they were his friends, although none of us saw them. They waited inside the car until he'd sent everyone else packing. Even me! He said an early night would do us all good."

"He might have a point," said Caroline, squinting at the leaflet in her hand. The girls had reclaimed some of the stolen bulbs, but the light was still very dim. "We've got to get up at the crack of dawn. B.B. has promised to take us all to Versailles."

"When was that announced?"

"At dinner, which was beyond disgusting. You weren't there, of course, you lucky thing. B.B. wants to get off to an early start to beat the crowds."

Chapter 7

Daisy's upturned face was soaked with sweat.

"I suppose you'll have to come with us," said Kate doubtfully. "It's not as though there's anything seriously wrong with you."

Rolling back into a tight ball, Daisy groaned. "That doesn't make it any less painful or messy. How on earth can I sort myself out down here with all the boys around? I'd never hear the end of it from Doug."

"But what if B.B. notices that you're not with us? You heard what he said the morning after we arrived. No one's allowed to stay behind on their own."

"I don't care. Just cover for me if you can and ask the others to do the same. Don't tell the boys why, though. Say that I've got a bad headache or something."

"What about the dogs?"

"Oh, I don't suppose they'll come down here. B.B. said that they're trained not to and there's nothing for them to eat anyway, but I'll keep the door shut just in case. Don't worry about me. I just want some time on my own. It's usually only a real problem for the first few hours."

"If you say so. Do you want any breakfast? I could probably sneak you down a couple of rolls."

"No thanks. I just want to be left alone to get over it."

Daisy vaguely remembered hearing the coach leaving before she fell back asleep. The cramps had lessened a little by the time she woke up again and she did her best to wash herself and her stained pyjamas. She couldn't hang them up outside, of course, but they might dry eventually on the end of her bed. Thank heavens she'd recently put her qualms aside and graduated to tampons. Although it had been a struggle to get used to them, at least they were easier to dispose of without embarrassment.

Her thoughtful mother had supplied her with a bottle of Dr Collis Browne's Mixture to help with the pain. With no measuring spoon at her disposal, Daisy took a mouthful straight from the bottle. The peppermint flavour was quite pleasant, although she didn't like the chalky after-taste. As the dose wouldn't take effect for a while, she crawled back into her sleeping bag and pulled her knees up to her chin. With nothing to do and only the rustling of the trees outside the window to break the silence, it was going to be a long day. Concern about running down the batteries without the means to replace them ruled out the option of listening to the tinny music from Maureen's transistor radio and she didn't even have a book or a pack of cards.

The Mixture had made her drowsy anyway and she dismissed the now familiar smell of Gauloises as a dream at first. It reminded her of Jean-Claude and she stretched out languorously, wondering when she would see him again. It was only when more smoke drifted towards her and someone coughed very close by that the hairs on the back of her neck stood up. The shaven headed man with the gold earring was standing right outside, his back to the window. That alone would have been frightening enough, but he had a pistol tucked into the waistband of his trousers. What if he turned round and saw her? She pulled the edge of her sleeping bag up to her nose and crossed her fingers. After what seemed like a lifetime, there was a long, low whistle, evidently a signal of some kind, and the man hurried off.

Daisy's heart leapt into her throat as she heard shouting, vehicle doors slamming and the frantic barking of the guard dogs. Even worse, heavy footsteps were tramping down the passageway towards the dormitories. As her door was flung open, Daisy shrank down so far into her sleeping bag that she could hardly breathe, trusting to the gloom to conceal her presence. It worked. Someone entered, paused for a moment and then withdrew. There was another low whistle, followed by a burst of activity.

"*Merde! Putain!*" Although the sound was muffled by the padded fabric around her ears, Daisy was aware of something being manhandled and dragged up the passageway. The manoeuvre was repeated several times before there was a loud clang. The last of the footsteps retreated and a heavy vehicle revved up in the distance.

More frightened than she'd ever been in her life, Daisy waited a full ten minutes before emerging red-faced and dishevelled from the sleeping bag and throwing on the first clothes that came to hand. She tiptoed to the door. Everything in the passageway looked the same as before, but it took her even longer to pluck up the courage to mount the steps and peep outside. Eyes narrowed against the sun, she was relieved to see that the whole area was deserted. Only the fresh tyre marks in the gravel bore witness to the fact that she hadn't overdosed on the Mixture and dreamed the whole episode. The dogs were chained up as usual and she wondered whether they ever really were released. It was hard to imagine that the poor animals would stick around if they had the choice.

Daisy hovered in the shadow of the entrance, jumping at the slightest sound. After a while, afraid to leave but even more afraid to stay there on her own, her thoughts turned to Jean-Claude. If only she could thread her way between the trees without being seen, she would be able to run straight across the main road to the garage.

"Daisy? What are you doing here?" Her eyes filled with tears of relief as she stumbled at last onto the forecourt and threw herself into his arms, taking comfort from his warm sturdiness.

"Fetch the cognac and a small glass," said a sympathetic voice. "It's the best thing I know for a girl at these times. *C'est normal, non?*"

Daisy blushed, but Jean-Claude's father had needed no long drawn out explanation for the dark circles under her eyes. She couldn't imagine an Englishman being as open about such a personal subject.

"Daisy. That's a pretty name." Monsieur Binard was so like his son that she felt at home with him straight away.

"It's a little white flower," she choked. Her throat, unused to spirits, was burning.

"So, my son has found himself a little English flower and with such lovely green eyes too." For a moment his expression was bleak, but he recovered himself as an impatient paw pushed him out of the way. An old spaniel had waddled over to rest his shaggy head against Daisy's knees. "Now, my dear, tell us what has upset you so much."

The worried glances exchanged between father and son as she stumbled through her story made it hard to believe their reassurance that she'd just witnessed the arrival of regular supplies.

"It has to be more than that. I've seen a lot of goods unloaded and they all go straight into the kitchen."

"Well, maybe Valentin has run out of space."

Daisy played her trump card. "Is it normal in France for delivery men to be armed?" That floored them for a moment.

"Many people in the countryside have guns, Daisy," said Monsieur Binard eventually. "Some for hunting and others to protect their property from vermin or poachers. I advise you not to mention what you saw to any of the staff. The *patron* isn't a man to appreciate questions. Let him believe that you were at Versailles all day with your friends."

"But..."

"Are you hungry, my dear?" The sudden change of subject startled Daisy, but she nodded.

"Good. We were just about to stop for lunch when you arrived."

Expecting sandwiches and a mug of tea in the garage, Daisy was amazed to be escorted to the old house that adjoined it. The spaniel had trotted ahead of them and was immediately jumped upon by the white kitten sunning itself by the front door.

"Minette! Leave poor Didier alone!" The kitten hung on grimly until Jean-Claude gently detached her claws from the dog's coat and pushed her little pink nose into a saucer of milk. Didier shook himself and went over to stand pointedly by his own food bowl.

Red wine, mineral water and a crusty loaf were waiting on the big square kitchen table with its patterned oilcloth. Daisy's nose twitched at the delicious aroma from a pan bubbling away on the cast iron range.

It contained a thick vegetable soup, which would have made a meal in itself but was followed by pork cutlets in a spicy sauce, crisp green beans and fried potatoes.

She had wondered how Jean-Claude and his father coped without a woman in the house. Well, whatever else they might lack, they certainly weren't badly fed. A soft cheese with a white rind was followed by a baked dessert of black cherries with cream. They hadn't been expecting visitors, so it looked as though they ate like that every day. Yet neither of them had an ounce of spare flesh. It was remarkable.

She pushed her coffee cup away with a sigh. "That was a wonderful meal. Thank you very much for inviting me."

Monsieur Binard smiled. "So, Daisy, you like French food?"

"Some of it. It's good here and at the café."

"But not up at the *chantier*, I've heard. Is it even worse there than in England?"

Daisy thought from the twinkle in his eye that he was teasing her but felt obliged all the same to defend her national cuisine.

"English food can be very good too. Have you ever tried it?"

"Sadly no." He reached for his pipe, his expression hard to read. Regret, maybe? Had she said the wrong thing? To make up for it, she asked,

"Please could I have the recipe for your delicious soup, Monsieur?" That did the trick.

With a rueful grin, he told her, "I'm afraid I can take no credit for that. My sister-in-law brought it over for us and the dessert also. You've met her son Victor, I believe?"

"Yes. He always calls English people *rosbifs*." Or worse, but she wouldn't go into that.

"Revenge, I suppose, for what you call us."

Worried in case he might be offended, Daisy said, "I'm afraid so, but it's only a nickname because frogs' legs are popular in France. It's like calling the Germans 'Krauts' because of their pickled cabbage."

His expression darkened. "That's not what we call them." Oh dear.

Had she had put her foot in it again?

Jean-Claude rescued her. "I'm sure my aunt would give Daisy the recipe for the soup."

His father relaxed, good humour restored. "Of course she would. Do you like to cook, Daisy?"

"Yes, indeed I do."

"Then maybe you could make a meal for us one day?"

"Papa," Jean-Claude protested, "Daisy's here on holiday. We can't expect her to do that."

"I was only joking. Of course we can't. Please accept my apologies, Mademoiselle."

"No, really, I'd love to." Daisy was thrilled by the idea of demonstrating the skills that her mother had taught her. Then, remembering the good manners also instilled by that lady, she offered to do the washing up and was turned down flat.

"Certainly not! You are our guest today. Take your friend into the parlour, son." Daisy was whisked out of the sunny kitchen and made to put her feet up on a long sofa. It was designed for elegance more than comfort, but Jean-Claude piled it up with cushions and she slumped back against them with a contented sigh. Minette had sprung up onto the top of a tall corner cabinet as they came in and was waiting to be coaxed down.

"She hasn't been with us very long," explained Jean-Claude. "Papa found her all alone down by the river and brought her home in his pocket." He tried to hand the kitten to Daisy, but she clung to his shoulder and licked his face as he carried her into the kitchen for some titbits.

The parlour looked little used, although both the furniture and the parquet floor were well polished. It was hard to see much through the lace covered window, so Daisy turned her attention to the photographs lined up on the sideboard and mantelpiece. Most of them were of Jean-Claude at different ages, including one of him in the arms of a pretty fair haired young woman at his christening. His mother, if the formal wedding portrait were anything to go by, had been much less attractive.

There was no accounting for taste, Daisy mused, but Jean-Claude must have got his good looks from his father.

Amongst all the family photographs was one of the village war memorial and she got up to have a closer look. To her horror, the old frame came apart in her hands and a small snapshot fell out. Retrieving it hastily from the floor, Daisy saw a strikingly beautiful woman, somewhat older than the other two, laughing into the camera as she fingered the locket at her throat. Her dark hair fell in neat waves and she had beautifully arched eyebrows, full lips and perfect teeth. Sensing that the photograph had been concealed for a good reason, Daisy hastily put the frame back together and pushed it behind all the others. She was sitting primly on the sofa when Jean-Claude came back into the parlour, his face full of concern for her.

"Papa has gone for a nap, but he says that he can manage alone this afternoon. Are you feeling any better?"

"Yes, very much, thank you." He glanced around the parlour for something to entertain her and Daisy tried not to look guilty as he went through the photographs one by one.

"This is my parents' wedding, of course, just after the war. These are my aunts before they were married. Aunt Yvette is Charlot's mother..." Oh dear! So he and Jean-Claude were cousins too. Ronnie seemed happy enough with him, but Daisy hadn't taken to Charlot any more than she had to Doug. The list went on and on. Jean-Claude seemed to be related to half the village and Daisy could just picture Kate's face and sarcastic comments about inbreeding.

"My grandmother Madeleine here," he said, pointing to a squarely built woman with a pleasant face, "understood more about engines than most men. I wish I'd known her, but she was killed during the war."

"By the Germans?"

"No. She was working for the Resistance, but it was an accident. I know it's hard to believe, but she was changing the wheel of a lorry all by herself at the time. My grandfather had already died. He went off right at the start and never came back. His name is on the war memorial, which is why we keep this photograph in his honour."

He pointed at but didn't pick up the frame and Daisy wondered if he'd ever seen the hidden snapshot. Whoever the mysterious woman was, it looked as though she'd inherited the late Madeleine Binard's locket, so why wasn't her photo also on display?

"They'd both be pleased to see Papa still running the garage," continued Jean-Claude, "and to know that it will be mine when he retires. That won't be for a long time, of course. I haven't even done my National Service yet." Images of him in uniform flashed through Daisy's mind. Whichever of the services he went into, he'd cut a very dashing figure.

"My other grandfather was a baker, but he was never the same after the war and has passed on. Grandmother Brigitte suffered a stroke a while ago and my Aunt Marie-Françoise, Victor's mother, runs the bakery now. Her brother Daniel was one of the deportees from the village and never came back, but you can see him in this group shot of the family."

Having run out of photographs to talk about, for which Daisy was very grateful, he produced a pack of cards and taught her a two-handed version of Belote. They were still playing when his father came back downstairs to start work again.

"I'll finish servicing the Renault," he said, "and keep an eye out for the coach returning from Versailles. You can get Daisy up there in time to mingle with the other young people. Baltzinger may think he knows this forest well, but we could teach him a thing or two about short cuts, couldn't we!"

Chapter 8

"They didn't miss you," said Ronnie, flopping down on the bed to massage her sore feet. "Raoul was supposed to be checking everyone onto the coach, but Kate fluttered her eyelashes at him and made him lose count. He looked as though he'd got other things on his mind anyway and so did B.B. He just got into the front of the coach for a few minutes before we set off to say that he'd booked the grand tour of Versailles, including all the gardens."

"We all thought until then that he was coming too," added Kate. "We spread out so that he wouldn't notice your empty seat, but he wished us a good day and got off the coach."

"Didn't Raoul go either?"

Kate pouted. "No. But I expect that they've both been there lots of times. They drove behind the coach in Raoul's car as far as the entrance and then handed us over to a friend of theirs called Marie-Jacques. Strange name! I wonder if her parents were hoping for a boy."

"How do you know she was a friend?"

"Because they both kissed her and called her *tu*. She was very glamorous for a tour guide. The boys' eyes were out on stalks."

Kate scowled at Ronnie. "I thought she looked like mutton dressed as lamb with all that make-up and flashy jewellery. She'll certainly never see thirty again. Anyway, she handed out the tickets and I took two, so she didn't have one left over and start to count heads. As for the château, it was much too crowded. You couldn't move inside the place for Americans and Japanese and it was all a bit tatty. Most of the furniture was sold off during the Revolution or taken to the Louvre."

"What about the famous Hall of Mirrors?"

"Disappointing. They were scratched and dusty. I liked the gardens better, especially the fountains."

Ronnie grinned. "They're good if you ignore the signs telling you to keep off. Caroline and Lucinda went for a paddle and Marie-Jacques was furious in case we were all asked to leave. When she threatened to tell B.B., Caro just put on her snootiest voice and told her to go ahead if it would make her happy."

"He certainly got his money's worth. Our tour went on for hours. Maureen had a big blister on her heel and wanted to take a local bus back here, but Marie-Jacques wouldn't hear of it. She handed her some sticking plasters and made her stay with the group."

"The whole thing must have cost a fortune. We were given lunch in a restaurant and afternoon tea and cakes, all paid for in advance."

"I can't imagine how B.B. does it, unless he gets some kind of grant to run this place. International good will or something like that."

"If that's the case, you'd think he'd employ a decent cook, wouldn't you? One who actually enjoys the job."

"Did you come straight back after your tea and cakes?"

"No, we were all shattered by then, but Marie-Jacques looked at her watch and said there was still time to look round the souvenir shops. These are what I bought." She held up a little plastic viewer with its set of slides.

"And I got this." Ronnie was brandishing a book full of colourful anecdotes about Versailles in its heyday. "Just imagine! Before the Revolution, queens of France had to give birth in front of dozens of people to make sure that the babies weren't switched. And did you know that Louis XV's mistress, Madame de Pompadour, started life as Mademoiselle Poisson and the first champagne glasses were modelled on her chest? And that he had someone called a *porte-coton* to wipe his backside when he'd done his business? Imagine that!" They were too excited about their day out to ask how Daisy had whiled away her time.

At dinner that evening, Hans-Peter was elected spokesman to express the group's appreciation for the trouble Monsieur Baltzinger had gone to in arranging the visit.

B.B. looked gratified. "Thank you, young man. I'm glad that you all enjoyed yourselves. There will be more excursions, I assure you, to reward you for doing what I ask of you and causing me no problems."

No one else remarked on the deep tyre marks in the gravel and must have assumed, if they noticed them at all, that they'd been made by the coach. Even to Daisy, once she'd had a good night's sleep, the whole business seemed much less important than seeing Jean-Claude again.

"Oh, stop looking at your watch, Daisy! You're getting on my nerves."

"It's all right for you!" Kate had forgiven Raoul for the night the two strange men had claimed his attention and was fretting over what to wear for their second date.

The morning passed slowly and Daisy was scraping out the remains of one of Valentin's burnt offerings into the bin outside the kitchen when Jean-Claude arrived.

"Papa's given me some extra time off. How about coming for a walk?"

She hesitated. "I'd love to, but I'm on kitchen duty again."

Valentin leaned out of the open window. "Pass me that dish, Daisy, and then you go and enjoy yourself."

"But Ronnie and Kate..."

He held up a hand. "Never mind about them. You work far harder than both your friends put together."

"But what if Raoul sees me leaving?"

Valentin winked. "No more 'buts'. I'll tell him that we needed more bread. Bring a couple of loaves back with you, just in case."

Daisy beamed at him. "Thank you. You're very kind."

"Think nothing of it, my dear." He lowered his voice to add, "I wasn't fooled for a moment by your sudden interest in our local garages, you know, and you'll come to no harm with that young man."

"I need to send a postcard to my mother," said Daisy, as they entered the square.

"OK, but how about a cake first to take away the taste of Valentin's cooking? Aunt Yvette will help you to find something even more delicious than the meringue you bought from her last time."

So he *had* noticed. She liked Madame Legoux, who didn't seem at all surprised to see them together. After a lecture on the superior health benefits of French chocolate, she gave Daisy a bar of Valrhona and let her sample a few different sweets before she settled for a lemon and honey variety called *bergamots*.

"I like those too," said Jean-Claude. "They come from the east of France."

"Like your Monsieur Baltzinger," added his aunt, "although he's from Alsace. The sweets are made in Nancy, which is in Lorraine."

"Really? I didn't know that," marvelled Daisy politely. Thank heavens B.B. didn't come from Nancy, she thought to herself. Ronnie would have had a field day with that.

"Well, you're not French, so you won't have picked up on his accent. He was only in his teens when he first came here, but he's never lost it. My late husband didn't like him from the start. He said one should never trust a man from Alsace and he was right."

"Why? What happened?"

Jean-Claude broke the charged silence that followed, as his aunt bit her lip. "Raoul isn't from round here either, you know, but his accent is from the Midi, from Marseilles, to be precise. That's why he talks about 'pang' and 'vang' instead of *pain* and *vin*. Anyway, that's enough geography for one day. Come on! Let's get you your postcard."

"And we'd better not forget the bread!"

In the bakery next door, Jean-Claude's other aunt seemed quite perturbed by Daisy's request and had to be reassured that the regular order hadn't been short that morning. She wouldn't take any money for the extra loaves either.

"Is she worried that she might lose the *chantier* business?" asked

Daisy as they left. "I suppose it must be worth quite a bit."

"No. It's nothing like that. She's still getting used to all the responsibility and wouldn't want to upset my grandmother by telling her that she'd made a mistake."

There was a stand of postcards under the striped awning of *Chez Pug*, as Daisy always thought of the *bar-tabac*. The boy himself was lounging in the doorway and gave Daisy a curt nod as she went inside to pay his mother for a view of the Eiffel Tower."

"No, there are no postcards of Saint-André-la-Forêt and I don't have any stamps for England either. Sorry." Turning her attention to Jean-Claude, she patted her hank of peroxide blond hair and said coyly, "I haven't seen Alain for a long time. What's he up to these days?"

"Oh, this and that. We're always very busy, you know."

"Is he still waiting for the right lady to come along?" The slash of red lipstick formed itself into a sly smile.

"I really wouldn't know. Please excuse us, Madame. The post office will be closing soon."

Daisy was curious. "Does your father really have no one? I mean, he isn't very old."

"And not bad looking either, I suppose," he grinned. "But no. There are a lot of widows in this village and he hasn't gone short of offers, I can assure you. I used to think it was because of me that he hadn't remarried, but he always says that no one could ever replace the love of his life."

"Your mother must have been a very special lady."

"I'm sure she was. I just remember someone soft and warm with a gentle voice. Everyone was very kind after she died, but it was never the same." His mouth twisted and Daisy squeezed his hand.

"I know how you feel. I'm missing Mum already. That's why it's so important to get this card into the post. I've never been abroad before, you know, and she's bound to be worrying about me."

He chuckled. "Tell her that a handsome French boy is taking good care of you."

"I think that would worry her even more!"

She was mortified when he took the remark seriously and pulled her round to face him. "I would never do anything to harm you, Daisy."

"I know. I didn't mean it like that and I will tell her. It's just that I'm all she's got."

He relaxed. "Have you really no other family? Not even cousins?"

"Not a single one."

"I sometimes wish I didn't have any, especially Charlot. His mother has always spoilt him. It would have been different, I suppose, if his father had lived long enough to belt his backside occasionally." He grinned and made a graphic gesture.

"As your father did to you?"

"Not often and only when I drove him to it."

Odile Vartan's fine boned face lit up as they walked into the little post office. She brushed a wisp of silvery blond hair out of her eyes and leaned forward to shake Daisy's hand. "I was just about to close up," she said, "but sit down there and write your postcard, Mademoiselle. Here's a stamp for it." She chatted to Jean-Claude until Daisy had finished and then invited them both upstairs to her flat for some refreshments.

"I hope you don't mind interrupting our walk," he said as she bustled about.

"No, of course not." His godmother was still recognisable as the girl in the christening photograph that Daisy was shown for the second time, although her face was now etched with deep lines. It was very obvious that Jean-Claude was the apple of her eye. The mantelpiece of the little parlour held several other photographs of him and Daisy particularly liked the one of a reluctant schoolboy in short trousers, struggling with an oversized satchel.

He gave her a rueful grin. "I was never much of a scholar. Always preferred working with my hands."

"His mother was my dearest friend," said their hostess. "Look, here we are in the dresses we made for ourselves out of some old curtains. It was during the war, you see, and there was no new material to be had."

"They're very pretty. Were they for a dance?"

"No, I'm afraid not. The Germans didn't allow that. Anyway, let's not talk about those terrible times. Tell me about yourself. Is this your first visit to France?"

"What a nice lady," said Daisy, as they set off back. "She's obviously very fond of you. Does she have any children of her own? There weren't any photographs and I didn't like to ask."

"No. She never married, although I think there was someone a long time ago. I overheard my aunts talking about it once, but they stopped as soon as they realised that I was listening. Papa wouldn't discuss it either. He said that some things were best forgotten."

"I like your aunts too. They seem very wary of Monsieur Baltzinger, though. I don't think your father's keen on him either."

Jean-Claude hesitated. "Look, I shouldn't say this, but Baltzinger has some shady connections. Raoul too, I think. Those two men who turned up the other night, for example. They had a look of the *milieu* about them."

"The *milieu*?"

"Oh, forget I said anything." He took Daisy's face in his big hands and drew her to him. As their lips touched for the first time, she hoped that it meant more to Jean-Claude than a convenient way of changing the subject.

Kate scoffed at Daisy's warning. "Put your dictionary away! You don't seriously expect me to believe that Raoul's mixed up in organised crime. Not everyone from Marseilles is a crook, you know."

"Well, he sent you off to bed pretty smartly when those men turned up."

"He explained that and apologised. They had some private business to discuss with B.B."

"Funny business, if you ask me," said Ronnie.

"Nobody did ask you!"

Daisy tried again. "Look, Kate, Jean-Claude thinks that they're part of the Parisian underworld, and he doesn't mean the Catacombs."

"Oh, do me a favour! He's been watching too many gangster films at that flea pit he dragged you off to. Raoul wouldn't be seen dead there. He's taking me to see a show at Le Grand Rex in Paris tonight."

"Big Rex?" scoffed Ronnie. "It sounds like someone's old dog."

"Well it's not. It's smart, expensive and we're having dinner afterwards. So there!"

"What about B.B.'s curfew?"

"Oh, please!"

"So screwing Raoul brings you special privileges, does it?"

Kate turned on her. "No one's screwing anyone." A rich blush rose in her cheeks and Daisy wondered just how far their relationship had progressed. Ronnie made a joke of how often she had to slap down Charlot's eager hands, but Kate had told them nothing.

Chapter 9

Daisy didn't have long to wait for her next kiss from Jean-Claude. He rode up through the trees after dinner and took her to a *fête foraine* in a village a few miles down the road. It wasn't a very grand affair, just a handful of rides and stalls set up around a temporary stage strung with coloured lights, but it had attracted a large crowd of all ages.

The teenagers hanging round the dodgem cars were a study in nonchalance. Jean-Claude shook hands with several of them before driving Daisy round, one hand on the steering wheel and the other resting on her shoulder. All the other young men were doing the same, more intent on impressing the girls with their expertise and not swallowing their cigarettes than bumping into each others' vehicles.

Glad to recover her land legs, Daisy took a deep breath. The combined smell of onions and fairground generators was reminiscent of all the times she had dragged her patient parents round from one stall to another. Jean-Claude needed no urging to load her up with treasures. By the time they reached the shooting gallery, he'd already presented her with a blue and white plush teddy bear, a boxed set of six emerald green glass cups and saucers and a wind up clown with a grumpy face. Although she was praying that he'd miss the target, he hit the bull's eye and added an Eiffel Tower lamp to her collection. Even if it all survived the journey back to Saint-André-la-Forêt, how on earth did he think she was going to get it back to England? As an accordion band took to the stage, she looked at her watch. "We really should be going."

"Just one more thing," he insisted. "Wait here a minute." As if the hot dogs, paper cones of *frites*, doughnuts and *crêpes* soaked in Grand

Marnier that they'd already eaten weren't enough, he came back with a stick of candy floss.

Hoping against hope that he hadn't bought it for her, Daisy asked, "Isn't that one of Edith Piaf's songs that they're playing now?"

He looked impressed. "I wasn't aware that she was well known in England. Yes, that's *Je ne regrette rien*. Papa says that her songs break his heart and he won't have it that she was a collaborator."

"And was she?"

"Well, some people condemn her for not refusing to perform for the Germans, even though she used to mock them to their faces."

"How?"

"By using Parisian slang they couldn't follow, but they even allowed her to sing for the prisoners of war sometimes. Papa says that some of the photographs she had taken with them at those concerts were then used to make false documents for men who managed to escape."

Daisy sighed. "I wonder if I'll ever be able to understand Parisian slang."

He grinned. "It's best that you don't, at least until you've taken those exams you're studying for. Then come back to France and I'll teach you all you need to know. Eat up your *barbe à papa* now!"

"Aren't you having any?"

"No. I don't like it, but I know that girls do." Daisy reluctantly sank her teeth into the pink woolly mass. It was even worse than drinking the *diabolo-menthe*, because a breeze sprang up and blew the wretched stuff all over her face and hair.

Before leaving her that night, Jean-Claude rested his cheek against the general stickiness before his mouth found hers again. "Bye, Sugar Lips," he said. "See you tomorrow."

Daisy's happy mood evaporated the following afternoon when Victor arrived with a note. Jean-Claude would be unable to see her that evening after all. What should have been a simple job on a customer's car had proved to be much more complicated and he was going to have to work until late into the evening to get it finished.

"Something wrong, Daisy?"

She gave Valentin a watery smile. "Not really, it's just that Jean-Claude has to work tonight and I was looking forward to seeing him again."

"I understand. He's a good sort, one of the best. I wish some of the other young men in the village were more like him. Of course, if so many of them hadn't lost their fathers, they might have been very different."

"That's exactly what Jean-Claude said about his cousin Charlot."

"Some of the girls are quite difficult too, of course, but no worse than English girls, I dare say. Your friend Ronnie, for instance. She's always so aggressive."

Daisy pulled a face. "She's not really my friend. We're just in the same French class at school."

"And Kate?"

"The same, really." He looked relieved, as though he'd seen them from the beginning as an unlikely trio.

"Do you enjoy your studies, Daisy?"

"Most of the time, especially French. We've got a very good teacher."

"Ah, so did I once upon a time. My father used to tell stories about his predecessor, an ogre who carried a big stick and used to shake it over the head of anyone he thought too lazy or too stupid to learn. The children were all terrified of him. Monsieur Kahn was just the opposite. He wasn't a big man and almost hunchbacked from all the hours he spent bending over his books, but we all loved him and he could keep perfect order without ever raising his voice. I'm afraid it didn't do him any good when the Germans came. He was Jewish, you see and... Well, anyway, I'm sure that Ronnie's more than capable of handling young Charlot, but Raoul is a very different matter. He and the *patron*..."

The words died in his throat as a large figure loomed over them. For such a big man, B.B. was very light on his feet and they hadn't heard his approach.

"He and the *patron* what?"

Daisy thought desperately. "Valentin was just telling me that you and Raoul are already planning the next excursion."

A heavy hand slapped Valentin on the back, nearly knocking him off his feet. "Quite right. So we are. Now then, young lady, are you busy after dinner or would you like to drive into Paris with me?" Daisy's startled expression must have said it all, because he roared with laughter. "I'm not asking you for a date, sweetheart. I've got to go to a business meeting and there's room for a few passengers in my van. Ask around your friends and find out who'd like to see our capital by night."

Although Daisy had accepted Jean-Claude's reason for cancelling their date, she was slightly put out and decided to take up the offer. Such was the lure of an evening in Paris that she could have filled the spare places twice over. Groaning with the extra weight, the old grey van set off down the track with Doug, Jaap, Maureen and Siobhan squeezed onto a couple of old mattresses in the back. There was no sign of Jean-Claude when they reached the garage, but his father looked amazed to see Daisy in the passenger seat. Maybe that was why he forgot to charge for the petrol? No. That was silly. As a regular customer, B.B. would most likely have an account.

A powerful thigh pressed against hers every time the van went round a bend, but the big man beside her made no attempt to take advantage of the situation. Ordinary conversation was made almost impossible by the noise of the engine. It sounded like marbles rattling around in a biscuit tin and they spent most of the drive in silence.

B.B. had much more to say once they entered Paris, but his running commentary was punctuated by so many colourful gestures and curses that it was hard for Daisy to follow more than the gist. By the time they reached the Arc de Triomphe, all pretence of joviality had disappeared. His brow was furrowed with anger and his thick fingers beat a tattoo on the steering wheel each time he was obliged to stop. Occasionally, his left arm bent into an L-shape and, with the right hand gripping it, he would gesticulate through the window to other drivers. A few replied in kind, but most took one look at his bulk and thought better of it.

B.B. left his young charges outside the brightly lit Moulin Rouge with a stern warning to stay together and keep out of trouble until he picked them up.

"I wonder what kind of trouble he had in mind," giggled Maureen.

"Take your pick! We're in Montmartre, where the Sacred Heart watches over the sins of Pigalle."

"Nice one, Doug."

"Shame we can't afford night club prices. Jaap and I wouldn't mind seeing some topless dancers, although they'd probably make his glasses steam up."

Doug certainly knew his way around and led the others up a succession of narrow streets lined with crowded cafés, bars, food and wine merchants' shops, most of them still open and doing a roaring trade. Even busier were the hundreds of steps, thronged with tourists and souvenir sellers, leading to the Sacré Cœur on the crest of the hill.

"It really does look like a big white wedding cake!" exclaimed a delighted Daisy. "And what a view!"

"Enjoy it, gel," said a cynical voice. "It's the only thing round here that's free."

"Oh, don't be such a misery, Doug!" With the whole of Paris laid out before them and lights twinkling everywhere, she wasn't going to let him spoil the mood. Resigned, he leaned on the stone balustrade and allowed his companions to drink in the scene for a few minutes before leading them round the back of the Basilica to the Place du Tertre.

Almost every inch of the cobbled square was covered with tables belonging to the different cafés, all full to bursting, that lined its sides. A number of artists had squeezed in where they could to set up their easels and several were at work drawing portraits of self conscious tourists. Others, on the lookout for potential clients, were trying to catch the eye of every passer by.

"I wouldn't waste your money!" advised Doug, who'd spotted Daisy wavering. "The genuine artists moved on years ago. If you want a picture to take home to Mummy, get Geoff or Danny to draw one for you." Daisy bridled but had to admit to herself that what he said made sense. Much of the finished work on display was both lurid and highly priced. All the same, she couldn't imagine what the two art students would make of her. Certainly not a sunflower!

Even the amounts quoted for drinks were eye watering, so Doug and Jaap ducked down a side street in search of something cheaper. One look at the *vin ordinaire* they brought back convinced the Senegalese carpet sellers to leave the little group in peace to return to the steps of the Sacré Cœur and enjoy the atmosphere.

Daisy thought it was like being on a film set. To their left, a man in a black leather coat and dark glasses was holding forth about revolution to the group of young people seated around him. To their right, a girl with hair down to her waist was singing softly to her own guitar accompaniment. Her voice was deep and throaty and the crowd around her was listening with rapt attention. Daisy could only make out that the song had something to do with the war, but she joined in the applause and threw a few coins into the pink beret on the ground beside the singer.

Maureen was unimpressed. "Isn't it time that the French moved on and sang about something more cheerful?"

Jaap sprang to his feet, his usual mild expression replaced by outrage. "It's easier to forget if your country hasn't been occupied within living memory. My parents saw innocent people beaten up in the street and taken away at gunpoint. It may seem trivial to you, but it broke my grandmother's heart when a German patrol searching for Jews used her crystal chandelier for target practice."

The Irish girl flushed. "I'm sorry, Jaap. You're right and I didn't mean to cause any offence."

"It's OK. Let's forget it. Just don't say things like that to any of the people in the village, especially the older ones. They were trapped in the Occupied Zone, you know, and must have some terrible memories of that time. I was quite serious when I told Hans-Peter that knowing the truth about his birth might be worse than not knowing. His mother could have been raped or, if she loved his father, been persecuted by her own community for collaboration."

"Maybe, but that wouldn't explain how her baby came to be adopted by a German couple."

"There is another possibility. Have any of you heard of the Lebensborn programme, the Fount of Life? No? Well, it was set up by Heinrich Himmler. You must know who he was."

"Of course," said Doug. "Who doesn't? Funny little bloke who ran the SS."

"Yes, but that isn't all he's remembered for. He wanted to increase the number of suitable babies brought up to be good Nazis."

"Suitable?"

"Strong, healthy Aryan types. Blond with blue eyes, preferably. Just like Hans-Peter."

"But not like himself."

"No. That's the irony of it. Very few of the Nazi leadership measured up to the standards they wanted for their 'master race'. Anyway, Himmler set up special mother and baby homes in Germany to begin with and then in some of the countries they took over."

"Including France?"

"Yes. If Hans-Peter was born in one of those, his mother may have had no choice about giving him up."

"How awful!" Daisy was nearly in tears.

"Ancient history," said Doug, anxious to lighten the mood. "Time to open these bottles, doncha think?"

All around them, young couples were holding hands and kissing. Daisy noticed Jaap shyly slipping an arm round Maureen's shoulders and wondered whether it was just to confirm that she was forgiven.

They'd all regained their spirits by the time they had to make their way back down to the Moulin Rouge. Daisy stumbled a couple of times on the slippery cobbles but veered away from Doug when he tried to link arms.

"Your loss," he shrugged, turning to Siobhan.

Although it was already well past midnight when he picked them up, B.B. didn't whisk them straight back to the village. Instead, he flashed his gold teeth in their direction and asked if anyone was hungry. Lips and tongues stained with the cheap red wine and, in Daisy's case at least, quite light headed, they all nodded.

"Into the van with you then," he said briskly. "And off we go to Les Halles."

Chapter 10

B.B. drove them into a scene straight out of *Irma la Douce*. Still in the front seat, Daisy had never seen so much fresh food in her life. Forced to slow down in the narrow cobbled streets, some already choked with produce laden lorries, the van crawled past arched iron and glass sheds that housed enormous quantities of fruit and vegetables, flowers, fish and shellfish, dairy produce, meat, tripe and other offal. Some burly porters, their smocks the same shade of blue as Jean-Claude's overalls, were striding over the cobblestones with whole carcasses slung over their shoulders. Others were pushing trolleys or carrying huge sacks and wicker baskets full of potatoes. Women were at work there too, a few in clean white overalls but most swathed in dirty blue aprons. The noise was incredible, with everyone shouting at everyone else and aiming kicks at the skinny cats and dogs chasing rats or just seeking refuge from the traffic.

"It's just starting to warm up," remarked their guide, as they stepped out onto a slippery mass of squashed produce, straw and mangled cardboard boxes. "It will be even busier by three o'clock."

Daisy's nose twitched. The stench of rotting cabbage leaves and the steady trickle from the well patronised iron urinal across the street was overpowering, although it hadn't put off the crowds spilling out of dozens of bars and restaurants, some of them no more than holes in the wall. Through one open door, she was amazed to see a middle-aged couple in evening dress drinking white wine and eating oysters. Viewed through another, working men in bloodstained overalls were laughing and clapping each other on the back as they waited for their food to be served by a harassed waiter. The only people who seemed to have nothing to do were the heavily made up women leaning on the wall outside and smoking.

"*Filles de joie*," hissed Doug, "and those men playin' cards inside and keepin' an eye on them are their pimps."

One of the women winked at B.B., but he ignored her and steered his little group towards the narrow frontage of the bistro opposite.

"Now you're going to taste the best onion soup in the world," he promised. "Make the most of it while you can. There are politicians who'd like to sweep all this away and the heart of Paris with it."

"More like the belly, according to Zola," muttered Jaap. "But it's worth seeing all the same."

Chez Solange didn't look very promising. Through the clouds of tobacco smoke, Daisy could just about make out yellowy brown cracked walls and a floor covered with sawdust.

"What a dump," said Siobhan. "Our hair's going to reek tomorrow."

"And I don't like the look of some of those fellas at the bar," agreed Maureen, pressing closer to Jaap as a man with a heavily pockmarked face leered at her. "They'd probably cut your throat for sixpence."

The premises stretched back a surprisingly long way. Daisy tried not to inhale any of the bitter fumes as B.B. hurried them past a sullen group gathered round a pinball machine and down towards the area where tables had been laid and the atmosphere was slightly less foul.

"Bertrand!" A fat woman in black, a double row of pearls round her neck, left her perch behind the silver coloured cash register and opened her arms to embrace him. The affection appeared to be mutual. He stooped to kiss the scarlet painted lips, whispered a few words into her ear and then turned her round to meet his young companions.

"Madame Solange," he boomed, "is very happy to see you all and will feed you royally."

"Eat as much as you like, my dears," she confirmed with a smile. "It's all on the house. Come along now, old friend, we have business to discuss." They sat down together at a separate table, too far away to be overheard but close enough for the *patronne* to keep a shrewd eye on her till.

The steaming bowls of thick onion soup were a revelation to Daisy, from the crust of melted Gruyère cheese on top to the thick slice of fried bread that lined the bowl. She ate ravenously, not caring how much dripped from her chin, and looking forward to telling her mother all about it.

The meal over, she wondered how long they would have to wait before B.B.'s business was concluded. He didn't seem to be in any hurry and merely looked irritated when he was approached by a boy in tight leather trousers and a black polo neck sweater. Waved away with an abrupt gesture, the boy slunk back to rejoin his friends by the pinball machine. His thin face looked almost bloodless to Daisy.

"I wonder what he wanted," she said to no one in particular.

"Or what he was offerin', more like."

"What do you mean, Doug?"

"Oh, Daisy, you're so innocent!"

"He looks like a vampire," giggled Maureen. "I'll bet he never goes out in daylight."

"Well I think he's hungry. I wish I could have shared my soup with him."

"He wouldn't thank you for it. Don't worry about him. He'll find someone to stand him a meal." Doug was right. Before long, a red faced man in a bowler hat had welcomed the boy to his table.

The noise and bustle had died down a little by the time B.B. ordered them back to the van, herding them in front of him like a flock of chickens. As they drove away, he narrowly missed a couple of black robed nuns collecting food for the poor. They were carrying an orange box between them and everyone seemed to be contributing.

It was already light as they drove across the city and the street cleaning machines were out in force. Torrents of water pouring down the gutters into the sewers below were the last thing that Daisy remembered about Paris before she fell asleep with her head on B.B.'s shoulder.

Chapter 11

Raoul had been told to let the group who'd been to Les Halles sleep as long as they wanted to and no demands were made on them for the rest of that day. Evening brought an interrogation from Jean-Claude, who wasn't at all happy to hear about Daisy's outing to the seedier parts of Paris.

"It was fine," she hastened to reassure him. "It would have been better if you'd been there, of course, but I enjoyed myself and I learned a lot. We all did."

"You still look tired," he said, making no attempt to hide his disapproval. "We'll just go for another little walk, shall we?"

The route he chose took them past his old school, a two storey building built out of the same pale stone as most of the village houses but with a red tiled roof. A shoulder high wall topped with a wire fence surrounded the grounds and the thick hedge growing behind it kept them private, but Jean-Claude lifted Daisy up to peep through the bars on the top half of the dark green metal gates. It all looked very pleasant. Heavy double doors on the ground floor led out onto a garden with several mature trees and a partially covered play area designed for all weathers. The dormer windows upstairs were shuttered.

"The teacher lives up there with his wife, but they won't be back until the start of the school year," he told her.

Daisy was surprised. "Is it usual in France for a teacher to live on the premises?"

"I don't know. It's always been so in this village."

"What will happen when he retires?"

"I don't know that either, but he's got plenty of time to think about it. He was only young when he took over the school during the the war. I hope trying to teach my cousins and me hasn't aged him too much! Let's move on now."

The long driveway they turned into was in a very poor state with tall weeds sprouting through the cracks. It led through an abandoned gatehouse towards some ruins that Daisy could just about make out in the distance.

"I've seen that coat of arms before," she said, "on the archway opposite your garage."

"Yes, of course. The family it belonged to owned most of the area once upon a time. This was their home, but it's been deserted since the war. We can take a look around, if you like."

"What a shame that the garden is so neglected. It must have been beautiful once."

"Yes. So I believe. Valentin's father worked here when it was in its heyday and remembers when the château was taken over by the Germans for their headquarters."

"Was it blown up by the Resistance?"

"No. By the British, actually. The old lady who owned it was killed."

"How awful! But what about the rest of the family?"

"She was the last of them, I think."

"Oh, that's a pity. Let's go back the other way. I don't like it here."

As they passed the little church, a voice called out, "I haven't seen you for a while, my son." The smiling priest bearing down on them could himself have been the heir to a great estate. Thick dark hair streaked with silver topped a narrow face with high cheek bones and he had what Daisy's mother would have called 'an air of breeding'.

"No, Father. I apologise for that, but please may I introduce you to my English friend?"

"Delighted, Mademoiselle. I was a great admirer of your Mr Churchill and very sorry to hear of his death last January. Perhaps I shall see you at Mass on Sunday?"

"I'm afraid not, Father. I'm not a Catholic, you see."

"You'd be very welcome, even so, especially if you can persuade this young man to accompany you. He used to be my best altar boy." The smile faded as he added, "I married his parents, you know, I baptised your friend here and then I had the sad task of conducting his mother's funeral service far too soon afterwards. Are you going to visit her grave today?"

It was some way from the church and Daisy doubted whether Jean-Claude had intended to take her there that evening. The neatly tended cemetery spread back towards the ruins, so that the giant oak that sheltered the Binard family plot had half its roots on the other side of the boundary wall. A stone urn held a fresh bouquet of mauve and yellow freesias.

The boy's lip trembled as he said, "Papa comes here every week. He lays flowers for my mother and for my grandmother Madeleine. Then he takes some to the war memorial for my grandfather Hervé, who doesn't have any grave that we know of."

To give him time to compose himself, Daisy bent over the inscriptions and was amazed to see that his poor mother had been only a few years older than herself at the time of her death. Tears in her eyes, she straightened up and suggested going for a drink, even if it meant having to sip another *diabolo-menthe*.

Life at the *chantier* had fallen into a comfortable routine. B.B. was rarely there and Raoul didn't demand much of the young people. Long periods of lazing around in the sun were interspersed with bursts of noisy activity and followed by a mass exodus to the village. Most evenings were spent at *Chez Thérèse* or *Chez Pug*, as the latter establishment was now generally known, and ended with everyone straggling back up through the forest, those who'd paired off taking a more indirect route.

With romance all around them, the German twins were growing desperate to slip the leash still firmly held by their brother. After careful consideration of the girls not yet spoken for, they settled on Lucinda to distract him.

Renate came straight to the point one morning. "Do you like our brother?"

Lucinda blushed. "Why do you ask?"

"Because he likes you. We know this, but he is shy, isn't he, Astrid?"

"Yes he is. Maybe you should ask him to go to the cinema with you. I believe there is a film by Jean-Luc Godard this week and our brother likes this director's work very much."

With no reason to suspect an ulterior motive, Lucinda plucked up the courage to follow their suggestion. Good manners prevailed over Hans-Peter's amazement at being asked out by a girl and off they went. Unfortunately for the twins, the projector broke down halfway through the film and everyone was obliged to find their evening's entertainment elsewhere. Passing *Chez Pug*, where his sisters were surrounded by Antoine and his friends, shocked the young German to the core and he'd have hauled them out by their hair if he'd been alone. That he didn't was down to Lucinda.

Grabbing his arm, she said, "For heaven's sake, Hans-Peter, be reasonable. Astrid and Renate are nearly as old as I am."

He glared at her. "Did you know that they were planning to meet these boys? Is that why you invited me to go to the cinema with you?"

"No, of course not, but they're not doing anything wrong, are they? Unless you consider drinking Coke and playing *baby-foot* to be a crime?"

He sighed. "I suppose you're right. They're not children any more." All the same, he stalked across to the bar and warned the French boys in no uncertain terms to treat his sisters with respect. Table football was all very well, but that was as far as it went. The twins were mortified, but Antoine gave him a rueful smile as he fingered his only recently healed lip and nodded.

The story did the rounds the next morning to general hilarity.

"Frenchmen can be just as protective," said Geoff. "Danny and I asked a couple of girls we met down by the river if there was anywhere a little more private to swim. They got the message all right and said that they knew a good place, if we didn't mind a cycle ride."

"Did they have tandems?" joked Caroline.

"No, of course not. They managed to borrow a couple of bikes for us."

"They must be very trusting to ride off into the middle of nowhere with you two."

"That's what we thought," chortled Danny, "until we found out that their *tonton* – that's 'uncle' by the way – was coming with us. You'll have met him. Gilles Petacque. He owns the grocery on the square. Anyway, the pond they took us to was a big one and he made us change behind the trees on the opposite side to the girls. Have you noticed, by the way, that French girls don't shave under their arms? I find those little tufts of hair really sexy."

"Yuck!"

"We behaved like perfect gentlemen, of course, and now we're allowed to take them out on their own. Only until ten o'clock, though, and he'll be waiting for them on the doorstep."

"And checking for grass in their hair, I expect," added Geoff. "Oh, by the way, something really weird happened while we were swimming. Danny was showing off his duck dives and came back up with a rusty old rifle he'd found at the bottom of the pond. He threw it over, but *Tonton* Gilles snatched it from me and looked so shocked for a moment that I thought he was going to pass out. He babbled something about his brother and the war, but I couldn't make head or tail of it."

"Yet you can understand the girls?"

"Well enough," he grinned. "We don't talk much, if you know what I mean."

Chapter 12

The announcement of an *excursion culturelle* to Saint-Germain-en-Laye came as a sharp reminder to Daisy of the fright she'd had before and she made a point of being in good time for the coach. Geoff was the next to arrive, clad in shorts and with the satchel containing his sketching materials over his shoulder as usual.

"Phew! It's going to be a scorcher."

"Where's Danny?"

"Oh, he's not coming with us."

"Why? He's not ill, is he?"

"No. It's all right. He's cleared it with B.B. His girlfriend is taking him to the Jeu de Paûme to see the Impressionist paintings. B.B. turned the idea down flat at first, even though Danny said he'd already been to Saint-Germain-en-Laye on a school trip."

"What made him change his mind?"

"Good old Uncle Gilles, oddly enough. He told B.B. that he'd be giving them a lift into Paris first thing in the morning and they wouldn't be back before dinner time at the earliest. Danny's already walked down to the village to meet them."

So nobody would be around during the day, thought Daisy. How convenient!

One passenger was already on board when their transport arrived. Standing beside the driver and sizing everyone up through the thick lenses of his gold rimmed spectacles was a strange man with a large round face and a slight squint. What was left of his hair was grey and greased back in tight strands. A white silk shirt, left open almost to the navel to show off a gold medallion, also revealed a pudgy and completely hair-less chest. Beneath dangerously tight black trousers, his small feet were encased in slip on shoes with shiny silver buckles.

"No need for formality," he lisped, moistening his lips with a thick red tongue. "My name is Pierre d'Aulnay, but my friends call me Pierrot."

"I wonder where he keeps the white suit and pompons," muttered Ronnie, tactful as ever.

When it was Daisy's turn to shake his hand, she caught a whiff of something that reminded her of her mother's face powder and recoiled. Poor Kate, she thought. With no sign of Raoul, Pierrot was bound to make a beeline for the spare seat next to hers. He didn't, though, choos-ing instead to sit next to Geoff, who had to move up to make room for him and didn't look too pleased about it.

The drive was a short one and Ronnie turned to Daisy as the coach lurched to a halt. "That's odd. I'm sure that's Marie-Jacques over there, so why do we need two guides?"

That was the least of Daisy's concerns. "Oh dear! I'd better stay at the back of the group. She might realise that she hasn't seen me before."

If that were the case, the elegant Frenchwoman gave no indication of it. Having greeted Pierrot like an old friend, she swung into action. Marie-Jacques certainly knew her stuff and was going to leave no inch of the château and its grounds unexplored. Pausing occasionally to round up stragglers, she bombarded the young people with information.

"Here is where Jarnac defeated France's best swordsman by craftily slicing his hamstring. Dumas, Offenbach and Delibes were inspired to write some of their best work here. Louis XIV was baptised on this very spot and here is where President Thiers died. Many famous people have resided here, including your King James II during his exile and Mary Queen of Scots when she was a girl."

They were made to walk along all eight thousand feet of Le Nôtre's terrace to admire the lime trees and take in the view of the western side of Paris. Only Jaap was really interested. He leaned over the iron balustrade to take photographs and asked lots of questions, which Marie-Jacques answered at great length. The rest of the group was entertained by Geoff's increasingly blunt attempts to shake off Pierrot, who had added no information to that supplied by Marie-Jacques and was evidently just along for the ride.

"He won't take the hint," snorted Doug. "He must have the hide of a rhinoceros. He even followed him into the Gents the last time we stopped. Geoff locked himself into a cubicle and sat there for five minutes waiting for him to go away, but Pierrot was still waiting patiently outside the door when he came out."

From that moment on, Patient Pierre became P.P., pronounced English style, and must have been thick skinned indeed not to be aware of the smirks and stifled giggles. Things took a more serious turn after lunch, when he put an arm round Geoff's shoulder to emphasise something he was saying. Geoff shrugged him off so violently that he almost bowled over an elderly Japanese couple walking by under their paper parasols. Shortly afterwards, while the group was climbing in single file up a spiral staircase, the English boy felt a clammy hand on his bare thigh and gave a bellow of rage.

The owner of the hand seemed quite unabashed, made an excuse about having lost his balance and ambled off to take in the view.

Marie-Jacques was furious, but not with Patient Pierre. Rounding on her charges like a spitting cat, she shouted, "How dare you all insult Monsieur Baltzinger's friend. Don't deny it. I've heard your *pipi* joke and it's very insulting. Monsieur d'Aulnay comes from a distinguished family, one of the best and oldest in France. He has the *particule*."

"Is that the same as in Germany?" asked Hans-Peter, trying to defuse the situation. "Our aristocratic families usually have *von* or …"

"Von Ribbentrop, for example?" interrupted Marie-Jacques and had the satisfaction of seeing his smile disappear.

Geoff wasn't impressed. "I thought your Revolution was supposed to have got rid of all that nonsense. Anyway, tell him that he'll get my boot up his *particule* if he touches me again."

She passed on the message to Pierrot who spread his hands theatrically towards Geoff as if he had no idea how he'd managed to give offence. All the same, he walked ahead with Marie-Jacques for the rest of the tour and sat by himself on the coach for the return journey.

Daisy was scanning the gravel for fresh tyre marks when she noticed him in conversation with Doug. They were half concealed behind a tall tree and had their backs to her, but she saw Pierrot passing something across before they shook hands. Whatever it was, Doug pocketed it and turned round with a look of satisfaction. Far from being embarrassed when he saw Daisy watching him, he gave her a broad wink.

Dinner was about to be served when Danny returned from Paris. If Geoff had been expecting sympathy, he was out of luck. Danny howled with mirth and refused to take Pierrot's unwelcome advances to his friend seriously.

"I'm more interested in why there's no fresh bread," he said. "Where's Victor this evening?"

"No idea." Geoff was keeping a wary eye on the door to the staff quarters, where he knew that B.B. was entertaining his friend and the coach driver. "He could throw me out, you know."

"No he won't. Pierrot's probably too embarrassed to mention it and the driver didn't come on the tour with us."

"What if Marie-Jacques turns up and tells him?"

"Then you just say that you both got the wrong end of the stick. Your admirer will have gone by the time we get back from the village. Hurry up and finish eating. The girls will be waiting for us."

Daisy thought Valentin looked worried and made a point of asking after Victor.

"It's kind of you to ask," came the cautious reply. "He's not ill. It's just that there are times when it's better for him to stay at home. Now then, dear, are you going out with Jean-Claude this evening?"

"Yes. Just for a drink."

"At my sister's place? And something to eat too?"

"Oh no," she lied, not wanting to hurt his feelings. "I'm quite full."

"Well, I shall be there too. I've promised to help behind the bar and the coach driver will give me a lift down to the village on his way back to Paris."

By the time Daisy arrived with Jean-Claude, Valentin was already busy. The café was packed and she was surprised to see Kate sitting at a table by the window with Raoul.

"They're really slumming tonight!" quipped Danny from the corner where he was sitting with his girlfriend on his knee. Slumming or not, Raoul was acting as though he owned the place.

"Pastis!" he shouted, snapping his fingers in the general direction of the bar. "Four parts of cold water to one part Ricard. No ice." Ignoring all the other customers waiting to be served, Valentin hobbled across with the drinks. His sister followed with a dish of olives and pickled vegetables.

Kate's face spoke volumes as she sipped her drink. Daisy knew how much she loathed aniseed and thought it served her right for laughing about the *diabolo-menthe*.

"Did you like your visit to Saint-Germain?" asked Jean-Claude.

"It was quite interesting." Keeping an eye on Raoul, she told him in a low voice what had happened with Pierrot and Geoff.

To her surprise, he whistled and said, "So that is why my aunt kept Victor at home today. Valentin must have warned her that this Monsieur d'Aulnay was expected."

"And that he's interested in boys? If they're friends, B.B. must surely know that."

"I suppose so, but maybe he's also a business associate that he can't afford to offend."

"What kind of business?"

"I don't know. Let's talk about something else. I've heard that you're all going to the seaside soon and that those of you with friends in the village can invite them along. I'll ask Papa for a day off, shall I?" His hand reached for hers and Daisy soon forgot about Pierrot.

So did most of the boys, until they went down to their dormitory that night and found a languid figure in maroon satin pyjamas occupying one of the spare beds.

Geoff couldn't believe his eyes. "That's it! I'm out of here!"

Danny grabbed his arm. "And where do you think you can go at this time of night? Don't worry. He's not going to jump on you with the rest of us here."

It took a long time for Geoff to fall asleep, but it was Danny who was in for the shock of his life. Woken up in the pitch darkness by a strange hand groping underneath his blanket, he heard a voice say,

"Danny? One has assured me that you're the sort of boy to be kind to Pierrot."

"What the hell!" Forgetting that he'd chosen a top bunk, Danny crashed heavily to the floor. By the time someone found his way to the light switch, Pierrot was back in his own bed and appeared to be fast asleep.

Geoff helped Danny to his feet. "Are you sure it wasn't a dream?"

"Of course it wasn't a bloody dream and I'll be covered in bruises in the morning. It's a wonder I didn't break my neck. Let's throw him out of here and let the dogs have him."

"You can't," counselled Doug. "Don't forget that he's B.B.'s friend."

"Well why isn't he sharing *his* room? And who on earth told him that I'd be up for it? I'll kill him or her, when I find out."

"I can't imagine," lied Doug, "but none of us will be able to get back to sleep now. I'll tell you what, let's leave him here by himself and join the girls. We could have a pyjama party."

"But I don't have any pyjamas." Howls of derision greeted Jaap's objection and he hastily reached for a pair of shorts.

"Pick up your blankets and any bottles you've been hiding and let's go."

Once over the initial shock of the invasion, the girls embraced the idea with enthusiasm. The door was barricaded with one of the spare beds, an impromptu bar was set up and music was provided by Maureen's transistor radio.

There was no sign of Pierrot when the party broke up at dawn and he didn't appear for breakfast either. Neither did Doug.

Doubled up in pain and gasping for breath, he waited for the next blow to land.

"Not laughing now, is he?" Raoul was leaning back against the wall, blowing on his knuckles.

"And he won't, if he knows what's good for him." Seizing the boy by the hair, Baltzinger straightened him up and then kneed him viciously in the groin. Doug collapsed, clutching himself and whimpering, as the *patron* threatened him with worse.

"This is just a warning, lad. Keep that big mouth of yours shut from now on. If you cross me or any of my friends again, you won't live long enough to regret it. Here, Raoul, you can have him back and make sure that you get Pierrot's money from him when you've finished." With that he strode off, brushing past Valentin in the kitchen doorway and confident that neither victim nor witness would dare to report what had happened.

He was right about Doug, who passed off his bruises as the result of a fall, but the night wasn't far off when Valentin would open his heart to Daisy.

Chapter 13

Très chic in his navy blazer, B.B. sat next to the driver at the front of the full coach. Despite the early hour and grey skies, almost everyone was in holiday mood and sang along to the radio whether they knew the words or not.

"Don't look so miserable, Caro," teased Ronnie. "You've got yourself a boyfriend now."

"Very funny!" She'd already had to remove Victor's skinny arm from her shoulders twice and they'd hardly left the village. "Do you and lover boy have to carry on like that at this hour of the morning? It's giving the kid ideas."

"He's just keeping me warm."

"You should have brought a jacket."

"Oh, shut up. And you, stop that!" Charlot had run a practised hand up the back of her T-shirt and twanged her bra strap. There were stifled giggles from the girls within earshot. Ronnie's updates on how far she'd allowed him to go were still nightly entertainment in the dormitory. Daisy glanced at Jean-Claude and wondered if the boys compared notes too. She hoped that he'd have more respect for her if they ever progressed beyond kissing and holding hands.

B.B. soon tired of pop music and ordered the driver to switch off the radio. "It's about time that our friends from abroad learnt some of our traditional songs." His powerful voice needed no microphone. He started with *Alouette* and encouraged everyone to join in. Pleased with the dutiful applause, he then launched into *Auprès de ma blonde*.

"Good God!" said Ronnie. "This must be his party piece. How

many more bloody verses?" As soon as the last chorus faded away, she leapt to her feet and began to bellow *We shall overcome.* Supporting the Civil Rights movement and the Ban the Bomb campaign was a feature of life in the Sixth form, rather like wearing a duffel coat instead of the regulation school gabardine, but Ronnie took it much more seriously than most. B.B. allowed her to take over, but his expression suggested that Ronnie had better watch her step.

By the time they arrived in Fort Mahon, the sun was out and the day was heating up. The holiday mood intensified as everyone scrambled off the coach.

"Look at that beach!" marvelled Danny. "Miles of sand and the seagulls still have it all to themselves."

"Yes, it's hard to imagine that this was once part of the Atlantic Wall. If it weren't for that grim looking concrete bunker up there..."

"Oh, pack it in, Jaap!" yawned Geoff. "Thank goodness Marie-Jacques isn't with us today. I just want to enjoy myself, not listen to a history lecture. It's rather different from Brighton, don't you think, Danny? You wouldn't find space for a deckchair there by this time of the morning."

His French girlfriend was pulling at his arm. "*Chut*, Geoff. I think that Monsieur Baltzinger is trying to tell us something." She was right. He was standing in front of a couple of big cardboard boxes and tapping his foot impatiently.

"Please pick up the food that Valentin has prepared for you and then you're free to do whatever you want. Enjoy yourselves, but make sure that you're back at the coach by half past five. If you're not..." He guffawed and brandished a fist at them.

"Someone else can have my packed lunch," said Kate, as B.B. and the driver headed into the nearest bar. "Raoul rang up yesterday and booked us a table at that restaurant over there. It was awarded a Michelin star last year."

"Well, lah-di-dah!"

"Oh, shut up! You're only jealous."

As Kate flounced off, Ronnie nudged Daisy. "I can't wait to see what the French boys are going to wear in the water, can you? Do you remember those pictures in *En Route* when we were in the First form? Bathing suits with shoulder straps!"

"Well, the book *was* published before the war."

Ronnie didn't have to wait long. Raoul's swimming trunks could have been sprayed onto his tanned and muscular frame and left very little to the imagination.

"Bloody hell!" she gasped.

"Don't forget that you're supposed to be here with me, not him!" snarled Charlot.

"Well, you can stop gawping at Kate, then."

Kate was a picture in her blue and white checked bikini with its frilly lace border. It looked quite demure until you realised that the bottom section was only held together at the sides by thin fabric ties.

Doug spoke for all the boys when he said, "Raoul's fingers must be itchin' to get at those knots!"

Daisy and Jean-Claude left them to it and walked down to the water's edge. Hungry already, they sat down on their towels to eat the fruit and biscuits Valentin had provided. The seagulls got the stale cheese rolls.

"Well then," she said when they'd finished. "Are we going in?"

He hesitated. "There's nowhere down here for you to change."

"That's all right. I put my swimming costume on under my clothes."

He laughed. "So did I."

She watched with interest as he shed his T-shirt and jeans. Not as showy as Raoul, he was certainly very well put together and his strong frame was the result of hard physical work. Valentin had confided in Daisy that Raoul's muscles owed much to the use of body building equipment at a gym he frequented in Paris. The same establishment had sun lamps to ensure an all year round tan for its clients.

Daisy was wearing a modest nylon one piece in emerald green. Self consciousness about an operation scar had ruled out buying anything more revealing, although her mother hadn't been keen on the idea anyway. Next year, maybe she'd be more daring. The scar had already changed from an ugly purple to pink and would in time, the surgeon had assured her, fade to white.

Jean-Claude dispelled any doubts she might have had about her appearance. "Very beautiful," he said, taking her by the hand and leading her into the water. It was warm and shallow and they splashed around happily for a long time, chasing each other in and out of the gentle waves before wading out far enough to swim.

The sands had started to fill up with families, many of them well equipped with deck chairs, parasols and windbreaks. A few even had brightly striped changing tents. Sun worshippers of all sizes and shapes lay as far as the eye could see, but Jean-Claude grimaced when he noticed that Daisy's shoulders and back were starting to turn pink.

"Your skin is much more delicate than mine," he said. "You'll burn badly if we stay out here." Brooking no argument, he picked up their things and led her away from the water. A noisy crocodile in identical *colonie de vacances* T-shirts and hats passed them on their way down to paddle and he clicked his tongue disapprovingly. "If I were in charge of those kids, I'd keep them in the shade until at least three o'clock."

"Are you fond of children?"

"Yes, of course. I hope to have at least a dozen of my own one day."

"A dozen?"

"However many come along. I didn't like growing up as an only one."

"Neither did I."

"Then we agree."

The sand was almost too hot to walk on and they had to pick their way through the thorny plants and sharp grass growing through the dunes. It was worth it to find a secluded hollow free from discarded cigarette packets and empty bottles.

"We'll spread our towels out here, shall we?"

In the intimacy of their private little world, the heady scent of sun kissed flesh and the gentle pressure of Jean-Claude's lips turned Daisy's legs to water. He was so unlike Charlot, she thought. Even now, wearing next to nothing and with her head pillowed on his rolled up jeans, she knew she could trust him. Propped up on one elbow and gazing into her eyes, he moved her damp tangled hair aside and stroked the soft skin behind her ear.

"Do you like that?"

"Mmmm."

"And this?" She hardly dared to breathe as he trailed his fingers down her neck and started to trace the curve of a breast as it strained against the taut nylon. Daisy jumped when his thumb grazed the sensitive tip and he withdrew his hand at once.

"I'm sorry. Was that too much?"

"No," she croaked. It was just that the sudden tingle of pleasure between her legs had caught her by surprise.

"May I go on a little?" She nodded dumbly and lay back to enjoy the butterfly play of his fingers and the new sensations rippling through her body as he bent his dark head to kiss what he'd already caressed.

The moment was ruined by the sound of angry voices close by and a loud slap. A moment later, Charlot crashed down the sand dune towards them, red faced and furious. The cause of his discomfort was all too obvious. Jean-Claude rolled hastily onto his stomach, not wishing his cousin to see him in a similar state.

"What the devil is going on?"

"That silly English bitch is driving me crazy," snarled Charlot, making no attempt to cover himself.

"Ronnie? Why? What's wrong?"

"You'd better go and see," said Jean-Claude quietly.

Daisy found Ronnie wriggling back into her bikini top, unhurt but defiant. "We had a row, that's all. He wouldn't take no for an answer this time."

"What did he want you to do?"

"Go all the way, of course. He said he'd be careful, but I wasn't going to risk it." Her face crumpled. "Now he's going to find himself someone who will."

"Don't cry, Ronnie. He isn't worth it." Daisy tried to give her a hug, but she wrenched away.

"When did you ever see me cry?" She stormed off towards the beach, leaving Daisy nonplussed.

"What did Charlot say to you after I'd gone?" Jean-Claude seemed reluctant to tell her and they sat in silence for a while.

"Well," he said eventually. "My cousin wants too much. That's to say, every boy wants it, of course, but it should only be when the girl wants it too and... Look, Daisy, I'm very hot. Let's go and get an ice cream." Springing to his feet, he picked up his own clothes and handed Daisy hers.

On their way back from the kiosk, they saw the colonie de vacances children being marched off the beach by a couple of grim faced teenagers.

"I wonder what they've done," said Daisy.

"No idea, but their *moniteurs* don't look very happy."

"Neither does Ronnie. Look! There she is."

Daisy rushed across to where a small crowd had gathered. In the centre was her classmate, sitting on the sand with a seagull in her arms. The bird's eyes were glazed and its neck was bent at an unnatural angle

"What happened to the poor thing?"

"It was two of those little bastards," spat Ronnie. "They threw down some bread for the gulls and then grabbed this one when it came to take it. They were hanging onto its wings and trying to stretch it as far as they could."

"Did no one try to stop them?" Daisy looked accusingly at the crowd, which included several familiar faces.

"Yes, I did, but they'd already broken one wing by the time I chased them off. The poor thing was in agony, squawking and thrashing about."

"It gets worse, I'm afraid," said Caroline. "B.B. was kicking a ball around with the coach driver and some of the boys and came across to see what was going on. Ronnie wanted to take it to a vet and he just laughed at her."

"He said that he couldn't see what all the fuss was about," added Maureen. "And then he just broke its neck and threw it onto the sand."

"What a horrible thing to do."

Jaap grimaced. "Well, he said it was only a damned bird and gave it a kick. That was when Ronnie hit him."

"She did what?"

"I'm afraid it's true, Daisy. She said she wanted to wipe the smile off his face. Well, she certainly did that. If the coach driver hadn't stopped him, I think he'd have hit her back."

"He wouldn't dare! Would he?"

Caroline shuddered. "I wouldn't rule out the possibility."

"Where is he now?"

"In the bar over there. I hope he's cooled down by the time we have to leave."

Word got round quickly and the mood on the return journey was very subdued. Charlot ignored Ronnie completely and pushed a disgruntled Victor off the seat next to Caroline.

"I'd better go and sit with Ronnie," whispered Daisy. "Do you mind?"

Jean-Claude gave her hand a sympathetic squeeze. "Of course I do, but you must. I think she's in shock. She looks dreadful." He walked up the coach to where Antoine was sitting with Renate and came back with a leather jacket to put round Ronnie's shoulders. The events of the afternoon had broken through her tough shell and she was shivering uncontrollably.

B.B. sat facing forward the whole time and spoke to no one, but the stiff set of his shoulders and bulging neck muscles did not bode well.

Chapter 14

There were moans of anguish in the girls' dormitory the following morning from those who awoke to the sting of raw flesh. Wiping the sleep from her eyes, Daisy wondered at first why so many of them were wearing white bikinis.

"Caroline doesn't look like the back of a bus this morning," remarked Ronnie. "She looks like the front with those big headlights."

"Shush. She'll hear you."

"Do you think I care, Daisy? She couldn't wait to get her paws on Charlot. Well, she can have him. Randy little sod! Doug told me what he'd said about me to the other boys."

"And what was that?"

"He called me an *allumeuse*."

"A match?"

"No. That's an *allumette*. According to Doug, the other word means a girl who leads a boy on and then refuses at the very last minute to go through with it. Charlot said that I'd left him in agony. He didn't really believe me when I told him that I was just frightened of getting pregnant, because he'd heard that English girls are mostly on the pill. The French can't get it at all yet, you know."

"What an idiot!" said Kate. "As if it's as simple as that! One of my cousins went to the family planning clinic just before her wedding and was put through the third degree before they'd give her a prescription. Anyway, let's change the subject. Where did you disappear to yesterday, Daisy? I hardly saw you after we got off the coach."

"Oh, we didn't stay long on the beach. Jean-Claude was worried that

I'd burn and took me up into the dunes to find some shade."

"Oh yes?"

"Yes. Look, Ronnie, don't you think you ought to apologise to B.B.?"

"To that cruel bastard? I'd rather die."

"Well, you did hit him and called him some very rude names."

"Not rude enough. I couldn't remember them all."

"I know you won't agree, but he probably thought that putting the gull out of its misery was the kindest thing to do. Country people look on these things differently, you know."

"How do you know he's a country person?"

"Valentin said so once when I was helping him in the kitchen. He said that B.B.'s family used to own a vineyard in Alsace."

"Who told him that?"

"B.B. himself, I suppose. They've known each other since they were boys. Seriously, though, tell him you're sorry. I'm sure it's the right thing to do."

"Over my dead body!"

The atmosphere at breakfast was tense, even though the man in question didn't put in an appearance. Catching Daisy's eye, Valentin beckoned her to join him in the kitchen.

"You must make your friend apologise to the *patron*," he whispered. "I've never seen him as angry as he was last night."

"I've tried," she whispered back. "So has Kate. But she won't."

"Then I fear for her."

When Daisy reported back, Kate put down her cup and said, "Look, Ronnie, you've paid to come here like the rest of us and I don't suppose B.B. could throw you out just like that, even if he wanted to. There must be some kind of official procedure and he might not come out of it too well himself if you told your side of the story."

Daisy agreed. "And he wouldn't be keen to draw attention to the way he runs this place either. I'm quite sure there's some funny business going on, whether Raoul's mixed up in it or not."

Ronnie had heard enough. "Oh, I don't really care what happens now," she declared. "After all, I only wanted to stay in the first place because of Charlot and now I can't wait to go home. Have you noticed how Renate keeps giving me dirty looks?"

"That's probably because you're still wearin' her boyfriend's jacket," suggested Doug.

"Well, it's quite chilly this morning."

"That's hardly the point. Now that you've finished with Charlot, she probably thinks you're interested in Antoine. Not that you're any competition for her, of course."

Ronnie scowled at him. "Thank you so much for pointing that out. Well, Renate can think what she likes, but I'm not handing the jacket over to *her*. I'll give it to Antoine myself when we go down to the village this evening."

"I wish I could go down there now," said Maureen, wincing as she leaned forward to take another roll. "Jaysus! Me shoulders are killing me. Kate, do you think Raoul would let me get some camomile from the pharmacy? I'm burning all over. Even me face."

"You mean calamine, don't you? Unless you want to make tea with it."

Maureen may have flushed at the sarcasm, but it was hard to tell. "Yes, of course I mean calamine. The biggest bottle of lotion you can find."

"Then I'll ask him, if you like."

"Get some for me too while you're down there," pleaded Danny.

Geoff laughed. "Just look at the idiot! He was too busy romping around on the beach yesterday to worry about catching too much sun. Even Pierrot wouldn't fancy him now."

Danny picked up a basket of bread rolls with every intention of pelting Geoff with them but thought better of it when he realised that B.B. was standing behind him. He'd entered the building through the back door into the kitchen and there was no knowing how much of the conversation he'd heard.

His full lips compressed into a thin line, he looked round the room and roared, "Some of you look like boiled lobsters this morning, but don't expect any sympathy from me. Your problems are self inflicted and I'll have no malingering. There's a lot of work to be done today and you should all have finished breakfast by now."

Only Ronnie dared to defy him. Jumping to her feet, she said, "That's ridiculous. Sunburn might be a disciplinary offence in the Army, but we're not bloody soldiers. We're supposed to be here on holiday!"

The room fell silent as he rounded on her. "You again? You've got some nerve after yesterday." Ronnie took a couple of steps back and, with what looked like an immense effort of self control, the big man unclenched his fists and disappeared into the office.

"You've really done it now," sneered Doug, as they waited for tasks to be allocated. "I wouldn't want to be in your shoes."

She stuck her chin out. "He doesn't frighten me. The only way to deal with people like him is to stand up to them."

"You reckon?"

"Of course it is. If he does try to make me leave, I'll threaten to go straight to the British Consulate. The French authorities would certainly hear about it and have this place closed down."

"I very much doubt that. It's hardly a diplomatic incident, after all."

"Oh, shut up, Jaap."

"If B.B. did get the sack," giggled Kate, "Raoul might be promoted to his job."

"And then Valentin would be second in command and Daisy would have to take over the kitchen."

The laughter died away as Raoul appeared with his clipboard. Ronnie's name was top of the list.

"You will clean the underground toilets. All of them."

"I certainly will not."

"You must. The *patron* will not change his mind and he wants to see them spotless."

Ronnie crossed her arms defiantly. "He can't make me do it."

"Oh yes he can," hissed Doug. "Take it from me. Don't make him even angrier with you."

"I don't give a fuck! Tell him I'm on strike." With that she pulled Antoine's jacket more tightly round her shoulders and sat down on one of the unpainted boulders.

Renate was outraged. "How dare you still wear that jacket. Antoine is not your boyfriend. He is mine. And remove that silly badge. It will damage the leather."

"Get stuffed!"

"What?'

"*Va te faire foutre!*'

"What nice idioms you English girls choose to learn!"

"I'm only sorry that I don't know how to say it in German." Renate was about to tell her when a warning look from Hans-Peter stopped her in her tracks.

Raoul shrugged his shoulders and carried on with his list. Daisy's and Kate's names were right at the end and he asked them to walk into the village to collect a few things that Valentin had forgotten to order for the kitchen.

"Couldn't Siobhan and I do that instead?" asked Maureen. "I really need to go to the pharmacy."

"No, but you can tell them what you need and I'm sure they'll get it for you." He didn't look disposed to argue and Maureen gave up.

Taking Kate aside, he pushed a banknote into her hand and muttered, "I don't want any change. Treat yourselves to something nice when you've done the shopping. There's no need to rush back. Stay down there all morning, if you like."

"How much did he give you?" asked Daisy. "It still looks like Monopoly money to me."

"A hundred francs," marvelled Kate. "He must be in a much better mood than B.B."

"I don't feel right about leaving Ronnie."

"Oh, she'll come round. You know what she's like. It's not just that seagull business yesterday. It's breaking up with Charlot as well. I expect she'll sulk for a while and then go and throw a couple of buckets of water around like Caroline did. We'll buy her a cake to cheer her up."

On their way back, Daisy spotted Monsieur Binard laying fresh flowers at the war memorial and told Kate what Jean-Claude had said.

"Do you want to go over and say hello to him?"

"No, I don't think so. He looks so sad that I shouldn't like to intrude. I don't think he's seen me."

"He must have been very fond of his father to do that every week."

"His mother too and especially his wife. Their graves are a picture."

"How wonderful to be loved like that!"

Was Kate imagining herself receiving similar devotion from Raoul? As for Daisy, Jean-Claude filled her dreams and most of her waking thoughts in a way that no one else ever had. Not even Billy Fury or any of the Beatles.

There was no sign of Ronnie when they got back, but Maureen came rushing towards them, her face even redder than before.

"Here's your calamine lotion," said Daisy. "We didn't forget."

"Never mind about that. Thank God you're back! You'd better get down to the dormitory as fast as you can. I found your friend in an awful state when I went to get me tranny, but she wouldn't tell me what had happened to her."

Daisy and Kate rushed down the steps, nearly tripping over an upturned bucket at the bottom. They found Ronnie face down on her bed and wrapped only in the thin towel that she'd brought from home. The clothes she'd been wearing that morning lay on the floor, filthy and soaking wet.

"What on earth has been going on?"

As Ronnie sat up, the towel fell away to reveal livid bruises on her shoulders and the tops of her arms.

"What do you think, Daisy? That I did this to myself? B.B. came back just after you'd both gone and told Raoul to scrap the rest of his list and take everyone down to the casemates to clear out all the rubbish and burn it. He kept me back, though, and dragged me down here as soon as the others had gone."

"I thought you were on strike."

"Look at me! He's three times my size and had both my arms twisted up my back. He said that Doug had told him what Tanner meant and I wasn't even worth that much. Then he gave me a bucket, a plunger and an old brush with half the bristles missing and said, 'Use those to clean up this mess, or you'll do it with your toothbrush.' He actually pushed me down onto my knees and stood over me until I'd finished. I don't know how I managed not to throw up. Then he started to finger his belt buckle and said that there were worse things he could do if I hadn't learnt my lesson. I didn't know whether he was threatening to beat me or..."

"Oh surely not," said Kate. "Look, get yourself washed and dressed and then we've got a nice surprise for you."

Ronnie stared at the contents of the little box in disbelief. "Do you seriously imagine that a chocolate eclair's going to make me forget about all this? No way! I'm packing my things and getting the first bus out of here. Will you two come with me? No? Oh, well, stay with your bloody Frogs if you must. I'll see you back at school."

"You might be able to change your Skyways ticket," said practical Daisy, "but have you got enough money to get to the coach terminal in Paris?"

Ronnie's face fell. "No. Not without changing a traveller's cheque. How about you? Could you help me out?" Daisy reached for her purse, but Kate said,

"No, don't do that. You might need it yourself. I'll find Raoul and ask if it's all right to give Ronnie the money left over from the shopping. He did say that he didn't want it back."

Much to Daisy's surprise, Raoul was with Kate when she returned. Frowning with apparent concern, he took Ronnie's grimy hands in his and said, "I'm so sorry that you want to leave us, little one, but I do understand."

"Has Kate told you that I intend to report what Baltzinger did to me to the British Consulate?"

"No, but you have every right to complain and I'll drive you to Paris myself. Kate will let me know when you're ready to leave."

"What about *him*? I don't want to see him again."

"Don't worry about that. He's gone off somewhere and you'll be well on your way before he misses you."

"Thank God! Could Kate and Daisy come along to back up my story?"

"With the deepest regret, I must say no. My car is too small, you see, and the *patron* has taken his van. There's no need to be nervous, though. I am a very safe driver, as Kate will tell you."

She nodded. "You'll be fine. He'll have you in Paris in a fraction of the time that the bus would take."

Ronnie's parting gesture was a two fingered salute towards B.B.'s office window as Raoul drove her away.

Chapter 15

The whole incident with Ronnie proved to be something of a damp squib. No one came from Paris to investigate and even some of the young people were sceptical about the story.

"I cannot see what all the fuss was about," said Renate. "This girl Ronnie came on a working holiday and then did not like it when she was told to clean some toilets."

Her twin agreed. "Yes. I believe that she made up the story to pay B.B. back for what he did to the seagull."

"Oh, come on, Astrid," protested Jaap. "She wouldn't do that."

Lucinda had never taken to Ronnie and thought it quite possible. "Did you actually *see* B.B. get rough with her, Maureen?"

"No. I can't say that I did, but he's a quare fella right enough and Kate and Daisy saw the bruises."

"Well no one else did. Surely if they'd been convinced that he was dangerous, they'd have gone back to England with her."

Renate had the final word when she told everyone that Ronnie had gone off with Antoine's leather jacket.

Their time in France was slipping by far too fast for Daisy and Kate, who had drawn closer together after Ronnie's departure.

"Look," said Kate on one of the rare occasions they found themselves alone in the dormitory, "Tell me to mind my own business if you like, but how far have you gone with Jean-Claude?"

"Only to a village a few miles down the road so far, when a travelling fair set up there. He has said, though, that he'd like to take me to Paris one day for a trip down the Seine on a *bateau-mouche*."

Kate stared at her in exasperation. "I didn't mean how far have you *been* with Jean-Claude. I meant how far have you *gone* with him."

Daisy blushed, remembering how close she'd come to throwing caution to the wind in the sand dunes, if only they hadn't been interrupted. Since then they seemed to have taken a step back. Furtive fumblings in the forest or the casemates didn't appear to be his style.

"Oh, I see what you mean," she said. "Not far at all, but why do you ask? Has Raoul been putting pressure on you?"

"No, quite the opposite, which was weird after all the warnings I'd had about his reputation. Until last night, I'd started to think that he just liked being seen out with me but didn't really fancy me at all."

"Don't be silly, Kate. I've never met a man who didn't."

"Except Pierrot."

"Yes, well that was different and Raoul certainly isn't like that! Maybe it was because he's a member of the staff here and quite a bit older than you. I suppose there are rules about that kind of thing. He and B.B. might be legally *in loco parentis*."

"I did wonder about that."

"So what happened last night that was so different?"

"Well, you know how he usually takes me out somewhere well away from here? Yesterday he suggested a quiet drink in his room instead."

"I thought the staff accommodation was out of bounds."

"It is, but B.B. had gone to Paris again and dropped Valentin off in the village."

"Did Raoul want to show you his etchings?"

Kate smiled. "No. His record collection, maybe. He's got dozens of them."

"Sounds harmless enough."

"That's what I thought. I felt a bit awkward sitting on his bed, but there weren't any spare chairs. Raoul gave me a drink and asked me to put on something by Charles Aznavour while he rolled a couple of cigarettes."

"Oh yes? You do realise that it's not always ordinary tobacco that he uses, don't you? Danny and Geoff told me. They smoke that stuff too when they get the chance and can recognise the smell anywhere."

"I know that! I'm not stupid, but I only had a couple of puffs. Raoul said that it would help us both to relax."

"Relax for what?" asked Daisy, as warning bells rang in her head.

"That's what I wondered. Anyway, it got really hot with the window shut and the curtains drawn in case anyone was snooping and Raoul asked if it was OK to take off his shirt. I could hardly object, could I? It was his room, after all, and it's not as though I hadn't seen him with even less on at the seaside."

"I remember. Some of the girls couldn't keep their eyes off him and the boys were all as jealous as hell. Nobody was going to kick sand in *his* face."

"Their eyes would pop if they saw the holiday photographs from Cap d'Agde he's got on his wall. He saw the look on my face and said that it's quite normal to romp around in the nude on some beaches in France and he wished it had been like that at Fort Mahon."

"I can well believe it!" said Daisy, remembering Doug's comments on the bikini that Kate had worn that day.

"Anyway, then he told me that he'd fallen in love with me and needed to know how I felt about him."

"And what did you say?"

"That I felt the same. That was when he started kissing me. Really kissing, you know, with tongues and everything. Not like before. When we came up for air, he confessed that he'd been dying to do that from the day he met me but had been holding back because I was so young. I told him that I was quite old enough to know my own mind."

"And he took that as the green light, did he?"

"Oh, Daisy, you're starting to sound just like Ronnie."

"But am I wrong?"

"Well, no. I was feeling a bit woozy anyway and before I knew what was happening, he'd unzipped my dress and ..."

"Flung it over his shoulder?"

"No. Linen creases badly, you know. He got up and put it on a hanger."

"How very neat! You must be kindred spirits."

She dimpled. "Maybe we are. Anyway, I didn't have much on underneath but, when you think about it, there's no real difference between that and wearing a bikini, is there?"

"Only psychologically, I suppose, and the fact that you were in his bedroom rather than a public beach! That's what your parents would say."

"It was too late to worry about them, I'm afraid. He started kissing me again. Up and down my neck and then...further down. He hadn't shaved and the stubble tickled my sensitive bits."

"You mean you let him get to 'second base', as Ronnie would say?"

"I hate that expression, but yes, I did."

"And was that it?"

"No, but it all seems a bit of a blur now."

"That's what happens when you smoke that stuff."

"Raoul said I could have my bra back later if I was a good girl. He'd hung it over one of the bedposts where I couldn't reach it. Not that I remember trying very hard."

Daisy wondered how many notches there were on that bedpost, but there was no stopping Kate now that she'd decided to spill the beans.

"Anyway, it wasn't long before I found myself letting him do whatever he wanted. To be honest, I was enjoying it too much to ask him to stop and afterwards I just lay there as if I'd been shot."

"Oh Kate! I hope he used something?"

It was the other girl's turn to look shocked. "Oh, we didn't go as far as *that*. He didn't even take his trousers off."

"So you're still a virgin?"

"Yes, of course I am. It didn't take him long to find that out and he was very pleased about it. He said that I was a good girl to keep the gate to paradise locked until the most fortunate man in the world claimed me for his own."

Daisy winced. "He really said that?"

"I know, but it sounds better in French. Then he promised that my birthday would be a day I'd remember for the rest of my life. I think he's going to propose."

"Propose what?"

"Marriage, you idiot!"

"And will you accept?"

"Of course I will. If I hadn't decided that Raoul was THE ONE, I wouldn't have let him take the photographs."

"What photographs?"

"Oh, don't look like that, Daisy. They're only for himself. He promised me that no one else would ever see them."

"And you believed him? Kate! What about the person who develops the film for a start?"

"Not a problem," she said smugly. "Raoul has one of the new Polaroid Swinger cameras!"

The following morning, a blue and white Dormobile with British number plates arrived while everyone was still having breakfast. Daisy was amazed to see Ronnie's parents framed in the doorway of the dining room and jumped up from her seat to greet them, closely followed by Kate.

"Mr and Mrs Tanner! What are you doing here?"

Scanning the room, Mr Tanner replied, "We're on our way home from the Loire valley and were passing so close by that we thought we'd drop in and surprise you."

"We can take some of your things back with us, if you like," added his wife, "so you won't have as much to carry next week."

"I'd be very grateful," said Daisy, thinking of all the fairground prizes stashed away under her bed. "It's very good of you to put yourselves out for us like this, especially since..."

Mr Tanner interrupted her. "Where's Veronica? Did she decide to skip breakfast this morning and have a lie in? That would be just like her."

Kate and Daisy looked at each other in astonishment before Kate said, "But Ronnie left for England a few days ago."

"A few days ago? No, she couldn't have. Her grandmother's staying at our house to take care of the dog and she'd have told me. I rang home last night from the phone box on the campsite to see if everything was all right. She said it was and she'd had our postcard, although she was disappointed not to have had one from Ronnie."

Daisy touched his arm. "I think you'd both better sit down." They listened with growing anger to what she had to tell them and then Mr Tanner sprang to his feet again, fists clenched.

"Where is this man? He needs locking up!"

"I'm afraid he's not here this morning and...Where *is* Raoul? Does anyone know?"

"I think he's driven into the village to get some more white paint," said Doug. "We ran out yesterday and there are still a lot more boulders to do."

"Boulders? Why on earth is anyone painting boulders? Well, never mind that. Is there anyone in authority here that we *can* speak to?"

"Only the cook."

As soon as Valentin appeared from the kitchen, Mrs Tanner seized him by the arm. "We must notify the police at once of our daughter's disappearance. Oh dear, I do wish that my French were better. *Où est votre téléphone, s'il vous plaît?*"

No one was even making pretence of finishing their breakfast. Silence had fallen and the attention of the whole room was focussed on the new arrivals.

"There isn't one, M-m-m-adame? B-b-but..."

Jaap took pity on him. "You'll be able to put a call through to the British Consulate from the post office in the village, Mrs Tanner. I'll go with you, if you like."

"And you can speak to the local Plod while you're down there or leave a message for him," added Doug.

Mr Tanner was grim faced when they returned. "We managed to get through to someone at the Consulate eventually and..."

"There was no record of our Veronica ever having been there," sobbed her mother. "Wherever can she have gone?"

A gasp ran round the room. The question was an impossible one to answer and Daisy, imagining her own mother in a similar situation, couldn't have felt sorrier for her.

The middle-aged policeman who cycled up from the village, the rest of his face so red from the effort that it almost matched the port-wine stain on his left cheek, had only just got his breath back when Raoul appeared with the paint cans and demanded to know what was going on.

"These are Ronnie's parents. She seems to have vanished and they think that something bad may have happened to her. Please tell them that it isn't true." Kate was clinging onto his arm in a way that made Mr Tanner raise his eyebrows.

"Well, of course it isn't true." Raoul gave her hand a gentle pat before detaching himself and offering his own to the frantic couple.

The policeman cleared his throat in a way that suggested a dislike of being upstaged. Removing his képi and taking out a notebook and propelling pencil, he said, "I am ready to take down all the details and then decide on the appropriate action, should any prove to be necessary."

"What?"

"He doesn't seem to think there's much of a problem," said Daisy.

"Our daughter's gone missing and this yokel doesn't think there's much of a problem!"

There was no denying that the policeman, having established that no one had actually *seen* B.B. lay his hands on Ronnie, was looking increasingly sceptical. "Let's move on for the moment," he said. "Who was the last person to see Mademoiselle Tanner?"

"That would be me," offered Raoul. "I gave her a lift into Paris and dropped her off on the Faubourg St. Honoré. It's impossible to park right outside the British Consulate and I didn't actually see her go in, but she was certainly heading in that direction as I drove away."

"For the record, what did you do then, Monsieur?"

"I visited some friends and then came back here."

"Will your friends confirm the time that you spent with them?"

"Of course. I'll be happy to give you their contact details."

"Thank you, Monsieur." With Jaap on stand by to translate where necessary, he turned to the Tanners and said, "We must take into consideration all the circumstances of your daughter Veronica's hasty departure and not just the version her friends have given you. She isn't a total innocent in this matter, you know. As her parents, you naturally see her in a different light, but she built up quite a reputation during the short time she was here."

"What kind of reputation?" asked her indignant father.

"Well, for one thing, a local boy has reported the theft of his expensive leather jacket."

"Our daughter, a thief? I don't believe it. Ronnie never stole anything in her life."

"Calm yourself, Monsieur! That is not all. Did you know that she assaulted the *patron*, both verbally and physically, on the day before she left? This happened in front of several independent witnesses on the beach at Fort Mahon and is therefore an incontrovertible fact. Monsieur Baltzinger would have had good grounds to press charges against her, had he wished to do so, but he is a generous man and put the incident down to adolescent hormones or maybe," he paused to cough delicately, "Veronica's time of the month."

That took the biscuit and Daisy couldn't let it go unchallenged. "I'm sure it wasn't anything like that. He killed that poor seagull right in front of her and laughed about it. And have you seen the state of the dogs he keeps chained up outside all day long?"

"Yes, yes, but there's no proof that he's ever harmed any of the young people staying here. If that had been the case, there would have been other complaints and none have been received."

"But he actually threatened her with his belt!"

"And you saw this, Mademoiselle?"

"Well, no. But I believe Ronnie. I've never seen her so upset."

Unimpressed, the policeman continued, "Your daughter seems to be a very strong minded and impulsive girl. Do you think it may be the case that she took herself off somewhere on the spur of the moment and just hasn't bothered to contact anyone in England?"

The Tanners looked at each other doubtfully and Ronnie's mother said, "Well, she knew that we wouldn't be back from our holiday just yet, so I suppose it's possible. She can be a little wild."

"All I can do then is to pass on your enquiry. Thousands of young people go missing in France every year, you know, many of them foreigners, but they almost invariably turn up again. Perhaps you would be so kind as to inform the authorities in Paris when you hear from Veronica, so that the case can be closed. Good day to you."

"Aren't you even going to wait and interview this Baltzinger chap?" protested Mr Tanner.

"No. I have many other calls on my time." Turning to Raoul, he said, "Please ask the *patron* to pop down and see me at his earliest convenience." With that, he replaced his képi, tucked away his notebook and departed.

The Tanners were speechless for a few moments and then Ronnie's mother said, "I think that you two girls should come away with us. I'm sure your parents would agree and we'll pay for your ferry tickets. Go and pack your things and say goodbye to your friends. We can be in Le Havre by lunchtime."

"I can't," said Kate, glancing at Raoul. "It's my birthday soon and…"

"Wouldn't you rather celebrate it at home with your family?"

"No!"

"And why not?"

Raoul gave Mrs Tanner a dazzling smile. "Because plans have already been made and it's too late to cancel them now."

"I see. Well, how about you, Daisy?"

"Oh, I think I'd better stay and travel back with Kate. Mum would understand."

"Very well. We can't force you to come with us, of course, but we shall be speaking to your parents about all this as soon as we get back to

Leeds. Do take care of yourselves. Goodbye then."

The last Daisy and Kate ever saw of the Tanners was their Dormobile disappearing down the track towards the village.

Chapter 16

Although concerned about Ronnie, Daisy had other things on her mind and went into the kitchen to consult Valentin. She meant to keep her promise to cook a meal for Jean-Claude and his father and was determined to make a good job of it, even if it cost her all the money she had left.

"Don't worry," he said, scanning the list of ingredients that she'd scribbled down. "You should find everything you need in the local shops. I'll tell Raoul that you're doing some errands for me." He was rewarded with a big smile and a hug from Daisy, who lost no time in heading down to the village.

It was the first time that she'd been shopping for meat in France and she was surprised to find the *boucherie* run by a woman. Did she do her own slaughtering? She certainly looked equal to the task. Quite indifferent to the queue backing up behind her, Madame Busselle insisted on giving Daisy chapter and verse on how her best beef should be cooked if one were not to suffer agonies of indigestion. Daisy thanked her for the advice, which she fully intended to ignore, and went off in search of horse radish.

By the time she'd bought everything she needed, including a pretty but inexpensive green apron with a gingham trim, the thought of an English girl let loose in the Binards' kitchen had raised eyebrows all over the village and Daisy wondered with amusement how many of their nearest and dearest would be praying for them.

Father and son looked on in amazement as golden slabs of Yorkshire pudding with onion gravy were placed in front of them and it was very satisfying to see their expressions change as they took the first bite. The roast beef that followed, they told all interested parties later, melted in their mouths and the vegetables were cooked to perfection. As her mother had taught her, Daisy had roasted potatoes and parsnips with the beef and also prepared mashed potatoes, mashed swede, green beans, carrots and peas.

"We were forced to eat so much swede during the war, that I never thought I could bring myself to try it again," remarked Monsieur Binard. "That, however, was delicious, Daisy." He sat back in a happy coma after the big helping of apple pie and custard that had completed his first English meal. As Jean-Claude beamed proudly, his father kissed the tips of his own fingers and then Daisy's.

"*Magnifique, ma petite!*"

She blushed. "I'm sorry I couldn't find any English cheese for you."

"Cheese? Who would have room for cheese after all that? Jean-Claude will do the washing up, won't you son? Come with me, Daisy!" To her amazement, he reached out to untie the bow at the back of her apron, pulled the halter over her head and led her into the parlour.

During the ritual filling of his pipe, which brought back a bittersweet memory of her own father, she took the opportunity to admire the family portrait gallery as though she'd never seen it before.

Her host sighed. "Memories, memories."

"They make you sad, Monsieur?"

"Yes indeed." Reaching for the little photograph of the war memorial and cradling it in his hand, he said, "It is only right that one should remember, but I hope that my son will have a happier life than mine has been. I lost my little flower so many years ago. Perhaps Jean-Claude will be more fortunate."

"Your little flower? You mean your wife?"

There was a pause and then he put back the photograph and said, "Yes. Of course, I mean my wife. Now then, Daisy, tell me about your family."

"Well, I'm an only child. Mum didn't have me until she was over forty and really shouldn't have done then."

"Why not? It's not so uncommon to give birth at that age, is it?"

"I don't know, but Mum was advised not to have any children at all. She was born with a heart condition, you see, and she's never been very strong."

"And your father?"

"He was away for most of the war, which is why they left it so late, I suppose. And then Dad died of cancer, so it's just the two of us now."

"I'm so sorry, my dear. Did your father suffer much?"

"Yes, I'm afraid he did. Mum wore herself out nursing him and now she worries all the time about what will happen to me when she's no longer around."

"And you worry just as much about her, I think."

Chapter 17

A couple of days before her seventeenth birthday, Raoul took Kate to a bistro in rue de Sofia, not far from the Sacré Cœur. They hadn't been sitting there long when they were joined by Marie-Jacques and two strange men.

"Marie-Jacques was very friendly," said Kate on her return. "She spoke to me in English quite a bit. Apparently working as a tour guide is something she only does occasionally as a favour to B.B. and the rest of the time she runs a lingerie boutique. She said that French ladies insist on privacy when they're buying their smalls and wouldn't dream of going to a place like Marks & Spencer."

"What about the two men?" asked Daisy.

"They were called Jeannot and Kadda. I didn't like Jeannot at all. He looked like a convict. Hard as nails with a bald head and silly ear ring." An unpleasant image stirred in Daisy's memory, but she let Kate carry on. "Kadda's from Algeria, but he lives in Paris now. He was much nicer than Jeannot and much better dressed too. He made a big fuss of me and said that he'd never seen such beautiful blond hair. His horrible friend just grunted and asked Raoul if he was sure it was natural."

"What a cheek!"

"I know. Raoul said that he had his personal guarantee and they all laughed. I didn't know where to put myself."

"I hope he apologised."

"Afterwards he did. He said that they're business associates of B.B.'s and he has to play along with them. They were making some kind of deal tonight, I think. Just before he left, Jeannot wrote something on the palm of his hand with a biro and showed it to Raoul. When he nodded, he spat into his hand and rubbed it out and then the two of them shook hands."

"Ugh! I wouldn't want to shake anyone's hand if they'd just spat into it."

"I don't suppose Raoul did either, but he wouldn't want to offend him. They didn't stay with us long after that, but at least they all wished me a happy birthday for Saturday. Marie-Jacques kissed me on both cheeks and said that I could count on Raoul to make it unforgettable."

The birthday began badly when Raoul knocked on the door of the girls' dormitory. "Sorry to wake you all, but I need to say something to Kate. No, please don't get up, *chérie*, it's just that I've had a telegram from home. My mother is very ill and asking for me. I'm so sorry not to be able to celebrate your birthday with you as I promised, but there'll be a nice surprise for you later on."

Bleary eyed and hardly able to take in what he was saying, Kate wished his mother well and sent him on his way. Only after he'd gone did her face crumple and she shed a few tears. Everyone felt sorry for her, especially Daisy.

"I know what," she said to Valentin, having raced up to find him before breakfast, "Do you think there's time for us to organise a surprise party for Kate? She was so disappointed not to be going out with Raoul tonight and I'm sure he wouldn't mind if we borrowed his record player."

"That's a very kind thought," he replied. "Would you like me to try and make a cake?"

"No, no," she said hastily. "You have enough work to do as it is and I'm sure we can get one from Jean-Claude's aunt. I'll go down and ask her myself."

Even B.B. entered into the spirit of the thing, offering to get out the bunting he'd bought for Bastille Day. The only remaining hurdle was how to stop Kate finding out.

That problem was solved when she opened an envelope waiting by her place at breakfast. Pink cheeked and smiling, she refused to show anyone the contents but announced that she needed to take the first available bus into Paris.

"I'm sorry, Daisy. I'll tell you all about it later, but I've got something very private to do. Don't worry. It's a nice thing and it shouldn't take long. I'll be back before dinner and perhaps you won't mind if I tag along with you and Jean-Claude this evening rather than stay here by myself."

Daisy could hardly keep a straight face. "Of course not. You'll be more than welcome to join us."

Once she'd gone, everyone set to work. Long before Kate was likely to be back, the whole area was a riot of red, white and blue and, despite the short notice, a big cake had arrived. Covered in pale lemon icing, it had the number seventeen and Kate's name picked out in a delicate pattern of mauve flowers and green leaves. Another floral tribute, a bouquet of two dozen red roses, had also arrived all the way from Paris. The delivery man told Daisy that Raoul had bought them at the airport and paid three times the standard rate to ensure a prompt delivery.

"It really must be love," marvelled Siobhan. "Who'd have thought it?"

By seven o'clock, the work camp was *en fête*. The decorated tables were piled high with fare of a much higher standard than usual and friends invited from the village had already arrived. All that was needed was the guest of honour.

There was general consternation when Kate failed to return. B.B., who had driven down to meet the last bus from Paris and returned alone, refused to cancel the party.

"*Bof*! Young people today! I expect she's gone off somewhere to sulk because Raoul was obliged to miss her birthday."

"She wouldn't do that," protested Daisy. "She was disappointed, of course, but she understood that he had to put his mother first."

"Well everyone else will be disappointed if all this goes to waste. Valentin! Put on another record." There was a general murmur of agreement as the music started up again and soon everyone was dancing.

Almost everyone, that is.

Daisy and Jean-Claude were the only young customers in the café. As she sat over her fourth coffee, he gave her hand a sympathetic squeeze.

"Kate will be all right, I'm sure. After all, she didn't know that you'd organised a party for her. She probably just missed the last bus and decided to take a room for the night."

"Then why didn't she find a way to let us know? Even find a post office and send a telegram? Kate must have realised that I'd be worried and B.B. would be furious."

"But he wasn't, was he?"

"No. Not really. That bothers me too. He seemed to take it too much in his stride."

Half past ten came and went, then eleven o'clock and half past. Even when the café closed for the night, Daisy couldn't bring herself to return to the party. Jean-Claude, who had been up since before six, stifled a yawn.

"Look, even the *bar-tabac* has closed early tonight. You'd better come home with me. I'll wake you up in time to get back before you're missed in the morning. Judging by all those bottles they had to get through, I expect that everyone will be having a lie in."

"But what about your father? Won't he mind if I just turn up?"

"Oh, he'll be asleep now and snoring his head off, but he wouldn't mind anyway." When she looked uncertain, he said, "Don't worry, Daisy. It will be fine. You can have my room and I'll sleep downstairs on the sofa."

Didier and Minette stretched sleepily in their baskets as the teenagers tiptoed past them up the creaky wooden stairs. Jean-Claude had been right about the snoring. The noises coming from his father's room would have drowned out a thunder storm.

Switching on the bedside lamp and turning back the quilt for Daisy, he said, "You'd be uncomfortable sleeping in your clothes, so you can share my pyjamas, if you like. They've just come back from the laundry.

Bonne nuit." Handing her the jacket, he kissed the tip of her nose and turned to leave, but Daisy threw her arms round his neck.

"Please stay. I don't want to be on my own tonight."

He detached himself gently and studied her face. "Are you sure?"

"Yes. Quite sure."

When she returned from the bathroom, he'd changed too and was lying on his back waiting for her. Although Daisy was the one who'd suggested sharing the bed, she was nervous when he switched off the lamp. The borrowed garment was more than long enough for modesty, but she'd kept her knickers on underneath in case it rode up during the night.

In the moonlight penetrating the thin curtains, she could see less of Jean-Claude than she had at Fort Mahon and yet this was much more intimate. They lay cuddled up together for a long time, feet touching and ankles rubbing together. He threaded his fingers through her hair and apologised as a day's growth of stubble rasped against her skin. He was kissing her far more deeply than ever before as his tongue sought hers and she pulled him closer, enjoying the feel of bare skin and hard muscles under her palms.

"No one will interrupt us this time," he whispered. "Now then, where were we? Ah, yes. I remember." It didn't take him long to reacquaint himself with her curves through the thin cotton of the pyjama jacket. Then, as he met no resistance, his hands strayed underneath. Soon the garment lay on the floor and every gentle stroke of his thumbs on her breasts was fuelling a throbbing echo lower down. Daisy's body knew what it wanted and she was beginning to understand why Kate had been unable to resist Raoul's caresses.

As if reading her mind, Jean-Claude said, "I think I know how to make you very happy, if you'll let me try?" When she made no move to stop him, he began to circle a finger tip round a tiny spot of perfect pleasure in a way that made her quiver with anticipation.

"It will be better with nothing in the way," he whispered, a question in his eyes. Too far gone even to think of refusing, Daisy raised her hips and let him remove the last shred of her clothing. Only then did she remember her operation and wondered if he would be repelled. Instead, he clucked sympathetically and kissed the scar.

"It was appendicitis, but it doesn't hurt any more," she reassured him. "Please don't stop."

"Not unless you ask me to."

He made the final intimate claim and soon had Daisy writhing in ecstasy. Wave after wave of exquisite sensation washed over her until she arched her spine and sank back in a blissful haze. "I didn't know what to expect," she stammered.

"But it was good?"

"Oh yes. It was good."

"You girls are very lucky, you know. You can enjoy yourselves many times a night. Not like we poor boys."

As he pouted in fun, Daisy reached out a tentative hand. A friend's brother at a birthday party had once tried to make her touch him and she'd been horrified, but surely it was different when you loved someone? She was quite disappointed when Jean-Claude groaned in the back of his throat and stopped her.

"No, Daisy, you mustn't. I'd like it very much, of course, but I wouldn't be able to control myself and there might be a baby."

Breathing hard, he disappeared into the bathroom for a few minutes. When he came back, he picked up the discarded pyjama jacket and buttoned Daisy into it as though she were a child. He was stroking the night out of her hair when she woke up at first light.

There was nothing to be heard but the dawn chorus as he escorted her back, taking the long way round to avoid passing the dogs. Down in the dormitory, the other girls were fast asleep. Kate's belongings appeared to be all there as usual, but she hadn't come back.

Chapter 18

There was still no word from Kate when Raoul returned that afternoon and found everyone clearing up after the party. Not seeing her with the others, he seized upon Daisy.

"Where's Kate? My mother isn't as ill as the doctor first thought, thank God, so I took the first plane back. I've booked a table for dinner in the restaurant at the top of the Eiffel Tower to make up for missing her birthday. Kate will love it there, I'm sure."

The usually laid back Raoul seemed so full of enthusiasm that Daisy found it difficult to break the news to him. When she did, the eager puppy dog expression disappeared and was replaced by one of cold fury. He burst into the office without even knocking on the door and yelled at B.B. at the top of his voice.

"What do you mean, Kate never came back from Paris? What was she doing there on her own in the first place? Why haven't you sent for the police? Do I have to drive down to the village myself and get Clavié up here?"

What happened next was almost a rerun of the aftermath of Ronnie's disappearance, except that the policeman seemed to take his cue from Raoul's menacing expression and made no dismissive comments. All the same, the results of his later enquiries weren't encouraging.

"Mademoiselle Fairbairn was definitely on the ten o'clock bus to Paris. Several of the other passengers have said that she looked well and very happy. My colleagues in the city have spoken to the driver, who recognised her from the day of her arrival in Saint-André-la-Forêt, and he's confirmed that she travelled with him all the way to the terminus at Porte de St.Cloud. No one met her and he watched her going into the Métro station alone. That's as far as it's been possible to trace her movements since she set off from here yesterday. Her details have been circulated and there is nothing else that can be done."

Raoul buried his head in his hands and muttered, "That's it, then. Kate has gone home like Ronnie and she didn't even leave me a note!"

Seeing him looking so bereft, his *patron* clapped him on the shoulder. "Maybe now you'll believe me, my friend. It was spite, as simple as that, because you let her down on her birthday. You'll just have to forget about this girl and move on."

Daisy couldn't believe her ears. "Kate wouldn't have done that to you, Raoul. She loves you. I know she does. She only set off for Paris yesterday morning because she received a message telling her to go there."

Raoul sat up and rubbed his eyes with his fists. "Did you see this message?"

"No, she wouldn't show it to me, but she looked very happy about it. I assumed it was from you. After all, I heard you tell her to expect a nice surprise."

"Yes, but I meant the roses."

"Then I've got no idea what it was about."

"You don't think it could have been from your other friend, do you," suggested B.B. with obvious distaste. "Maybe she's still in Paris."

"No. Kate would have told me and she wouldn't have looked so pleased about it either. They never really got on, you know. Ronnie was always jealous of Kate and teasing her about the way she fussed over which outfit to wear. That's a point, actually. If Kate hadn't been planning to come straight back, she wouldn't have gone off with only a handbag. All her other things are still down in the dormitory."

"Then we'd better collect them and keep them in the office until we hear from her."

"And if you don't?"

Raoul turned his red rimmed eyes up towards B.B. and spread his hands in a gesture of despair. Did the big man wink? Daisy was almost sure that he had, but he muttered something about *chagrin d'amour* and signalled to Raoul that they should continue their conversation in private.

"So much for Kate," said Doug, who hadn't missed a word of the exchange. "By this time next week, Raoul will have found another girl and it won't take Jean-Claude much longer. I hope you're not foolin' yourself that he'll pine away when you've gone back to England."

All the other young people expressed sympathy, but Daisy paid little more attention to that than to Doug's spite. Oscar Wilde would probably have said, "To lose one friend may be regarded as a misfortune; to lose both looks like carelessness." Nothing about this latest business rang true and she was determined to get to the bottom of it. With that thought in mind, she went straight down to the dormitory after lunch. Going through Kate's belongings felt intrusive, but she wanted to satisfy her curiosity before they were taken away. In as far as the limited space available to her permitted, everything was as neatly arranged as usual, but Daisy was shocked to find no sign of a passport, folder of traveller's cheques or return tickets. Could B.B. and Raoul be right after all? In that case, Kate was a better actress than Daisy would ever have given her credit for. Needing more time to think, she ran back up to work with Valentin in the kitchen. They'd become good friends and he often complimented her on the improvement in her French.

"Don't worry about Kate," he said, handing her a tea towel. "She's the type who can look after herself."

"I hope so. I'm not surprised that you don't like her, but do you think Raoul really will forget her in a week? Doug's sure that he will and he said the same to me about Jean-Claude." Valentin turned towards Daisy and took both her hands in his.

"Not Jean-Claude," he said earnestly. "No one could ever accuse *him* of being two-faced and he dotes on you. He'll write and I'm sure that you'll see each other again."

"But Raoul doted on Kate, didn't he? She thought he was going to ask her to marry him."

"Well, I w-w- wouldn't know about that." Valentin let go of her hands and changed the subject. "As for that boy Doug, did you know that the *patron* has offered him a job?"

"Doug?"

"Yes. Apparently he doesn't have anything to go back to in England."

"But the *chantier* is about to close down, isn't it?"

"Of course, but Monsieur Baltzinger has his finger in many pies and thinks that the lad might be useful."

"Do you think the *patron* might have a vacancy for an assistant cook?" She was only half joking. While longing to see her mother, the thought of being parted from Jean-Claude was unbearable.

Valentin smiled. "If he had, Daisy, you would definitely be my first choice."

With just one full day left, and a wet and gloomy one at that, Daisy was growing desperate. All she had to cling to was a vague promise from Jean-Claude to teach her Parisian slang if she came back to France after her exams. They'd only spent one night together and she almost wished that he'd been as pushy and selfish as his cousin Charlot. With a grandchild on the way, her mother, although shocked and disappointed at Daisy's behaviour, would have done her best to get them to the altar.

Maybe it wasn't too late? He'd promised to take her out for a farewell dinner and there were plenty of secluded spots in the forest. Could she tempt him to the point of no return or was that a silly idea? He might not want to marry her and, even if he did, his father might convince him that eighteen was too young to tie himself down. Daisy could end up as just another sad teenager in one of the bleak mother and baby homes that she'd heard about and forced to give up her 'mistake' for adoption. The minutes to her departure were ticking by far too fast and she just couldn't make up her mind.

As some of the young people had already left, Raoul gave the rest the task of clearing everything from the unoccupied beds.

"God Almighty!" said Doug. "Have you seen the junk that some of your friends shoved under their mattresses!" He pointed to the growing pile of items on the table in the centre of the girls' dormitory. Magazines and tourist brochures, broken sunglasses and half eaten biscuits, a sandal with a broken strap, old bus tickets and odd socks, shampoo bottles and sticking plasters, an empty Tampax box, a whole collection of used tissues and a rusty pair of eyebrow tweezers. "And you girls always say that we're the untidy ones. Daisy, are you listenin' to me?"

"What?"

"Never mind. Wotcha got there?" Daisy must have looked as though she'd seen a ghost.

"Oh, Doug, I've just found these things wedged between the springs of Kate's bed."

He yawned. "What things? False eyelashes? Pan Stik? A couple of extra mirrors?"

"No. Her passport and ticket home. And the traveller's cheques that she never got round to cashing because Raoul paid for everything. Don't you see what this means? If she didn't take them with her, she can't have been intending to go back to England after all."

"Yes, I do see," he replied slowly. "Well, you'd better hand them over to the *patron*, hadn't you?" It was the first time that Daisy had heard Doug refer to B.B. with such deference and a shiver went down her spine.

"Not likely. I don't trust him. Or Raoul."

"So what do you plan to do with them?" She didn't trust Doug either, especially not now that he was about to join the staff.

"I don't know. I'll have to think about it."

"Suit yourself." Much to her relief, he heaved a mattress over his shoulder and sauntered out.

It didn't take Daisy long to come to a decision. She would make her way secretly down to the Garage de la Forge and ask Jean-Claude to phone the number on Mr Fairbairn's business card. If he and his father were both out, she'd go to his godmother at the post office or even the priest, who was bound to have a telephone.

Although she'd never taken Doug's short cut to the village by herself before, she decided to give it a try. Tucking the things she'd found into the pockets of her jeans, she made her way up to the top of the steps and peeped out into the rain. When she was sure that no one else was around, she ran at full pelt towards the clump of trees that shielded the ruined building. So far, so good! Soaking wet but relieved, she was almost halfway through the casemates when she heard heavy footsteps behind her and the hair stood up on the back of her neck. It was too late to escape. A hard blow to the side of the head sent her reeling towards the straw covered stone floor. The fall knocked the stuffing out of Daisy and she lay helpless as her attacker shoved a knee into the small of her back. Then a large hand was clamped over her nose and mouth and she blacked out.

The slightest movement made Daisy's head throb harder. Eyes open or shut, it made no difference. There was nothing to see anyway. Sandwiched between a thin bare mattress and a scratchy blanket and shivering in her wet clothes, she knew only that the air in the dark space around her smelled stale. Whoever had tied her up had known his business. Thin cords bound her wrists to one end of the bed and her ankles to the other. The coarse cloth of the gag tasted salty against her tongue and she tried in vain to spit it out. Had she been dreaming about muffled voices in the distance? There was nothing but silence now.

At last she heard someone approaching and the jangle of keys. A dim glow allowed her to see two shadows moving along the wall. The smaller one was carrying a tray; the larger, a bucket.

Valentin reached her first. "Lie still, Daisy. I'm going to untie you." Almost dizzy with relief, she looked up at him. This was no rescue, though. His eyes were full of apology as he finished dealing with the knots, but the other man merely looked amused. He reached under Daisy's armpits and hauled her up to a sitting position.

"You've caused us quite a dilemma, young lady," was all B.B. said to her before leaving them alone and locking the door behind him.

Valentin pulled the gag away from Daisy's mouth as gently as he could and held out a cup. Terrified now of the one staff member that she'd come to think of as a friend, she shrank away from him.

"Oh Daisy, dear," he whispered, "I wouldn't hurt you for the world, but I'm just as afraid of him as you are. More so, probably. You've no idea what he's capable of. What he's already done. To me and to many others. Please drink this. You must be parched."

She shook her head violently and winced at the pain that shot through it. "Where are we?"

"In the third dormitory."

"You mean on the other side of that big gate from ours?"

"Yes, I'm afraid so."

The only sign of the chamber's intended function was a stack of iron bedsteads against the far wall. The rest of the space was taken up with rows of wooden crates and cardboard packing cases. The merest chink of daylight showed through the boarded up window.

"What's going on, Valentin? Was it he who attacked me?"

"Yes."

"Why? I haven't ever done anything to him."

"It wasn't anything that you'd done. It was what you were about to do."

"But how did he know? Oh, of course. Doug."

"Yes. He ran straight to him with the information and the *patron* guessed that you'd take the quickest route you knew to the village. Raoul went the other way, just in case. You were never going to make it."

"How did he manage to get me down here without anyone noticing?"

"There are hidden entrances to some of the tunnels and he knows this part of the labyrinth very well. Your weight meant nothing to him and he just carried you over his shoulder."

"But everyone will wonder where I am, won't they?"

"No. The *patron* sprang a final outing on them as a 'special treat'. They've gone off to Fontainebleau with Marie-Jacques. Doug was under orders to spread the word round at lunch that you weren't feeling well enough to go with them. When they get back, they'll be told that you're in hospital and too ill to see anyone. They wouldn't have time to visit you anyway. They'll all be busy packing to go home."

At the mention of home, Daisy's face contorted. "What about my mother?"

"I'm afraid that she'll never find out what happened to you. By the time enquiries are made, all the other young people will be back in their own countries and this place will be closed up."

"But Jean-Claude..."

"Will believe what he's told, if he knows what's good for him. Alain Binard wouldn't dare to cross the *patron* and neither would anyone else in the village. They're all in his pocket, you see." As she sat in stunned silence, he said, "I'm so very sorry, Daisy. Do have something to eat." He held out a half baguette spread with pâté. "I don't know when you'll next get the chance."

Trembling, she shook her head again, not caring any more about the pain. "How can I possibly eat? I'm too frightened and very cold."

"Come here, then." He sat down on the bed, put his arm round her shoulders and aimed a clumsy kiss at her hair.

Daisy clung to him. "Please help me. There must be something you can do." Downtrodden as he was, Valentin was her only hope.

"I only wish that there were."

Chapter 19

Valentin sprang to his feet when the door opened. Clicking his teeth, the big man whose nickname Daisy would never use again looked down at her and said,

"I suppose you're wondering what we're going to do with you. Left to me, you'd probably go the same way as your ugly friend with the big mouth, but Raoul may have another solution."

"She won't eat, *patron*, and she'll catch her death of cold if we leave her down here like this."

"Oh, stop fussing, you little softie. She'll eat when she's hungry and you can get her some more blankets if you must."

While Valentin was gone, Baltzinger seized Daisy by the hair and pulled hard enough to bring more tears to her eyes. "Don't try and get smart, girl," he said evenly. "If you behave yourself, we'll leave the gag off and you can stretch your legs. If not, well, I think you know that I don't make idle threats."

By the time that Valentin returned with the blankets, he'd tied a cord round Daisy's waist and fastened it to an iron ring in the wall. She could get to the bed or the bucket but neither the door nor the window.

"Sweet dreams!" he said, reaching for the light switch.

"Please don't leave me in the dark again!" Daisy begged.

He hesitated. "Oh, all right. I've always been too kind for my own good."

Once they'd gone, she didn't dare to scream for help in case Baltzinger heard and came back. Sick with fear, she started to retch and had to rush for the bucket. Later on, mainly to get rid of the sour taste of bile, she turned to the tray that Valentin had brought for her and drank the cold coffee. It tasted strange and soon Daisy was unconscious again.

Three men were standing round her bed when she was roughly awoken. A Raoul that Kate would scarcely have recognised seemed to be in charge. Without the easy charm, he looked much older. His blue eyes, diamond hard, were glittering down at Daisy in a calculating way that petrified her.

"Put the gag back on," he ordered. "I don't want her waking up any of the other kids while I check her out."

Baltzinger pulled Daisy to her feet and held her in a tight grip while Valentin reluctantly obeyed. Only then did he undo the rope around her waist. "All right, Raoul. Let's get her clothes off. I don't want to be down here all night."

Valentin turned away as Daisy struggled uselessly against the other men. She might have been a carcass from Les Halles for all the emotion they showed until Baltzinger spotted her scar and swore obscenely.

"That's a pity. Will she still do?"

"I suppose so, although it's going to knock quite a bit off the price. More importantly, Doug reckons that lad from the garage has had first crack at her, but there's only one way to find out for sure. Spread her legs for me." Although tears of humiliation were pouring down Daisy's face and she was moaning into the gag, Raoul made no attempt to be gentle.

"All right," he said, wiping his fingers disdainfully on one of the blankets. "Tie her back onto the bed when she's dressed."

Left alone once more but knowing that only a few feet away were girls she'd come to know well over the last few weeks, Daisy couldn't sleep. Rocking her bed from side to side didn't make enough noise to attract their attention and there was nothing else that she could do. If only her captors hadn't tied her up again! She could have picked up the rusty bucket and banged it on the wall, but they must have thought of that.

Valentin, setting down a heavily loaded tray, wouldn't look Daisy in the eye. Baltzinger had no such inhibitions. Having removed her gag and released her wrists and ankles from their bonds, he sat down heavily on the end of the bed and smiled unpleasantly.

"Now then, Daisy, I suppose you'd like to know about your future. It may not be a long one, I'm afraid, unless you're very lucky. Here, try some of this excellent Brie de Melun." He took a piece and held it out to her.

She recoiled from him. "What do you mean?"

"Well, that scar of yours has reduced your market value, which wasn't in the highest category to begin with. Raoul's associates will have no choice but to pass you on to one of their less discriminating clients."

"Pass me on for what?"

"Oh, my dear, don't be so naive. Why do you suppose that he went to the trouble of establishing your virginity? I might have known that Alain Binard's son wouldn't have the balls to take it. Your friend Kate, of course, was in a different league entirely. Natural blondes still fetch the best price. It's funny how some things never change. It was exactly the same under the Third Reich, as some girls around here found out to their cost, eh, Valentin? Rich and powerful men won't accept anything artificial or second hand. Even so, they soon get bored with their new toys."

"Surely there's no need to go into that now, *patron*," mumbled Valentin.

"Oh, anticipation is half the fun, don't you think? I've always found it so. Anyway, the longer our little Daisy can please her new owner, the longer it will be before she's passed on to one of the *maisons closes* in Algiers or Cairo. Maybe you haven't heard of those, sweetheart? They're charming establishments where girls just like you service dozens of men a day. That's until they reach the point where they're so worn out and diseased that they're only fit for the back streets in the meanest parts of town."

Daisy blanched as the full horror of what he was telling her sank in. Poor Kate, with all her dreams of a happy marriage to Raoul! And Ronnie? What on earth had they done with Ronnie? In their eyes, she'd have been strictly bargain basement material to begin with.

"Anyway," Baltzinger concluded, checking the knots that secured the cord round Daisy's waist to the iron ring, "Don't even think of trying anything foolish. Valentin will be keeping an eye on you down here until you're collected, but Raoul and I won't be far away. Don't worry. It may be some time, but there's enough food and drink to keep you both going."

As soon as he'd gone, Valentin burst into tears. "This shouldn't be happening to you, Daisy. I didn't care half as much about the others, but you're different."

"Then won't you help me to get out of here?"

He shook his head. "It's impossible. I don't only have myself to consider, you see. Have you ever watched a house of cards collapse or dominoes topple? You can't imagine how many lives would be ruined if I let you escape and put Baltzinger's whole operation in danger."

"But how does he think he's going to get away with it? Our parents will never stop looking for us. And what about the people of Saint André-la-Forêt? Surely they'll realise that three disappearances are too much for coincidence."

"Perhaps, but I told you how it was. They know that strange things go on up here, but they keep their thoughts to themselves."

"Why? Are they all as chicken as you?"

He flinched at the insult without defending himself. "I suppose you could say that. I've often heard you and the other youngsters wondering why you receive so much for the tiny amount of money you pay to come here. Well, it's because the local businesses never charge Baltzinger for the supplies and services they provide. He knows everyone's little secrets, you see."

"And blackmails them? I suppose I'll have to believe you, but surely a decent man like Monsieur Binard can have nothing to hide?"

"And yet the *patron* never pays him for the repairs to his van."

"Raoul's car too?"

"No, but only because he's too fussy to let Alain touch it. They both get free petrol from him, though."

"Well how about your sister? Madame Gaudet doesn't look like the sort of woman who'd be frightened of anyone."

Valentin gave a hollow laugh. "You're right. It isn't fear that keeps her on side. It's gratitude."

"Gratitude for what?"

"Oh, for doing her a huge favour years ago. Thérèse wouldn't lift a finger to help you, anyway. She hates Englishwomen as much as she hates the Germans. More so, probably. Look, we're going to be down here for hours, so I'll tell you all about it, if you like. It's not as though you're going to be able to pass it on to anyone who matters."

While Valentin's mind was fixed on the past, thought Daisy, she might be able to think of a way to save herself from what her mother would surely call 'a fate worse than death'. With or without his help, she was determined to escape. If it came to it, she didn't think that he would actually hurt her any more than she wanted to hurt him, but that was a risk that she would have to take.

"All right, if you want to. It might help to pass the time."

"Well," he began, pouring himself a glass of wine, I was only fifteen years old when Bertrand Baltzinger arrived in our village."

Part Three

1937-1950

Chapter 1

Valentin's new brother-in-law was the first to spot the hefty fair haired youth peering in through the café window and taxed him with making eyes at his bride.

Luc Gaudet was a lucky man and he knew it. The sound of him claiming his conjugal rights had kept Valentin awake almost every night since the wedding. Knowing the basics of what happened in a marriage bed, he could scarcely bring himself to look at his heavy eyed sister over the breakfast table. From the affectionate glances exchanged by the couple, it seemed that whatever went on in their room suited them both well enough, but thinking of Thérèse in that light made Valentin at the same time excited and ashamed.

"I assure you, Monsieur," protested the strange boy, who stood several inches taller than the irate husband, "that nothing was further from my mind. Madame, your wife, is very beautiful, of course, but I was only plucking up the courage to ask for a glass of water and maybe a piece of bread. I have no money, you see, although I'm willing to work for whatever you may be kind enough to give me." Luc grunted and released his grip on the ragged collar. Not taken in by the polite speech, he would have sent him on his way if Thérèse had not come out to see what was going on.

Pulling Luc aside, she said, "Oh, come on, *chéri*, just look at the state of the poor lad. He looks as if he hasn't eaten for a week. We can find something for him to do, surely."

"I've already taken Valentin in to please you and your family. Isn't that enough?"

"You know I'm grateful for that, but this is quite different. It would only be for a little while." She squeezed his arm and whispered, "I'll make it up to you tonight."

Luc knew when he was beaten. "Well, all right, but I'm not having a young drifter with his accent serving our customers. The older ones wouldn't like it." He had a point. The boy's speech was quite guttural and memories of close encounters with Germans in their trenches were still fresh in the minds of the veterans.

"They'd get used to it, but he can work in the kitchen to begin with."

"And sleep in the attic?"

"No. He can share with Valentin. He'll be company for him. I worry sometimes that he might be homesick for the other children."

Having been given a room and indeed a bed of his own for the first time in his life, company was the last thing that Valentin wanted. He resented the intrusion from the moment the stranger sat down on the bed to take off his down at heel shoes and holey socks. The large feet thus revealed were covered in cuts and blisters, which would have aroused his sympathy under different circumstances, but he couldn't help noticing the change in the boy's demeanour the moment Thérèse left them alone together. The mattress sagged under his weight as he flopped back against the bolster with a self satisfied grunt.

"So where have you come from?"

"Paris."

"You don't sound like a Parisian. Luc says that you're from Alsace."

"You asked me where I'd come from, not where I was born."

"And my sister feels sorry for you. She thinks you've run away from home?"

"Got it in one."

"Why?" Valentin waited to be told to mind his own business. Instead, the other boy shrugged and said,

"Because my old man's a brute and I got tired of being his favourite punch bag."

"That's tough." His own father could be harsh, but he was generally fair. "Where did you live?"

"My family has a vineyard near Mulhouse. Twelve thousand hectares. The grapes go into the best wines in the district. You'll have heard of Riesling and Traminer, I expect? Anyway, he got fighting drunk most weeks and took it out on me. I'm the youngest, you see, and my brothers just let him get on with it. Glad that he wasn't picking on them, I suppose."

"Didn't your mother ever try to stop him?"

"*Her?*" he said with loathing. "She was frightened of him too and turned a blind eye to everything he did to me. It wasn't only the beatings, you know."

"What do you mean?" In Valentin's experience, nothing could be worse than a hiding from Papa's well oiled razor strop. He was hoping that his new life at the café had removed him from that threat for good. He didn't think that Thérèse, who'd always stood up to the village bullies on his behalf, would ever allow Luc to strike him.

"Oh, maybe I'll tell you about it later, when we know each other better."

"Does that mean that you're planning to stick around for a while?"

"Maybe. Would that bother you, Shorty?" The blue eyes gazing into his were suddenly fierce.

"No," he lied. "That would be fine with me." The intimidation had begun.

Luc and Thérèse kept both boys busy during the days that followed and it was in their shared bed that Valentin learnt the rest of the story. Although he neither liked nor trusted Bertrand Baltzinger, he was mesmerised by his tales.

"There came a time when I just couldn't take it any longer," he said one night. "I ran away and hid at a friend's house, but the police came looking for me. The old man had told them that I'd pinched the cash box he kept under his bed. He didn't trust banks, you see, and the money from a whole year's crop of grapes was in it. I knew that no one would believe that I hadn't taken his lousy box, so I climbed out of the window and legged it.”

Valentin was agog. “So who did steal the money?”

The other boy laughed at the naive question and tapped the side of his nose before continuing his story. Aware that the police would be watching the railway station in Mulhouse, he'd taken his friend's bicycle and ridden nearly fifty miles to catch a train from Strasbourg. A few hours later, he strode confidently out of the Gare de l'Est to begin a new life in Paris.

With money in his pocket, it was easy at first. Looking older than his sixteen years and avoiding smarter areas where too many questions would be asked, he had no difficulty in finding a comfortable room. From there, he set off daily to eat well and enjoy the sights of the capital. As funds started to run out, he moved to cheaper accommodation and asked around without much success for casual work. By the time the winter set in, he was homeless and jobless, living on his wits and riding around all day on the Métro in an attempt to keep warm.

“I had a real stroke of luck though,” he said with a gleam in his eye. “The trains stop running in the early hours of the morning, so I used to wander around Les Halles to see what I could pick up. A lot of the stuff that falls off the stalls is perfectly fine to eat, you know. Then I'd find a doorway to shelter in until the Métro opened again. That's how I met Manon and Solange.”

“Who were they?”

“My guardian angels. A couple of whores with big hearts.”

“Whores?”

He sighed. “Women who'll do it with anybody for money. You know what ‘it’ is, don't you?”

Valentine flushed. “Of course I do. I just didn't know that you could pay for it. I thought you had to get married first, like Thérèse and Luc.”

“Do they keep you awake too? Sorry, I know she's your sister and all that, but I wish they'd make less noise when they're at it. Anyway, the girls took a fancy to me and bought me a meal.”

“You mean they took pity on you?”

"A bit of both, probably. They were working out of a bistro in rue Montorgueil. Solange wiped some steam off the window and saw me standing outside in the cold. She signalled for me to come in and got me a bowl of onion soup. It was the best thing I'd ever tasted in my whole life. I've never been able to forget it."

He licked his lips and paused so long that Valentin grew impatient. "Go on! Tell me more about them."

"Well, they were having a good night, so they stood me some drinks as well. Every now and then a punter would approach one of them. It made no difference whether it was a market porter or an old fart in a suit. She'd go off with him for a while and then come back to tidy her hair and touch up her lipstick. When the girls both left, arm in arm with a couple of drunken soldiers, I didn't expect to see them again that night, but they were back even faster. After it started to get light, Manon said that they'd done enough business for one day and were going home to get some sleep. That was when Solange asked me if I'd got a bed to go to. When I told her that I hadn't, she said I could go back to their place if I liked. It had to be better than the Métro, so I did."

"Did they have a nice apartment?"

"Are you kidding? I'd never seen anything like it! My mother was useless in other ways, but our home was always spotless. Those girls only had one dingy room and it stank."

"Stank of what?"

"Sweat, damp and sex, I suppose. They tried to cover it up by spraying some cheap scent around, but it didn't do any good. The carpet was so messy that my shoes stuck to it and the wallpaper was peeling away in places. It was a muddy red colour and cockroaches came out from behind it as soon as the light went off.

"Ugh! I can't stand cockroaches and they're really hard to get rid of. My sister says..."

"Never mind what your sister says. Are you still listening to me?"

"Yes."

"Well, the girls' bed filled most of the room. The quilt didn't look too bad, but the sheets underneath were disgusting."

"Was that all the furniture they had?"

"Not quite. They'd squeezed in a couple of chairs with wonky legs and a dressing table mirror that they'd bought at the big flea market at Porte de Clignancourt. It was propped up on an old cabin trunk so that they could see to do their hair and make-up. There was a tap on the landing next to the WC and they had a big enamel basin for washing in and doing their laundry."

"It doesn't sound as though there was enough room for two people, let alone three. Where on earth did you sleep?"

"With them, of course."

"What?"

"Yes, honestly, and I didn't get much sleep either. Not for the first couple of hours or so, anyway. I thought they'd have had enough of all that, but I woke up the next afternoon too knackered to count the bites from the bed bugs." He paused there and yawned. Incredulous but desperate for details, Valentin begged him to continue.

"Well, the first time it was just a straight fuck."

"With both of them?"

"Well, not at the same time, obviously. Don't you know anything? Solange first. After she dozed off, Manon insisted on trying me out. They both seemed satisfied," he added smugly.

"So what happened after you woke up?"

"Oh, that was the best part. They couldn't cook in their room, but they refused to give me my clothes back and told me to stay in bed while they went out to buy some food. They came back with several bottles of wine as well and we all got plastered together. The girls were very giggly and told me all sorts of tales about their clients. They were back in bed with me by that time and had fun showing me some of the tricks of the trade."

"What do you mean?"

"The sort they use on men who can't get it up fast enough. Time's money in their profession, you know."

Valentin felt as though his head would burst with curiosity. "Will you tell me about their tricks?"

"I can do better than that. I'll show you one, if you like." Without waiting for a reply, he dived underneath the bedclothes.

Chapter 2

The following morning, Valentin had a new reason for not wanting to look his sister in the face at breakfast. The sexual revelations of the night before had been followed by a deep sense of shame. His parents had warned him to steer clear of the more forward village girls, not that they ever spared him a glance anyway, but they'd never said anything about other boys. The fact that the one who'd destroyed his innocence was sitting calmly across the table and eating a *pain au chocolat* with noisy enjoyment made him feel even worse. If self abuse were a grave sin, then what two boys did together must be at least twice as bad. On the other hand, the wrath of God didn't frighten him nearly as much as that of his earthly father or his brother-in-law. If Luc refused to let him stay at the café, he might not be welcomed back home either.

"I w-w-won't say anything, but p-p-please don't ever m-m-make me do anything like that again," he said as soon as the boys were on their own. Sly amusement written all over his face, Baltzinger heard him out and then ignored him for the next couple of nights, at least as far as was possible when sharing both room and bed. It wasn't long, though, before he continued his tales about the seamy side of life in Paris.

"The girls had a Corsican pimp called Marco and he was waiting for us in the bar the next evening. 'Don't get me wrong,' he said. 'I don't mind my girls keeping a pet, but everyone works around here. I've fixed up for you to meet a restaurant owner in rue Saint Sauveur. You're a big strong country lad, just the kind he likes, and you'd better be on your best behaviour. Do as you're told and we won't have any problems.' I thought he'd found me a job washing dishes."

"And hadn't he?"

"No, thank God. I started to wonder when he took me for a haircut and to buy some new clothes. No one cares what a *plongeur* looks like."

"That was very generous of him."

"So I thought, at first. He bought me a white shirt, a leather jacket and a pair of black trousers so tight that they nearly cut my balls off. I hardly recognised myself in the shop mirror and it didn't come as much of a surprise when the interview took place upstairs in the guy's apartment."

"Why?"

"Because I knew what he was after, of course. I earned more in half an hour up there than I'd have made in a week in the kitchen, although Marco took most of it."

"What did you have to do?"

"Use your imagination." When he realised that Valentin hadn't a clue what he was talking about, he explained in the crudest possible terms and the younger boy was still reeling when he continued, "He was a lot gentler than my father and even thanked me afterwards. I saw him regularly after that and quite a few other men too."

"Didn't you mind them doing that to you?"

"Not really. Some of them were a bit rough, but most of the time I was the one in control, especially of those who paid me to do it to them or asked me to thrash them."

Valentin's jaw dropped. "Why would they want you to do that?"

"Because they enjoyed the pain and it was the only way they could get themselves off. They'd even have their own equipment ready for me to use. Whips, canes, riding crops..." He grinned at his bedmate's open mouthed amazement. "That reminds me. There were some punters who only wanted oral."

"What?"

"Well, it doesn't mean that they just wanted to talk about it and I'm getting bored with that too."

That night he forced himself onto Valentin for the first time, pushing his face into the bolster to stifle his cries. There was no pretence of mutual pleasure and yet the younger boy could see no way out of the situation and gradually resigned himself to what he was powerless to prevent. It took him years to realise that his father and Luc would almost certainly have come across similar behaviour during their time in the Army. If only he'd had the courage to confide in them, they would have sent his tormentor packing.

Valentin found out eventually why Baltzinger had left the city life that seemed to suit him so well. For all his boasting, he'd been naive enough to believe that he could outsmart a thirty year old Corsican who cleaned his nails with a flick knife. Not only was the teenager caught lying about how much a client had paid for his services, for which he was roughed up by Marco and his friends, but he tried to persuade Solange and Manon to move to Pigalle and work for him instead. Unfortunately for the people of Saint-André-la-Forêt, they were tipped off by another of Marco's stable of girls that the boy was about to end up in the Seine with his throat cut. That being so, they smuggled him out of Paris and bade him a tearful *au revoir*.

Chapter 3

Relieved and envious at the same time, Valentin watched Baltzinger depart for a live in job on a farm just outside the village. Georges Perthuis, crippled at Verdun, needed someone to replace an only son who'd recently moved away. It was rumoured in the village that the son's choice of bride was to blame for the rift in the family, although no one could say what was wrong with the girl. Her mother-in-law took to the new farmhand straight away and the veteran's death a couple of months later could have suited both of them very well, had it not been for French inheritance law. Vincent returned for the funeral and stayed on to take over the farm. His new wife, more perceptive than he, saw straight through Baltzinger's glib charm and had him sent off with only a week's wages in his pocket.

Back at the café, he told an uneasy Valentin, "I don't really blame Vincent, you know. He'd have kept me on. That bitch Judith had better watch out though. I'll get my own back on her one of these days. You just see if I don't."

Valentin put down the tray of crockery he was carrying back to the kitchen. "Why bother? Her mother-in-law has found you another job, hasn't she?"

He grinned. "Yes. Geneviève gave Madame Signac her personal recommendation, as widow to widow. Jacqueline's much younger and not bad looking either. We'll be able to do it with the light on!"

"You didn't with the other lady?"

"Not likely. She's as old as my grandmother. I kept my eyes closed most of the time."

"From what I've heard of Madame Signac, you might not find it an easy life up there. It's a bigger place, I know, but men who've worked for her before say she's very stingy and has a tongue that can take the skin of your back. She led her late husband a dreadful life."

Thérèse, coming out of the kitchen to see what was holding him up, caught the remark and nodded. "She only married him to get her hands on his farm, you know."

"Just like you married Luc to get yours on his café? Not that I don't think that he got the better end of the bargain."

She swiped at him playfully with her tea towel. "No, you cheeky thing. I love Luc, although I'd have thought twice about marrying him while his mother was alive. Anyway, the first Madame Signac, God rest her, was a gentle soul and the poor old chap was overheard one day in the confessional saying that he couldn't wait to join her. He died a week later with a smile on his face."

"I'm not a Catholic, but I thought confession was supposed to be private."

"It is, but Father Ferdinand's housekeeper is forever polishing the brass in that part of the church. I always make sure that she's not around when I go."

"I can't imagine that you've got anything to confess, Thérèse, a happily married woman like you." He raised a quizzical eyebrow and she blushed.

"No one's perfect, Bertrand."

"Well, you're closer to it than most. I'll never forget the way you took me in when I had nowhere to go. Let me know if you ever get tired of Luc. You and I are about the same age, aren't we? He's getting on a bit and might start running out of steam soon."

"Really! What a thing to say! He's only just turned thirty." She gave him another playful swipe but looked pleased.

"Well, anyway, you know that I'll always be there for you if you need me, even if I do marry Madame Signac to get *my* hands on the farm!"

That ambition was never realised. Despite all that went on between them, about which Valentin was given regular updates, the young widow had no intention of giving up her new independence.

It was during his time with Jacqueline Signac that Baltzinger made an enemy of Alain Binard. Most of the villagers were unsentimental about animals, especially those they classed as vermin, but Alain was different and would never willingly hurt any creature. Baltzinger, on the other hand, revelled in cruelty.

"Maybe it was the way his father treated him that made him that way," suggested Valentin after the event.

Alain dismissed the idea. "No. Some people are just born evil in my opinion and I'm sure that your friend is one of them. I'll have to watch out for him for the rest of my life."

"He's not my friend!"

"Well he's always round at your place and your sister seems fond of him."

"That doesn't mean that I am. Luc isn't either. We'd both be very happy never to see him again."

The trouble had started when Baltzinger, paid no more than other farmhands despite his intimate relationship with his employer, decided to make some extra money. He set traps in the big barn and waited until he'd caught enough rats to make sport for the village boys and their dogs. Then he built a cage big enough to hold one dog and three rats at a time. He intended to hold the stakes while everyone else gambled on how long it would take each dog to make its kill.

Alain wasn't invited but found out anyway and sprang into his father's car. He could hear the commotion from half a mile away as the proceedings got underway. By the time he arrived, the first dog had already dispatched two of its rats. Alain wrenched open the door of the cage and yanked it out by the scruff of its neck. As the third rodent took the opportunity to escape, Baltzinger launched himself at the young blacksmith, his face contorted with fury, but he'd met his match. Although he wasn't as powerfully built, Alain's work at the forge had made him a formidable opponent. He sidestepped neatly and caught the other boy a blow to the side of the head that sent him stumbling forward. He would have left it like that, if Baltzinger hadn't whirled round to attack him again. Spotting a glint of metal, Alain grabbed his wrist and jerked it up behind his back, forcing him to drop the knife. Then his fist slammed into Baltzinger's face, knocking him to the ground. No one dared to intervene and most of the audience had melted away by the time the fight was over.

"You've broken my bloody arm," snarled the loser, spitting out a tooth.

Alain was already intent on releasing the rest of the rats, some of which had been held for days without food and water. "No more than you deserve," he called over his shoulder. "It will be your neck if you ever pull another stunt like that."

To add insult to injury, Jacqueline Signac docked Baltzinger's wages for the time he was out of action and it wasn't long before he moved on. Although on the face of it they remained on cordial terms, she'd joined his family in Alsace, Marco the pimp, Judith Perthuis and Alain Binard on the ever growing list of people he intended to make sorry one day for the way they'd treated him.

Baltzinger's third widow was very different from the other two. Henriette Tilleray was a kindly soul who took him on to help with the heaviest work on the farm, having learnt to cope with the rest herself. Despite the loss of her husband on the Meuse and both sons two years later on the Somme, her Catholic faith had remained as strong as ever and she spent a good deal of time helping Father Ferdinand in any way she could. Her piety was well known but of a kind quite different from that of his sour faced housekeeper, being matched by a generosity of spirit unrivalled in the village.

"I've landed on my feet with this one," boasted Baltzinger during one of his regular free meals at the café. To all intents and purposes, he was Valentin's only friend, so how could Thérèse deny him that, whatever

Luc thought of him?

"She doesn't want any hanky panky, of course," he continued. "But I know how much she misses her boys. If I play my cards right, she might adopt me and then…"

"You'll be lucky!" said Valentin. "She'll be leaving everything to the Church. Just you wait and see!"

"You don't know that!"

"Well ask her, if you don't believe me."

"Don't be bloody ridiculous. How on earth could I do that?" He couldn't, of course, but he found an opportunity to go through the personal papers in his employer's desk. There seemed to be no point in staying with her after that.

During the months that followed, he moved from job to job. His good looks and the boyish charm that he could turn on at will were often sufficient to get him through the door, but it was never long before suspicion grew of something darker behind his innocent expression. His employment at the bakery ended abruptly when Robert Bail caught his wife emerging from the stockroom red faced and with her hair all over the place. Henri Devane at the hardware store dismissed him for telling his schoolboy son about the aphrodisiac power of raw oysters.

"Some whores in Paris explained it to me," he was overheard saying to the fascinated youngster. "You've only got to look at the shape or sniff them to understand why. They're very moist and if you've ever been with a girl…"

He continued to exploit Thérèse's fondness for him whenever he needed food or a bed for the night. She dimpled at his compliments but otherwise treated him like an extra brother. Although his so-called friend's hypocrisy sickened Valentin, for Baltzinger often made lustful comments about the young wife behind her back, he still couldn't think of a way of exposing his true nature without admitting his own shame.

Then, with war in the air and many local men volunteering for service or being mobilised from the reserves, his luck changed. An assistant general handyman was needed at the château to work under Arnaud

Garnier, who was also the family chauffeur. Luc seized the opportunity to recommend Bertrand Baltzinger for the position.

Chapter 4

"We'll all be murdered in our beds if we stay here," said Madame Morcel.

"But where would we go?"

"South, like everyone else, of course."

"And who's to say that the Boche wouldn't follow us?"

The question posed by Thérèse was a reasonable one. The unthinkable had happened. The Dutch and the Belgians had admitted defeat, the Maginot Line had failed to keep the Germans out and they were advancing so fast that they were overtaking French troops trying to retreat. Panzers were roaming the countryside, many thousands of soldiers had already been taken prisoner or couldn't wait to get rid of their ragged and filthy uniforms and it looked as though Rommel had a clear run to Paris. Who would stop him? The British had been driven into the sea at Dunkirk.

"Look, *Maman*," said Valentin. "You must have heard on the radio that the roads south are already choked with refugees. We don't have any transport, I can't walk far and the little ones certainly can't."

"Then we'll borrow a cart and push them. I'll carry the baby on my back if I have to."

"With another one on the way? How far do you think you'd get in your condition?"

She flushed with embarrassment. "How dare you speak to me like that? If Papa heard you, he'd..."

"Agree with Valentin," said Thérèse. "I'm sure we'll be better off staying here and I couldn't leave anyway without knowing what's happened to my Luc." She paused to wipe away a tear and then pulled herself together. "According to Bertrand, the Countess refuses to move, even though most of her friends have high tailed it to Biarritz or Geneva. Both her sons are still missing, you know."

"Monsieur Kahn says that the way our armies fell apart has been the most humiliating defeat in the history of France and..."

"Oh well, far be it from me to disagree with the fount of all wisdom." Their mother waddled out of the café, watched enviously by Thérèse.

"I know that she isn't happy to be expecting again, especially now, but when will it be my turn?" Valentin could say nothing to comfort her. There had been no word from Luc since the so-called Phoney War turned into a real one.

The café was full every night and the till rang merrily as arguments raged to and fro. Older men who'd served their time as front line riflemen in the trenches still worshipped Marshall Pétain. They thought that the hero of Verdun was just playing the enemy along as part of his master plan to reclaim the glory of France. The leaders of that camp included Michel Massot, who juggled the roles of mayor and notary, and his friend Benôit Aubier, the pharmacist. They had detested Léon Blum's Popular Front government and bored everyone to tears about the influx of Jews into the administration and the professions. Aubier had been particularly bitter since his son failed to get into medical school.

"It makes me sick to see that Abraham boy swanning off with his briefcase every morning. Calls himself a Frenchman, but he's just another bloody Hebrew. Some of them can't even speak our language properly and yet they've swamped the universities and taken all the best jobs. Have you been into Paris lately? The last time I was there, I felt like a foreigner in my own country."

His views were echoed by a young policeman, newly appointed and full of his own importance. Despite the port-wine stain that had been the bane of his life at school, Armand Clavié's new status had greatly enhanced his prospects and he was shortly to be married to a girl he had known all his life. "Didn't I say that it was mad to let all those Jews into the country before the war? Everyone knows that some of them are Bolshevik agents sent here to stir up trouble. Well, my fiancée and I would rather be ruled by Nazis than Communists any day. At least they don't burn down churches."

"Just synagogues, or so I've heard."

He ignored Valentin's comment and continued, "Look what happened in Spain, eh, Gaston?"

Everyone turned to look at the big man at the end of the bar, who shrugged and said, "Don't ask me. What do I know?" His world had shattered when Joseph Stalin signed a non-aggression pact with Adolf Hitler. To make matters worse, he'd been slapped down at a meeting in Paris for insisting that Hitler was persecuting German Communists and must be resisted. The chairman, a professor from the Sorbonne, had refused to be lectured by a village butcher and told him to leave policy decisions to those who knew what they were talking about. Gaston Busselle and his friend Henri Devane had torn up their party membership cards and walked out.

"My sister-in-law would agree with you," said Robert Bail, a rueful look on his face. "You could paper our bakery with the copies of La Croix that she leaves lying around to improve us. I can't stand the woman." There was a grunt of agreement from most of the other men and Thérèse, who'd been silently topping up everyone's drinks, said,

"I don't know why our dear Father Ferdinand ever took her on as his housekeeper. He's so kind and yet she never has a good word to say about anybody. She's younger than your Brigitte, isn't she, Robert?"

"Yes, Corinne's a couple of years younger, but you'd never know it."

"I take it she's never been married?"

"No, despite the widow's weeds she insists on wearing. Years ago, there was talk of her taking the veil, but nothing came of it. Brigitte and I had only been married a few months when she followed us down here from Normandy."

"And now she sees herself as the moral guardian of the village!"

"That's about the size of it."

The moral guardian was one of only two women present at the meeting called by the priest immediately after the fall of Paris. Corinne Dupré sat as far away as possible from Madeleine Binard, who, to her horror, had arrived wearing a rolled up pair of her husband's old work trousers. A dab hand with a spanner, Madeleine was determined to keep their business going during Hervé's absence and ignored those who thought that a woman had no business to be tinkering with engines. Her calm strength inspired confidence in her customers, who'd become used to seeing her legs sticking out from underneath a different vehicle every time they pulled in for petrol. The blacksmithing she was content to leave to Alain until his father returned. She seemed amused by the awkward expressions on the faces of those who normally never set foot inside the church. Just about every man remaining in the village and most of the older boys had responded to the call.

Valentin was glad to see Father Ferdinand resolved to calm down the hotheads. Some of the veterans had even brought their guns with them into the church. Alain was examining a particularly horrible old German Mauser. The outside was rusty, the rifling inside badly corroded and the wooden barrel guard was split.

"This is only fit for scrap. Are you planning to hit the Nazis over the head with it, Monsieur?" he asked before his mother could stop him. Old Jules snatched his property back with a few well chosen words and brandished it at him.

Father Ferdinand shook his head in mild reproof. "Please put it down, my son. We're all on the same side here. If we're to support each other through the difficult times to come, we need to set aside our different religious and political views and greet the occupying forces with a quiet dignity."

There was a chorus of protest and one old soldier nearly choked. "You want us to be nice to the Boche?"

The priest raised his hand for silence. "Not at all. Have as little to do with them as possible. Don't speak or give them any kind of help unless you have to. Just realise that they have the upper hand for the time being and we're not yet in a position to do anything about it. Any ill thought out acts of resistance could provoke a massacre."

Massot stepped forward. "Father Ferdinand is right. Random attacks on the Germans will only result in hostages being taken. This has already happened not far from here and some of the hostages have been shot."

The doctor and the schoolmaster were sitting together for the first time that anyone could remember. The strain on the older man's face was obvious to all, matched by the agitated way in which he was fingering his long grey beard.

The Abrahams were relative newcomers to the village. The decision of Dr Simmonet to retire from the family practice before his son Jean-Pierre was ready to take over had created a temporary vacancy. Dr Abraham, highly qualified but frustrated by his failure to find a more suitable position in Paris, had accepted the offer with as good grace as he could muster. At least Peter, through whose friendship with Jean-Pierre the arrangement had come about, would be able to continue his medical studies. All the same, the Abrahams had never really fitted in and they were considered to give themselves airs. A woman they employed to help with the cleaning told everyone about the solid silver candlesticks they used on Friday nights and from the laundry came descriptions of their fine monogrammed linen, second in quality only to that owned by the Countess. Still worse, they withheld their other custom from local businesses, preferring instead to drive to Paris and patronise Jewish shops in the Marais, the district in which their children also received their education. A few stones had already gone through their windows, something that had never happened to the only other Jewish family in the village.

The Kahns had long been part of the community and had sacrificed sons for France. The only survivor of his generation, badly wounded on the Western Front, wore his Croix de Guerre with enormous pride. Old Guillaume's face had as many lines as a map of the Métro, but he always wore a smile and children loved the way his sightless eyes disappeared into his wrinkles when he laughed.

It was only because the meeting was taking place in the church that his son Marcel had changed out of the old overalls he wore to tend his little vegetable patch. With no religious beliefs of his own, he was always careful to respect those of others. His and Rachel's older boys attended lessons with everyone else, ate the same food and fished from the river banks or played football on the old parade ground in the forest. In the winter, when a fire was lit in the casemates, they were very happy to pair off with any willing girls. How Valentin envied them all that as well as having the kindly schoolmaster for their father! To the irritation of his parents, he respected Marcel Kahn's opinions over those of anyone else in the village and was sitting close enough during the meeting to hear the exchange between him and Dr Abraham.

"Well, Doctor, I expect you've also read *Mein Kampf*."

"Yes, I'm afraid so. Hitler set out his plan very clearly and I can't understand why his ambitions weren't nipped in the bud when he marched into the Rhineland in '36. He might just as well have had himself filmed tearing up the Versailles Treaty."

"I don't understand that either, but you were right to move your family to Paris when you did."

"My wife didn't think so. Not at the start, anyway. It took the first pogrom in Berlin to convince her. I don't deny that giving up my practice in Metz was a wrench. I was a visiting consultant at the hospital as well, you know. We had a comfortable home and many good friends, but it seemed inevitable that our region would pass back into German hands together with Alsace. Now the nightmare's about to catch up with us and the upheaval I put my family through may have been pointless."

"Surely not! My heart bleeds at the plight of the foreign born Jews left in Paris, but you and I are Frenchmen, for heaven's sake! Would my eldest boy have enlisted otherwise?" Valentin winced, recalling how useless he'd felt when he saw Roger Kahn marching off proudly with other men from the village.

"Peter wanted to as well, but I persuaded him not to interrupt his studies. Now I can only wonder if I did the right thing."

Dr Abraham was not the only one to feel uncomfortable in the presence of so many born and bred inhabitants of Saint-André-la-Forêt. A few hostile glances had been aimed at Bertrand Baltzinger and he decided that he'd had enough. Springing to his feet, he shouted,

"Look, if you've got anything against me because of my name and where I come from, just have the guts to say so."

"You know exactly what I've got against you," retaliated Alain Binard. "But it's got nothing to do with your background."

"Well, you can't blame us for wondering," piped up a voice behind him. It was Hubert Morcel, who had sneaked in at the back.

"You should be in bed!" threatened Valentin. "Just wait until Maman finds out. Sorry, Father."

The priest smiled. "Don't be too hard on your brother. He'll be leaving school soon, won't he, and a lively curiosity is not a sin."

"No, Father, but it's lucky for him that Papa's still missing." Silence fell as the import of what he'd just said sank in and Valentin wished that the stone flags would open up and swallow him. Father Ferdinand made no comment, preferring to turn back to the matter in hand.

"I'm sure that young Bertrand here is just as loyal to France as the rest of us."

"Of course I am, *mon père*." The polite term of address flowed easily from his lips, even though he had only a passing acquaintance with the priest. "The fact that I come from Alsace and can understand German doesn't prove anything. There wasn't much that my family agreed about, but our Frenchness was never an issue. Do you think I wanted Mulhouse to become Mulhausen and to imagine my family having to walk down Adolf Hitler Straße?"

Valentin marvelled at the barefaced lie, knowing that Bertrand would be quite happy to see the rest of the Baltzingers filing through the gates of Hell. Only the other day he'd confided his heartfelt desire to see his father and brothers conscripted by the Germans and killed in action. As for his mother...

"And the Boche to invade France?" he continued with one of his wide eyed boyish looks. "If I liked them so much, why didn't I head for Freiburg when I left home? It's only just over the border and would have been a damned sight easier."

"Of course you're French, young man," said Massot, taken in by the passion in his voice. "And your knowledge of German may be very useful to us to find out what's going on."

"Thank you, *Monsieur le Maire*. But what if they ask me to tell them what's happening in the village?"

"Then you do," smiled the priest. "Harmless things, of course, and maybe a little misinformation from time to time."

His housekeeper was shocked. "You'd encourage the boy to tell lies, Father? France has been laid low by sin and only prayer will lead to her liberation. Prayer and more children. Marshall Pétain was right. It's partly the selfishness of French women that has led to this defeat. Fewer children mean fewer soldiers. The Church's view of contraception is quite clear and as for abortionists... I'd send them straight to the guillotine." She'd strayed so far off the point that her audience was left speechless until raven-headed Marius Duval, recently forced by her meddling into a loveless marriage, shouted,

"And how many have you contributed personally, Mademoiselle?"

She bridled. "If it had been God's will for me to marry, I should have been happy to bear a dozen children or more."

"Then I should pray for them *and* their father."

"Now, now, my son, that's quite enough of that. We *will* pray, of course, those of us who believe. As for those who do not, they will also have their part to play for the good of all before France once again casts off her chains. In the meantime, it's best that we all keep our heads down."

Chapter 5

It wasn't long before the Germans were goose stepping down the Champs-Elysées and putting big signs in Gothic script over the buildings that they'd commandeered, but taking over the capital seemed to keep them happy for a while. Maybe they wouldn't bother with a little backwater like Saint-André-la-Forêt?

Valentin was washing the café windows the morning they arrived. A couple of motorcycles with sidecars swept past, followed by armoured vehicles full of soldiers in greenish-grey uniforms. Their highly polished steel helmets were dazzling in the sunlight and every man was heavily armed. The convoy went straight through the Place de Verdun and up to their chosen *Kommandatur*. Baltzinger reported later that he'd stood with the rest of the staff as the Countess, elegant as always with her silver chignon and fine pearls, handed over her keys without a word.

"Sensible lady. Practical as well as proud," was Thérèse's verdict. "What else could she do?" What indeed? End up like a certain Madame Bourgeois, tied to a tree and shot for haranguing the German soldiers requisitioning her home?

"So what's he like, the new *Kommandant*?" asked Valentin.

"Colonel von Achten? Could have been worse, I suppose. In his late forties, I'd say, or maybe early fifties. He speaks excellent French and was very polite to the Countess. Clicked his heels and bowed to her. He even apologised for the inconvenience and said that she could keep a whole wing of the building for herself and the staff who live in."

"Well, that's something at least."

"He was very tactful too. Didn't say a word about what had happened this time around but praised the French troops he'd seen in action when he was a young lieutenant."

"The Countess would like that. Her husband died in 1918, just before the armistice, and she still mourns him."

The French flag over the *mairie* had been taken down and replaced by a black swastika swimming in a blood red background. To add to the state of shock in the village, notices started to go up all over the place threatening the death penalty for acts of sabotage or attacks on the German troops. They were certainly taking no chances. The tall sergeant in charge of the operation had a submachine gun and some of his men had sacks of grenades slung casually over their shoulders in addition to their rifles.

Even so, when they realised that only women and children were in the little crowd watching them, the soldiers started to relax. One or two of them, clean shaven and confident, even winked and offered sweets. Stony faced and conscious of the scrutiny of their neighbours, the mothers held their children back, but the Germans knew that time was on their side. They didn't even look offended when Madeleine Binard, who'd been brought up near the Belgian border and lived under German occupation before, pointedly turned her back on them.

The miracle that many prayed for seemed a forlorn hope. The Americans had no plans to intervene this time round, the British had fled back to their island and the French government was holed up in Vichy with no say in what happened to fellow countrymen left behind on the wrong side of the dividing line.

All the same, it wasn't too bad at first. It took time for the new authorities in Paris to get organised and even longer for all their orders to filter down to the countryside. The soldiers under the Colonel's command were, according to Baltzinger, under orders to treat civilians with courtesy and their presence soon ceased to be a novelty. They spent their pay in the local shops and seemed to enjoy trying out their schoolboy French. There were sinister rumours about an elite corps in black, but it was some time before they made their presence felt in the district.

When the Germans attempted to flirt with Thérèse, she always pushed Valentin forward to serve them and scuttled back into the safety of the kitchen. The NCO who'd been in charge of putting up the notices the day they arrived and whose French was better than most, made a point of engaging him in conversation. He wouldn't tolerate any mocking of Valentin's awkward gait and leaned across the bar one night to say,

"I shouldn't really tell you this, Monsieur, but a lot of the propaganda about the perfect Aryan specimen comes from Dr Goebbels, who was born with a disability just like yours. How ironic is that!"

Valentin poured the drink he'd requested and dared to joke, "Well, you could easily be one of his poster boys."

When he'd stopped laughing, Sergeant Stracke ran a hand through his straw coloured hair and said, "Tell me something, Monsieur. Are any of my men really bothering your sister or any of the other local girls? If so, I'll make sure that it doesn't happen again. I know they're a long way from home, but that's no excuse. They can find what they want in Paris when they're on leave."

"Thank you for your concern, Sergeant."

"It was kindly meant. We Germans aren't monsters, you know, and we don't need the Allies to teach us civilised behaviour." He wasn't alone in that sentiment, at least at the beginning of the Occupation.

"I haven't any time for the English," snapped Corinne Dupré one day, as the butcher was wrapping the cutlets she'd just bought for Father Ferdinand's dinner. "We still hate them in Rouen for martyring Joan of Arc." Valentin, waiting behind her in the queue, was about to argue that there was more to it than that, when another voice chipped in.

"They're our traditional enemy and we shouldn't forget it. Did you hear what Paul Ferdonnet said on the radio before they sank our fleet at Mers-el-Kébir? He said that Britain would fight to the last Frenchman. Well, he was right, wasn't he?"

The butcher spluttered with rage. "Don't you mention that traitor's name in my shop! He was broadcasting from Stuttgart, you fool! Anyway, it only happened because they thought the entire fleet was about to be handed over to the Germans."

"Try telling that to the families of the sailors who were killed!"

The curfew that first year ran from nine o'clock in the evening until six in the morning, but the area remained quiet and it was not very strictly enforced. The first civilian to fall foul of it was young Hubert, caught out poaching by a German patrol. Luckily for him, Stracke was the duty sergeant that night. He made the boy work until dawn polishing boots and peeling potatoes and then delivered him to his startled parents with a stern warning. Monsieur Morcel, only recently returned home after an exhausting and hazardous trek across northern France, didn't enjoy the humiliation of apologising to the enemy for his son's behaviour. As a consequence, Hubert didn't enjoy what followed as soon as the door closed on the big German, but it did serve to rein in his activities for a while.

His father had more than one reason for wanting to keep a low profile. He'd managed to slip back into his former life without any awkward questions being asked, but a search of his home might well have turned up the shotgun he kept hidden on a beam in the attic. Almost to a man, the hunters and farmers of the village were determined to defy the order to hand in all their weapons, although an attack on an enemy soldier a few miles away had just resulted in the shooting of some French hostages. As Hubert scuttled off to perch gingerly on a hard school bench, his parents were discussing whether to bury the gun in the forest or wrap it in a tarpaulin and lower it into the bottom of the well behind the house.

"*Vous avez du feu, Monsieur?*"

The café fell silent as the polite request was greeted by a snarl and an obscene gesture. Fired up by a report of one of Churchill's speeches but too frail to fight on the beaches, landing grounds or anywhere else for that matter, Old Jules could at least refuse the enemy a light. Sergeant Stracke, who had made the request, hesitated for a moment but was painfully aware that he would lose face with his own soldiers as well as the local people if he failed to take action.

His mind made up, he barked, "Corporal Meyer! Arrest this man." As a scowling blond giant bore down on the veteran, Thérèse ran out from behind the bar and threw herself between them.

"Please don't hurt him," she pleaded. "He's just a bit touched in the head." The corporal hesitated, but Stracke signalled that he should rejoin his friends and then said for all to hear,

"I assure you, Madame, that it is not my intention to teach your customer better manners in that way." He turned to the old man and prodded him gently in the chest. "And you, Monsieur, will kindly show more respect in future to members of the Wehrmacht." Badly shaken despite his bluster, the veteran shambled off as fast as his legs could carry him.

"Here you are, Sergeant. Take these." Matches were already in short supply, but she handed him a whole box. As Stracke took it from her, he muttered,

"I wasn't going to let any harm come to him, you know. A night in custody would have sufficed to make the point. The weather is still quite mild, but I'd have made sure all the same that he got a decent blanket and some hot soup." He lit his cigarette and gave back the matches. Their hands touched only briefly, but the ice had been broken.

Another German it was hard to dislike was Private Jelling. No older than Valentin and with an eager face sprinkled with freckles, he was thoughtful enough to leave the odd cigarette, sometimes even two, in the packets he discarded. This was generosity indeed, as each one, whether Eckstein No. 5, Salem or Juno, contained only six cigarettes and represented his daily ration. Repelled by the swastikas on their tax labels, Thérèse threw them away at first. Later, with hardened smokers reduced to drying nettle leaves in their ovens, every flake of tobacco became valuable currency.

As for the rest of the soldiers who flocked into the café most evenings, some were polite enough and did their best to be friendly. Others, despite their orders, were loud and arrogant. Amongst those were the giant corporal and his cold eyed friend Rankert, a much smaller man with a vicious tongue. They demanded instant service and never thought of leaving a tip.

Thérèse's attitude towards Germans in general hardened when she heard what Luc had been through since his capture. He tapped at the back door one night after curfew, worn out and filthy. He'd lost so much weight that she hardly recognised him and he ate half the contents of the larder before he'd tell her and Valentin anything about his ordeal.

"I was taken to a stadium on the outskirts of Paris," he said finally, spitting out crumbs as he spoke. "There were hundreds of us, maybe thousands, both French and British. So many prisoners that the Germans didn't know what to do with us all. There wasn't much food and precious little shelter or sanitation. The place stank to high heaven and most of the sick and injured didn't get any medical care."

Thérèse handed him a napkin. "That's shameful. If they couldn't look after you properly, they should have let you go."

"Well, the guards kept telling us that we'd be released after the armistice, but then word got round that we were going to be sent to Germany. That was enough for me. I managed to sneak under the tarpaulin of a delivery truck with some other men. The driver spotted us, but he was a patriot and kept his mouth shut. As soon as we were safely away from the stadium, he let us out and I set off to walk home."

Thérèse had knelt down to pull off what remained of his boots and socks. "Your poor feet are in shreds. I'll get a bowl for you to soak them in."

He leant forward to kiss the top of her head. "My feet are the least of my problems, *mon amour*. The Germans will be looking for me. I need to find a safe place to hide."

She looked up, alarmed. "Of course you do. How silly of me!"

"But we'll take care of that tomorrow. Even if this is my last night on earth, I'm going to spend it with my wife in our own bed. Food and drink aren't all I've been missing."

"Are you sure you're not too tired, my love?" Without another word,

Luc picked her up and headed for the stairs.

It may be that the sheer number of prisoners in the stadium had prevented the Germans from making accurate lists. In any event, no one ever did come looking for Luc and he didn't feel the need to hide out for long. Furnished by a contact in Paris with some fake demobilisation papers, he resumed his place behind the bar as though he had never been away.

Not every family was so lucky. Amongst those men who never came back were Hervé Binard, husband of Madeleine and father of Alain, and the Countess's much beloved sons.

Chapter 6

As the weather grew colder, the situation in the village became much worse. Just about everything that made life worth living was rationed and the Germans had even taken away the few decent horses that hadn't been commandeered by the French army at the start of the war.

"How am I supposed to get my fields ready?" complained Jacqueline Signac on one of her rare visits to the café. "They've only left me that skinny old nag I was going to send to the horse butcher. It's lame and it's a devil of a job to get any work out of it."

"I feel sorry for the poor creature," muttered Luc, who'd been listening to their conversation from behind the kitchen door. "Better to be shot than worked to death by that harridan!" His wife and brother-in-law, hard at work on preparations for the evening meal, nodded their agreement.

"Be grateful you've still got a horse," Baltzinger was saying. "The Perthuis haven't been left a single one and Vincent's tearing his hair out. He'll have to yoke that wife of his to the plough. I wouldn't mind putting a whip to her hindquarters." His eyes glistened at the thought and Jacqueline reached across to squeeze his knee.

"I don't suppose you'd like to come back and work for me, Bertrand? I could do with another pair of hands and I'd really make it worth your while this time."

"Well, I suppose I could put in a few hours," he said, feigning reluctance, "but only when I'm not needed at the château. At least I can show that old horse who's the boss." They left the café arm in arm.

Madeleine Binard, who had caught the last few words of their conversation as they passed her table, drained her glass and frowned.

"It's lucky for him that my Alain didn't hear that."

"In the meantime, what are we supposed to do about supplies for this place?" Luc's face was creased with worry. "The Germans requisition all the good stuff and what they can't eat they send back home to their families. Just come into the kitchen and see how little we have left to carry on with."

Looking round, Madeleine sighed and said, "It's even worse for the Parisians, you know. Greens, swede and a bit of fish or tripe if they're lucky. All washed down with a hot cup of *café national*, as we're supposed to call it."

"Revolting stuff! At least we're not reduced to that yet," said Thérèse with a shudder.

Valentin grimaced. "It might not be long."

"Cheer up, you three. There's always something to eat in the countryside and not as many questions asked. If you've got anything to spare, I can take it with me next time and try to barter it for something you need."

"Isn't that dangerous?"

Madeleine shrugged and they all understood why. The brave woman brought back anti-Nazi pamphlets each time she drove into Paris in search of spare parts. Oily from being hidden at the bottom of her tool bag, they were passed round and read until they fell apart. With private radio sets now forbidden, everyone was desperate to know what was really going on and you couldn't trust the collaborationist publications subsidised by the Germans. The paper they were printed on was of much better quality than the rest, though, and put to good use when torn into strips and hung on a nail.

"Does your Hubert still do a bit of poaching?"

"Yes, but not after curfew any more. He learnt his lesson last time. He couldn't sit down comfortably for a week."

"Well, tell him that even acorns are in demand to mix with the chick peas. The cafés and hotels in Paris will pay for them when they can't get proper coffee. People are getting desperate. There are queues everywhere and women are selling their wedding rings to buy food on the black market. Some people are even eating their pets."

"Eating their pets!"

"Jean-Pierre! I didn't see you coming in. Yes, I'm afraid so. Tell them about it. You spend more time in Paris than I do."

The young medical student's face was grave. "You're probably right, Madame, and it's getting worse. I've seen posters warning people about the dangers of eating rats."

"Rats!" Thérèse turned pale at the thought.

"Yes, rats. There's a fuel crisis too. Hardly any coal and the squares are full of people collecting anything that will burn. Branches, dead leaves and even chestnuts. At least we've got proper fireplaces and chimneys. The Parisians are having to make braziers out of old tins and flower pots."

Valentin was intrigued. "Where does all the smoke go?"

"Oh, I can tell you that," said Madeleine. "I've seen pipes sticking out of their kitchen windows and the outside walls are getting covered in soot of all colours."

"It sounds as though we're much better off living here," said Thérèse with a smile. "If we all stick together and help each other where we can, we'll be fine."

"I wouldn't like to be in young Clavié's shoes," said Luc, jerking his head towards a table in the corner where a hunched figure sat alone. The village policeman was having to walk a very fine line. Ordered by his superiors to cooperate with the Germans, he was anxious for his neighbours to understand that he was acting under duress. Despite his earlier opinion, he'd become sickened by the increasing focus on the Jews. After the round up and deportation of all those foreign born and resident in Paris, it had now been made illegal for Jewish citizens of the occupied territories to emigrate. If the Germans hated them so much, why didn't they just let them go? Instead, they were doing all they could to make their lives miserable. They were already banned from practising in courts of law and the collaborationist press had called for them to be forbidden to teach in French schools. Where was it all going to end? The young man buried his head in his hands, dreading what he had to do the following day.

Followed by two German soldiers with hessian sacks over their arms, Clavié walked into the little bookshop attached to the newsagent's.

"All books by undesirable writers, especially Jews, must be purged," he announced at the top of his voice. "I have a full list here. More suitable stock will be delivered to you shortly." As the soldiers set about their work, he slunk into a corner and looked at his boots.

The next day, Father Ferdinand stopped in his tracks. Displayed prominently in the window was a large framed photograph of Adolf Hitler next to a pile of copies of *Ma Doctrine*, his infamous book translated into French. Shaking his head sadly, he went inside and picked one up.

"So, my son, it has come to this?"

The proprietor was scarlet with embarrassment. "It isn't my fault, Father, but at least I haven't sold any yet."

"I should hope not, indeed. Pernicious rubbish from start to finish."

"But these are going well, I'm afraid." He pointed to a selection of textbooks on the German language. "People are hedging their bets in case the Allies lose the war."

"Trust in Allah, but tether your camel," said the priest, fighting against the urge to tear the offending volumes to shreds.

"What?"

"It's an old Arab saying."

"I've heard it before," said a young customer. "Monsieur Kahn quotes it to us at school when a test's due. 'Pray if you like,' he says, 'but don't forget to revise.' It always makes us laugh."

"It's your teacher you need to pray for now, my child."

"The Colonel's compliments, *Madame la Comtesse*," said Bertrand Balzinger, "and please would you step into his office for a few minutes?"

The former library had not changed very much, if you discounted Hitler's portrait and the swastika over the fireplace. The loss of her sons had hit the Countess very hard, but her chin was up and her back straight as she approached the figure behind her late husband's desk. Seated before him on carved and gilded walnut chairs were Massot and his clerk, a bright eyed young man by the name of Louis Lenoir. A third chair stood empty.

Colonel von Achten rose sharply at her approach and greeted her, as Baltzinger later recounted to Valentin, with his usual courtesy.

"Please take a seat, Madame," he said pleasantly, as if he had every right to offer her hospitality in her own home. "Would you like some coffee." The aroma of freshly ground beans hung in the air, but the old lady looked as though the very thought made her feel sick. How could it be otherwise when the ornate silver coffee pot that had been in the family for generations was now presided over by an unsmiling and very plain young woman in grey? Massot, who had also scrambled to his feet, had spilled his own drink and was trying to rub it into the priceless antique carpet with his foot.

"First of all, may I offer you my condolences for the loss of your sons."

The Countess inclined her head. "Fallen for the glory of France."

"Indeed." He left it to her to break the silence that followed.

"You have other business with me, Colonel?"

"I'm afraid I do. You know everyone in this village, do you not?"

"I believe so."

"Then I require you to tell me if there are any omissions in the list already compiled for me by the Mayor. You will see that there is particular reference to the religious persuasion of each family."

"I beg your pardon?"

"I need to know how many Jews reside in Saint-André-la-Forêt and the surrounding district, Madame, so that I can check if they have registered with the police. The Kahns and the Abrahams are already noted, but there may be others?"

"Not to my knowledge," she said firmly and threw him a challenging look. "Tell me, Colonel, is it true that Jewish homes in Paris have been raided and property confiscated?"

He reddened. "May I enquire who told you that?" His clerk shuffled her feet, trying not to catch the eye of the well built young handyman still hovering in the doorway. Since what she believed to have been a chance meeting in the grounds, they had been become very well acquainted.

The Countess pursed her thin lips. "I'm afraid that I don't recall."

"And what else did you hear, Madame?"

"That the soldiers had stolen whatever took their fancy and arrested anyone who tried to resist. Some homes were stripped completely bare."

The Colonel frowned. "Oh, I doubt if it was as bad as that. The first Jews to receive one of these unfortunate visits would have been able to alert the others in time to conceal their valuables."

"And how would they do that? Aren't they forbidden to have private telephones now?"

"You have been well informed, Madame."

As the sparring continued, Louis Lenoir leaned forward and said with a polite cough, "Please excuse the interruption, Colonel, but I've just recalled an appointment this afternoon for the redrafting of a will. I'm quite capable of handling the preliminaries, if you don't need us both to stay?"

Permission was granted. As soon as he was safely out of sight, the young man took to his heels and sprinted towards the church.

"Father, I must speak to you urgently." The priest rose from his knees and dusted himself off. The smell of lavender polish was strong, although no one else was to be seen. "Alone, if you please."

"Then take a walk outside with me, my son, and tell me what troubles you."

As he absorbed the information, Father Ferdinand thought rapidly. "Some of us have seen this coming for quite a while," he said, "and plans have been made. For your own safety as much as theirs, I can't give you any details, but we shall do our best to help both families." As he spoke, he was tucking the end of his soutane into his belt. Mounting his old black bicycle, he added, "If the Germans want to know why I'm in such a hurry, I'll tell them that one of my parishioners is in urgent need of the last rites." Then he was off, pedalling so fast that he had to steer with one hand and hold on to his biretta with the other.

Early the next morning, before most people had opened their shutters, a patrol arrived on the Abrahams' doorstep. With dirty dishes from the previous evening's meal still on the table, every sign pointed to a hurried departure. The Colonel was obliged to order a search of the district, but his heart wasn't in it and he reported later to his superiors in Paris that no trace of the family could be found. Sad to say, it wasn't long before the house was ransacked, windows broken and doors wrenched off for firewood. Amongst the many items stolen was the magnificent brass plate that Dr Abraham had brought with him from Metz.

Marcel Kahn gave up his post only when, stiff with humiliation, he was escorted out of his classroom and ordered to vacate the accommodation over the school for the new teacher. The soldiers, maybe because they found nothing worth stealing in his home, vented their spleen on his precious book collection.

During the hand to mouth existence forced upon the family from then onwards, he must have wished many times that they'd agreed to escape with the Abrahams. Although the Kahns were popular and well respected, most homes were overcrowded already and people feared getting on the wrong side of the Germans.

It was rumoured that Corinne Dupré threatened to resign when Father Ferdinand wanted to take them in. Instead of seeing it as a heaven sent opportunity to get rid of her, he knocked on every door in the village and even went up to the château in a vain attempt to reason with the Colonel.

"The *Kommandant* said that his hands were tied," he told Thérèse later, "and it was young Bertrand who came up with a solution. He stopped me on the way out and said that there was an empty cottage on Henriette Tilleray's land. God bless him! He even offered to cycle up there and ask her if the Kahns could use it. She agreed at once, of course. It's pretty ramshackle, but at least they'll all be together."

"Do you think they'll be left in peace now, Father?"

"I can only pray that they will, but who knows?"

The ever lengthening list of anti-Jewish laws, some petty in the extreme, was greeted with consternation by most villagers but with ill concealed delight by others.

"What else could I do?" said Madame Joubier, when Thérèse upbraided her for refusing to accept the Kahns' laundry or allow them entry to the public bath house. "It made me feel bad, of course, but I can't risk any trouble with the Germans."

"Especially now that they've given you a nice fat contract."

"That's got nothing to do with it, although I don't suppose the Colonel would want his linen sharing the same tub as theirs."

"You know that Rachel would do her own washing if she could, but they've got no running water at the cottage."

The other woman gave a contemptuous sniff. "Not my problem, I'm afraid."

"You're a disgrace to France!"

Chapter 7

As soon as she heard that Jews were no longer allowed to own bicycles, Madeleine Binard offered to dismantle those belonging to the Kahns and hide them until after the war. Pets were also now forbidden to them, so Alain promised to take care of Bijou, the little black poodle that seven year old Aimée had been given for her last birthday.

"But why can't I keep him?" wailed the little girl. "I've always fed him and taken him for walks and he loves me."

"Of course he does, darling," said her distraught father, folding her into his arms. "And when all this madness is over, you'll get him straight back. Won't she, Alain?"

"Of course she will."

"But what if he forgets me?"

"He won't. I promise. And you and your brothers can call in to see him each day on your way to school."

"But Papa says we won't be going to school any more. It's too far to walk."

Marcel's lips were set in a grim line. If only that were the genuine reason! He wouldn't have his children exposed to the ordeal of being singled out and their so-called Jewish features pointed out to the rest of the class. The collaborationist newspapers were full of vile cartoons and Radio Paris was no better. Worst of all were the compulsory school visits to the Palais Berlitz, where an exhibition had been mounted to present the Jews as responsible for all of the nation's ills. They were depicted as a giant spider feeding on the blood of France.

"I assure you that I would never take my pupils to anything so appalling," his replacement had protested. "I feel bad enough about the way you were forced to leave your post and your home, Monsieur."

Marcel looked into the earnest young face and pitied him. It was good of Templier, newly qualified and only recently married, to seek him out and offer his apologies.

"You might not be given any choice, my boy," he said simply.

Knowing how much his old teacher missed his books, Valentin collected all the reading matter he could lay his hands on and sent Hubert up to the farm with it. Always hungry for news, Marcel read every word, quite often with one of Private Jelling's cigarettes hanging from his lips.

Luc and Thérèse contributed as much as they could spare from their own supplies and others did the same. Valentin was pleased to see that his parents' earlier hostility to Marcel had evaporated in the light of what had happened to him. With a large family of their own to feed, they had less than most to give, but came up with something most weeks. Quite aside from the fact that the Kahns no longer had any source of income, the long list of items that they were no longer allowed to buy meant that they would have starved to death without the help of well wishers.

"Do you realise that I'm committing a criminal act right now?" said Marcel one evening as he faced Father Ferdinand across the latter's chess board. The fact that Jews had been forbidden to play had made him more determined than ever to improve his game.

At least they were left alone by the Germans. Colonel von Achten had done what was required of him and hoped to leave the matter there. As the area under his command remained peaceful, he came down to the village occasionally to watch a game of *boules*, allowed fund raising activities to send parcels to prisoners of war and was even keen to organise a football match between his soldiers and the local men.

Chapter 8

"He can't be serious!" spluttered Luc. "Cultural evenings at the château? I thought the Colonel would have taken the hint when Massot couldn't find enough volunteers to form a football team."

The young clerk grinned. "You'd rather stay at home and listen to all that crackling on your radio?"

"You bet I would. The Germans don't manage to jam every broadcast from the BBC."

"And you're not worried about being caught?"

Luc hesitated. "Of course I am. We all are. But it's the only way to find out for sure what's going on. You don't suppose that German newsreels are going to tell the truth, do you?"

"Of course not. Jean-Pierre says that the heckling's so bad when they're shown in Paris cinemas that they have to keep the house lights on."

"Doesn't that make them unwatchable?"

"I suppose so."

"Well, I shan't go and I don't suppose anyone else will."

"I don't want to either, but my boss insists. He's worried that an obvious snub might have repercussions. The Colonel went to a lot of trouble to have a projector and screen set up in the ballroom to entertain his men and he thinks that laying on some films in French for the locals will improve relations and be good for morale. There's no charge and maybe even some free refreshments."

Luc sighed. "You go if you want to, but you'll be sitting there by yourself."

He was wrong about that. With little other entertainment available, the *Soirées Culturelles* proved remarkable popular. Nicholas Garnier, son of Baltzinger's boss, never missed a single one. Amused by the teenager's avid interest in the equipment, the NCO in charge taught him how to operate it.

The presence of so many enemy soldiers in the audience was sufficient to prevent heckling, even though the news reels were full of spectacular victories by the invincible German forces, all achieved virtually without loss.

"Tell me, Bertrand," said Thérèse one evening. "Do you think that *they* believe it all?"

He glanced around the almost deserted café and leaned towards her across the bar. "That most major British cities are being wiped off the map while the pilots of the RAF cower in their hangars? Maybe the squaddies do. Who doesn't want to think himself on the winning side? But most of them are more interested in chatting up girls than watching the screen. Even those who say they're only trying to improve their French."

"How about the officers?"

He laughed. "Von Achten listens to the BBC with his door closed."

"How on earth do you know that?"

He tapped the side of his nose and winked. "I have my sources."

"What he means," added Hubert, "is that he's got into the knickers of the Colonel's clerk."

"Hubert!"

Valentin cuffed him gently. "What a thing to say in front of our sister! You're growing up far too fast."

"That's hardly the point," scowled Baltzinger. "Who told you about Sabine and me?"

"No one," was the smug reply. "I overheard you talking to Valentin."

"Well don't you dare tell anyone else."

"So you don't deny it?"

"No, Thérèse, I don't deny it, but there'd be hell to pay if the other Germans found out."

Her cheeks were pink. "Aren't you ashamed of yourself?"

"Not a bit. I'm gathering intelligence, just as Father Ferdinand said I should do. Whatever I get up to with Sabine Lohner is part of that."

"I don't think he meant you to go to that extreme. Sleeping with the enemy!"

"Who said anything about sleeping? We don't do much of that. She can't keep her hands off me, you know."

"Bertrand!"

Luc had heard enough. "Can we please change the subject? Is it true that the Colonel isn't well?"

"Yes, his blood pressure is sky high and he's got to go to Paris for a medical next week. If he doesn't pass, he'll be replaced."

"Oh dear! For a German, he isn't a bad sort. We could do a lot worse."

Chapter 9

Colonel Erhardt Köstler had worshipped Adolf Hitler since the day of their first meeting in a Munich beer hall. Twenty years later, strutting down the Champs-Élysées as a fully paid up member of Hitler's master race, he was beside himself with joy. German currency, once worth less than the paper on which it was printed, was now eagerly accepted by everyone from waiters to whores and he intended to gorge himself on every delight that Paris had to offer. It did not trouble him in the least that the Louvre had been stripped of its paintings and the museums were being systematically looted. Fine restaurants, brothels set aside for the use of German officers, theatres, music halls and cinemas were all open to him. He might even arrange for his wife and younger children to pay him a visit and Georg, of course, when he got some leave. Paris must be the safest posting on offer. Even Hitler himself had been driven round in an open car and no one had taken a shot at him.

How proud he was of his eldest son. Tall, fair and as callous as he was handsome, Georg Köstler had been the ideal candidate for the SS and was in his element when Germany launched its attack on the Soviet Union. How his father relished his enthusiastic accounts of the total destruction of villages, hanging and shooting of civilians at the slightest excuse and the rounding up of enormous numbers of prisoners. Herded into hastily set up internment camps, they would die of starvation or disease behind the barbed wire. Every letter from the Russian front was cherished.

You'd love it, Father. My detachment has orders to execute all Communists, particularly commissars, officers and Jews. They try to hide what

they are, but I can pick them out easily enough. Spectacles and a book in his
pocket = a commissar. Big nose and gold fillings in his teeth = a Jew. Dares
to protest about the conditions = an officer. Nobody really cares whether I
get it right or wrong. Sub-humans, the lot of them.

Displeased at first when the order came through for him to take
over from Colonel von Achten, it was not long before Köstler saw the
advantages. He would be moving from a middle range hotel to a fine
château within easy reach of the capital and with the added attraction
of a community of subservient peasants to lord it over. Having been
obliged to read *A Tale of Two Cities* as a schoolboy, his sympathies had
always been with the Marquis St. Evrémonde rather than his milksop
of a nephew Charles Darnay. The inhabitants of Saint-André-la-Forêt
had better watch their step if they knew what was good for them. If
they didn't, then he would soon teach them. His French might not be
as elegant as that of his predecessor, but it was certainly adequate for
giving orders.

"He hasn't got any respect for the Countess," reported Arnaud Garnier.
"He's taken over her Daimler, even though he's got his own staff car."

"Well," said Valentin, "at least you won't have to wash and polish it
any more. You're always complaining that you've got too much to do."

"That hasn't changed. I'm just not allowed behind the wheel." A
wistful look came over his face. "It's a 1931 Double Six, you know."

"We know." The black and brown Daimler with its white walled
tyres had been a familiar sight since its arrival a decade earlier.

"The Colonel's driver thinks it's a sniper's dream," said Baltzinger,
but Köstler won't have anything changed."

"It's hardly ever there now anyway. He gets dressed up in his best
uniform and medals almost every evening and has himself driven to
Paris. He doesn't care how much petrol it uses. I think that's part of
the pleasure, anyway. He's even used it to take other officers and their
whores to Longchamps."

Derision written all over his face, Luc said, "Longchamps? The race meetings are only kept going by the Germans."

"He fancies himself on a horse too," continued Baltzinger. "He's ordered some riding breeches lined with leather and a new whip."

"Well, I hope he falls off and breaks his neck."

"If he does, he'll probably have the poor creature shot and my son with it. Poor Nicholas is under orders to keep the horse's coat as shiny as Köstler's best riding boots."

"A parcel for you, Colonel," said his clerk, her hands trembling as she put it down in front of him. Köstler's face had a pale waxy look and he had barely spoken a word since the news arrived of his son's death. Dazed with grief, he'd spent whole days sitting at his desk and staring at the framed photograph of Georg in his dress uniform. "Shall I open it for you?"

The slim box contained only two things; a handwritten letter from one of Georg Köstler's brother officers and a black handled SS dagger with the inscription *Meine Ehre heißt Treue.* My honour is loyalty.

The knuckles gripping the desk were white and the Colonel's lips moved without sound for a few seconds. Then he pushed the letter towards her and said,

"Read it to me. I don't think I can." The tone was brusque, but the stricken look in his eyes, as she reported later on to her lover, was one that Sabine Lohner would never forget.

"Of course, Colonel."

After the formal greeting and expressions of condolence to the bereaved father came the following:

I know that you will want the full facts of your son's death, however painful. We had had a typical day chasing the retreating Russians through clouds of yellow dust on their atrocious roads. The weather kept changing; tremendous heat, heavy showers and then sunshine that baked the mud into crumbly clay. We were not far from Smolensk when a group of men appeared from nowhere and opened fire on our convoy. Their weapons were no match for ours, of course, and we soon drove them off, but Georg was determined that a handful of illiterate Slavs with rusty rifles would not be allowed to get away with challenging the SS. He insisted on taking some men to hunt them down and that was the last time I saw him alive. The Russians are barbarians and your son's death was not an easy one. The search party we sent out when he failed to return could identify his remains only by the blood group tattooed in his armpit. I enclose his dagger which, I regret to say, had played a part in the butchery and been deliberately left behind for his friends to find.

Köstler's whole stance had changed. Sitting bolt upright, he snatched the letter from her. "Enough!" He would make sure that his wife never knew how their beloved son had died. Only revenge could assuage his own grief. With any luck, the harsher measures in the pipeline might stir those within his jurisdiction to a revolt that he would take great pleasure in crushing. The French forces had fled like scared rabbits at the beginning of the war, but there might be more sport to be had with the civilian population. He turned to the clerk with a tight lipped smile that looked as though it had been stitched on.

"Fetch me the latest orders from Paris."

"According to Sabine," said Baltzinger, "since his son was killed, Köstler's out for blood and doesn't much care whose. Would someone mind passing the cheese?" Thérèse had invited him to join her family and the priest for lunch after Mass.

"Well, I never understood why the Germans attacked Russia in the first place. Napoleon's supposed to be one of Hitler's heroes, isn't he, and just look what happened to him!"

With a sigh, Father Ferdinand put down his glass. "You're right, Valentin, but history teaches us that people have never learned anything from history."

"That's very profound, Father," said Luc.

"Not original, I'm afraid. The German philosopher Hegel said it first, well over a hundred years ago. His works weren't approved reading in the seminary, but I was always rather a rebel."

"All those poor soldiers," shuddered Thérèse, pulling her cardigan more tightly round her shoulders. "I remember from school, that only about ten thousand of Napoleon's men came back out of half a million. Those who weren't killed by the Russians died of starvation or frostbite and..."

"Never mind about all that," interrupted her father. "Let's stick to the here and now. I don't want your brothers ending up in front of a firing squad like those poor young fellows the Germans caught cutting their telephone cables."

"They were true heroes, weren't they, Papa?"

"Don't even think about it, Joseph, or else you know what to expect from me."

"Things are starting to move, though," remarked Luc. "It's going beyond pamphlets and slogans now and the British have promised..."

Monsieur Morcel stamped his foot in frustration. "Don't talk to me about the British! They just want us to distract the Germans from their invasion plans. Let them sacrifice their own sons first!" The argument might have gone on all afternoon, had it not been overtaken by events.

Valentin spotted them through the open doorway and this first sight of the Kahns wearing their yellow stars would stay with him for the rest of his life. About the size of the palm of his hand and outlined in black, the vile things were made of cloth, six pointed like the Star of David and with the word *Juif* in the centre. Not since the Middle Ages had such humiliation been inflicted on the Jews.

The family was dressed in the best outfits it could muster. Guillaume, decked out in all his medals and with his beret at a jaunty angle, was holding Marcel's arm. His older grandsons were just ahead, their set expressions defying anyone to mock. The little ones walked behind with their mother. Aimée, whose position as the only girl in the family meant that she never had to wear hand-me-downs, looked too nervous to take any pleasure from the bright ribbon in her hair or her shiny black patent shoes with their straps and bows. How could she, with the memory fresh in her mind of *Maman* weeping as she sewed the star onto

the front of her best frock? Only Alphonse, the baby of the family, had
no idea what was going on and was smiling and waving to everyone as
the little procession crossed the square. After the long walk down from
the farm, he was looking forward to a cool drink and a slice of cake.
He hadn't believed his sister when she told him that they wouldn't be
allowed into the café."

"Bertrand," asked Madame Morcel, "do you know why Alphonse
isn't wearing a yellow star like the rest of them?"

"Because the new law states that children under six are exempt. For
the moment, anyway."

Marcel took his family across to the war memorial and settled his
father onto his favourite bench. Although the old man couldn't see the
inscriptions, knowing that his brothers' names were amongst them was
some consolation for the darkness he endured without complaint.

The square was busy with families strolling about in what remained
of their Sunday best and several games of *boules* were going on, yet the
conversation was unusually subdued. People were exchanging embarrassed glances and wondering whether to acknowledge the Kahns. It
took Madeleine Binard to put the rest to shame. She strode across to
embrace every one of them in turn, even the startled grandfather. Others
took their cue from her and soon the family was surrounded by their
former neighbours.

Madeleine caught Hubert's arm. "Run up to our house and tell Alain
to bring Bijou down to see Aimée." A few minutes later, the little dog
was hurtling joyfully towards his mistress, who beamed and threw her
arms round his neck.

Obeying the letter of the law if not the spirit, Luc took over a tray of
drinks and then some chairs from outside the café. Thérèse sliced up an
apple tart intended for that evening's diners and handed it round. Little
Alphonse's smile as he received his share was all the thanks she needed.

"Why don't you fetch your accordion?" she called out to Arnaud
Garnier, who was just putting his set of *boules* back into their case. "We
could do with some music."

Winning his game seemed to have put Arnaud in a good mood, because he agreed at once and disappeared. He never returned, though, and the sound of heavy boots approaching put paid to the happy atmosphere. A German patrol marched onto the square, accompanied by a breathless policeman who'd been ordered to get there on the double.

Focussing his gaze on a distant cloud, Clavié gasped, "This area is henceforth forbidden to Jews. Any such persons here now must leave at once or face arrest."

Fear and anger were there in equal proportions during the shocked silence that followed. Unwise though it would have been, Marcel might have defied the order if he'd been alone. As it was, and with his wife in tears, he slowly got to his feet and helped his father to stand. That could have put an end to the incident if one of the soldiers hadn't deliberately stuck out a foot to trip up the old blind man. Guillaume stumbled and fell to his knees, dropping his walking stick. Aimée rushed to pick it up, but the jeering soldier snatched it away from her and brandished it over her head. That was enough for Bijou, who bared his teeth and rushed to her defence. The brave poodle was no match for jackboots and it took the combined strength of four of his friends to hold Alain Binard down until the Germans and the policeman had escorted the Kahns off the square. Then, tears pouring down his face, he took off his jacket and wrapped it carefully around the little body. Madeleine was waiting for him and they went off together into the forest to bury the only pet that Aimée Kahn would ever have.

Chapter 10

Luc was busy in the cellar and Thérèse in the kitchen when Private Jelling arrived that evening. Valentin, although obliged to serve him, made no attempt to be civil and everyone else in the café turned their backs.

Plainly upset, the German said, "Look, Monsieur, I'm really sorry about what happened this afternoon, but I couldn't do anything to stop it. Those Jews were lucky to be allowed to get away without being punished, you know."

Valentin couldn't contain himself. "Without being punished? Don't you think that seeing that poor little animal kicked to death by your friend is punishment?"

"Of course I do, but Rankert's no friend of mine and most of the men hated what he did. All the same, you know, it's nothing compared to what could have happened today. An attack on a German soldier by a Jew's dog would be sufficient reason to arrest the whole family and round up everyone else present at the scene for good measure. You're lucky that Sergeant Stracke was in charge of the patrol. He won't report the incident to the Colonel unless he has to. If I may offer you and your family some advice, and it's for your own sake, steer clear of the Jews in future. Things can only get worse for them and anyone seen as their friend."

He'd raised his voice for the last two sentences, which rang out across the café. That very night, the names of Marcel's brave uncles, who'd sacrificed their lives for the country they loved, were crudely erased from the war memorial.

Most people fell into line after that, but Hubert Morcel made himself a yellow star to wear to school and persuaded more than half of his classmates to do the same. Once there, they turned deaf ears to their startled teacher's appeals.

"The Kahns are still my friends," announced Hubert, "and I don't care what the bloody Boche think! If they've got to wear these things, then so shall I."

"Bravo!" shouted the others. "So shall we."

Not daring to leave his pupils alone for fear of what they might do next, Monsieur Templier sent his wife in search of their parents. The revolt was short lived. Irate fathers and older brothers hauled the rebels out of school by their collars and berated them in no uncertain terms for putting their whole families at risk. It was a much chastened group that returned to its studies the following morning and there was no more talk of wearing yellow stars.

Although unaware of it at the time, Hubert and his classmates were not alone in remaining loyal to the Kahns. An anxious meeting took place at their temporary refuge later on that same day.

"I've had a phone call from a friend in Paris to say that French Jews are being rounded up by the busload," said Father Ferdinand, his face creased with anxiety. "Your family has to go into hiding right away, Marcel. It can't be put off any longer."

"You're right, of course, but how? We haven't the money to pay anyone to smuggle us out of the Occupied Zone, let alone out of France."

Madeleine Binard squeezed his hand in sympathy. "Neither have we, unfortunately. It was expensive enough when we got the Abrahams away, but so many groups are fleeing now that the *passeurs* can charge anything they like."

"I suppose you can't blame them when they know that they'll be shot if they're caught."

"Oh yes I can blame them. Some are making a fortune out of other people's despair. Even so, it would be hard to find anyone to lead such a large group."

Old Guillaume leaned forward from his armchair near the stove.

"Please say what you mean, Madeleine," he said quietly. "There's no need to spare my feelings. Who'd risk taking an old blind man on such a journey? Well, as far as I'm concerned, no one needs to worry. Leave me here and go with my blessing. You've got to think of the young ones. I've had enough of this world anyway and you'd be doing me a favour."

His daughter-in-law reached for his hand. "Never, Papa. 'Whither thou goest, I will go and whither thou lodgest, I will lodge'. Isn't that what it says in the Book of Ruth?"

"I don't know," he retorted. "I've never read it."

"Well I have. If we go, we'll go together. If you stay, we'll all stay and hope for the best."

"Your sentiments do you credit, Rachel," said the priest, "but none of you can stay here a day longer. What we've got to do is to convince the Germans that you've all left the area. I've got an idea, if Henriette will help by doing a little play acting. It won't be easy, mind."

"Of course, Father. You know you can count on me. Just tell me what I need to do."

Madame Tilleray was as good as her word. The next morning, she tottered into the village, dishevelled and apparently distraught. Her anguished cries had people running out of homes and businesses to see what was going on. As soon as enough spectators had gathered, she dried her eyes and launched into the agreed speech.

"After all the help I've given them, the Kahns have done the dirty on me! While I slept, they broke into my house and stole everything they could carry. Even my ration coupons. How am I supposed to manage now? Do they expect me to live on thin air?"

"Calm yourself, Madame," said the Mayor, who'd arrived on the scene with his clerk at his heels. "They can't have got far with the old man and the little ones."

"Yes they can. Didn't I mention that they also took my car? I don't know where they found the petrol to fill it up, but it's gone."

Corinne Dupré, who had bustled to the front of the crowd, took her by the arm. "They must have been planning this for a long time," she hissed. "Haven't I always said that the Jew is never to be trusted?"

"You have, and you were right. I'll never trust one again."

"It's shameful," said Louis Lenoir, who'd been present at the meeting the previous evening and was desperately trying to keep his face straight. For dramatic effect, Henriette had smeared her own with dirt and threaded a few twigs through her grey locks. "Everyone knows, Madame, that you'd give your last crust to anyone in need."

"And now I have. The Kahns emptied my larder before they left. I've got nothing to bless myself with. Not a drop of milk. Not a crumb of bread." It was a bravura performance that brought tears to the eyes of some of the onlookers.

By mid-morning, Henriette was on her knees in the church. "Was that all right, Father? I've never told a lie in my life before."

"You did a fine thing, my daughter, and God will understand. How could telling a lie in such a good cause be a sin? The search parties will find no trace of the Kahns, I can assure you of that. As for your car, I think I can safely say that it will turn up again one day."

"This area is now completely cleared of Jews," dictated Colonel Köstler. Without his having lifted a finger, thought his clerk, eyes firmly fixed on her shorthand pad. "But there are still Jewish sympathisers left in the village and they will pay for that."

"No matter how old they are?"

"What's that? Oh, you mean that business at the school? Mmm. Wasn't the gardener's boy the ringleader?"

"Yes and a fine thrashing he got for it from his father. He's probably learnt his lesson, Colonel."

Köstler's bloodless lips tightened. "You think so? Just to make sure, I'll send him a little reminder."

"We want eggs, Madame," said Meyer in his fractured French.

"And what makes you think we've got any? This isn't a farm, you know."

"Information received," replied Rankert smoothly, elbowing the heavily pregnant woman aside. "Now call that son of yours. Not the cripple, the cheeky one. He can get them for us."

Leaving his mother surrounded by the younger children, Hubert reluctantly went out to check on the scrawny hens they kept in a coop at the end of the garden. When he came back with a couple of eggs in each hand, Meyer took them from him, passed them to Rankert and slammed the boy up against the wall. Slowly and deliberately, Rankert broke each egg onto Hubert's head and sneered as the contents trickled down his face.

"Nice and yellow," he said. "Just like that star you wore at school. We have a list of all you little Jew lovers." Laughing, the Germans sauntered off. Madame Morcel slammed the door behind them, fighting the temptation to box Hubert's ears.

"You see?" she scolded. "That's what comes of trying to be a hero!" Then she hugged him and cried with relief that he was still there.

"What's for dinner, *Maman*?" asked one of the little ones as her mother bent Hubert over the sink to wash the mess out of his hair. "I'm hungry."

"I don't know yet," she replied, "but it won't be an omelette."

The requisition of goods became relentless and carried the threat of severe penalties for any attempt at concealment. It wasn't just the farmers and shopkeepers who found the enemy on their doorsteps each week. Every home in the village was searched, every kitchen, cellar and outbuilding, and it wasn't only food that was taken. A treasured piece of jewellery or a small ornament was just as likely to disappear into a uniform pocket.

"They've even taken my gramophone and all my records," protested the bookseller one evening. "Just because Hitler thinks that jazz is decadent. It took me years to build up that collection."

"Oh, what a shame," sympathised Valentin. "I suppose it's because most of the musicians are black."

Baltzinger smiled. "You're right there. Jazz has been banned on

German radio ever since he came to power. Beethoven, Wagner and Bruckner are the composers he favours."

"Then I expect my collection will have been destroyed like the books they took from my shop last time."

"Don't you believe it! There's going to be a party at the château tomorrow and they'll all be kicking up their heels to your records."

"Bloody cheek!"

"I won't be invited, of course, but Sabine's been ordered to go, although there's talk of bringing in some whores from Paris to make up the numbers. That will wipe the smile off her face."

"You mean she actually cracks a smile occasionally?" asked Nicholas Garnier in wonder. "I never get so much as a *bonjour* when I collect the new film reels from her."

"Oh, there's more to that woman than you'd think. She's not much to look at, I know, but separate her from that uniform and..."

Nicholas held up a hand. "Please, I don't even want to think about it."

"Well, *you* haven't been told that it's your patriotic duty to screw sensitive information out of her."

"I don't think Father Ferdinand put it quite like that, Bertrand," chided Thérèse, who was still just as uncomfortable with the idea.

"Maybe not, but the end justifies the means, eh, Gaston?" The butcher put down his glass.

"Only as long as there's something that justifies the end."

Chapter 11

Thérèse was puzzled. "I don't understand the need for soldiers to be billeted in the village. Surely there's enough room for them all at their *Kommandatur*."

"There is. More than enough since the Colonel sent so much stuff back to Germany. He's requisitioned furniture and paintings that have been in the family since well before the Revolution."

"Requisitioned, indeed! It's theft, pure and simple, and I'll bet it hasn't all gone to Berlin."

"You're right there. Sabine does the paperwork and thinks that the Köstlers will have the best furnished house in Munich."

"Until the Allies drop a bomb on it."

"The Countess has threatened to report him to his superiors, but he's got friends in high places and doesn't care."

"Poor lady! She'll be heartbroken."

"Anyway, with all that space he's created, there must be plenty of room for extra beds, so why do we have to house his soldiers?"

"Because he wants his men dotted around to keep a closer eye on everyone. He's sending out the best French speakers, so you'll have to watch what you say. Father Ferdinand was up there this morning, trying again to convince him that there just isn't room for an extra person in most homes, but Köstler's got no more respect for the clergy than he has for the aristocracy. He threatened him with deportations as a way of freeing up enough beds."

"Oh my God! I thought only factory workers were being rounded up and sent to Germany."

"That was so in the beginning, but there weren't enough of them to meet the demand."

"We'd better make some room, then. I don't suppose they'd choose you, Valentin, but I couldn't bear it if they took Luc."

In her anxiety, Thérèse didn't seem to notice that she'd cut her brother to the quick.

It was hard not to warm to a lodger as unfailingly considerate and polite as Sergeant Stracke. During the first awkward week, he ate his meals separately, but then he asked if he might join the family at the kitchen table when the café was closed. He even offered to help with the washing up, which was more than Luc ever did. He showed them photographs of his family back in Lower Saxony and spoke with obvious longing about walking in the mountains and fishing for carp in the Weser. Only when other people were around was there a return to chilly formality.

No doubt it was the same in many other homes, but what went on behind closed doors was only revealed after the Liberation and not always then. Some Germans treated their unwilling hosts with contempt and were loathed. Others became almost part of the family once the mothers sensed the homesick boys behind the hated uniforms. One such was the daughter-in-law of the veteran who'd had such a narrow escape during the first weeks of the Occupation. Old Jules nearly burst a blood vessel when the young soldier, touched by her kindness, insisted on assembling the entire household on their doorstep for a photograph to send to his *Mutti*.

"What must our neighbours think?" he grumbled to Luc. "We can't even get rid of the copy he had framed for us."

"Well, I've seen it," Thérèse reassured him, "and only a fool would imagine that any of you were comfortable with the situation." The cheerful young man in the centre of the group, his arms around the shoulders of two of the grandsons, was the only person whose smile looked genuine. "Just be grateful that you've got that lad and not some of the others who come in here!"

She was relieved that her own lodger preferred music to photography. Sergeant Stracke treated the old upright piano in the café with respect, unlike the soldiers who hammered the keys and stood their glasses on the polished top. The popular tunes of the day he left to others, preferring the works of Bach and Mozart, and he always waited until the café was quiet before he sat down at the instrument. It hadn't been tuned since before the war and he was sadly out of practice at first, but Thérèse loved to listen and always left the kitchen door open when he was playing.

This pleasure, shared to an extent by Valentin and Luc, went some way towards making up for the irritation he caused during the night. Sergeant Stracke's snoring, which never woke *him* up, reverberated throughout the whole building. He sheepishly admitted that his own family had often threatened to make him sleep in the garden. As that wasn't an option open to the Gaudets, he tried to make it up to them by offering extra rations, which they always refused.

Such scruples weren't shared by everyone. Angèle Duval, who had tricked her husband into marrying her in the first place, had broken her wedding vows long before Rankert and Meyer managed to get themselves billeted together at the couple's *bar-tabac* and she was very happy to accept anything they brought home. Marius, long past caring what his wife got up to, turned a blind eye and a deaf ear.

"Doesn't it bother him that you call your Germans by their Christian names?" asked Thérèse one day as they waited in the patient queue at the bakery.

"No, and I'll bet you do the same with yours when no one's listening."

"I most certainly do not and I'm always Madame Gaudet to him."

"Oh, hoity toity!"

"The difference between us, Angèle, is that I know my duty to my husband and my country. Don't judge me by your own low standards!" There was a round of applause from everyone else in the shop and Angèle never forgave her.

As another Christmas approached, it seemed as though the Occupation would go on forever and it was hard to find anything to celebrate. The Germans had taken over the whole of the country, the French fleet had scuttled itself at Toulon and the winter promised to be even harder and hungrier than the two that had gone before.

The death rate was rising everywhere as semi-starvation took its toll of the elderly, who often gave up their own rations to feed their younger relatives. Severe vitamin deficiency was inevitable on a diet where swede was the only vegetable readily available and citrus fruit a distant memory. Newborn babies were dying at a far greater rate than usual and tuberculosis was on the increase. Some people, desperate for food, continued to claim rations for relatives who had died. Discovery meant imprisonment and informers were never in short supply.

"Do you think there's any point in going into the forest for a Yule log?" Valentin asked his sister one morning as they were getting ready to open the café. "It's probably the only sort of log we'll be getting this year. No hope of a chocolate one, I suppose?"

Thérèse gave a hollow laugh. "Not for us, but there's going to be one for each table at the château."

"I thought they'd be having German specialities like they did last year."

"No. Bertrand told me that it's going to be French style, a true *réveillon* feast with nothing left out."

"Except French people to eat it?"

"Of course. Philippe and Yvette Legoux have been ordered to go up there to make all the desserts."

"Why can't they make them in their own shop?"

"Because the ingredients are coming from Paris and Colonel Köstler doesn't trust them not to set some aside for themselves or their regular customers. Can you just imagine? Whole trays of petits fours, eclairs... It makes my mouth water just to think about them."

Delicious as those treats sounded, they weren't what Valentin most yearned for. Before the Occupation, the Christmas displays in the window of the pâtisserie had been spectacular and the centrepiece had always been an enormous *bûche de Noël*. The chocolate coating had lines and knots, just like a real log, and was decorated with a drift of icing sugar, little images of Father Christmas, nuts, roses, elves and a big sprig of holly. The Busselles had tried to compete with a *bûche* made of colourful vegetables in aspic or chilled pâté, but Valentin had a sweet tooth and those had never appealed to him half as much.

After more thought, he decided that they really shouldn't go without a Yule log to light before they went to midnight Mass. No *réveillon* would await their return, but at least there would be some warmth. His parents thought the same, so he accompanied two of his brothers into the forest. They would have accomplished the task much faster without him, but Joseph hero-worshipped Hubert and Valentin was under orders to keep them both out of trouble. He needn't have worried. Unlike in previous years, when people had almost come to blows over the best logs and everyone had returned with armfuls of holly and mistletoe, there was hardly anyone else about. Dragging their finds back down to the village was hard work and Joseph insisted on stopping for a rest.

"Don't you know that sitting on a Yule log will give you boils?" teased Valentin. Hubert, who knew full well that it was an old wives' tale, backed him up.

"Valentin's right and the doctor will have to lance them for you. Your bum will hurt a lot more than when you get on the wrong side of Papa." Joseph sprang to his feet immediately at the thought of Dr Simmonet, forced out of retirement since the disappearance of the Abrahams, wielding a scalpel over his nether regions.

On a bitterly cold and windy Christmas Eve, Valentin and Thérèse picked their way carefully across the square towards the church. Luc had stayed behind in the café, part of a small huddled group deep in conversation, and promised to join them as soon as he could. The ice squeaked under their worn boots as they walked along and their breath formed clouds in front of them. It was beyond the power even of the Germans to impose a blackout on the full moon and they could see throngs of people heading the same way. In a rare good mood because of his party or because he thought the locals too cowed to cause any trouble, Colonel Köstler had lifted the curfew for one night to allow the traditional service to go ahead. In other areas, the Mass had had to be celebrated a day early and in the afternoon at that. The few soldiers supposed to be on patrol were sheltering in shop doorways, stamping their feet in attempt to keep warm. Their rifles were slung casually over their shoulders and they had cigarettes cupped into their palms like convicts.

"I could almost feel sorry for them," said Valentin.

"Well I couldn't. I just wish that Bertrand hadn't told me what's on the menu for the Germans tonight. Oysters, canapés, pâté de foie gras, goose with prune and pâté stuffing, cheese, fruit, nuts..."

"And they'll be drinking the wine cellar dry."

"There can't be much left in there now. Don't you waste your sympathy on the Germans! The Countess is the one who needs your pity. She'll be all alone in the east wing with nothing but her memories. Do you remember those wonderful Christmases before the war, when she used to hold open house for friends and relations from all over France?"

"Of course I do, especially when you were old enough to help out with the extra work and Papa took you up there with him. You always came back with lots of leftovers for the rest of us. We missed those after you married Luc."

Father Ferdinand, who had changed his Advent purple for white, wore his usual expression of good humoured tranquillity. He had done his best to make the church look festive. Every candle he could lay his hands on was blazing and the crèche was as magnificent and ornate as ever, but the spirits of his parishioners were very low. How could it be otherwise with no feast to return to and only disappointment in store for the children.

Valentin couldn't get the face of his youngest sister out of his mind. He'd found her in tears after she'd been told that there was no point in putting her shoes by the hearth because no one would be coming. It was a cruel blow and so unlike previous years. Their father could make almost anything out of a few pieces of wood and left over paint and the older boys never forgot the toy farm he'd made for them one year. Complete in every detail, it had been the talk of the village. Their mother usually dressed dolls for the girls and sewed, knitted or crocheted enough gloves, hats and scarves to keep everyone warm throughout the year to come. Now, though, they had nothing left to work with.

"It's not fair," the little girl had sobbed. "I've been ever so good and *Père Noël* hasn't even seen my new shoes." Having already been worn by two of her sisters, they were shabbier than those she'd outgrown, but she was proud of them. "Do you think he'll change his mind if we leave out a drink for him and something for his donkey to eat?"

"I don't know, sweetheart." What else could he say? Of all the deprivations his family had suffered so far, that had to be the worst.

Hungry, exhausted and humiliated, they needed a miracle: an angel to come down from the heavens with a fiery sword to put the enemy to flight. Anything to restore hope and dignity. Little did Valentin know then that his angel was already preparing to land.

Chapter 12

Valentin was on his knees, acutely conscious of the damp rising from the stone flags, when the big oak door at the back of the church creaked open and the sudden draught blew out the nearest candles. There were footsteps, whispering, more footsteps and then the door closed again. Father Ferdinand carried on with the Mass as though nothing had occurred, but his housekeeper pursed her lips and peered suspiciously into the gloom.

There was still no sign of Luc when they left the church and went home. Thérèse wouldn't hear of going to bed without knowing where he was and Valentin, although weary, was unwilling to leave her on her own. Fortified by a glass of mulled wine with a pinch of precious cinnamon in it as a special treat, they settled down by the hearth to wait. The embers of the Yule log were still sending out plenty of sparks, sign of a good harvest in years gone by, when Luc returned. He was accompanied by a short bulky figure in camouflage colours. A hand reached out in greeting and, like a butterfly from its chrysalis, a slender young woman emerged from her parachute suit. It was love at first sight for Valentin, peering at her in the firelight. The newcomer had a classically beautiful face, oval with a straight nose, high cheekbones and the liveliest green eyes that he'd ever seen. They sparkled whenever she laughed, which she did a lot.

"Good morning. I'm very pleased to meet you. My name is Fleur. Sorry about the outfit. I'd have buried it with my parachute at the rendez-vous point, but your reception committee was very punctual and there was no sign of any Germans. Intelligence knew about the party and there was plenty of time for London to plan the perfect drop." She paused for breath and laughed again as Luc unselfconsciously raised his overcoat to warm his behind at the hearth.

Thérèse recovered herself. "Please, Mademoiselle, come and sit by the fire. You must be chilled to the bone as well."

Fleur beamed at her. "It's very kind of you, Madame, but I'm quite warm already." It was no wonder. The parachute suit was roomy enough for her to wear both a raincoat and an overcoat on top of her other clothes. From a pocket inside, she pulled a battered brown leather briefcase. "I was supposed to have a special pad in here to protect my spine, but I thought this would be more useful. Luc was kind enough to carry my two little suitcases. They came down after me and I'm glad they didn't land on my head."

Waving away Thérèse's offer of food and wine, she continued, "No, thank you. I'm still a little queasy and just need to sleep it off. My air sickness pills weren't much good and the flight was rather bumpy. I'm grateful to have landed safely, though. Not like the poor chap who broke his leg and had to be trundled off in a wheelbarrow. The farmer who found him had the nerve to tell the Germans that he'd been knocked down by one of their vehicles and their own doctor set his leg for him."

Sergeant Stracke was spending the night at the château, so there was no need to tiptoe around. Luc disappeared into the darkness again on some mysterious errand of his own and Fleur shared the big bed in their room with Thérèse. When Christmas Day dawned bright and sunny, she was still asleep.

"She looks as though she hasn't a care in the world," said Thérèse over breakfast.

"Well I have," retorted Valentin. "I'm twenty years old now and yet you and Luc still treat me like a child. You could have told me what was going on."

"I didn't know myself until she arrived. Only that there was a chance of a British agent being sent here."

"British?"

"Yes, I know. Her French is as good as ours. Better, probably. But she's British all right."

"Well, I still think you could have told me."

Thérèse reached over to pat his cheek. "I'm sorry, Valentin. It's just that I'm so used to seeing you as my little brother."

"Is that why I was the last to know that you're expecting? You think I'm too young to know how babies are made? The way your bed squeaks sometimes is worse than Stracke's snoring. I can hear it from the attic."

She flushed with embarrassment. "Then this is your lucky day. You won't hear it from the store room."

"What do you mean by that?"

"She means that Fleur will be moving into the attic when she wakes up." Luc had returned, dark circles under his eyes and failing to suppress a yawn.

"Are you mad?" protested Valentin. "You can't have a British agent and a German NCO under the same roof."

"Yes we can. While he's here, none of the others will bother us. We're going to pass Fleur off as a distant cousin of mine who's just lost her husband. She's here to help us out at least until the baby's born. Well, you know everything now, Valentin. Can we trust you to keep your mouth shut?"

"Of course you can. Don't be ridiculous."

"Who's ridiculous?" Fleur walked in, rubbing her eyes and apologising for having overslept. "Merry Christmas, everyone. I've brought you some presents. I hope you smoke, Luc, because yours is my dear departed's cigarette case with his initials on it." Luc was delighted and lost no time in discarding his crumpled Gauloises packet. He offered one of his precious cigarettes to Fleur who hesitated and then declined.

"Better not," she said. "I've been briefed that most French women don't smoke and I need to blend in."

"You're right about that," said Thérèse, "and only men get them as part of their rations."

"Do you smoke in England?" asked Valentin, curious to find out as much as he could about the newcomer.

"Like a chimney, I'm afraid," she confessed, "but I'm sure that I'll be able to manage without while I'm over here. Look, I've got some hand-kerchiefs for you. They've got my late husband's initials on them too."

The airy way in which she was disposing of the poor man's property seemed rather cold blooded to Valentin.

"Thank you, but I'd rather not."

There was silence for a moment and then she said, "Oh, my dear, I'm so sorry. You don't understand about these things or about the scarf that I've brought for your sister. See, the label is French."

"But where did you get them all from?"

"The same place I got everything else, including my excellent papers. There are a lot of French refugees in England and they help the war effort by donating items to back up our agents' cover stories. Now then, do you have a cup of coffee for me?"

"Not proper coffee, I'm afraid," apologised Thérèse. "Our lodger offered to get us some, but we turned him down."

"Quite right." All the same, Fleur pulled a face at the horrible brew the others had become used to and settled for a piece of bread and a glass of milk. Breakfast over, she picked up her two little suitcases and set off for the attic.

Valentin, desperate to help, reached out to take them from her and found them much heavier than he'd expected. All the same, he refused to admit defeat and struggled up the narrow staircase with one in each hand.

"Thank you so much. You're a real gentleman. Oh, what a lot of books you've got!"

"You're welcome to read them. Do you like French literature?"

"Very much and it's kind of you to leave them here for me. You must hate being turned out of your room. I'm sorry about that."

"This isn't really my room anyway," he confessed. "I lost that when Sergeant Stracke moved in. It's my pleasure to make way for you, though." Valentin was quite sincere about that. Just the thought of her lying there with one of his books at her elbow left him in a happy glow that continued all day.

The German looked a little worse for wear when he came back from the party, but he was as polite as always. Before he disappeared upstairs, he wished everyone a merry Christmas and casually dropped something onto the kitchen table. It was almost a whole *bûche de Noël*, carefully wrapped in greaseproof paper. Just for once, their principles went to the wall, although they saved a share for the rest of the family.

When Fleur was introduced to Stracke later that day, he gave her papers only a cursory glance and said that he was very sorry to hear of her loss. She cast her eyes down and thanked him for his kind words.

Once everyone's curiosity about a new face had died down, Fleur was able to fit into village life as easily as she'd hoped. She certainly looked the part with clothes and shoes as shabby as anyone else's. To be well dressed and shod in those days was a sure sign that you were in the enemy's good graces. Garments were patched and darned until they fell to bits; shoes stuffed with cardboard and resoled with wood when leather became impossible to obtain.

Although very well briefed, Fleur was still aware that the tiniest mistake could give her away. One such occurred when she started to spoon her soup away from her in what Valentin assumed to be the English fashion. While Thérèse distracted Stracke with the offer of a second helping, Luc nudged her elbow and filled his spoon correctly. She caught on at once and followed his example. It was hard to believe that the genial German could send them all to their deaths, but they feared that his sense of duty might overwhelm any feelings of good will towards his hosts.

From that point onwards, Fleur's table manners were impeccably French and she was as unobtrusive as possible. She busied herself around the living quarters during the day and rarely entered the café. It was a different matter at night, once Stracke was asleep. Valentin was made to sit at the top of the stairs during the secret meetings to warn those below if the snoring, now seen as a blessing, should stop. Usually the German was only turning over in bed, but once or twice the nocturnal visitors had to leave hurriedly when he clattered downstairs for a glass of water.

There was no shortage of potential volunteers for even the most dangerous acts of resistance. The countryside was beginning to fill up with young men determined to avoid being sent off to Germany as forced labour. Many, later to be known as the Maquis, took to the woods by day, slept in barns and empty farmhouses and went raiding for food. Trusting a stranger was a very risky business and stories were circulating of betrayals by informers and double agents.

Luc was very cautious at first and only the friends who'd accompanied him the night Fleur landed were invited to the first meeting. They gathered round the kitchen table and spoke in such low voices that Valentin had to strain to catch their words. If ever he edged closer, Luc waved him impatiently back to his post. Valentin very much resented being allocated such a subordinate role, especially as Alain Binard, not much older than he, was a member of the inner circle. It felt just like being back at school and unwelcome in the big boys' playground.

Fleur did most of the talking and soon inspired respect and confidence in all the men, even those old enough to be her father. "The day is coming," she said, "when the Germans will be driven out of your country for good, but it will be necessary for loyal French people to do the groundwork. You're needed principally to sabotage transport and communications. Every soldier the enemy has to take from the front line to guard a railway bridge, canal lock, petrol storage tank or telephone line is another blow struck for France. The RAF will drop everything you need: plastic explosives, guns..."

"That's all very well," said a doubtful voice. "We all know about guns, but who's going to train us to blow up bridges and the rest? I've never even seen plastic explosive."

"London is aware of that, Monsieur. I've been sent in first to liaise with you. Soon an *instructeur-saboteur* will be arriving to direct operations in the field. Until a third agent can be spared, I'll be doubling as a courier and radio operator, but I'll need your help. You've got a bicycle for me already, Luc, haven't you?"

"Yes, of course, and this young man here has made sure that it's road worthy."

"Thank you, Monsieur. That's very good of you."

"Not at all, Mademoiselle."

"Oh, please call me Fleur."

"Then you must call me Alain."

"Your cover story is good," continued Luc as the two smiled at each other and Valentin experienced an even deeper pang of jealousy. "Everyone will understand a young widow sick with grief needing to spend time alone and so you should be able to walk or cycle around without exciting suspicion. I never thought to ask, but I suppose you do know how to ride a bike?"

"I certainly do, but the question isn't as silly as you might think. One girl I heard about, who'd done umpteen courses on demolition and weapons training, had never learnt and nearly broke her neck on the dreadful old machine she was given when she first arrived in France. It had no brakes and the tyres were stuffed with hay, but she refused to give up and mastered it eventually." Fleur waited for the laughter to stop and then continued, "As for other equipment, I brought as much as I could and the *instructeur-saboteur* will bring more as soon as it can be arranged. In the meantime, I'll need assistance to reconnoitre suitable landing grounds and find farmers willing to store arms and help with transport. Then I'll transmit the co-ordinates to London."

"I'd be happy to help you in any way I can." Valentin had nearly fallen down the stairs in his eagerness to volunteer. The men around the table looked sceptical, but Fleur peered up into the gloom, smiled and accepted his offer.

Thérèse was curious. "Why has our area been chosen? It's put up no serious resistance to the Germans so far."

"That's exactly why. They'll be caught completely off guard to begin with. Also, the location is ideal. It's close to Paris and yet the proximity of the forest will give everyone involved an excellent chance of getting away after an operation."

So it began. Although the weather continued bitterly cold and there was snow on the ground most of the time, the following few weeks were the happiest of Valentin's life. He and Fleur went out together nearly every day on some pretext or other. Bundled up in the warmest clothes she had and wearing Thérèse's rubber boots with Luc's spare socks underneath, she still enchanted him. He was acutely aware at first of slowing her down, but she didn't seem to mind and never once referred to his disability. Sometimes they went into the forest to collect bundles of firewood and one day Valentin took her up to the old fort. The Germans had checked it out when they first arrived, but there was no indication that they'd been back since. The place looked as grim and deserted as ever and theirs were the only footsteps in the snow.

"It's just as well that your brother can't walk very fast," she told Thérèse one evening. "I've been told that Englishwomen take longer strides than Frenchwomen and you never know who's watching!"

"Also, he looks so harmless that the Germans would never suspect him of anything untoward."

Soon Fleur knew everyone in the immediate area and was ready to go further afield. It was the cause of much private mirth when Stracke stopped a German soldier from requisitioning her bicycle and smilingly assured her that it wouldn't happen again as long as he remained in the village. She was part of his host's family, after all.

It only took her a few days to choose a landing ground and then she sent the information to London while he was on duty. Valentin watched Fleur in fascination as she unpacked and assembled her radio. Once the crystal was inserted, she threw the end of the aerial out of the window and started to tap out her message in Morse code. Before long, her dark head bent in concentration, she was scribbling down the reply. She pored over it for a few minutes and then burnt the scrap of paper in the kitchen fire. The radio parts disappeared back into her suitcases and the attic returned to normal.

"Did it take you long to learn how to do all that?" he asked.

"Not really. I suppose I've got flexible fingers after all the piano lessons my parents made me have."

"Will you play for us some time?"

"I'd better not. It might cause suspicion, especially if your German lodger asks me to play a duet!"

Chapter 13

By the next full moon, Fleur had struck up a friendship with Judith Perthuis and Vincent was persuaded to allow a plane to land in the flat meadow behind his farm. His mother wasn't happy with the plan and added it to the long list of things she had against Judith. The only positives were her little grandchildren, upon whom she doted.

Before the daylight faded, the landing ground had been cleared of obstacles and then Valentin was sent back to the café, boiling with frustration at not being allowed to do more.

Luc had been blunt. "Look, you'd put us all in danger if the Germans turned up. You couldn't run away and we couldn't leave you." Being forced to experience all the excitement second hand was yet another blow to his manhood.

Just before two in the morning, the little group laid out most of the bicycle lamps they'd been able to collect into a long straight line, with just two forming a right angle at one end. Then they waited in the doorway of Vincent's barn to listen out for the plane. As soon as they heard the drone and saw the Lysander coming over the dark line of the forest, Fleur switched on her torch and flashed the agreed signal. The pilot flashed back and everyone ran out to switch on the lamps.

To their relief, the plane landed smoothly and taxied along the line laid out for it. A passenger in a long beige raincoat and battered trilby came down the fixed ladder, several boxes were thrown out after him and then the plane ran back down the line into the wind for take-off. It climbed steeply and disappeared into the night sky.

Sick with fear that the Germans might be on their way, everyone rushed to pick up the boxes and carry or drag them into the shelter of the barn. They pushed most of them under the straw and hay behind Vincent's cows and the others joined Adolphe in his sty. Then the group scattered and headed homewards.

Having two British agents under one roof was considered far too much of a risk and the Binards had offered to help out, so it was the following day when Valentin met the new arrival. He was much older than Fleur, with silver tips already showing in his dark hair. A neat moustache gave him an air of authority that overrode the ill fitting suit and stained shirt with its frayed collar and cuffs. Fleur greeted him warmly. They chatted for a few minutes in their own language and then switched apologetically into French. The new agent spoke fluently, although he'd never have been able to pass for a native speaker in the way that Fleur did.

"Brave men, those Lysander pilots," he said. "The chap who flew me over hates it when the bomber crews call them taxi drivers. According to him, any clot can strut around in a leather jacket and fly four engines." Valentin laughed uncertainly and Fleur had to explain to him later how British airmen used mocking humour to keep up morale. It was their way of staving off nervous nausea and the explosive diarrhoea stirring in their bowels every time they climbed into their planes.

When the rest of the men arrived, Paul said, "Fleur has already given you some idea of what lies ahead. Plans are already in hand for the Allied invasion and people like yourselves are needed to sabotage the enemy from within, even at the risk to your own lives and those of your families." There was a pause as he studied each face in turn and added, "If you wish to back out, do so now, but be warned. If information about our activities reaches the Germans, you'll be at the top of our list of suspects. Luc feels sure that he can trust every one of you and I hope he's right, but no one can know for certain what his neighbour will do under pressure or when faced with temptation." No one moved. "Fine," he continued, "I'll train you and the volunteers you recruit in the use of Sten guns, Bren guns and plastic explosives. I'll demonstrate how to lay charges, blow up targets and carry out ambushes. In addition, you'll learn how to stalk a sentry and knock him out without making a sound."

"You mean by using a silencer?" asked Alain.

"No. He might cry out and alert his colleagues. I mean by covering his mouth from behind with one hand while you bring your knife round into his stomach. That way, you still have him gagged when he collapses. Do you think you could all do that?"

"No need to ask a butcher!" joked Gaston Busselle.

Henri Devane nodded too. "I've got some excellent knives in my shop."

Alain was less sure. "It would be with no warning and in cold blood. I don't think I could bring myself to do it."

"Well I could," said his mother. "I'd only have to remind myself what the Boche did to my home town during the last war and this lot are much worse. Just give me a Bren gun and I'll take out a few of them myself." Paul looked at her in admiration, seeing a rare woman with the strength to shoulder and carry round such a heavy weapon.

"You're an example to us all, Madame. Now then, the most important thing to bear in mind for the moment is that new members of this group can be vouched for. Any weak link in the chain could get us all shot or worse."

"What could possibly be worse?" asked Valentin.

"Being arrested and taken to Paris to face the torturers of the Gestapo. We've had terrible reports of what goes on in their headquarters."

There was silence for a few seconds and then Luc spoke up. "You can count on everyone in this room and on my wife too. Thérèse is in a delicate condition and wouldn't hurt a fly in any case, but she'll help in other ways and you can certainly rely on her discretion."

Leaving his wife and brother-in-law to watch over Stracke, Luc sneaked out most nights and joined the others at Paul's new base in the old fort. Occasionally Valentin accompanied Fleur up there during the daytime, always with a cover story of gathering kindling or foraging for edible plants. He knew better than to put himself through the humiliation of being rejected for combat missions but eagerly took part in the cleaning and greasing of weapons, using olive oil or bacon fat to make up for any lack of gun oil.

Madeleine Binard was never allowed to fire a Bren gun at the enemy. Despite what Paul had said at the meeting, he feared that the men, particularly her son, would lose focus in a tight corner and try to protect her. It was left to Fleur to tell her that in as tactful a manner as possible.

"There will be plenty of other ways to help, you know. Alain tells me that you can build just about anything. Perhaps you'd look at these diagrams I brought over with me." Furious at first, Madeleine rose to the new challenge and turned her attention to keeping the radio transmissions going once the Germans sensed active resistance in the area. By that time, it would be far too dangerous to send messages from anyone's home and the radio operator would have to move around a lot.

One evening she drew everyone into a dark recess at the back of the garage to demonstrate a pedal generator she'd built from spare parts, mostly taken from an old bicycle. It was a weird but effective contraption, the first of many ingenious devices she came up with.

The radio equipment was hidden in a bundle of sticks collected from the forest. Madeleine stuck some short ones into the holes she'd bored into each end of the box containing the radio and then made an outer casing of longer sticks to nail on top. The aerial was used to bind the whole thing together and not even the sharpest eyed onlooker would have spotted anything out of the ordinary. Everyone needed fuel and people walking or cycling around with firewood were a common sight.

By moving constantly, Fleur was able to keep to what she called her *skeds*, messages sent three times a week using pre-arranged wavelengths and codes. This was much easier in the countryside than in Paris, where many radio operators were caught by German direction finding equipment. There were stories about Gestapo officers lurking on street corners, the turned up collars of their heavy overcoats concealing earphones. Agents in the capital received urgent orders to transmit for no more than five minutes at a time and no more than twenty minutes a day altogether.

More supplies were needed before the group could carry out its first assignment and the parade ground was chosen for the drop. That it was very overgrown didn't matter, because the Halifax wouldn't need to land.

Thérèse had been feeling unwell for several hours and went to bed as soon as Fleur and Luc set off that night. It was just as well that Valentin had promised to stay awake and let her know as soon as they were safely back. A gentle but persistent tapping on the kitchen window alerted him to the unexpected arrival of Bertrand Baltzinger, sweating despite the cold weather and out of breath.

"Where's Luc?" he gasped. "I've got to warn him."

"Warn him about what, for heaven's sake? He's been asleep for hours."

"You don't need to pretend with me, Shorty. Colonel Köstler has received some intelligence about a parachute drop on his patch. He doesn't know where it's going to be, but he's got patrols ready to set off at the first sign of a plane. You're just going to have to trust me, if only for your sister's sake. You haven't got a hope of getting to Luc in time yourself. Now where is he?"

Valentin had no choice but to tell him and Baltzinger took off into the darkness. He got there in time, the drop was aborted and everyone returned home unscathed.

From that point onwards, Baltzinger was an accepted member of the group.

"Why don't you ever use your friend's Christian name?" Fleur asked Valentin once, but she only got a shrug in reply and didn't pursue the matter. Baltzinger's strength and contacts were invaluable and he helped with the next drop, which was a complete success. The supplies arrived in heavy cylindrical metal drums with flat lids. Two hinged handles on each made them easy to carry and they soon disappeared into the tunnels. Then the secret entrances were camouflaged again and all traces of recent activity erased from the area.

The Germans had grown more suspicious, though, and outsmarting them was becoming very dangerous. Sergeant Stracke remained as pleasant as ever, if a little more guarded in his manner, but some of the soldiers became increasingly belligerent towards the locals. The curfew was enforced earlier and more rigorously and there were extra patrols. Nevertheless, the founder members of the resistance group risked taking more people into their confidence.

When it became impossible to get petrol except on the black market, Madeleine converted the baker's van into a *gazogène* that ran on a charcoal burner. Robert Bail used to hide rifles in between the long loaves when he was making deliveries to the outlying farms. Sometimes he even had the nerve to begin his round at the château, where soldiers would help him to unload the Germans' daily order.

The priest risked his life many times carrying messages around his parish. Many of the clergy were collaborators but not Father Ferdinand. He was always dashing around on his bicycle and it never seemed to occur to the enemy that he was on any other but church business.

Fleur was the most resourceful of all. One day she stumbled as she was crossing the square and dropped her handbag in front of a passing soldier. As always, it contained a loaded pistol. The German gallantly picked it up for her and commented on its weight. She gazed up at him, her eyes dark and deadened with grief.

"Well, you know, Monsieur, there are so many things that we poor widows can't bear to part with. I carry all my mementoes of my poor husband everywhere I go. I expect that your wife will do the same if she ever finds herself in my sad situation."

"I sincerely hope that she will never have to." His face started to work and he hurried away.

The British agents were sure that German search parties would home in on the fort sooner or later and wanted to delay them for as long as possible. Paul introduced the group to tyre bursters, mini mines disguised with papier mâché to look like animal droppings or local rocks.

"We're going to lay them at intervals along the track," he said. "Where the earth is soft, it's necessary to put a stone underneath to stop them from being pushed in without exploding."

"What will happen if an animal treads on them," asked Alain, worried that some innocent forest creature would be blown up. Gaston snorted in disbelief and the other men guffawed too.

Only Fleur shot him a sympathetic glance and said, "No. That won't happen. I'll show you how they work." She found a stick and drew a diagram in the soil. "This outer case has overlapping halves; a ring of high explosive and a pressure switch. It takes at least seventy kilos to make the two halves telescope and set off the charge." Alain thanked her and held out one of his big paws with its permanently black nails. A bolt of jealousy shot through Valentin when he saw Fleur's tiny hand disappearing into it.

The morning after the group's first attempt to sabotage a railway line, Luc was in tears at the kitchen table. He wiped them away when he saw his brother-in-law staring at him in horror but was too choked up to speak.

Valentin refused to be put off. "What's happened? Was somebody killed?" His greatest fear was that it might have been Fleur, but a tiny part of him that he felt guilty about hoped that Alain might have perished.

"No!" said Luc at last. "I just can't believe that I was so stupid. All that work for nothing and the others will probably never trust me again."

"Why? What went wrong?"

"I made a silly mistake. We were after a troop train on its way to Paris. The others rigged up some dummy fog signals and laid the charge and it was my job to fix the spring adaptors holding the detonators. I put the bloody things the wrong way round on the rail. The flange of the locomotive just cut them off and made the charge useless. We stood there like idiots watching the train disappearing into the distance. The whole operation was a complete failure, a waste of time and materials, and it's all my fault."

Thérèse refused to let him wallow in self pity. "Pull yourself together, Luc!" she said sharply. "I'm sure you'll do better next time." She placed a comforting hand on his shoulder to make up for the harsh words.

"Listen to your wife!" said Fleur, who'd walked into the kitchen unnoticed. "We were disappointed, yes, but no one is as angry with you as you are with yourself. The only failure, you know, would be if we all stopped trying." In an attempt to cheer him up, she went on to tell him about another group who'd waited all night in the freezing cold for trains that never arrived. Unknown to them, patriots at the other end of the line had already siphoned abrasive grease into the lubrication points of the engines.

"Imagine their frustration!" she concluded.

"Does that often happen," asked Valentin, "that different groups get under each other's feet?"

"Unfortunately, yes. Lack of liaison is the price we must pay for secrecy."

A few days later, the scene at the breakfast table was a happier one. The local group had chalked up a modest success, managing to derail a goods train on a branch line some way from Saint-André-la-Forêt. They all got away safely and there were no immediate repercussions. Unfortunately, success bred ambition and it wasn't long before a chain of events was set in motion that would touch every family in the village.

Chapter 14

Baltzinger was breathless with excitement. "I've found us some sitting ducks! You know how Colonel Köstler likes to show off? He's just invited some Nazi bigwigs for the weekend and promised to send the Daimler up to Paris to collect them."

Paul was sceptical. "Surely not. They wouldn't risk driving around the countryside in anything less than an armoured car."

"They might, you know," said Fleur. "Some of them are arrogant enough. Heydrich refused an armed escort and used to travel round Prague in an open top Mercedes."

"Yes, until someone tossed a grenade into it and killed the bastard." If he'd mentioned how many innocent Czechs had died in the reprisals, the group might have thought better of it, but he just said, "It might be worth a try. See what else you can find out, lad."

Baltzinger was soon back with the news that the enemy's desire to show off was to be tempered with caution. The Daimler would be escorted by soldiers on a pair of motorcycle combinations. Each of the sidecars would have a machine gun mounted across it on a bar.

"Piece of cake," said Paul. "We'll lay charges on that narrow bridge just before the garage."

"What about the outriders?"

"Don't worry. We'll take care of them. Now, that isn't a straight stretch of road and we're going to need someone to give us a signal before the convoy gets too close to the bridge. Someone who's good at climbing trees."

"That sounds like young Hubert," said Luc.

"No!" protested his wife. "My brother's too young to get involved in this and our parents wouldn't let him anyway."

"Then we won't tell them. He's old enough now to make his own mind up and he's been dying to have a go at the Germans ever since that business with the eggs."

Hubert jumped at the chance to be the lookout man and joined the others as they blackened their faces and hands with burnt cork. As soon as it grew dark, he clambered high into the gnarled branches of an old oak and settled himself down for the long wait. Not only did he have an excellent view in both directions, but he was equipped with Fleur's torch and a brand new battery that he was strictly forbidden to waste. The torch had coloured filters and she hoped that her trust in him would overrule any boyish desire to play with it.

Paul's preparations complete, he settled down in the undergrowth on the right hand side of the road, ready to detonate the charges. Alain and Luc took up their positions on the left. About five hundred metres beyond the bridge, Gaston and Henri had fastened one end of a steel cable round the trunk of a tough old hornbeam and were ready to stretch it across the road to knock the leading rider off his motorcycle. They all lay motionless for two hours, although very few vehicles went by. By the time Hubert's signal came, it took a big effort to force their cold, cramped limbs into action. As soon as the first motorcycle escort had passed, Alain and Luc sprang up and threw their tyre bursters into the middle of the road. The driver of the Daimler saw them too late to stop, fought to keep control of the big car and skidded to a halt in the middle of the bridge. There was a flash and a tremendous explosion. The rear escort was too far behind to be caught in the blast, but there was so much smoke and confusion that the soldiers were unable to give chase and everyone got away safely.

An innocent game of Belote was going on at the kitchen table when Stracke appeared later that same night.

"There's going to be hell to pay," he said simply. He'd never sworn in

Thérèse's presence before and she gave him a reproachful look. Putting down her cards, she said,

"Why? What's happened?"

"Are you trying to tell me that you didn't hear all the commotion?"

"Well, we did hear a big bang, now you mention it. We wondered if there'd been an accident, but then we're not allowed out after curfew, as you well know."

"It was no accident. There's been an attack on some guests of the Colonel. An old friend of his and one other passenger in the car are dead, as well as the driver. Not only that, but a soldier from the escort was also killed and another very badly injured." He slumped onto a chair to pull his boots off.

"Did no one in the Daimler survive?" As the words left his mouth, Valentin realised his mistake in being so specific, but Stracke didn't seem to notice.

"Only one person did. A Gestapo officer called Lichtenberg. He was blown clear by the blast and only has a few cuts and bruises."

"That was lucky."

His mouth set in a grim line, Stracke said, "I'm glad you think so, but it certainly won't be lucky for the people responsible."

No one slept that night. When the soldiers banged on the café door just before dawn, Stracke helped them to escort Thérèse, Luc and Valentin into the square and allowed them to join the rest of the Morcel family. The youngest children were clinging to their mother, who was trying to keep them warm under her threadbare coat. It had been a clear night and there was frost on the ground. The area soon filled up with bewildered people, herded like sheep and guarded by troops with fixed bayonets.

Black clouds and a cold wind were coming in from the east and it started to drizzle. Some of the soldiers had allowed people time to dress, but others had turned them out into the street straight from their beds. Old Jules, dressed only in his long winter underwear, stood shivering and humiliated in front of his neighbours.

It was a good hour before a black Mercedes arrived on the scene and two men stepped out. Colonel Köstler was warmly wrapped up in the grey leather coat issued to officers of his rank. His companion, dressed from head to toe in the black favoured by the Gestapo, had a badly bruised face and one arm in a sling. He was shorter and slighter than Köstler, but there was no doubting who was in charge. As he raised the megaphone to his lips, his cold grey eyes swept the waiting crowd in a way that increased their trepidation.

In flawless French, Lichtenberg said, "An outrageous crime against the Third Reich was committed yesterday evening and I have excellent reason to believe that men from this village were responsible. You will remain here until every one of your homes has been thoroughly searched, however long that takes. Be in no doubt that the perpetrators of this atrocity will be tracked down and brought to justice, with or without your cooperation. However, anyone who comes forward with information to speed up this process will be suitably rewarded." He paused for a moment and gave a humourless smile. "Be assured also that any individual attempting to assist these criminals to escape will be considered equally guilty and will pay the full price for his or her actions." With that, he turned on his heel and got back into the car. Colonel Köstler followed him and they were driven away.

Everyone was kept standing for a long time afterwards, but eventually the soldiers allowed the old people to sink gratefully onto the benches around the square and the children to sit cross legged on the ground. Thérèse was in agony with her swollen ankles and Angèle Duval spitefully mimed a pair of horns behind Luc's back when Sergeant Stracke found her a seat. It was brutally cold, nobody had had any breakfast and many were desperate to relieve themselves. There was nowhere for them to go and embarrassing accidents added to their misery.

It was two o'clock in the afternoon when the Mercedes reappeared in the square and old and young alike were ordered back onto their feet. Baltzinger reported later that the search parties had returned before noon, but that had been seen as no reason to postpone lunch in the officers' mess.

Lichtenberg, alone this time, came straight to the point. "We have found no evidence of direct involvement in last night's atrocity. However, all my instincts tell me that there is support in this village for anti-German hostility. It has also been brought to my attention that some incidents haven't been investigated with the necessary rigour and others have been dealt with far too leniently. From today, all this will change. For each of my fellow countrymen killed or badly hurt in the attack, two of yours will be selected." There was uproar and the soldiers guarding the villagers took a tighter grip on their weapons.

Lichtenberg held up a leather gloved hand for silence and continued, "Many of my colleagues would have ordered a firing squad by now. However, the Third Reich needs young, fit labourers and I shall leave the choice up to your leading citizen. *Monsieur le Maire*, please step forward. All eyes turned to the unfortunate official, who was open mouthed with horror. "Of course," added Lichtenberg smoothly, "if you feel unable to perform this little task, I can always double the number and invite someone else to choose."

"No, no. I'll do it."

"Remember, now. No weaklings and no cripples." Valentin flushed, wondering whether someone had pointed him out to the German.

As Massot moved along the stunned ranks of his neighbours, his lips moved in silent apology to the family of each person he chose. The young men and women were lined up, unable to believe what was about to happen to them, when Madame Morcel let out an audible *Dieu merci* that none of her brood had been chosen.

"Oh, it isn't over yet," said a cold voice. "Only ten have been selected, two for each of the other victims of the attack. I too was hurt and claim the right to choose for myself." Looking down his nose at Valentin, he tapped Hubert on the shoulder. There was mayhem as his mother screamed in protest and did her best to hold onto the boy. Thérèse, rushing to grab his other arm, slipped on the wet cobbles and fell flat on her face. As Lichtenberg laughed, Luc took a desperate swing at him, missed and was felled by a single punch from Corporal Meyer.

"When this idiot comes round, tell him that he's just volunteered to be number twelve. And don't treat him too gently."

Each of the deportees was allowed to return home under guard to pack a small case. With Luc still unconscious, Thérèse had to entrust his things to Hubert. He and Jean-Pierre Simmonet, who had also been selected, carried him to the waiting lorry and propped him up between them in the back.

That night, a grief stricken Thérèse miscarried. She hovered between life and death for weeks afterwards, only surviving because Fleur spoon fed her with the extra rations provided by Sergeant Stracke. Her strength returned eventually but not her spirits and she asked Valentin to burn all the little garments intended for her baby. This he couldn't bring himself to do and Fleur offered to keep them out of sight for as long as might be necessary.

As the year dragged on with no word of the deportees, their grieving families had to adjust to life without them. New faces appeared behind the counters of many of the shops as younger brothers and sisters stepped into the shoes of those who'd been taken and Berthe Bail began to help her parents in the bakery. The way she blushed every time Alain Binard passed the window became a standing joke in the village.

"She's wasting her time," said the women in the queue. "Everyone knows that he's only got eyes for the young widow at the café."

Baltzinger reported that the Gestapo officer was staying on indefinitely and keeping everyone, including the Colonel, on their toes. More soldiers were billeted with local families and the pattern of patrols was staggered to catch off guard anyone out after curfew. With no sign of the long hoped for Allied invasion, frustration led to petty quarrels, resentment and a trickle of letters to the enemy authorities. Most were anonymous, others signed and a few written in newly acquired and very bad German.

The Colonel's clerk had the task of sorting through them, sometimes with her young lover sitting on the floor by her desk and running a casual hand up her stockinged leg to distract her.

"Stop that, *Liebchen*! I've got to work. Oh, throw this lot away for me. They're just the usual niggles about shopkeepers showing favouritism to some customers at the expense of others. Oh, and there's one here about that slut at the *bar-tabac*. She's showing off with a new lipstick, so naturally she must have got it on the black market."

"Would you like three guesses as to where she did get it?"

"I only need two. Meyer or Rankert. They share her, so what does it matter? How about a cup of coffee?"

"Yes please. Something nice to go with it?" His hand was probing underneath the elasticated leg of her pastel-blue Directoire knickers.

"Yes, you naughty boy, and maybe some of the Colonel's favourite petits fours afterwards?"

"Lovely. I'll just put these letters on the garden bonfire for you," he lied.

Chapter 15

Unfortunately Baltzinger was at work in the grounds when the note came denouncing the butcher, although he retrieved it later from the office files. At first, Sabine took it as just another complaint about the meat ration, but then she read the rest and laid it before the Colonel.

With enormous relish, he read out aloud, "I suppose it's only to be expected that Gaston Busselle would favour his fellow Communists over good honest Catholics."

Köstler had been waiting for a chance to redeem himself with the Gestapo, Lichtenberg having been scathing in his criticism of the way the Jews of Saint-André-la-Forêt had been allowed to escape. Not only that, he could avenge his son's death at the same time. As soon as the patrol had gone off to arrest the butcher, he unlocked the drawer of his desk and took out Georg's SS dagger.

Gaston, still in his blood stained apron, was dragged out of his shop in full view of his horrified customers. Interviews of a gentler kind had usually taken place in the Colonel's office, but this time the prisoner was marched down to the cellars. The Germans didn't seem to notice Arnaud Garnier repairing a faulty valve in the boiler room, and it was his account of what happened next that Baltzinger passed on early the next morning.

"Arnaud couldn't bear to tell you himself," he said. "He's worried that everyone will blame him for doing nothing to help Gaston."

"You mean that...?"

"Gaston is dead. Yes." Valentin's face was ashen. As Thérèse burst into tears, he asked, "How? I mean..."

"Your sister really doesn't need to know the details. May I suggest that…"

"No. You may not! It could have been any one of you…of us." Thérèse recovered herself and sat down firmly.

"Well, Gaston denied ever having known any Communists, let alone being one. That was before they went to work on him. Eventually he couldn't take any more. They'd broken some of his ribs, both his arms and his face was so swollen that he could have hardly seen them by the time he spoke. He admitted that he'd been drawn to the Party as a young man but said that he'd become disillusioned and put it all behind him. He must still have had his wits about him, because he gave them a couple of names of men he'd known in Paris who'd already been executed."

"How did Arnaud know that?"

"Because Lichtenberg recognised the names and told the Colonel so. Then Köstler said, 'We know that you have Communist friends in the village. Who are they?' Gaston denied it and they started on him again. Every time he passed out they brought him round with a bucket of cold water and still he refused to give them any names. It was only when the Colonel held a dagger to his face and threatened to gouge out his eyes that Gaston broke and told them what they wanted to know."

"But they killed him anyway."

"Yes. Just for their own amusement, Arnaud thought, and some of their own men looked quite sick by the time they'd finished. Then they went off laughing to change for lunch."

"Was Sergeant Stracke there?" asked Thérèse.

"No. I don't know if he's even heard about it yet."

"I'm very glad that he played no part in what happened to poor Gaston. I don't think I could ever have looked him in the face again if he had."

His fury spent, or so it appeared, the Colonel gave his permission for a funeral. The coffin lid was nailed down straight away to spare the mourners the sight of Gaston's mutilated body. Although the butcher had been a non-believer, Father Ferdinand did his best to comfort his widow and the remaining children, the eldest having been one of the deportees. Madame Busselle was in complete despair and could barely stand by the graveside. With enemy soldiers looking on, no one dared to place a *tricolore* on the grave of the village's first martyr. It was a final insult to a brave man driven beyond endurance.

Henri Devane had gone into hiding, so a patrol was sent to the hardware shop to pick up his wife. When she was released, she stumbled back to the village and made her way straight to the church. There it was that Father Ferdinand came upon her, shivering and soaking wet, before the altar. Without asking any questions, he half carried her to his own home, sent his housekeeper for towels and a blanket and settled Florence down before the fire in the little parlour. After a while it became clear to him that she would rather confide in another woman but not the one closest to hand. Sending a furious Corinne Dupré away on a concocted errand, he telephoned the Garage de la Forge. As soon as Madeleine arrived, the priest withdrew discreetly to his study.

"Take your time, my dear," she said, "and tell me what has happened. It's all right. No one else can hear."

Florence shuddered. "I've never been as frightened in my life. Köstler threatened me with his fist when I said that I'd got no idea where my husband was and that I'd never shared his political views anyway. Then the other man, the one from the Gestapo, took him by the arm and whispered something into his ear that made him laugh. The next thing I knew, I was upstairs with that big corporal who's billeted with the Duvals. He was standing there in nothing but his drawers, grinning at me and fingering his...well, you know. It was sticking out like a tent pole and I was sure that he was going to rape me, although I couldn't understand why we were in a bathroom. Anyway, the others came in then and it turned out that he'd only taken off his uniform to keep it dry. The bath was full to the brim with freezing water and he forced my head into it over and over again."

"Your face is very swollen. How did you get all those bruises?"

"From the rim of the bath tub each time he pushed me back down. He held me under until I nearly blacked out and then pulled me out by my hair."

"Did you tell them anything?"

"How could I? Even when they threatened to arrest the children, I couldn't tell them where Henri is hiding. I just don't know. Eventually they seemed to believe me and said I could go. I ran straight down to the church to thank the Blessed Virgin for my release and that's when Father Ferdinand found me."

"What will you do now?"

"Well, I'll just have to keep the shop going on my own and hope for the best. It will be hard without Henri, but I've got to do it for the children's sake."

Madeleine gave her a hug. "You'll all be together again one day," she said. "This bloody war can't go on forever."

The Duvals' suspiciously fair haired baby was the talk of the village, but fear of Meyer, Rankert and their friends prevented a confrontation. Marius wore his usual air of indifference and the baby had been given his name. It took a snide comment from Angèle one day when they were waiting for their clean laundry to make Thérèse lose her temper.

"I wish you'd stop parading that brat around as if it's something to be proud of! We all know that it doesn't belong to Marius and I'll bet you don't even know for sure which of the Boche fathered it." Angèle turned on her, arms folded across her still swollen stomach.

"Well, look who's talking! You've got the pick of the bunch to keep your bed warm."

"You bitch! How dare you say that? I didn't ask to have the Sergeant billeted with us, but his behaviour has always been impeccable. You can ask my brother, or Luc's cousin or anyone else who knows me if I'd ever betray my husband." One or two of the other women in the queue gave watery smiles, but most looked at their feet and no one backed her up.

Encouraged by their silence, Angèle went further. "It's just as well that you lost your own baby before anyone could see who it took after!" That was enough for Thérèse, who promptly slapped her hard across the face. The argument descended into a violent brawl of hair pulling, scratching and punching until the two were pulled apart by a scandalised Madame Joubier and her daughters. Even then, they fought to get at each other and hurled the sort of abuse commonly attributed to fishwives.

Deeply ashamed, Thérèse was still weeping when Stracke walked into the kitchen and came to attention before her.

"I have heard what happened today, Madame, and I am mortified. Knowing that you were forced to accept me into your home, I have always tried to cause you no unnecessary inconvenience. Now it is obvious that my very presence is a great embarrassment to you."

Thérèse turned her tear stained face towards him. "It's not your fault," she said. "You've always been the perfect gentleman, both before and after my husband was taken away. It's that woman's evil mind and the lies she's spreading about us."

"Trying to justify her own behaviour, I should imagine. Soldiers talk, you know, and she has quite a reputation."

Thérèse flinched. "What do the soldiers say about me?"

"That Monsieur Gaudet is a very fortunate man and will find you waiting for him with nothing on your conscience when he comes home. I've always made it very plain to all that you've been courteous towards me but nothing more. However, to spare you any further problems, I've applied for a transfer. I'm just here now to collect my things. I have also requested that no other soldier be billeted in your home while your husband is away." He hesitated for a moment and then said, "Madame... Thérèse, if the situation had been different, I think we might have been friends."

She nodded dumbly and took the hand he held out to her. When he'd gone, she locked the piano and told anyone who asked for the key that the instrument had too many broken strings to be playable.

Chapter 16

No one was looking forward to the fourteenth of July. With all celebrations of the *Fête Nationale* strictly forbidden, there would be no procession, no fireworks and no dancing. Still brooding about her reputation in the village, Thérèse decided in a moment of madness to show her patriotism.

Fleur had cycled off that morning to visit Judith Perthuis and Valentin had a message to deliver to the old fort. Dodging patrols had led to a very roundabout route and then Paul had kept him hanging around for a long time while he composed a reply. It was very hot, even under the trees, and the tunnel entrance looked cool and dark, but Valentin didn't like to follow Paul inside uninvited and could only guess at who else might be concealed in the shadows.

There were no Germans in the café when Thérèse brought out the champagne. Luc had hidden their last few bottles behind a false wall in the cellar to await the time when France would be free once more. Everyone was happy to accept a glass with their meal and Thérèse had several. The effect on her empty stomach, for she generally ate after her lunchtime customers had gone, was catastrophic. Throwing all caution to the wind, she rapped on the bar for silence.

"It is the fourteenth of July and I should like you all to join me in a toast to our beloved country. *Vive la France!*" The response was subdued as people looked over their shoulders and the café cleared rapidly when she launched into the Marseillaise. She was still singing loudly when a German patrol halted at the open door.

Rankert, newly promoted and very proud of the silver lace on his collar and shoulder straps, swaggered in. He was followed by his friend Meyer and half a dozen other soldiers. Surprised to find Thérèse alone at what was usually a busy time of day, he demanded to know what was going on.

Very tipsy, she replied, "It must be my birthday, Monsieur."

"Indeed? Seizing a glass from one of the tables, he drained it and said, "I congratulate you, Madame, on celebrating your birthday with such an excellent vintage. A farewell present from Sergeant Stracke, was it? Are you missing his other attentions? Never mind. My men and I are always happy to oblige a lady. Especially one who's made it very clear in the past that she thinks herself too good for us." As Meyer bolted the door and pulled down the blind, Rankert started to unbutton his trousers. The other Germans lined up behind him.

Fleur would have been back half an hour earlier if she hadn't met Valentin on the road and got off her bicycle to walk with him.

"That's odd," he said as they entered the square. "Thérèse wouldn't normally close up as early as this."

"Well, the blind's down. She must have. Come on. We'll go in through the back and see what she's up to."

There was no sign of Thérèse in the kitchen and she didn't reply when they called her name. It was only when they went through the connecting door to the café that they found her lying spreadeagled and semi-conscious across two tables that had been pushed together. All around were signs that her attackers had helped themselves to drinks while waiting for their turn. Valentin's first thought was to cover his sister's violated body with a table cloth.

"Run for the doctor, Fleur!" he said. That brought Thérèse to her senses and she tried to sit up, wincing from the pain of her bruises. The Germans had not been gentle.

"No! I don't want him to see me like this."

"*Maman* then?"

"All right. But only *Maman*. Just help me upstairs."

Valentin couldn't understand why his sister refused to see the kindly man she'd known all her life, but he soon found out that their mother was of the same mind. After she'd done all she could for Thérèse, she left Fleur sitting with her and came downstairs to talk to him. He'd never seen her look so sorrowful or so stern.

"Nobody else must ever know about this," she said. "Your sister would die of shame. It's bad enough that you've seen her in a way that no brother should. You must pray every day to put that image out of your mind and never mention what has happened to anyone, even the rest of the family. Papa would seek revenge and I couldn't bear to lose him too."

"But the soldiers will boast about what they've done."

"Maybe not. They'll not want their superior officers to find out."

"Do you really think that any of them would care?"

"There must be some with a sense of decency like your Sergeant Stracke. This would never have happened if he hadn't left."

Thérèse stopped going to confession and then to church altogether. She blamed herself for the entire incident and resolved never to let another drop of alcohol pass her lips for as long as she lived, not even communion wine.

Valentin had his own reasons for staying away from the church. The sight of his sister that day had awoken more emotions than pity in his lonely heart. Despite having a small and overcrowded home, his parents had always insisted on modesty and he'd never seen a naked woman before. Her body was quite different from the nude statues he and the other boys had giggled at in the pre-war days when Monsieur Kahn took them on cultural excursions to Paris. Armpit hair was an everyday sight, of course, but what lay further down had been a mystery to him until then. Did Fleur look like that? Well, she must do, he supposed, although her hair was thick and dark and his sister's fine and ash blond. In his feverish dreams, the two women he loved most in the world merged into one for his pleasure and he was consumed with guilt the following morning.

To purge himself of the confusion, he sometimes waited until he heard Fleur go downstairs and crept into her bed while it was still warm. There he would lie for a few precious minutes, burying his nose in her nightgown and imagining them together.

"I overheard a couple of corporals talking about the black market the other night," said Baltzinger. "They said it would be easy enough to lay their hands on some of the good stuff the patrols requisition, but there wouldn't be any point without having contacts in Paris. Do you think that I should offer to help them? There might be a way that we could turn it to our advantage."

Paul agreed. "I can see a lot of potential there, lad, if you can convince them to take you along. Do a few trial runs and then we'll see."

The Germans agreed to everything he suggested and looked forward to making their fortunes. To convince them that they were right to trust him, he canvassed local farmers for surplus food to sell in addition to the goods the corporals had already stolen. The Perthuis disagreed with the scheme and Henriette Tilleray insisted on sharing anything she had to spare with local families, but Jacqueline Signac embraced the idea with enthusiasm. Her rabbits, poultry, butter, eggs and cheese went up to Paris with every load.

"How does she do it?" wondered Alain out loud. He was hanging around the smoky throng near the bar and hoping for Fleur to appear. "It must take more than one pair of hands to produce all that."

"I asked her once how she managed," said another man. "She just tapped the side of her nose and asked me if I'd never read *The Elves and the Shoemaker*."

"Well I don't think little men in green are coming out at night to do all the work. Baltzinger must still be giving her a helping hand."

"I'll bet that's not all he's giving her. I wish I knew where he got his energy from."

"So do I," said Valentin. "He's got that German woman and he still sees a couple of whores he knows in Paris as often as he can get up there."

Thérèse was shocked. "That's quite enough from you. Don't let Papa hear you talking like that." Would his family ever accept that he was a grown man?

Baltzinger's old friends, busily financing their future respectability, were doing very nicely out of a war that saw Germans and black marketeers queuing up for their services. Marco was dead, killed in a territorial dispute between rival pimps. There were plenty of customers ready to buy at prices that would have seemed ridiculous in the past. A couple of kilos of butter could fetch more than most people spent on food in a month. Baltzinger was also good at bartering for things needed in the village and even found some new bicycle tyres for Fleur. Trying to replace the old ones with pieces of garden hose had been beyond even Madeleine's capabilities, as had another attempt to stuff them with old wine corks.

"I don't know how Bertrand manages to remember everything," remarked Thérèse after one of his trips. "He's a marvel. He never writes anything down, does he, Fleur?"

"He won't dare to, in case it falls into the wrong hands. I do agree, though, that he has an amazing memory. He only has to glance at a document and he can dictate it to Paul word for word. He remembers every detail of maps and plans as well."

The relationship that gave him the run of the Colonel's office stood him in very good stead one day. He nearly choked into his coffee when Sabine showed him a draft recommendation for him to be accepted into the Waffen-SS. Some other young Frenchmen had already been given that dubious privilege, but it was the last thing that he wanted. His wits didn't desert him and she told the Colonel that a childhood bout of rheumatic fever had weakened his heart and made the young man, despite all outward appearances, unfit for active service.

Valentin thought secretly that Baltzinger might have fitted in rather well. Rumour had it that even amongst Himmler's supermen there were candidates for the dreaded pink triangle imposed on homosexual prisoners.

The British called off their heavy bombing of the Ruhr to turn their attention to Hamburg, although there was no mention of that in the German newsreels. The Occupation seemed to have been going on forever and the film shows now played to a packed room. A lot of flirting went on as soon as the lights were dimmed. With so many local men and boys still missing, it wasn't hard for the soldiers to find what they were looking for. Teenagers, their heads full of romance, were bowled over by the handsome, vigorous young men. Their older sisters, tired of mourning lost loves or the endless wait for those who might never return, also succumbed. Some got more than they bargained for and unwanted pregnancies weren't the worst of it. Many of the soldiers had stood in queues three or four deep in Paris, where business was so brisk that the women weren't even bothering to get out of bed between clients, let alone worry about personal hygiene.

Angèle's sister, Nathalie Joubier, dyed her hair blond, plucked her eyebrows to extinction and replaced them with thin pencil lines. In return for her favours, a besotted young soldier by the name of Poth kept her supplied with black market nylon stockings and toiletries. Still technically a virgin, although by an increasingly narrow margin, Nathalie loved to show them off to her friends.

"You won't catch me in ankle socks again," she boasted to one of Valentin's younger sisters, "and why should a girl be expected to ruin her complexion with that horrible cheap soap?"

"Sometimes we can't even get that. *Maman* tried making some at home from caustic soda and leftover fat, but it smelled rancid and no one would use it."

"Well my soap smells lovely. You could have some yourself if you did what I do and have a lot of fun at the same time instead of staying at home every night."

"Not likely. Papa would kill me."

"Mine often said that he'd kill Angèle when she was our age, but he didn't and now he wouldn't dare to cross her Germans."

Shortly after that conversation, some of the late Georg Köstler's friends came to pay their respects to his father and were invited to spend their leave at the château. They'd arrived in style, with SS pennants flying. Although their dress uniforms with the lightning bolts on the collars were superbly tailored, the death's heads on the caps were enough to keep most girls away during their visit.

Nathalie ignored the warnings and went up there as usual to meet her boyfriend. She was reapplying her expensive lipstick when one of the new arrivals homed in on her. Poth, just coming round the side of the building and spotting the tall figure in black, smartly changed direction and made himself scarce.

"Good evening, Blondine," said a harsh voice. "Are you waiting for someone?"

Caught off guard, the girl stammered. "Yes. That is, he was here, but now he isn't."

"Good. Come inside and keep *me* company." It was an order.

An amused Sabine Lohner, the only other woman in the officers' bar, watched with amusement as the nervous girl sat on his lap, trying with unaccustomed modesty to pull the skirt of her skimpy floral dress down over her knees.

Pouring her a second glass of champagne, the SS Hauptsturmführer stroked her hair and said, "Now then, my little Lorelei, are you going to drive me out of my mind?" Nathalie, having never heard of the golden haired siren of the Rhine, had no idea what he was talking about and replied uncertainly,

"No, Monsieur. I don't think so."

He drained his glass. "Oh, but you will." Tilting her head back, he kissed her full on the lips. By the time he let her up for air, a determined finger had worked its way between two buttons on her bodice. This wasn't like the cosy darkness of the film shows and she looked around, hoping desperately that no one was watching. Instead, amused faces followed the progress of the finger inside her underwear and saw her jump as it found its target.

"Monsieur, I'm very sorry, but I have to go home now. My parents will be expecting me." His response was to put his hand up her skirt and stroke the flesh above her stocking tops.

"Then they will have to wait. I too have expectations of you and it wouldn't be wise to disappoint me." With that, he seized her hand and forced it down onto his bulging crotch. Turning to the soldier on bar duty, he shouted, "You there! Have another bottle of champagne and two glasses sent up to my room."

As it was recounted to Baltzinger later that night and to the trio at the café the following morning, Nathalie followed the swaggering figure upstairs with as much enthusiasm as a condemned woman on her way to the guillotine. Her ordeal was short and brutal. Not only did he force himself upon her but, irritated by her feeble protests, punched her so hard that he broke her nose.

"She was lucky to get away with just a fist in her face," Baltzinger continued to a horrified Thérèse. "That guy's got quite a reputation. Sabine told me that he once shoved a broken bottle up a woman he met at a party in Paris."

"For the same reason?"

"No, for singing a rude song about Hitler and the other Nazi leaders."

"She must have been mad to think she could get away with that!"

"Just very drunk, I'm afraid." He looked sideways at Thérèse, who blanched.

"I think I know which song that would be," said Fleur in an attempt to lighten the mood. "It's rather crude but very popular in England."

Valentin was curious. "How does it go?"

"To the tune of *Colonel Bogey*. I'll teach you the words if you like." He was still singing *Hitler's only got one ball* under his breath when it was time to open the café for the day.

It turned out that a broken nose was the least of Nathalie's sufferings. Poth would have nothing to do with her after that night and she discovered later on that the SS officer had infected her with gonorrhea. It was left to Dr Simmonet, who had no effective remedy at his disposal, to break it to her that she was most unlikely ever to become a mother.

That was a very bitter pill to swallow, especially as the birth rate in France, despite all the deprivation, was rising. Some blamed it on the lack of heating in most homes, others on the curfew that kept husbands indoors on long winter nights. Either way, Valentin's mother was unpleasantly surprised to find herself pregnant yet again.

Chapter 17

One girl longing to embrace marriage and motherhood was Berthe Bail. Hopelessly in love with Alain Binard, she haunted the café after her day's work in the family bakery. He always greeted her pleasantly, as he did most people, but he was only ever interested in Fleur.

Jealous as a man could be at every smile he saw pass between them, Valentin was happy to lend Berthe a sympathetic ear. "Here again, I see."

"Oh, Valentin, what does Alain see in Luc's cousin? She's already had one husband. It's just not fair. How can I make him notice me?" Looking into her homely little face, Valentin was at a complete loss. "Do you think make-up would help?" she persisted.

Compared to Fleur's effortless beauty? "I shouldn't think so."

"Well, perhaps it would make him jealous if he saw me with someone else."

She was looking at him so hopefully that he stammered, "Who? Me?"

"No. Not you. I don't mean to be rude, but being seen with you wouldn't make anyone jealous."

Not in the least attracted to the mousy teenager, he tried not to feel too insulted. "How about the brother of one of your friends?"

"No. Those still here are all too young. It has to be someone older and really handsome. Someone he'd be surprised to see me with."

"There's only one place that you'll find men like that, Berthe. Don't even think about it. I can assure you that Alain wouldn't be impressed. He'd be disgusted with you."

Berthe stuck out her bottom lip. "At least he'd notice me for once."

The next day she arranged to meet her friend Odile Vartan and go to the film show. Well aware that she was no competition for the pretty blonde, who'd daringly stated her intention to redden her lips with beetroot juice, Berthe decided to go one better and cadged a precious stump of lipstick from Angèle Duval. Highly amused at such audacity from Corinne Dupré's niece, Angèle taught her how to draw fake stocking seams down the backs of her legs with an eyebrow pencil.

The plan was doomed to failure. To get to the château, the girls had to pass the priest's house and they were spotted through the window by the last person Berthe wanted to see. She was marched straight back home and didn't stand a chance between her aunt and her mother.

"What an example to set your little sisters! Flaunting yourself like a cheap painted floozy!" shouted Brigitte, without even bothering to close the door behind her. An interested crowd gathered outside the bakery as she shrieked, "Just wait until your father hears about this! And what about your poor brother? We don't even know if he's dead or alive and you were going to invite a German to have his evil way with you." Berthe howled and danced about as each point was accompanied by a ringing slap to whichever part of her body her furious mother could reach.

"Now get upstairs and wash off that muck."

"But..."

"Don't give me any buts! Get out of my sight!"

As a sobbing Berthe obeyed, her aunt said, "You should send her to a convent, sister, if she's going to carry on like a guttersnipe. She's more than old enough to be a postulant and the nuns would soon straighten her out."

Brigitte rested her tingling palm on her lap. "Oh, I don't know about that, Corinne. I'd miss the silly girl and it would be hard for Robert and me to run the business without her. He's not getting any younger, you know."

"Is that more important than saving her immortal soul?"

"No, of course not, but I'd like to see what Father Ferdinand has to say. If he agrees with you, then I'll think about it."

To her relief and her sister's disappointment, the priest took the view that experimenting with make-up didn't automatically turn an innocent girl into a scarlet woman. As for becoming a bride of Christ when she had absolutely no vocation, that was quite of the question. He warned Berthe, though, to keep herself pure until she found a husband amongst her fellow countrymen.

"It will happen, my daughter," he concluded. "You just have be patient and bide your time."

"I will, Father. I promise."

"There's nothing else I can do," she complained to Valentin later. "I'm not allowed out on my own any more."

"Well, at least Alain's sorry for you now. He says that no one should blame you for trying to make the best of yourself."

"It isn't his pity that I want."

No one could understand that better than Valentin. If Berthe were ill equipped to compete with Fleur, he was doubly so with regard to Alain. Even apart from physical considerations, his rival would one day inherit the family business that he loved, while Valentin would continue to trip over Luc's old *rondeau* in a café that he would never own. The long apron was the bane of his life, but Thérèse was superstitious about shortening it. It would be like admitting to herself that Luc might never come back.

Paul's group had been keeping a low profile since the deportations. With no sign of an imminent invasion, he didn't want to risk any more reprisals. Paris was swarming with security police of all descriptions. Penalties for even the most trivial of offences were becoming more brutal by the day and he heard with dismay that Jean Moulin, the greatest resistance leader in France, had been betrayed and had died after weeks of torture.

Then came the news that he'd been waiting for. Supplies of arms were being dropped to groups all over the country in preparation for the arrival of the Allied forces. Fleur set off immediately to scout out a new landing ground and came back unusually flustered.

"I've just been up to Jacqueline Signac's farm to see if she'd help, but she turned me down flat and wouldn't even discuss it. It was as though she couldn't wait for me to leave. Just as I was getting back on my bike, a big lout I'd never seen before came out of the barn and made a lunge at me. I've never pedalled as fast in all my life."

Baltzinger sprang to his feet. "I wonder who that was. I'll go and sort him out for you, if you like."

"No, no. We don't want any trouble of that sort."

"What did he look like?" asked Thérèse.

"Younger than Jacqueline. Tall. Thick set. Red nose. Big chin."

"It sounds like Christophe. I didn't know that he was back."

"It's just as well that she doesn't have children," added Valentin.

"You're right there. Christophe is Jacqueline's only weakness, Fleur. He's her brother and she practically brought him up. He's a drunkard and a bully, but she wouldn't ever hear a word against him. Not even when he was sent to prison for a sexual assault on a little girl. Her father and brothers threatened to castrate him if he ever came back to these parts, but they're all dead or deported now. I expect that's why he's dared to return."

Fleur frowned. "That's odd. I didn't think that Jacqueline had any children, but I could have sworn that I heard one crying."

"It must have been one of the animals."

"Yes, I suppose you're right."

Fleur didn't like to use the same landing ground twice, but in the end she was obliged to approach the Perthuis family again. Vincent, backed up by Judith, agreed straight away. Only his mother was vehemently against the idea.

"Please don't risk it again, son. I've got a very bad feeling about this. It's not just your own life. You're putting the children at risk too."

"I notice that you don't mention their mother. My wife. What sort of a future do you think that any of us will have if we don't get rid of the Germans? What will our children think of us later on if we don't do our bit now? We *will* have the arms dropped here and we'll hide them for as long as necessary."

The following week, Vincent heard the whistling sound but didn't know which way to run. All around him were gentle thumps as heavy canisters whose parachutes had opened successfully hit the ground. The only one in free fall killed him instantly. Despite the consternation, everyone rallied to get the remaining canisters under cover before they carried Vincent's body back to the farmhouse. His hysterical mother railed at everyone that night, especially Judith. The new widow, her dark eyes brimming over with sorrow, was too stunned to defend herself.

Vincent's head and body were so badly crushed that she wouldn't allow the children to see inside the coffin when their grandmother brought them in to pay their last respects and the lid was nailed down before the other mourners arrived. At the funeral, Father Ferdinand spoke of a tragic tree felling accident.

During the week that followed, he visited the farm every day, but the grieving mother's tight lips offered no hope of forgiveness or reconciliation. She spent hours brooding near the spot where Vincent had died. It was from that vantage point early one morning that she saw a black Mercedes heading towards the farmhouse. By the time she got back, Lichtenberg and the French policeman taken along to add legitimacy to the arrest were already inside. Clavié, uncomfortably aware that Geneviève had been at school with his grandmother, shuffled awkwardly when he saw her and could not look her in the eye.

It was ominously quiet. Judith and the children were still seated at the kitchen table, their half eaten breakfast in front of them. The little ones were looking up at the two men with friendly curiosity. They'd known the young policeman all their short lives and he'd attended their father's funeral.

Lichtenberg, his grey eyes bright with satisfaction, took out a sheet of paper from his pocket.

"Judith Perthuis? Born Judith Goldenberg? It has been brought to my attention that this area has not been completely cleansed of Jews after all. You and your spawn will come with us at once!"

As Judith's eyes widened in horror, her mother-in-law rushed to the drawer where the family papers were kept.

"My grandchildren are not Jews! Look, Monsieur, I have proof." Baptismal certificates were worth their weight in gold in those days and parish priests turned out many false ones, but those belonging to the Perthuis children were genuine. "They're good Roman Catholics. You can take Judith with my blessing, but you must leave the children with me."

Lichtenberg smiled unpleasantly. "Must I indeed, Madame. If I thought for one moment that you were knowingly harbouring Jews under your roof, you would be accompanying us to Paris. Your late son deceived you when he brought that woman into your house. It's not a question of baptism but rather one of blood. Allow me to quote: *The Jew almost never marries a Christian woman; it is the Christian who marries a Jewess. The bastards, however, take after the Jewish side.* Your grandchildren carry the poison in their blood and must be segregated with their own kind. French translations of the Führer's wise words are available in the village bookshop. I suggest you purchase a copy and study it with care. You will find it very instructive. Good day to you, Madame."

Judith wasn't even allowed time to fetch the children's coats before they were all bundled roughly into the Mercedes. Geneviève ran screaming after them until the car was out of sight and then collapsed by the side of the road. She'd never known that such grief could exist and it was only the arrival of the priest on his daily visit that stopped her committing a mortal sin. Sobbing and quite incoherent at first, she unburdened herself to him.

"I knew from the start that Judith was a Jewess. That's why we didn't see Vincent for a long time. I've always hated her for driving a wedge between us, but I couldn't hate my own grandchildren."

"How did Judith's family feel about the marriage? Did they also object?"

"Yes. They even had the nerve to say that Vincent wasn't good enough for her. They're orthodox Jews and Judith was dead to them from the day she left home to marry him. I expect they'll have been brought down a peg or two by now, wherever they are."

"Yes indeed. I'm afraid that's very likely the case. Poor Judith! It can't have been easy for her to see the children brought up in the Catholic faith."

"She thought it better for them to have their father's religion than none at all."

"And Judith must have converted as well before she came to live here. She was a regular attender at Mass."

"For all the good it did her!"

"Indeed. To the monsters of the Third Reich, even a Catholic priest of Jewish origin is still a Jew. I don't suppose we'll ever know who denounced Judith to the Germans, but you must pray for God's grace to help you to forgive."

Chapter 18

"There's something I've got to tell you both. I'm expecting."

Fleur put out a comforting hand. "I did wonder, my dear. I've heard you being sick a couple of mornings this week."

"I've been trying to convince myself that this couldn't be happening to me. Pregnant to a Boche and I don't even know which one. It makes me no better than that Duval woman."

Valentin wouldn't have that. His beloved sister, no better than Angèle? "Don't be silly. It wasn't your fault that those animals took advantage of you."

"Who's going to believe that when even our mother thinks I brought it on my own head. It's bad enough, according to her, that I've always been too pretty for my own good, but I had to make it worse by getting drunk and making an exhibition of myself."

"That's no excuse for what they did to you. If Colonel von Achten had still been in charge, they wouldn't have dared. Soldiers in other areas have been hauled up in front of military courts and sent off to the front line for crimes like that."

"How do you know?"

"Private Jelling said so. He considers men like that a disgrace to the Wehrmacht."

"But he doesn't know what happened to me? Oh, please, tell me that he doesn't!"

"Not unless Rankert and his friends have been showing off and I doubt that. Baltzinger would have heard all about it from his lady friend."

"The question is," said Fleur, "what you're going to do about it. You'll start to show soon."

"Oh, God! What can I do? Use a knitting needle maybe? Throw myself down the stairs?"

"No, of course not. You could bleed to death or at least do yourself permanent damage. What if you want to have a baby when Luc comes back?"

At the mention of her husband, Thérèse started to cry and Valentin turned helplessly to Fleur.

"What other way is there?"

"Other than a bungled amateur abortion? Well, there are qualified doctors in England who take care of that kind of thing if they're paid enough, so there must be some in Paris as well. I wonder who would know."

"Baltzinger, of course. I don't suppose he's ever told you how he lived before he came here, but his friends from those days will have contacts, I'm sure."

"Then we'd have to confide in him. How would you feel about that, Thérèse?"

"I'd trust him," she said simply, "but I don't know if I could go through with it. Could you, if you were in my position?"

"In your position? Yes, I think I could. It must be wonderful to have a child with a man you love, but this is quite different."

Valentin agreed. "What else can you do, sister? You couldn't keep it. Luc doesn't even know yet that you lost his own baby and how do you think he'd react to a half German bastard? He's not a doormat like Marius Duval."

"Yet getting rid of it would be murder. How could I live with myself afterwards? Don't speak to Bertrand yet. I need more time to think."

Thérèse agonised over her situation for weeks and still couldn't bring herself to agree to Fleur's suggestion. She was clinging to the hope that she might miscarry again before her situation became obvious. When that didn't happen, she refused to be seen in public and a cover story had to be thought up. The word went round that she was suffering from nervous exhaustion brought on by anxiety about the deportees and would need complete peace and quiet for the foreseeable future. Some people were sceptical but most expressed sympathy.

Her mother guessed the truth almost straight away and it wasn't long before Monsieur Morcel, refusing to be kept away from his eldest daughter, came banging on the back door. Instead of the furious reaction that Thérèse had dreaded, he took her in his arms and cried with her.

Keeping the café going, even with Thérèse preparing the food late at night for him to heat up and serve the following day, fell largely to Valentin and business suffered accordingly. Fleur, who seemed capable of existing on very little sleep, helped whenever she could, but she generally disappeared as soon as the door was closed behind the last customer and was often out all night. As well as continuing to collect and transmit information, she was obliged to ensure supplies for the growing number of men hiding out at the old fort. There was new hope in the air. The war was going badly for the Germans in other parts of the world and, although there was still no definite news of the promised invasion, a lot more people all over France were joining the Resistance. When another hard winter came round, everyone dared to hope that it would be the last one of the Occupation.

The unwelcome child Thérèse was carrying clung to life and Valentin sometimes fantasised about how wonderful it would be to see Fleur's slim body swelling with his own son or daughter. Then reality would strike as Alain appeared and her face lit up. Even Thérèse's expression was often wistful when she saw them together and he wondered how differently things might have turned out if she'd married Alain instead of Luc.

Their mother was feeling guilty that her prayers for Thérèse hadn't been answered, although those for herself had. She really hadn't wanted to go through another pregnancy, but slipping on the ice and losing the latest baby had been a pure accident. While attending to her, Dr Simmonet had asked after Thérèse and been assured that there was no need for him to call.

With the spring, things started to hot up. A flood of messages came through on the radio and the number of arms drops was greatly increased.

"We've got to get everything away faster," said Fleur. "The Germans have stepped up their patrols and they're stopping and searching everyone they come across."

Paul agreed. "We have to find a way to bring everything up here. It won't be easy, though. There's a lot more stuff than we can shift in carts and wheelbarrows and anyway it's too far from the drop zones. How can we get hold of a roadworthy vehicle, though, with so few left in French hands?"

Baltzinger, as usual, had the answer. "I'll get you something. Just give me a day or two." He told his business partners at the château that he had another consignment ready to go up to Paris. When they arrived at the pick up point, they found themselves confronted by a group of armed men.

Up at the fort, it was easy enough to camouflage their prize and park it alongside Henriette Tilleray's old car. Baltzinger was fast asleep in his own bed by the time the Colonel was notified that two of his men were missing. As they'd taken the lorry without the correct authorisation and their bodies were never found, it was assumed in the end that they'd deserted.

Not everyone was capable of handling such a heavy vehicle, but Madeleine Binard was in her element. Knowing that Paul had given her the task very much against his better judgement, she was determined to prove herself the equal of any of the men. That was why she didn't go for their help on the night the lorry veered off the track, although the rain was torrential and she wasn't far from the fort. Propping her torch up against a tree, she started to change the wheel. Some of the nuts must have slipped through her wet fingers, because she was crawling underneath the lorry to find them when she dislodged the jack.

Once again there was no question of mourners filing past an open coffin. Everyone knew that Madeleine had been in robust health, so a fall at home was given as the reason for her death. She'd often been seen leaning out at perilous angles to wash the windows and the story wasn't questioned by the authorities.

Sensing that Alain dreaded going back home on his own after the funeral, Fleur went with him and didn't return. Valentin lay in bed racked with envy and cursing the blacksmith with every foul word he could think of. Was his sister also lying awake and wishing that the English-woman had never come to the village? Certainly the atmosphere the next morning when the pair came through the back door hand in hand was laden with undercurrents.

"None of us know if we'll survive this war," said Alain proudly, "but, if we do, Fleur has agreed to be my wife. I don't have a ring for her yet, so I've given her this instead. I know my mother would have wanted her to have it." Fleur displayed the gold locket briefly and then tucked it back into her blouse. "I'll have her real name engraved on it one day," he continued. "I can't yet, because she still won't tell me what it is."

"It isn't that I don't want to," she said with an affectionate smile. "It's that I mustn't. You do understand that, don't you?"

"Of course I do. Your *nom de guerre* will have to do for now and I also accept that we must keep our engagement between the four of us."

"Yes indeed. If Paul finds out, he'll arrange for me to be picked up and sent back to England with a flea in my ear. Falling in love during an assignment is the last thing I was supposed to do."

Valentin choked back his feelings long enough to kiss Fleur's cool cheeks and congratulate the big happy man beaming down at her. The brawny arm he'd placed possessively round her slim shoulders served to rub in the fact that he, his sister and Berthe had nothing left to hope for from either of them but friendship.

Although Berthe knew nothing of the engagement, she was as wretched as Valentin. Odile Vartan, allowed more freedom than she, had met and fallen in love with a German officer.

"Her parents don't know a thing about it," she told Valentin. "He says he wants to marry her as soon as it can be arranged."

"But what about her poor brother?"

"That's another thing. Her precious Hartmut has told her that deportees are very well looked after in Germany. He even hinted that he might be able to get him released if she'd... Well, you know."

"Yes. I know."

Odile's sudden disappearance from the village was overshadowed by another mystery. It was only a few days after their very private engagement that Alain had to cancel plans to take a walk with Fleur.

"I'm sorry, my darling, but I've got to report to the château straight away."

She turned white. "What for? Could they suspect you of something?"

"Of course not. The Colonel sent me a note, not an armed escort. I expect there's something wrong with the Daimler."

"And he wants you to fix it?"

"I wondered about that too. He usually sends for a specialist, but maybe he couldn't get anyone at short notice and needs the car tonight."

Alain was quite looking forward to the novelty of working on such a fine machine, even if he might be called upon to sabotage it again at some point in the future, and he went off whistling with his tool bag.

When he failed to return, an anxious Fleur asked Baltzinger to find out through Sabine Lohner if he'd been arrested. She was distraught to discover that the Colonel had been genuinely surprised by his clerk's enquiry.

"I didn't send for him. Have you any idea how difficult it was to get my Daimler fixed after the attack on the bridge? Do you really think I'd let the village blacksmith loose on it? He's lucky I allow him to shoe my horse." In actual fact, it was the Colonel who was fortunate in that respect. Alain had always rejected suggestions that he might put the odd nail in the wrong way round to make the poor animal buck and throw off its rider.

Fleur shed many a tear over Alain in the weeks that followed, but her anguish over his disappearance didn't diminish her determination to finish the job she'd been sent to do.

Thérèse had a long labour with only her mother in attendance. It was made worse by the need to keep noise to a minimum and only a rolled up cloth to bite on when the pains came. No matter how bad it got, neither of them would hear of sending for the doctor and Valentin's nephew was born just before midnight. His grandmother did what was necessary, although she could hardly bear to look at him. Thérèse, despite everything, felt a huge surge of love at the first sight of her son and named him Sébastien. He was a beautiful baby with enormous blue eyes and a fuzz of blond hair. Valentin, as soon as he was allowed into the room, was pleased to see that his limbs were perfect. He wouldn't have wished a club foot like his own on any child, not even one fathered by the enemy.

"But what are you going to do with him, Thérèse?" wailed their mother. "You won't be able to keep your doors and windows shut all day when the warm weather comes." It was true. The best baby in the world will cry sometimes and no sound on earth is more difficult to ignore.

"Well I'm not giving him up." Thérèse, although exhausted by the ordeal of giving birth, looked ready to take on the world to protect the newborn.

This pull of maternal love, so strong and so unexpected, left them all at a loss. Thérèse was overjoyed to get back the baby things she'd rejected after her miscarriage, including a striped blanket that she'd knitted herself. The pale blue wool had come from an old pullover of hers and the dark blue from one of Luc's. The fact that Thérèse didn't scruple to wrap another man's son in it proved what a fight they had on their hands.

Help came from an unexpected quarter.

"I could take care of the baby for you."

"You, Bertrand? But how on earth did you find out about him?"

"So it's true, then?" Realising that she'd fallen into a trap, Thérèse turned pale, but he hastened to reassure her. "By putting two and two together. The fact that you were still working behind the scenes in the café most of the time you were supposed to be ill, for one thing. Valentin never convinced me that *he* was doing the cooking. Fleur wouldn't have had the time and your mother's always too busy at home. Not that it's stopped her smuggling out all your extra washing these last few weeks, I'll bet. How long do you think that can carry on before the neighbours get wind of it? She can't take it to the laundry, she can't hang it outside, so she must be drying it round her kitchen fire. None of your brothers and sisters is still in nappies and it would only take one nosy parker to call round and see them all. Even without that, I'm convinced that people can see through walls in this village."

"But what else can I do?"

He smiled. "Well, for a start you can show him to me. I'll bet he's just like you, isn't he?"

"Yes, I suppose he is rather."

"And not at all like Luc?"

"Oh, Bertrand, if only he were! The whole village would take one look and believe that he's Sergeant Stracke's son. That would be bad enough to live with, but the truth is far worse. You might as well know about it." She told him exactly what had happened to her before sitting back to await his reaction.

His face showed only sympathy as he said, "You know I've always been very fond of you, Thérèse. Let me help you now. I can take your baby to some Carmelite nuns in Paris. They're already hiding a few Jewish children and I'm sure they'll take him too. He'll be well looked after, I promise."

"But I want to keep him with me."

"You can't. You're living on a knife edge as it is and your life won't be worth living if your secret comes out now. Be sensible. This war can't last forever. Maybe only a few more months. When it's over, things will be different. People won't be so hasty to judge."

"Are you sure that the nuns will give him back to me then."

"Of course they will."

"And do you think that Luc will accept him?"

"If you make it clear that your marriage depends on it. He'd be a fool to risk losing you. Any man would." Plausible as ever, he bent to kiss her hand. "Just let me make the arrangements."

A couple of nights later, with the greatest reluctance and many tears, Thérèse wrapped up her tiny son in his striped blanket and handed him over. The moonlight shone for a moment onto the baby's placid face as she said her last goodbye and Baltzinger disappeared with him into the shadows.

Chapter 19

The next day, Thérèse got down on her knees in church for the first time since her violation by Rankert and his friends and said a grateful prayer.

A few hours after seeing Sébastien on his way to safety, she'd been awoken by a series of explosions that had rocked the village, knocking shutters off their hinges, breaking windows and cracking walls. Most significantly for the young mother, the wooden cradle in which generations of Gaudet babies had slumbered had been showered with broken glass.

The RAF had recently stepped up the campaign against railway installations around Paris and a Lancaster bomber, badly damaged by German flak, had gone wildly off course. As the pilot circled round and jettisoned his remaining bombs, he must have looked desperately for somewhere clear of trees to make an emergency landing and seen the imposing driveway of the château as a godsend. Unfortunately, it proved to be not quite long enough and the plane was still travelling very fast when it hit the building. An inferno of exploding fuel tanks and tracer bullets followed the impact. When the fires were out and the smoke cleared at last, it was discovered that only the wing where most of the Germans slept was still standing. The Countess and her personal staff had died in their beds, as had a young woman only recently arrived.

"You know, Bertrand," sighed Thérèse, to whom he'd been describing the damage as he helped her to board up the café windows, "I feel quite sorry for the Colonel. I'll get my little boy back one day, but he'll never see his daughter again."

"Don't waste your pity on him. They didn't get on and she only came to visit because her apartment in Hamburg was destroyed in the fire

storm. Since her brother was killed, she's been his only hope for grandchildren and he's never hidden his contempt for her husband. He even
went so far as to accuse her at dinner of marrying a eunuch to spite him."

"That poor woman! What a horrible thing to say."

"Yes. And in front of everyone else too! She pointed out that her
other half was a U-boat commander and had been away at sea for most
of their married life. The Colonel just sneered at that and said that he got
leave, didn't he, and there must be something wrong with his wedding
tackle. She stormed out then and asked Sabine to find her a room as
far away from her father as possible. That's why she was sleeping in the
other wing. I helped to move her things across and she told me that her
husband had been awarded an Iron Cross for bravery and would make
a wonderful father if he ever got the chance. She hadn't heard from him
for several months, though, and didn't even know if he'd received any
of her letters."

Thérèse patted his hand. "You're so kind, Bertrand. A woman can
always talk to you and you'll make someone a wonderful husband
yourself one day."

When Fleur came home, she turned the conversation to more practical matters. "I wonder if the *Kommandatur* will be moved now."

"More than likely, especially since the raid on the aircraft factory at
Meulan-les-Mureaux. I'll keep my ear to the ground and let you know
as soon as I hear anything."

Baltzinger's vigilance paid off and he soon had plenty to report. "The
Colonel will be staying put for the time being, but he's planning to move
most of his men and their equipment into the fort. He wants to hide
them from the Allied bombers."

It had been years since the Germans had shown any interest in Paul's
headquarters and he grimaced. "He's copying Field Marshall Rommel.
He recently moved his General Staff into La Roche Guyon."

"I've heard of that," said Fleur. "It's north-east of Paris, isn't it? An
old fortress built into the rock."

"That's right. Rommel's secretly equipping the casemates and I suppose that Köstler wants to do the same. He can't have any real idea of the extent of the labyrinth, but he does know that there's plenty of room inside."

"Why would he want to copy Rommel, though?" asked Valentin. "Didn't you once tell us that he despised him for refusing to kill the Free French prisoners at Bir Hakeim?"

"Yes. And for losing at El Alamein as well, but Rommel's still in Hitler's good books and the Colonel would like to be there too."

"I'll just bet he would," agreed Baltzinger. "He spent ages dictating a letter to Sabine, because he kept changing his mind about how to sound well prepared but not defeatist. It went something like this: In the very unlikely event of any invading forces breaking through our massive coastal defences, the brave men under my command would be in an excellent position to strike a devastating blow for our beloved Führer and the Third Reich."

"You'd better start moving out pretty quickly," counselled Fleur. "He won't be dragging his heels on this one."

"I will, but those booby traps we laid last year should give us a little breathing space. The Germans won't be expecting anything like that."

He was right. After the first couple of explosions, the Colonel called a halt until a bomb disposal team arrived from Paris to sweep the whole track. A few pieces of burlap stained with gun oil were found, but no one could say how long they'd been lying around and there was no immediate witch hunt.

The soldiers did what they could to make themselves comfortable. They installed lighting, stoves and bunks and laid poison for the rats. Non-military personnel were excluded from a wide area around the fort, now regarded as top secret.

Deprived of their base, Paul and his men had to take shelter where they could. They were always on the move and often cold and hungry. The married men longed for their families but knew how dangerous it would be to make contact. If Paul had a family of his own, he never spoke of it, but then neither did Fleur. After all the time that they'd lived under the same roof, Valentin knew no more of her background than on the night she arrived and could only assume that she'd been free to accept Alain's proposal.

There were further explosions as the Germans sent in a team to deal with the bombs that the British pilot had jettisoned.

"Did you hear that?" asked Henri Devane. "It's just as well that our kids aren't allowed in the forest any more."

"It doesn't stop all of them, though," said another man. "I spotted Joseph Morcel out setting snares the other night, but I don't suppose he left this." He held out a piece of gaily striped ribbon that he'd found tied to a tree and Henri turned pale.

"My Nina had one just like it. If anything has happened to her or little Roselyne, my wife will be out of her mind. It was bad enough when we lost our son. I've got to go home and make sure that they're all right."

"Paul won't let you. What if you were caught? It's far too dangerous. Not just for you but for all of us."

"I wouldn't be caught."

"You can't guarantee that. Just forget the idea."

Henri nodded curtly and said no more, but that night he took the group's only bicycle and headed for the village. In the moonlight, the deserted square was a depressing sight. Few repairs had been done since the Lancaster came down and his own premises looked particularly in need of attention. Some of the heavy wooden shutters were hanging loose over the broken windows and there was a big crack in the wall.

Henri propped up the bicycle round the back of the building and fumbled for his key. Pulling off his heavy boots, he tiptoed through the dark shop and up the stairs, trying to avoid those that creaked. The girls' room was in darkness, but he was surprised to see a light under the other door. Florence must have fallen asleep over a book. Perhaps he could creep into bed beside her and lose himself in her arms before sleeping off some of his own weariness. What a wonderful surprise that would be for his wife after all this time!

In the event, it was Henri who got the surprise. Rankert's collar was undone and he'd taken off his boots. The sight of the German sprawling on his marital bed enraged Henri, but he had no chance to reach for his gun. A large fist crashed into the side of his head and he knew no more until he was brought round by a bucketful of icy water.

The Devane family sat in a neat row, their wrists tied together behind the backs of their chairs and their legs secured by another piece of rope. Henri's head throbbed. Florence and the girls were in tears, terrified by the dimly lit and unfamiliar surroundings.

"We heard that you'd found the ribbon and might be on your way home," said a soft voice eventually. "What a wonderful shop you have, Monsieur. It has supplied me with everything I needed. Look!" Lichtenberg pointed with satisfaction at the wooden box in front of him.

Henri, well used to the Germans' so-called requisitions, didn't care what they'd pillaged this time. "Why have you brought my wife and children here. What have *they* done?"

"Nothing yet," was the Gestapo officer's reply. "But they're going to be very useful if you don't co-operate." He advanced on Henri and jabbed him so hard in the chest that he nearly fell over backwards on his chair. "Now then, where is your nasty little gang of Communists and other criminals holed up these days? Tell me and I might consider allowing your family to return home. They're not going to be very comfortable here, I assure you."

Henri looked around hopelessly. The curved ceiling of the stone chamber was all too familiar and he knew that there could be no escape for him. The best he could do was to delay the inevitable. If he held out long enough, Paul might realise what had happened and move camp.

"Nothing to say?" Henri shook his head and braced himself for a beating, but Lichtenberg had moved on. "I'm spoilt for choice this morning. I wonder if Madame is in need of another hair wash. No. I've got a better idea. Do you smoke, Corporal Meyer?"

"Not on duty, Sir."

"Well, I'll make an exception on this occasion. Go ahead."

The man had barely lit up before Lichtenberg said, "No, you're right. You'd better stub it out. Oh dear, there's no ash tray. You'll just have to find something else."

Grinning broadly, Meyer shambled round behind the row of chairs and paused behind sixteen year old Nina. When Lichtenberg gave the nod, he took a final draw at his cigarette and slowly pressed the glowing tip into one of her palms. Nina screamed with pain, but her wrists were too tightly bound to allow her to move the hand away and the acrid smell of her singed flesh filled the nostrils of her anguished parents.

"Oh dear, oh dear," crooned Lichtenberg. "Did that hurt? Maybe your father has something to say to us now, before Meyer moves onto more sensitive parts."

Florence's eyes were wide with terror. "Henri! Make them stop. Tell them what they want to know."

Henri shook his head. "I'm so sorry, sweetheart, but I can't do that."

Lichtenberg gave a dramatic sigh and turned his attention to Roselyne, twelve years younger than her sister and rigid with fear. "Your father doesn't seem to care much about Nina, does he? Do you think he loves you more?"

"I don't know," she whispered, looking like a field mouse cornered by the farm cat.

"Well, we'll see, shall we? Untie her, Rankert, and take her pretty dress off. It would be a shame to spoil it." Henri swore violently as his daughter's skinny arms and legs came into view. The patched underwear made her look even more defenceless.

Florence cried out in desperation. "You can't! She's only a baby." Her plea was ignored.

"Let's see what we've got to play with. Wire, knives, screws, meat hooks, a blow torch..."

Henri Devane couldn't take it any more.

Chapter 20

The Germans struck just before dawn and the sentry had no time to shout a warning before he was shot in the head. He toppled backwards into the pond, still clutching his rifle. Some of the men and boys sleeping under the trees managed to grab their guns and shoot back, but the battle was a short one and only a handful managed to get away. The dead Germans were carried back to the fort; the French left where they lay.

Among the men marched past her for interrogation, Florence was amazed to see Marcel Kahn and two of his sons, their faces full of despair. Whatever was going to happen, they knew that it was the end of the line for them. She tried to cover Roselyne's ears as the defiant shouts and shrieks of agony echoed down the tunnels. In the end, Lichtenberg tired of the sport and had all the prisoners hanged from the meat hooks that the soldiers had screwed into the ceiling. It was so low that the taller men could almost touch the floor with their tiptoes. He left Henri until last and made Florence watch as her husband slowly choked to death.

"Time for a late breakfast, I think," said Lichtenberg cheerfully, as the soldiers started to cut down the lifeless bodies. "Oh, you and your children can go now, Madame. You're of no more use to me."

Was this a cruel joke? Looking over their shoulders the whole time to see if the German had changed his mind made the walk through the forest seem interminable, but at least it gave Florence time to think. No one appeared to be about when they reached home and she hurried the girls inside. Closing the door behind them, she said, "We must tell no one about this. People would call Papa a traitor and a coward."

"But he couldn't help it," protested Nina, her tears breaking out afresh. "I'd have told them anything they wanted to know to stop them hurting Roselyne. Wouldn't you?"

"Yes, of course, but the dead men's families wouldn't understand. Safeguarding Papa's good name is the only thing we can do for him now."

They were able to do that only because the Germans kept strangely quiet about the men arrested, tortured and executed that morning and their remains were never found. Maybe even monsters like Lichtenberg were starting to cover their tracks in case the Allies caught up with them.

A gun battle in broad daylight was a different matter and they had no compunction about rounding up local men to collect the bodies. Gilles Petacque was ordered to retrieve the dead sentry and came out of the water weeping with his older brother in his arms. Paul had died as anonymously as he'd lived, although Fleur promised that his relatives would be informed of his fate once the time for secrecy had passed.

Father Ferdinand, allowed to say a few words over the graves, was horrified by the strength of his own emotions. His very un-Christian desire for vengeance was echoed throughout the whole community and Valentin's father even dug up the old hunting rifle that he'd buried in 1940.

Florence and Nina had to nurse their grief in private and pay lip service to the hope that the members of Paul's group unaccounted for had escaped. Little Roselyne, whose silence couldn't be relied upon, was sent off to stay with an aunt in Sèvres and eventually persuaded that the whole ordeal had been nothing but a bad dream.

Looking back on it, Valentin recalled that it was round about that time that a growing lack of confidence led to the soldiers' helmets, formerly so shiny, being covered with a matt field grey or a camouflage pattern.

The projection equipment destroyed when the Lancaster hit the château was replaced and installed in the school. According to the German news-reels, the Allied air attacks were an outrage against defenceless French civilians, but through Fleur it became known that they were the run up to a general call to arms.

The pre-arranged signals began on the first day of June 1944. Preceded by the opening bars of Beethoven's 5th Symphony, the words *Les sanglots longs des violins de l'automne* put every Resistance group in France on the alert. Four days later, *Blessent mon cœur d'une langueur monotone* spurred them into action. At least one thousand attacks took place that night. Without Paul, Fleur didn't want to mount a separate operation and so she obtained permission from London to send men and supplies off to help other groups. They carried out some of the many ambushes that helped to disrupt the German transport system. D-Day had arrived at last and the gloves were off. Overnight, and as the Allied troops swarmed up the beaches of Normandy, the news spread far and wide and caused consternation among the Germans.

"The Colonel is in a real panic," reported Baltzinger. "He's started packing and told Sabine to burn all his papers. I've been helping and managed to save quite a few for Fleur to pass on."

Thérèse wasn't sure whether to laugh or cry. "Oh, Bertrand, what will happen to all the deportees now? What about my Luc?"

He shook his head. "All I know is that political prisoners held in France are being sent to Germany, to the camps they call *Konzentrationslager*."

The Germans weren't the only ones to panic. A few collaborators still tried to curry favour with them but, as convoys of plunder and members of the Vichy government headed east, most rushed to turn their coats and associate themselves with the Resistance. Believing the enemy to be on the run, some groups rushed in far too fast and died for it. Fighting went on for a long time as areas were liberated, recaptured and liberated again. The humiliation of defeat after all the years of triumph drove some of the enemy to respond to acts of aggression even more viciously than before.

"We don't want any more bloodshed here," said Fleur one day. "I've ordered everyone to give the Germans no excuse for reprisals before they pull out of the area. It shouldn't be too long now. Oh, Thérèse, I know how much you're missing Luc and worrying about your baby, but you must hold on for both their sakes."

"You miss Alain just as much, don't you?" She nodded, as controlled as ever, but reached for the locket she still kept concealed under her blouse. The chain, always fragile, chose that moment to break. Seeing the chagrin in her green eyes, Valentin felt ashamed of himself for hoping that Alain was dead.

"Give me your locket," he offered. "I'll mend the chain for you." She'd kissed his cheek in gratitude and disappeared into the night before he realised the impossibility of doing such fine work with only the contents of Luc's toolbox at his disposal.

In the early hours of the next morning, a patrol marching across the square stumbled over a motionless figure in black. Whoever was responsible for the attack had made a very thorough job of it, as the soldiers discovered when they turned the man over and removed his hat. One fist was clenched as though ready to strike, but several hard blows from a heavy instrument had reduced the head to pulp.

Colonel Köstler felt obliged to put on a big show of respect before sending the corpse, still fully clad, to Paris. He insisted on placing it in the church, where it lay under a large swastika until an elegant coffin arrived from the capital. He did not dare to have a member of the Gestapo transported in anything less impressive.

In case any of Lichtenberg's colleagues came to check if he were being treated with sufficient dignity, a guard of honour surrounded him and the silver candlesticks that usually stood on the altar were placed at his head and feet. Not even Father Ferdinand was allowed into the church until the hearse had driven away.

The next day, Mass was well underway when the door at the back was kicked open and the Colonel strode in. He was followed by a bewildered crowd of non-churchgoers, herded inside by a squad of soldiers armed with machine guns. Köstler ignored the priest and raised his hand for silence.

"An officer of the Gestapo has been murdered. I could hold you all responsible for this outrage against the Third Reich, but I'm going to offer you one chance to save yourselves. The body of my esteemed fellow countryman was examined in Paris and something of great significance was found in his hand. It has been sent back to me and here it is." He held up Fleur's locket and demonstrated how it could be opened. "The piece of paper inside this piece of jewellery contained some very interesting information. I've long suspected the presence of a British agent in this area and now I have proof. She is masquerading as a Frenchwoman and living amongst you. You will all take a good look at the locket and someone will tell me who owns it."

Only a few nervous coughs broke the silence as it was passed round from hand to hand and every head shook.

"I see," said the Colonel grimly. "Then you leave me no choice. Just be grateful that my men are going to shoot you *before* we lock up your church and set fire to it. Some of my colleagues would be less merciful."

There was a stunned silence for a few seconds and then pandemonium. Old Jules sprang to his feet shaking his fist and was shot where he stood. Father Ferdinand tried to reach the dying man and was clubbed unconscious by a single blow from a rifle butt. Mothers tried to shield their children as Köstler ordered his execution squad into position. A few people were defiant and cursed the Germans. Others fell onto their knees and cowered on the floor of their pews.

It looked as though some of the soldiers were struggling to hide their emotions. Would they really shoot down the girls they'd flirted with on warm summer nights? Wipe out young and old without exception? Florence Devane for one didn't doubt it and burst into noisy tears. Jelling's eyes were wet too and he was staring at the big crucifix over the altar as though he hoped for a miracle. To Valentin, it seemed just like that Christmas Eve when they'd needed an angel and there was a strange inevitability about what happened next. As Köstler raised his hand to give the order to fire, a clear voice rang out.

"Stop this at once. The locket is mine. I'm the one you want." Fleur looked so small and vulnerable as they led her away that no one could imagine her standing up to interrogation.

"She did, though," said Baltzinger the day after her arrest. "The Colonel tried his best to break her before he sent her to Paris, but she didn't give anything away. She even managed to convince him that Luc had fooled you two into believing that she was his distant cousin, so you should be all right."

All right? Valentin was heartbroken. Thérèse, too upset to be rational, could talk only of the new danger to her husband. What if Luc, wherever he was, were to be convicted of aiding a British agent? Why couldn't Fleur have concocted a story to exonerate him as well? He might be under arrest already and waiting to be shot. If the bloody Englishwoman hadn't parachuted into their lives in the first place, none of this would have happened. The help and kindness she'd received from Fleur counted for nothing. It was all down to her that Luc's life now hung by a thread.

Chapter 21

One morning in August, the village woke up to discover that all the Germans had gone, swallowed up amongst the hundreds of motorised and horse drawn columns heading eastwards to defend the Fatherland. Hitler, who'd only visited Paris once and didn't think much of it, ordered the commander of the German garrison to destroy the whole city. It was to Von Cholitz's credit that he stalled on purpose until it was too late. Everyone swelled with pride when the news broke that General Leclerc's French 2nd Armoured Division had entered the capital at the head of the US forces. There was still danger from enemy snipers hidden on roof tops, but the population went wild just the same. General de Gaulle strode down the Champs-Élysées where a German military band had marched only a few days before.

The period after the Liberation brought its own nightmares. In August and September, before some semblance of order was re-established, there was anarchy in many places and a rush to settle old scores. Much of the venom was reserved for women found guilty of *collaboration horizontale*, although a prostitute's dealings with the enemy were sometimes dismissed as merely a matter of business. Baltzinger's old friends had done very well out of the war. Solange had made enough money to buy her own establishment and Manon went to Chicago as a G.I. bride.

The women most reviled were those who'd fallen in love with Germans, but the finger of suspicion could be pointed at anyone who'd worked for them, however unwillingly, or had a soldier billeted under her roof. Her accuser could be anyone, from a woman who really did have something to be ashamed of to a rejected suitor. There was a carnival atmosphere with flags, banners and drums in some places as groups of shaven headed women were driven around in open vehicles to be mocked. It was a very ugly carnival, during which even those with babies in their arms were pelted with rotten fruit and dung. Some were paraded stripped to the waist or completely naked through the streets to be punched, kicked and spat upon.

The short lived vigilante group in Saint-André-la-Forêt was led by Jacqueline Signac's brother. Having lurked at the farm until all possible danger to himself had passed, he rode the old plough horse into the village and joined forces with some other last minute converts to the Resistance. They strutted into the square looking for free drinks and amusement. Their first port of call was closed and shuttered, Angèle having anticipated retribution and disappeared with Marius and the baby.

Clavié stood up as they entered the café, took one look at the guns over their shoulders and sat down again. How could any policeman be expected to take them on without back up? The other customers had frozen in their seats. Pushing Valentin aside, Christophe swaggered over to the bar and seized Thérèse by the arm.

"Look, everyone," he shouted. "Here's the German sergeant's whore. She was carrying on with him even before her poor sap of a husband was deported."

"I don't know who told you that, but it isn't true," protested Valentin. "My sister's done nothing to be ashamed of."

"Sit down, cripple, and shut your mouth unless you want us to shut it for you!" One of the men forced Valentin onto a chair and held him there. It was obvious that they were in no mood to listen to Thérèse either as she tried to defend herself.

"It's all lies. I never wanted the Sergeant here in the first place and he moved out straight away when he heard what the Duval woman was saying about us."

"That's not what we've been told and you're going to get what you deserve." Christophe and his friends plundered the bar as ruthlessly as the Germans had done and then dragged Thérèse into the kitchen.

"Hold the bitch down and give me those clippers." It wasn't long before all her lovely blond hair was on the floor and the brute paused to admire his handiwork. "Throw this lot onto the fire. Your lover wouldn't think much of you now, would he, Madame? Now then, lads, what else shall we do? Did you hear about that girl who was branded with a swastika made out of bent nails? How about doing the same?"

"We've got the fire, but we haven't got any nails," objected one of his companions. "Shall I get some from the hardware shop? Madame Devane will be delighted when I tell her what I want them for."

"No, don't bother. These scissors will do. Just keep her head still."

Thérèse screamed as Christophe used the point of a blade to gouge out a swastika on her forehead. Then they took her into the middle of the square and hoisted her up onto the back of the horse for everyone to see. Blood dripping into her eyes and down onto her torn dress, she wasn't there long. Although nobody had dared to confront the gang, at least someone had the wit to alert her parents. Before Monsieur Morcel could load his gun, his wife had picked up a cast iron frying pan and raced to the scene. Christophe just laughed when she brandished it at him, but her courage seemed to be rubbing off on the bystanders and he shambled off with his friends in search of fresh victims.

The cuts he'd inflicted on Thérèse became infected and took a long time to heal, but the scars on her forehead were nothing compared to those on her mind. Convinced that her blond hair was a curse she was born with, she dyed it black as soon as it started to grow back and darkened her eyebrows and lashes to match.

Thérèse wasn't the only woman in the area to be treated so unfairly. When the deportees started to return, some women who had been shorn in the camps were terrified of appearing in public in case their closely fitting scarves made them targets for abuse. Like Thérèse, they became prisoners in their own homes for many months.

Many deportees were so broken in health and spirit that they died not long after their return to France and others were never really well again. Luc Gaudet was one such. He weighed only forty kilos when he was brought into his home on a stretcher. The hand he held out weakly for well wishers to shake was scarred and the fingers thickened from the years of forced labour. Luc remained an invalid for the rest of his short life and Thérèse nursed him with unflagging devotion.

"He was heartbroken about my miscarriage," she sobbed one evening not long before he died, "and I've never found the right time to tell him about the other baby. Now it's too late." Baltzinger had been round to inform her that the nuns had placed Sébastien with a good Catholic family to bring up as their own.

Valentin tried to comfort her. "It's better this way, sister. What kind of an existence do you think he'd have had here, even if Luc had accepted him? No one will be able to point a finger now or call him cruel names the way they'd have done to Angèle's little boy if he'd lived. She's pregnant again, by the way, but at least this time there's a good chance that the father's a Frenchman. Or maybe an American." With no reputation left to lose, Angèle was back in business.

When Alain Binard burst into the café, he was in far better shape than Luc and desperate for news of his fiancée.

"What happened to me? Oh, that doesn't matter any more. Someone banged the bonnet of the Daimler down on my head that day the Colonel sent for me and I woke up in the back of a lorry heading east."

"Did you have a dreadful time?" asked Thérèse, releasing him from her welcoming embrace.

"No. Not really. I couldn't get away, but the Boche found my skills useful. Mind you, I fouled up as many of their engines as I repaired. I just want to forget that it ever happened and marry my Fleur. Where is she? Safely back in England, I suppose, and waiting to hear from me."

No one knew what to say and Alain's smile faded as he looked at all the sombre faces.

"I'm so sorry, my dear," said Thérèse at last. "She didn't make it."

Alain's own face crumpled as he heard about all the lives that Fleur had saved. "But she might still be alive somewhere?" he said, a gleam of hope in his eyes.

"No. I'm afraid that Fleur died in a concentration camp called Ravensbrück. Father Ferdinand found her on the Red Cross lists under her assumed name. The Germans must have tired of trying to force her true identity out of her."

"Then I've got nothing left to live for," he said as he walked out of the door.

All hope gone, Alain Binard lost interest in everything and everybody. The garage and the forge remained closed and he took to the bottle. As for food, he would have starved himself to death if it hadn't been for Berthe, who brought round his meals and sat over him while he ate them before drinking himself into a stupor.

She took her chance and he woke up one morning to find her curled up beside him in bed, proud of having 'given herself' to him. With no memory of the event, he ordered her out of the house, but it was too late. He had to marry her when Jean-Pierre Simmonet, who had been able to pick up and complete his medical studies, confirmed the pregnancy.

"It only takes once, you know," the young doctor had said to his furious former classmate, "but you could do a lot worse than young Berthe."

"Thanks for nothing!"

"I know Alain doesn't love me yet," she told Valentin, "but he will. I'll make him so happy that he'll forget her."

She was wrong. Her new husband dreamed of Fleur every night, cried out for her in his sleep and woke each morning to fresh disappointment. Berthe saw the look on his face and realised that Alain could hardly bear to touch her when he was sober. Even when they walked down the street together and she took his arm in a gesture of affection and possession, he shrugged her off as often as not. It all came to a head one morning when she came into the café, Jean-Claude toddling by her side, and burst into tears.

"I can't stand being at home, Valentin. Do you know what day it is today?"

"Yes, of course. Look, there's a calendar behind the bar."

"Oh, I don't mean the date! It's the *fête* of bloody Saint Fleur." Valentin had never heard Berthe swear before and waited for her to explain.

"Alain's just sitting there, staring at his precious little photograph. It's so stupid. Fleur wasn't even her real name, but he says that it's all he's got. Oh, Valentin, I know now that he'll never love me the way he loved her and I'm so tired of being second best."

He poured her a cup of coffee and sat Jean-Claude on the bar between them. As the little boy beamed at them both and stretched out his chubby arms to his mother, she dried her eyes and stood up to take him.

"I'm determined not to give up on Alain, but I won't go home just yet. I think I'll take a walk in the forest to clear my head."

"Would you like to leave the little one here with me for a while?"

"No. It's kind of you to offer, but you'll soon be busy getting everything ready for lunch. I'll take him round to the post office. Odile will be closing for a couple of hours and she's always happy to look after him. It's funny, that. Before she went away, she didn't have much interest in children, but something's changed. She loves Jean-Claude almost as much as I do."

"Did she ever tell you what happened while she was away all those months?"

"No, only that things didn't work out for her the way she'd hoped. She gets upset if I raise the subject and I've learned not to question her about it."

Berthe did leave the little boy with her friend, but she never returned to collect him. After a frantic search, her body was found up at the fort, hanging from one of the same meat hooks that the Germans had used to execute their prisoners. Father Ferdinand couldn't bring himself to add to all the grief of the past few years by refusing her a Christian burial and her apparent suicide was passed off as yet another tragic accident.

Berthe's death finally made Alain pull himself together, not for his own sake but for Jean-Claude's. He sold off the blacksmithing equipment and put all his energy into the garage.

It was around that same time that Balzinger proposed to Thérèse. Despite the medal he'd been awarded for his work with the Resistance, many people in the village still saw him as an outsider and she was the only one who was genuinely fond of him. All the same, and much to Valentin's relief, she turned him down.

"I'm sure you've done the right thing," he said. "He probably does love you as much as he's capable of loving anyone, but I still think that his main motive is getting his hands on the café. In any case, it's too soon. You're still grieving for Luc."

His sister shook her head. "It's not just that. I'll never remarry." Did she cast a wistful look at the piano or was she thinking of Alain with his double burden of grief and guilt.

The next day, Baltzinger was gone and it was many years before they saw him again.

Part Four

1965

Chapter 1

"Why don't you try to get some sleep now?" The suggestion was a kind one, but fear of what the next few hours might bring made sleep the last thing on Daisy's mind.

"No. You can't leave the story there. I want to know where Baltzinger went, why he came back and especially why everyone in the village seems so afraid of him. You were all on the same side during the war, weren't you?"

Valentin gave a hoarse laugh. "Baltzinger was always on his own side, whatever he did. You've got no idea."

"Then tell me! You've got nothing to lose, have you?"

"All right. Just give me a breather first and then I'll tell you the whole sorry tale. Have some wine. It's the only thing that's keeping me going."

"No thank you. I'd rather stick to water." Daisy, although heavy-eyed, was determined to keep as clear a head as possible.

"Well, Baltzinger loves to talk of his adventures, especially when he's had a few drinks. He's dropped any pretence of friendship between us but, after what happened when we were boys, he still thinks he can trust me with all the details, however unsavoury."

"And can he?"

"Yes, I'm afraid so. I'm as susceptible to threats and blackmail as anyone else. I don't have any money or goods to give him, so I've become his dogsbody. You must have noticed that." Daisy nodded.

"You know what a cruel sense of humour he has. It amuses him to see the mess I make of cooking for young people like yourself, brought up here only to provide cover for everything else he gets up to. But I'm getting ahead of myself. Baltzinger headed south after my sister rejected his proposal.

He wanted to try his luck in Marseilles. His devious mind and complete lack of scruples were ideal for the post-war black market. He was happy to deal in anything, from penicillin stolen from American army stores to heavy artillery, and he built up a very successful business. When his activities attracted the attention of the authorities and put him in danger of a long stretch in Les Baumettes, he crossed over the Mediterranean to Algeria. There he might have stayed, if President de Gaulle hadn't handed over the country to the nationalists. As it was, he slipped back into France and lay low for a while, all the time looking out for fresh opportunities. It was during his second stay in Marseilles that he went into a tattoo parlour down by the docks and met that handsome good-for-nothing layabout that you know as Raoul Favrin.

What a piece of work *he* was as a boy! Born in a tiny ramshackle old house overlooking the sea, or so he told me once, he didn't give a damn about the things I'd read about but had never been able to see for myself. The thick scent of herbs growing wild, the sunlight reflecting off the gilded Madonna of Notre-Dame-de-la-Garde and the clouds of flamingos heading home to the Camargue were wasted on him. All he ever saw from his cliff top home were the bright lights of the Canabière. Before he left school, which he rarely attended anyway, he was a well known figure in the dark bars of the back streets. On nights when naval ships were in port and their crews were swarming into town in search of a good time, he'd point them in the right direction. Whores and bar owners would tip him for every man he sent their way. Most of the sailors wanted women, but he was happy to oblige those who preferred boys and would do anything for the right price.

Seeing Baltzinger splashing money around, he latched onto him straight away. They were still together when things started to become too hot once again and Baltzinger proposed a move north. The pickings, he assured Raoul, would not only be better but all the sweeter when mixed with revenge.

An unhappy stir ran round the village at the news that Baltzinger was back and planning to make use of the fort in the forest. He lost no time in renewing old acquaintances and reminding them of things that they had thought were buried for good. One person after another was stunned into compliance by how much he knew and his scarcely veiled threats. He seemed to bear no ill will to Thérèse, though, and she smiled at him indulgently when he asked her a favour.

"Would you mind if I borrowed Valentin to help me to get organised? I need someone I can trust."

"Of course not. That's fine. I'm sure he'll be glad to lend a hand," she told him. The truth was the exact opposite, but Baltzinger wouldn't take no for an answer.

"I wonder what everyone would think of you if they knew what you'd done," he said to Valentin.

"If you mean what you forced me do when we were boys, you couldn't talk about that without making yourself look bad."

"I don't mean that, Shorty. I must have been desperate in those days. No, I mean that other business. Do you still think about *her* and what you did? How long do you think you'd last if Alain found out, eh? I thought so. Well, you're working for me now and you won't be the only one to call me '*patron*' by the time I've done the rounds."

Some of the information that Baltzinger threatened to make public, Valentin already knew or suspected. It came as no surprise that several villagers had plundered the Abrahams' home straight after their flight or that Massot and Clavié in their respective roles as Mayor and police-man had helped the Germans rather more than they'd been forced to.

"Still washing dirty linen, I see," he said to Madame Joubier. "What a shame that there are no more German uniforms to launder at inflated prices. Oh, and no more Jewish customers to insult."

"How can you say that? You know that I had no choice about work-ing for the Germans and it broke my heart to have to refuse Madame Kahn."

"It didn't look like it the day you told her that you'd no longer let dirty *Youpins* soil your premises with either their vile bodies or their laundry. Do you remember turning off the water when she and Aimée still had soap in their hair? Just remember that the Kahns had a lot of friends in this village. I wonder how many customers you'll have left if everyone hears about the way you treated them. On the other hand, I'll be needing a lot of laundry done soon and free access for everyone I send to you for a shower. By the way, how's Nathalie these days? Not given you any grandchildren yet? I wonder why. Still got the clap, has she?"

People who blustered at first were silenced when Baltzinger produced the notes they'd sent to the château.

"Do you remember that time when some of the schoolchildren made themselves yellow stars in sympathy with the Kahns?" he asked the pharmacist. "Your daughter didn't join in, but you sent the Germans a list of those who did, just to make sure that she was in the clear. Very neat writing, isn't it? Everyone would recognise it from the labels on their medicine bottles. Now then, I shall be requiring a few things from you."

"Madame, here's the complaint you sent in about your meat ration just before the butcher was arrested. I'll need some groceries for my new enterprise and I'm sure that you'll be able to provide them for me."

Threats to have Henri Devane's name dragged through the mud ensured a constant supply of hardware, a suggestion that he might inform Jean-Claude of the true circumstances of his mother's death gave him free access to all services offered by the garage and so it went on.

Baltzinger's former boss had thought that he was untouchable. After all, he'd boasted to everyone after the Liberation about the part he'd played in the Abrahams' escape.

"The Countess let me take her car and I risked my own life driving the Jews all the way down to the Loire to meet the *passeur*."

Baltzinger smiled. "Indeed you did, Arnaud. The old lady just wanted to help, but I'll bet you never told her about all the extra money you made the good doctor pay to get his family away safely; the money that you and the other man split between you. You know what happened to the Abrahams afterwards too, don't you?"

"No. How could I?"

"Allow me to put you in the picture. There was another family on board the little boat. When their baby started to cry, they were told to throw it into the river. They refused, of course, so the whole party was stranded before they reached safety, rounded up and arrested."

"You can't blame me for that!"

"No? Well, never mind. How about that Sunday afternoon when Thérèse asked you to fetch your accordion? It was no coincidence that the German patrol was on the square a few minutes later to turf out the Kahns, was it? Alain Binard was very upset about what happened to that little girl's poodle and I don't think your son would be too impressed either."

"Leave Nicholas out of it."

"Well, I suppose I can for the moment. He doesn't know that his cinema was financed out of blood money, does he?"

Arnaud, whose face was by then resembling a boiled beetroot, shook his head. "No. Of course not. He thinks I'd been scrimping and saving to give him enough to start it up."

"Well, you'd better carry on with that. I'll need some work done soon and I won't be paying you for it. Oh, and tell your son to give free passes to the young people I'll be sending his way. Call it a gesture of international good will, if you like."

Odile Vartan's secret was more painful than most. She'd been amazed by the delight of her German officer when she told him that she was expecting his baby.

"That's wonderful, *Liebchen*," he'd said. "We'll just have to bring forward our wedding plans. I'm sure I can get permission. In the meantime, I know a safe place where you'll be very well looked after. Don't tell anyone. Just pack a few things and I'll send a car round for you tonight."

"But what shall I say to my parents?"

"Leave them a note saying that you've eloped with an officer of the Third Reich and they're not to tell anyone. I can guarantee that they won't. They'll probably make up an excuse about your having gone to look after a sick relative or something like that. After the war, they'll be proud to have a son-in-law with influence."

The car arrived as promised and Odile was ushered into a seat next to a stony faced nurse who didn't speak a word to her on the long journey to Chantilly. Their destination was Westwald, one of Himmler's *Lebensborn* breeding farms. Odile was given no work to do and the living conditions for herself and the baby she produced were very good, but it broke her heart that his father never came to see them. Worse was to follow. She was allowed to care for the little boy for only a few months before he was taken away from her and sent off to his new parents in Germany.

"Stop crying, you silly woman," said the Matron. "Just be grateful that your baby is perfect."

"Why do you say that? What would happen if he weren't?"

"It's better that you don't ask."

Odile prayed for years to be reunited with her lover and their baby. Not all the Germans were faithless, she knew, and there were occasional tales of men tracking down their girlfriends and children after the war, but that never happened to her.

Angèle Duval was defiant at first. After all, her chequered love life was very old news and her son Gérard, born a couple of years after the war, was to all intents and purposes legitimate. She only came to heel when Baltzinger brought up the subject of Fleur's locket.

"Everyone has always wondered how Lichtenberg came to have it, but we know, don't we? It was given to you to have its chain repaired. Who else would still have eyebrow tweezers in good condition after all those years of Occupation? You poked around with those long nails of yours until you found out how to open the locket and saw what was inside."

"So what? It was only a scrap of paper."

"True, but you thought it might interest the Germans. You were trying to get Thérèse into trouble and have the café closed down. Or maybe take it over yourself? I've got the note you wrote to one of your lovers. It must have been a shock when Lichtenberg turned up instead."

She tossed her head. "It certainly was and I still don't know why my message went to the wrong man."

"Oh, I can tell you that. I hope you like the irony. Lichtenberg suspected you and your husband of running a Resistance group from your bar. There'd been a series of leaks and he'd noticed how much time Meyer, Rankert and their friends spent there, so he thought you might have been using your wiles to get information out of them. The village tart and her cuckold of a husband! What better cover could there be!"

"That's ridiculous."

"I know, but when he intercepted your note he decided to take Rankert's place. Do you remember what you wrote? 'Meet me in the church porch at eleven. This time, I'm the one who's got something useful for *you*.' How could Lichtenberg resist an invitation like that?"

"I thought the locket might help Rankert with his next promotion," she pouted.

"And then he'd be able to afford more expensive gifts for you. Secret information was never on your wish list, but Lichtenberg didn't know that. He suspected everyone, even the Colonel. That's why he came on his own to meet you. He thought his Luger would be adequate protection against a lone woman."

"He didn't need it for me. We only exchanged a few words before he grabbed the locket and told me to go home and consider myself lucky not to be arrested for breaking the curfew."

"So you didn't kill him?" Her finely plucked eyebrows shot up.

"Me? What do you think I could have done? Knocked him out with my handbag?"

"Relax! I know you didn't, but you started the ball rolling that got Fleur killed. Old Jules too and his family still lives here in the village."

"All right. I get the message. Free drinks and whatever else you want for keeping your mouth shut." Baltzinger accepted a glass of her best cognac as a down payment and strode off to call on his next victim.

Chapter 2

"So who did Baltzinger pick on next?" asked Daisy. "Did he really know who'd killed Lichtenberg?"

"Oh yes, and it was the last person anyone would have thought of. Corinne Dupré. She was completely taken aback to see him walking into the church and taking a seat in one of the pews.

"Are you wanting to confess? Father Ferdinand isn't here yet."

"Oh, I'll get round to him later. It's about confession, all right, but not mine. Sit down beside me, Mademoiselle. You and I are going to have a little chat about old times."

"Don't be ridiculous! Can't you see how busy I am? Now stop talking nonsense and let me get on with my work." She frowned at him as she reached for her lavender polish, but he seized her wrist in a painful grip that made her drop the waiting duster.

"Sit down right now and listen to me! I want you to cast your mind back to that night in 1944 when you killed the Gestapo officer."

"I don't know what you're talking about. Let go of me!"

He tightened his grip. "Don't try to deny it, you old bitch. I followed him to his meeting with Angèle. You and I both overheard their conversation. I was behind the old yew by the porch and you were in here, although I can't imagine why at that time of night."

She was glad to sit down then and swallowed hard. "I couldn't sleep. I was on my way downstairs to get a glass of milk from the kitchen and happened to glance through the window on the landing. The Duval woman was just disappearing into the church porch and a man was walking down the path to meet her."

"And you thought you'd catch them at it."

She pursed her bloodless lips. "Everyone knew that woman had no shame. Can you blame me for thinking the worst of her?"

"But it was even worse than the worst, wasn't it?"

"Yes. I went in through the vestry as quietly as I could and tiptoed to the back of the church. There's a big old keyhole in the door and I could hear every word they said. There was no one else around and they didn't bother to keep their voices down. When the man had packed her off, I put my eye to the keyhole and saw him shining his torch onto a locket and a little piece of paper. He was smiling as he read the words aloud and I knew that they spelled trouble. He put the paper back inside and turned to leave."

"You didn't really care about Fleur, did you, but you thought he'd make her talk and then come for your precious priest."

"Yes. He never told me about his work for the Resistance, but I knew that he was involved. You can't keep house for someone without noticing things."

"So that's why you grabbed one of those big silver candlesticks and clouted Lichtenberg with it. You certainly didn't leave anything to chance, Mademoiselle. You must be stronger than you look, but they say, don't they, that hatred adds strength?"

"Not hatred. Love. Something I'm afraid that you've never understood, my son." Father Ferdinand was standing behind them.

Baltzinger spun round and said, "I've been better off without it, *mon père*. It always lets you down in the end. Your arrival is very timely, though. We were just getting to the part where she ran for you because she couldn't move the body on her own. You decided to hide it in the forest, but it was a dead weight – sorry about the pun - and you hadn't got very far when you heard the patrol coming."

"If you saw all that, why didn't you help us?"

"I was going to, but it was a windy night and I was enjoying the sight of Mademoiselle here trying to hold onto Lichtenberg's legs and keep her skirts down at the same time. Then it was too late. You'd dropped the body and taken to your heels."

"Yes. There wasn't time to hide him, but we hoped that the patrol would march straight past in the darkness. We intended to return later to try again or at least search him for the locket. We'd already tried his pockets but, as you know, it was in his fist all the time. Even the Germans didn't find it straight away."

"If they hadn't and just wanted to find out who killed Lichtenberg, I expect you'd have done the Christian thing and taken the blame."

The priest nodded sadly. "There was no point after I regained consciousness and found that they'd taken Fleur away. I knew that she was as good as dead and other people needed me, especially Mademoiselle Dupré here. She wouldn't stop talking about how she'd committed a mortal sin and wanted to confess it to another priest. She could hardly confess it to me."

"As her partner in crime? No, I suppose not. And once she started confessing, you were worried about what else might come out."

Father Ferdinand turned white. "What do you mean?"

"Oh, come on! I had you figured out from the beginning. It takes one to know one, as they say. Of course, it took much longer for her to realise what you were and it must have been one hell of a shock."

"How on earth do you know that?" spluttered Corinne. "I only ever told my sister and she wouldn't say anything."

"Have you never heard of pillow talk? Losing their son knocked the stuffing out of her husband and we had some unfinished business, Brigitte and I."

"I don't believe you. My sister would never have let you lay a finger on her."

"Much more than a finger, I assure you. She went a very funny colour when I called on her this morning, but the bakery will be giving priority to my requirements from now on. To get back to the point, I was curious back then to know why a priest of such refinement had ended up in a little village like Saint-André-la-Forêt and with the housekeeper from hell. Brigitte couldn't wait to change the subject, so I became even more intrigued. It only took a hint that I might feel the need to confess about our little trysts to get the whole story out of her. She was terrified that you'd find out, Mademoiselle, and even more so that everyone would learn what a hypocrite she was. Half the village remembers her thrashing poor Berthe just for wearing a little make-up."

The priest was shocked. "That would never have happened. Even if she had come to me, it's my absolute duty to disclose nothing revealed under the seal of confession."

"Yes, but have you never wondered, Father, why the confessional is always so well polished? Now then, let's just run through the facts. Do tell me if I miss anything out. A very pious but plain girl, who might otherwise have become a nun, fell desperately in love with a student at the seminary next door to her convent school and started to follow him around like a lap dog. He did nothing to encourage her, quite the reverse, but she wouldn't be put off. Knowing that he was going to be a priest only added a delicious piquance to her dreams. However, it wasn't only because of the vows he was going to take that Ferdinand de Rosnay wasn't interested in girls. She was horrified to come across him one day sharing a lot more than a prayer book with another student but thought it through and gave him an ultimatum: her silence in exchange for a permanent place by his side."

Father Ferdinand nodded sadly. "It's all true. I did give way to temptation when I was young, but I've regretted it more than I can say and led a celibate life ever since. That includes my relationship with Mademoiselle Dupré, in case you're wondering, but I doubt whether the pleasures of the flesh ever played a part in her calculations. I dreaded and still dread exposure, above all because of the shame it would bring to my family."

Baltzinger smiled with satisfaction. "And that is why the two of you will make no public objection to a little scheme I have in mind. Let me tell you all about it."

The farms surrounding Saint-André-la-Forêt received visits from Baltzinger too. He had nothing at all on kindly Henriette Tilleray, so he painted a glowing picture of his new enterprise and persuaded her to support it out of the goodness of her heart. With no grandchildren of her own, she would be more than happy to see an influx of young people into the area each summer.

Geneviève Perthuis was quite another matter.

"You'll have to ditch those mourning clothes and get this place up and running again," he told her.

"What's the point?" she moaned. "I've got no one left to work for."

"Yes you have. Me. You wouldn't want me to tell any tales now, would you?"

The widow pursed her lips. "If you mean that little affair we had when you first came here, forget it. I have and no one would believe you after all these years anyway."

"I don't mean that, distasteful as it was to me at the time. I'm referring to the way you betrayed your daughter-in-law to the Germans."

She gasped and clutched the black serge of her bodice. "But what happened to Judith wasn't my fault."

"Oh yes it was. Everyone knew that you had your knife into her from the start."

"So did you," she protested, "for making Vincent sack you. It's true that I didn't like her, but I'd never have done anything to hurt my grandchildren."

"Ah, but you didn't know that they'd be taken away too."

"I didn't, but nor would I have deprived them of their mother."

"Oh yes you would. You told Lichtenberg that he could take Judith with your blessing. He told the Colonel all about it afterwards. What do you think your neighbours would make of that?"

"They'd only have your word for it and no one around here trusts you."

"How about this then?" Geneviève had to admit defeat when he produced the note she'd written to the German authorities all those years ago. The ink had faded a little, but the handwriting was still clear.

Jacqueline Signac was pleased to see him and her gaze was shrewd as he outlined his plan. "That sounds like a very good idea, Bertrand," she said. "What would you like me to supply you with? Oh, you've brought a list. Good. And how much are you offering to pay for all this?"

"Nothing," he replied, his eyes bright with amusement. "You should have married me when you had the chance."

"Marry you? It never even entered my head to accept your ridiculous proposal. I didn't want to marry anyone then and I still don't. But what makes you think that I'd agree to an outrageous demand like this? Blackmail? It was hardly a secret that we were carrying on while you worked for me."

"Maybe, but people don't know how you and your brother treated the Kahn children, do they?"

"You have the nerve to bring that up, when it was you who brought them here. Knowing that I couldn't stand kids!"

"Only because you couldn't cope with all the extra work on your own. It would have been fine if your brother hadn't shown up. How many years is he serving this time, by the way?"

"Ten, but it was all a misunderstanding."

"I'll just bet it was."

"Anyway, that's not the issue. Christophe would never say anything and how else could you prove that the brats were ever here?"

"It shouldn't be too difficult to convince people. Do you remember that day when Fleur came to ask for your help and you turned her away? She saw Christophe and thought she heard a child crying. Valentin and his sister were told about it and they won't have forgotten."

Despite herself, Jacqueline chuckled. "Yes, I do remember. Alphonse had wet his pants, so I put a bunch of stinging nettles inside them to remind him not to do it again. His mother was far too soft with him. With all of them."

"It was lucky for you that she wasn't ever able to visit and find out how they were being treated."

"How could she? She didn't even know where they were."

"That was her idea. She said that if she didn't know, she couldn't be made to tell. She was just grateful to me for placing them with a kind family and never found out otherwise. Poor Rachel! She looked after the old man on his deathbed and followed him to the grave three weeks later, half starved and worn out with all the moving around. At least she had the consolation of thinking that her children were being well fed and cared for. She'd have killed you with her bare hands if she'd seen the scraps they had to live on. They always looked hungry when I saw them."

"They were spoilt! Aimée especially. Didn't like this and didn't like that. She started bringing her food back up again, but I soon put a stop to that little habit."

"By slapping her and saying that you'd make her eat it if she did it again. You told me. Then Alphonse started to bawl as well and his brother just stood there. Mathieu didn't dare to say anything in case you threw them all out."

The trip down memory lane was starting to amuse Jacqueline and she added, "Yes, and then Aimée complained about having to share a bed in the attic with them. Rachel had told her that a girl needed privacy."

"So that's why you made her live in the barn with the animals you were fattening?"

"Of course. And that's another thing. The little madam was always trying to tell me my business. Do you remember when she said that it was cruel to keep the rabbits cramped up in those little cages you made for me?"

"I do. She was always trying to make pets of them until I fished one out and killed it in front of her. You told her to skin it and said that we'd skin Alphonse instead if she didn't."

"She hated plucking poultry too, but she had to get used to that as well."

"You certainly got some work out of them. If I'd been in their shoes, I'd have run away."

"The younger ones couldn't and Mathieu wouldn't leave them. Anyway, he wouldn't have known where to go."

"Well, that took care of itself when you had them all arrested."

Jacqueline's smile faded. "Only after Mathieu attacked Christophe with a spade."

"Because he found him up to his old tricks with his little sister?"

"No, of course not. It was nothing like that."

"Do you really expect me to believe that? What else would have given the lad the courage to go for someone twice his size? And then Christophe took the spade from him and battered him with it. You gave Clavié a cock and bull story about your brother having to defend himself when he found the children hiding in your barn, knowing full well that he'd hand them straight over to the Germans. How do you think that would go down in the village, especially after what your brother did to Thérèse later on?"

Chapter 3

"So, Daisy," concluded Valentin, "you know it all now. Saint-André-la-Forêt dances to Baltzinger's tune and he only set up the *chantier* as a convenient cover for his other activities. It never had any official status or sanction, you know."

"What about the famous French bureaucracy that we learned about in school?"

"It would have come down on him without a doubt if he'd placed his advertisements in French newspapers, but he was too clever for that."

"The application forms we got certainly looked the part."

"That's because he based them on genuine ones issued by the French Youth Hostelling Federation and all correspondence went through an office in Paris that he'd rented using a false name. I've got to hand it to him that having you foreign kids here as a smoke screen was a brilliant idea."

"A smoke screen for kidnapping girls?"

"No. That's just a sideline of Raoul's. It's more of a game to him really, albeit a profitable one, and he's very selective. Kate was the only one to fit the bill this summer."

"Is that so? How about the Swedish girl the others told us about? Lena, wasn't it?"

"Lena? No, she's safely back home. Oh, the story he told everyone about her brother wasn't true. The fact is that she was so upset when Raoul suddenly lost interest in her that she insisted on leaving straight away."

"And why did he lose interest, or should I guess?"

"If you like."

"Not pure enough for him?"

"No. When he got to the big seduction scene, she was just as keen as she thought he was and could even teach him a thing or two. He went through with it for appearance's sake and then told her the following morning that it was all over."

"And the German twins?"

"He never got close enough to either of them to find out, but I doubt if he'd have risked it with their big brother around."

"So what really *is* going on?"

"Well, Baltzinger doesn't flaunt his wealth around here, but you should see the car he keeps in Paris and his big house in Neuilly! That old boneshaker of a van is just part of the image that he likes to portray. He's one of the best middlemen of the *milieu* and he'll deal in anything that can make him a profit. Can you imagine a better place than this? His dogs guard a lot of the stuff, stored behind genuine supplies for the *chantier*, and the more sensitive items are kept down here. Only he has the keys to the gate and knows the full layout and extent of the tunnels beyond. No one else, not even Raoul, goes any further in than this."

Daisy shuddered at the memory of Raoul's hard face and intrusive fingers. "I still can't understand how he could treat Kate like that. She loved him so much and trusted him too. Doesn't he have any conscience at all?"

"Conscience? He'd pimp his own mother if the price was right."

"But he didn't have Kate locked up down here, did he? He wasn't anywhere around when she set off for Paris."

"No. He set the trap and then flew off to Marseilles to fix up his alibi."

"What do you mean? What trap?"

"Do you know why Kate decided to go to Paris that morning?"

"Only that she'd got something very private to do."

"And that came out of the blue?"

"Not exactly. There was an envelope waiting for her at breakfast, but she wouldn't tell me what was in it."

"I thought so. It's not the first time that he's pulled that trick. She'll have found a loving message telling her to go to the lingerie boutique owned by Marie-Jacques."

"Why?"

"To choose her birthday present. Some very special items for Raoul's eyes only, or so she'd think."

"No wonder she wouldn't tell me." A vision of Kate happily thumbing through racks of flimsy garments in anticipation of wearing them for the man she loved brought tears to Daisy's eyes.

"She'd have been invited to try them on, of course, and been shown into the changing room. Another member of the gang would have been waiting in there with chloroform. They wouldn't risk marking her. By the time Raoul returned, she'd already be on the other side of the Mediterranean with the client who'd ordered her."

"Ordered her? How?"

"Through Jeannot and Kadda, his friends. He agrees a price with them and they pass on the details and photographs."

"Photographs?" Daisy was horrified to have her worst suspicions about Raoul confirmed.

"Oh yes. I'm afraid so. Raoul can charm any girl out of her clothes. As I've already told you, Baltzinger was much the same when he was young."

"And yet they're both really more interested in men? Even each other? I just can't get my head round that."

"You've led a sheltered life, Daisy. It suits them to be discreet around here, but what they get up to in Paris, together or separately, is a very different matter."

"Is that where that awful man came from who tried it on with Geoff and Danny?"

"In a way. He was one of Baltzinger's clients in the old days. He's very rich, which is probably why they're still good friends. His taste is for the youngest boys he can lay his hands on and I make sure that Victor isn't anywhere near during his visits."

It took Daisy a while to absorb all that information, but something else was preying on her mind. "Valentin, now that I know what evil men they are, I'm even more worried about Ronnie. That story we were told about Raoul dropping her off near the British Consulate wasn't true, was it?"

He thought about it for a moment and then said, "I honestly don't know what they did with Ronnie, but I doubt if she ever reached Paris. To be truthful, she was always so nasty to me that I never asked. You're different, Daisy. I'm very fond of you and so sorry that you've been caught up in all this. If Doug hadn't given you away..."

"Well, he did. He's a nasty piece of work just like the others and I suppose that's why he's on the pay roll now. He'll fit right in."

"You're not wrong there. He's been on the run for a couple of years, including some time sleeping rough in Pigalle. He says that nothing Baltzinger puts him through can be worse than the 'beatings and bug-gery' of an English Borstal. He's already had one beating here that I know of and I'm not sure about the other, but he's still determined never to go back."

It sounded like 'out of the frying pan into the fire' to Daisy, but she was more interested in learning why Valentin was unable to extricate himself from a situation he obviously loathed. Taking his hand in hers, she told him so.

He sighed and said, "I have no choice, Daisy. I thought you under-stood that."

"No. I don't. Everyone would blame him, not you. In any case, homosexuality isn't illegal in France, is it? Even in England, there's talk of changing the law."

"No. That's not why." His voice tailed off, but Daisy had to know.

"Is it the other thing he said? 'Do you still think about *her* and what you did?' What did he mean? Did you do something to your sister?"

"No. Of course not."

"To Fleur then?" Valentin went scarlet and Daisy knew that she'd hit the nail on the head. "What did you do? Were you the one who lured

Jean-Claude's father up to the château and had him taken away?"

Valentin was shocked at the very idea. "No! How could I have arranged anything like that, even though I admit that I wasn't sorry to see the back of Alain."

"Then it must have been something to do with the locket. Did Angèle get it from you?"

His eyes filled with tears. "Yes. I tried to mend the chain myself, but my nails were blunt and split and I couldn't do it with the tools I had. The only person I could think of who would still have fine tweezers was Angèle, who was forever messing around with her eyebrows. She refused to lend them to me, even when I offered to pay her, but said that she'd fix it for me herself as soon as she had time. If only I'd given her the chain on its own and not the whole thing! I didn't even know that the locket could be opened, let alone that Alain had put a tiny note inside to make up for the fact that engraving would have to wait."

"What did it say?"

"It said 'To my little English flower'. Just five words, but they were enough to get her killed."

"Then it was his fault as much as yours?"

"Yes, and he's been torturing himself with it ever since. But he doesn't know about the broken chain and how the Germans got hold of the locket. Any guilt Angèle might have felt has been well and truly painted over, but I've scarcely been able to look him in the eye since it happened."

He was racked with grief and Daisy, putting aside her own fears, found herself comforting him. The hot sting of his tears had soaked the front of her T-shirt by the time he fell asleep in her arms, exhausted by weeping and the effort of telling his long story.

Chapter 4

Despite everything, Daisy dozed off too. A little daylight was penetrating the cracks in the boarding over the window when she woke up and gently disentangled herself. The sleep had done her good and a plan that just might succeed had formed in her mind. Knocking Valentin out with the big metal tray on which he'd brought the food was part of it, but he looked so defenceless as he slept that she couldn't bring herself to do it. He'd been as considerate as their situation allowed, even building a makeshift screen with some of the packing cases to spare her embarrassment when either of them needed to use the bucket.

He didn't stir when she manoeuvred herself into a standing position on the bed. Even with the still damp T-shirt wrapped around her hand, unscrewing the hot light bulb was painful, but she gritted her teeth and got on with it. The next task was to use the T-shirt to muffle the sound as she swung the bulb onto the concrete floor. One of the shards was big enough to saw through the cord that held her prisoner and she was past caring about the pain when the glass cut into her burnt fingers.

Valentin made a noise like a rusty hinge, grunted and turned over as she tiptoed to the door. With herself tied to the iron ring and her guard too frightened to leave, Baltzinger hadn't bothered to turn the key on them. Even better, the big gate was also unlocked. Daisy couldn't believe her luck until she crept past the other dormitories and realised why. The bedsteads, all stripped of their mattresses, were piled up against the walls. The season was over and everyone had gone. Everyone, that was, except the owners of the footsteps she could hear in the distance. Their approach could bode nothing but ill for her and there was nowhere safe to hide.

In desperation, Daisy ran back the way she'd come and into the darkness beyond. Heart pounding, she had a flashback to a mining museum visit, when their guide had led the group underground and turned off all the lights. The inky blackness had terrified her then, although she knew that her classmates were all around her and she was quite safe. All she could do now was grope her way along the stone walls, guessing which way to go each time she came to a junction and hoping against hope to stumble across one of the secret entrances she'd heard about. The footsteps were getting nearer and she quickened her pace until something warm brushed past her ankle and squeaked. Rats! Oh God! Kicking off her sandals, Daisy held out her arms in front of her and ran, not caring how much the rough surface punished her feet.

Her pursuers had heavy shoes and torches and were rapidly gaining on her. A few more yards and her outstretched hands banged into a stone wall. It was a dead end and maybe the end for her too. Cut and bruised, she wouldn't be any good to the evil men hunting her and she knew too much about them to expect mercy. Not daring to turn round, she sank to the ground, arms covering her head and shaking with fear as the light panned over the wall.

"*Merde!*" Big hands seized hers and she was pulled into the safe harbour of Jean-Claude's embrace. His father was close behind, holding Valentin by the scruff of the neck.

"How did you know where I was?" sobbed Daisy, tears of relief streaming down her cheeks. Monsieur Binard, who only needed one hand to keep a grip on his prisoner, handed her a large handkerchief.

"I didn't until half an hour ago," said Jean-Claude. "You were supposed to be on your way back to England."

"What?"

"I was told when I came to pick you up for dinner that the others had gone to Fontainebleau, but you'd been taken ill and had to go to hospital. *He* couldn't tell me *which* hospital." Jean-Claude turned round to glare at Valentin, who looked terrified. "I was really worried, so I waited for the coach to come back. Only Doug said that he'd seen an ambulance, but he didn't know where you'd been taken either. I had to hang around for ages until Raoul showed up."

"What did he tell you?"

"The same thing. Only Baltzinger knew and he'd gone to Paris. Raoul did say, though, that your mother had been informed and would be flying over to take you home as soon as you were discharged. He wouldn't give me your address and said that I'd just have to wait for you to get in touch later on, if you wanted to. You can imagine how disappointed I was not to see you before you left France.

Anyway, I didn't make much of it at the time but, just as I was getting back onto my bike, I noticed Valentin heading for the dormitories with a big tray. Everything started to fall into place this morning, when I saw Doug in the village and asked him if there'd been any news from the hospital. He looked very shifty and said, 'Oh, she'll be all right. It turned out that it was only a grumbling appendix.' He wanted to gloat about his new job, but I'd heard enough."

"Because you knew..."

"That you'd already had your appendix taken out. Yes, of course. I remembered Valentin and his tray and wondered if they had you hidden somewhere. I knew it was possible, but I didn't know why. It even crossed my mind that you might have come down with food poisoning from Valentin's cooking and they were trying to cover it up."

"It was much worse than that," said Daisy in a shaky voice. "You can't imagine."

"Maybe not, but all my instincts told me not to blunder straight in to look for you. The stories you'd told me about this place and others that I've heard made me think that I might need back up. I waited for Doug to disappear and then went straight back to the garage for Papa."

"It was just like the old days," said his father, patting the big spanner sticking out of the pocket of his overalls. "I only wish that I still had a gun. Come on! We'll soon get you out of here and then you can tell us exactly what's been going on. Oh, put your T-shirt on first. I've shaken all the glass out of it and you can't walk out of here half naked."

Jean-Claude held his torch for Daisy as she reached out to take it and part of the beam fell onto a little bundle tucked into a niche in the wall.

"What's that?" he exclaimed, peering at it. "Oh God, Daisy, don't look! One of the girls from the village must have hidden it years ago."

A howl of anguish echoed round the walls as Valentin saw what the torchlight had revealed. Wrenching himself from Alain's grasp, he lunged forward to pick it up and cradle it in his arms. The tiny skeleton was partially wrapped in the remains of a woollen blanket, its pale and dark blue stripes instantly recognisable to the man who'd watched his sister knit it. Rage pushed all fear out of his mind and he could only think of revenge.

Defiant and grim, he said, "That monster! I'll pay him back if it's the last thing I ever do. Come on, you two, let's get Daisy away. They'll be coming for her soon."

"Who will? If it's just Baltzinger, Raoul and maybe Doug..."

"It isn't just them, Alain. Some thugs from Paris will be with them and they're always armed. They've paid good money for Daisy."

"What? For heaven's sake, Valentin, I know that Baltzinger's a nasty customer, but even he wouldn't get involved in white slavery. This is the 20th century, for heaven's sake!"

"You've got to believe me! You've no idea what he's capable of."

"Yes, but..."

"For God's sake, man, he's the one who banged you over the head and had you deported."

"What?"

"And I think he may have murdered your wife too. Berthe loved you both far too much to take her own life. She must have walked in on something she wasn't supposed to see."

Jean-Claude's eyes were wide with horror. "*Maman?* But you told me that she died in an accident."

His father was stunned too. "Do you mean that I've lived all these years thinking that I'd driven her to suicide?"

"Yes, but you need to pull yourself together now and decide what to do. Either you and Jean-Claude take Daisy with you and disappear or we can work together to set a trap for them."

"No, don't," whispered Daisy. "You can't trust him. He was far too frightened to let me escape and he's never dared to help anyone else from under Baltzinger's thumb. How can we be sure that he's really changed sides?"

"Because of my poor little nephew here," said Valentin quietly. His grief seemed to have given him a new dignity. "Now that I've seen what Baltzinger did with Sébastien, I don't care any more what happens to me."

"Sébastien? Your sister's baby? It can't be. You told me that he was adopted during the war."

"That's what Baltzinger told us, but I'd know that blanket anywhere."

"Hold on a minute," said Alain. "Do you mean that the accusation about Thérèse and Sergeant Stracke was true all the time? I'd never have believed that of her. Poor Luc!"

"No. Stracke wasn't the father. He always treated her with the utmost respect."

"Then who was?"

"It's impossible to say, because my poor sister was gang raped by some more soldiers after he'd left. The one thing I can tell you for certain is that Baltzinger either killed her little boy or just left him here to die. No one else could have done it. You can ask her later, if you don't believe me. Now are you going to help me or not?" Father and son looked at Daisy.

"I think we have to," she said slowly. "Someone has to stop him. Go and get help. If he gets back first, I'll stall him for as long as I can."

The Binards hurried off and Daisy followed Valentin back to her former place of captivity. Once he'd kicked the broken glass into a corner and re-attached the cord, she lay down on the bed and Valentin threw a blanket over her to hide the injuries to her hands and feet. Then he fetched a light bulb from one of the other dormitories to replace the one she'd broken and closed the door.

It seemed an eternity before they heard quiet footsteps and muffled voices. Then all was silent again until the arrival of the men that Daisy had most dreaded seeing.

"Any problems?"

"No problems, *patron*."

"Good. I didn't think she'd dare to try anything. Well, you can go now. I expect you need some sleep after your first ever night with a girl." Valentin slipped away without a backward glance and the gale of laughter continued as the gang surrounded the bed. Even if she hadn't seen them before, Daisy would have recognised Jeannot and Kadda from Kate's description. Doug's face was taut with excitement and anticipation. Whatever his own past sufferings had been, it was very clear that he was relishing hers.

"Here you are, my friends!" With a flourish, Raoul whipped away the blanket. "What the hell?"

As they all stared down at Daisy, a group of men surged through the door and surrounded them. Jeannot was shot down as he reached for his gun. The sound echoed round the stone chamber and Baltzinger looked at the policeman in disbelief.

"Clavié? You won't point your gun at me if you know what's good for you."

"Shut your mouth and put your hands up. All of you! Valentin, untie that poor girl and bring the cord with you. We're going to need it. Now move!"

"Where do you think you're taking us?" snarled Raoul.

"You'll see." It wasn't a long walk.

Leaving Jeannot where he lay, the rest of the gang was herded into the girls' dormitory, which was crowded with silent people. Hunting rifles, knives and even a pitchfork shone in the afternoon sunlight coming in through the little window. Madame Devane had an axe in her hand and Nina was clutching a claw hammer.

The table had been set at right angles to the door, and behind it sat Massot in his mayoral sash. He was flanked by the doctor and the priest. In front of them on the table was a small box, closed but with a wisp of blue protruding from one corner.

The Mayor spoke first. "Clavié, have those three tied up over there, if you please." Raoul, Doug and Kadda were seized and fastened to the bars on the window, leaving only one man to stand before the tribunal.

Ignoring his cynical sneer, Massot said, "Bertrand Baltzinger, you stand accused today of a more terrible crime than any of us could have ever have imagined. It has brought our whole community together and no longer will you crack your whip over us like the evil ringmaster you've become."

Unruffled, Baltzinger retorted, "Is that right? Might I ask what you plan to do with me, you and your newly dutiful policeman? You wouldn't dare to put me in front of a proper court with all the stories I could tell. I'd take you down with me and well you know it. The name of every family represented here would be blackened. They're all guilty of something, as you well know. Theft, black marketeering, betrayal, collaboration... They'd have to open a new wing for you all in Fresnes."

"Some of us might go to prison, it's true, but we won't be following you to the guillotine."

"Is that what you think? Look around you! You might not have killed the little Kahns with your own hands, Jacqueline, but you were responsible for their deaths all the same. And how about you, Geneviève? Do Judith and her children haunt you at night?"

As the two women hung their heads, Dr Simmonet intervened. "Enough of that. What have you got to say about this poor baby?" He removed the lid of the box.

At the sight of its pitiful contents, the sneer left Baltzinger's face and he looked bleak for a moment before denying that the baby had anything to do with him.

Thérèse stepped forward, her eyes red rimmed and bloodshot. "Bertrand, how can you say that?"

It didn't take him long to recover. Looking her full in the face, he asked, "Why try to pin it on me? You're the one who had a little bastard to get rid of before your poor husband came back." A ripple ran round the silent crowd and Angèle Duval straightened up.

"What did I tell you all?"

"You promised me that the nuns would take care of him," insisted Thérèse. "Then you said that he'd been adopted by a kind Catholic couple with no children of their own. And all the time my little boy, my Sébastien, was lying abandoned in the cold and dark."

Father Ferdinand raised a hand. "I can't believe," he said, "that even you, my son, would kill a baby in cold blood. What have you got to say for yourself?"

"You mean before I get on to your grubby little secret? What if I were to tell you that Thérèse was the one who brought him into the labyrinth and dumped him?"

"I wouldn't believe it. She told me just after Luc died, how grateful she had been and always would be for your help."

"And I can confirm that. She trusted you and really believed that you were her friend." Valentin was supporting his sister, who looked as though her legs might give way at any moment.

"Trying to be the big man now? Who'd believe anything you've got to say?"

"I would." Every head turned towards Daisy as she hobbled forward on her lacerated feet. "He told me all about it during those long, long hours we were left alone together. Why would he lie? He was sure that I'd never be able to pass it on to anyone who mattered."

Baltzinger was looking less confident. "I should have known that it was a mistake to leave the two of you together. Did he tell you his whole bloody life story?"

"He did and there was plenty about you in it too. Raoul as well and those other two over there. Even Doug." The older men looked defiant, but the boy's face was ashen. Maybe he wasn't as tough as he'd made out. In any event, he gave Daisy an appealing look and held up his bound hands, palms together. She shook her head. If he ended up back in Borstal, it was no more than he deserved.

Father Ferdinand tried again. "Tell us about the baby. His mother has the right to know. She's in agony over this."

"All right. I don't suppose it matters after all these years. I was going to sell him to Hildegard Köstler."

"You were going to sell my little boy to a Boche?"

"Why not? His father was a Boche too, wasn't he? Anyway, he started to cry and it was too dangerous to smuggle him into the château, so I brought him here instead."

"You left my helpless baby alone? With no one to feed him and nothing to keep him warm?"

Did Baltzinger's face express a little regret? It was hard to tell, but his tone was less defiant the next time he spoke.

"You'd just fed him and he had his blanket. I was going to bring Hildegard to collect him in the morning and then she was taking him straight back to Germany."

"And that was the night the château was destroyed?" asked Valentin.

"Yes, there was so much confusion and running up and down to do that I couldn't get back here for some time. When I did, I found him dead."

"And you didn't even bother to bury him? You just left him to rot?"

"He'd have rotted anyway. What do you think happens to bodies in coffins? At least I left him out of reach of the rats." Everyone flinched. Thérèse was beside herself with grief and the atmosphere was turning very ugly.

The Mayor raised his hand for silence. "Weren't you worried that the little one would be found?"

"No, because no one else ever went as far into the labyrinth as that, not even Paul's men or the Germans when they took over the fort. Anyway, there was nothing to connect him with me. Hildegard was dead too and we hadn't told anyone about our little deal."

Father Ferdinand spoke again. "And didn't your conscience trouble you at all? Not even when you were with his mother, who had always been so kind to you and thought you were her friend?"

He shrugged. "Not really. Thérèse was still young enough to have a dozen more babies. I didn't think it would take her long to get over that one."

What happened next took everyone by complete surprise. There was a low growl as the grieving mother bared her teeth and grabbed the axe from Madame Devane. Running straight at Baltzinger, she hacked at him before anyone could stop her. Daisy had never seen anyone killed before. However well deserved, it was butchery. He caught her eye as he went down and the last thing she saw was the glint of the blade as the axe was raised again...

Epilogue

1987

Daisy had cried herself to sleep at last in the bed that she'd shared with her husband for so long and Laura was dozing with her head on the kitchen table when the men came home. Jean-Claude shook her by the shoulder.

"Wake up! Where's Margot?" There was no time for a more considered response.

"If you mean Daisy, she's upstairs."

"Daisy? There's no Daisy here."

"Oh, you can stop pretending. She's told me the whole story. Her name is Daisy Dobson, she's English and I know that you've held her a virtual prisoner here for more than twenty years."

"It's all over, son." Alain sat down by the fire and buried his head in his hands.

"You've no idea what you've done," said Jean-Claude, his face contorted with worry. "We've protected her all this time, loved and cared for her, and now you've ruined that with your meddling. God only knows what state she's in now." He stumbled out of the kitchen, closing the door behind him.

"I didn't mean to cause any trouble," said Laura, trying not to sound too self righteous, "but you can't put the genie back into the bottle. Daisy knows who she is now and will want to go home where she belongs."

Alain raised his head and looked her in the eye. "If she really has told you the whole story, you must know that it isn't as simple as that. If it were only up to my son and me…" He would say no more until they were summoned upstairs.

Daisy was sitting up in the big bed, her hands clasped round her knees so tightly that the nails had turned white.

"She's frightened," groaned her husband. "Frightened of *me* of all people! There are things that she still doesn't know, but she won't listen. You have to make her understand that what Papa and I did was the only way to keep her safe. She might trust you, although Doug was from England too and look what *he* did to her!"

"I'll try, but only if you promise to tell us both the whole truth."

"We will."

"All right then." Laura sat down on the bed and took one of Daisy's trembling hands between hers. "I won't leave you, love," she said in English, "but I think we both need to hear what they have to say." At first she thought that Daisy was going to refuse, but then the grip on her own hand tightened and she nodded.

"Go on then, son," said Alain. "You start."

"Well, Margot…Daisy, you hit your head on the stone floor when you fainted that day from the horror of what you'd just witnessed. All we cared about then was getting you out of there as quickly as possible."

"With blood on your hands?" asked Laura.

"No! I swear that neither of us had anything to do with Baltzinger's death. Nobody could have stopped it, except maybe Clavié, and he'd have had to shoot Thérèse. She had the strength of a dozen women at that moment and Baltzinger didn't stand a chance."

"I believe you," said Laura and meant it. "But what happened to Daisy then?"

"She was out cold for a long time and when she came round she was in a complete panic and making no sense, so Dr Simmonet put her under heavy sedation. He's never ruled out brain damage, either from that fall or the one in the casemates when Baltzinger hit her, but he thought it more likely that she was suffering from something called hysterical amnesia."

"I've heard of that. It's a way of repressing painful memories, isn't it?"

"Yes. That's how he explained it to us. They never completely disappear but lurk like shadows in the background. My wife has experienced them mainly as nightmares. It only took that little badge you found in the forest to reawaken the rest and bring them back into focus." As he spoke, he reached for Daisy's other hand, but she snatched it away from him and shrank back into her pillows.

As his son's eyes filled with tears, Alain turned helplessly to Laura. "You mustn't judge us too harshly. We thought that what we did was for the best and she's been very happy with us."

"Until today, Papa. We've always claimed to know nothing about her past, so how can we convince her to trust us now? It may be too late after we've lied to her all these years." His handsome face the picture of despair, he turned to Laura in mute appeal.

"Why did you do it?" she asked. "You knew her full name and that she came from Leeds. Surely the British police could have found her mother."

"We couldn't go to the police. Too many other people were involved and her safety depended on our silence."

"But the story about the killings that day must have got out. Even if the villagers were prepared to hush it up, Baltzinger's friends would have talked." The two men looked at each other and shook their heads.

"It was like this," said Alain. "After we'd carried Daisy out of there and Dr Simmonet confirmed that Baltzinger was dead, Raoul, Doug and Kadda were taken into the boys' dormitory under guard and there was a huge argument about what to do with them. There were only three choices, each with considerable drawbacks. The first was to hand them over to Clavié's superiors, in which case Saint-André-la-Forêt would be featured on the front page of every newspaper in the country and all its secrets exposed. The second was to set them free, knowing full well that they'd be back for revenge. The third? Well, I'm sure you can guess. Feelings were running very high and that's the way that the vote went in the end."

"Father Ferdinand and Dr Simmonet spoke against what was going to happen," said Jean-Claude, "but the Mayor said that the community would never live down the disgrace. Clavié said the same. He was just as worried about his own position, of course, and damaging his son's prospects of following in his footsteps. He might have got away with shooting Jeannot, but he'd stood by and watched Thérèse hack Baltzinger to death."

"Just as he stood by while she was attacked by Christophe after the Liberation."

"Yes."

"So what did happen in the end?"

"They were brought in one by one and shot through the back of the head with Jeannot's gun."

"Who did the shooting?"

"No one would ever say, only that it was three different people after they drew lots. It was done in cold blood, you see, to silence them. There would have been a queue to shoot Baltzinger, but the other three hadn't directly harmed any of those present, so it was quite different. Raoul and the other man just looked resigned when they realised what was going to happen to them and never said a word. I suppose they'd have done the same thing if the situation had been reversed."

"And Doug?"

"Didn't believe until the very last minute that he was going to die and then he cried. It was all very quick. Father Ferdinand said a few words over the bodies, including that of Jeannot, and then everyone left. Later on, some of the men who'd learnt about explosives during the war set charges and blew up the whole section. To be on the safe side, they bricked up all the entrances to the labyrinth, removed every trace of the *chantier* from the clearing and shot the dogs."

"Poor things! I suppose that they were too savage for anyone to take them on, even you two."

"Yes, I'm afraid so. They're buried in the forest."

"But what happened to the poor dead baby?"

"He was given a decent but very private funeral."

"And Valentin?"

"It was decided that he was a victim too, more to be pitied than blamed. Then the village closed in on itself. Baltzinger had gone, but there was always the danger of the whole thing being raked up again."

"Did no one ever come to make enquiries about the people who'd disappeared?"

"Yes, but everyone stuck together to deny that the *chantier* had ever existed. When pressed, they said that the name of the village must have been picked at random to cover up some kind of fraudulent activity that had nothing to do with them. I don't suppose the hard cases who came down from Paris were convinced, but they didn't know whom to threaten and couldn't tell the *gendarmerie* or the *police nationale* what they knew without implicating themselves. Everyone gave up in the end."

"But Ronnie's parents actually saw the place in operation."

"And they didn't live to tell the tale, I'm afraid. Their vehicle was run off the road halfway between here and Le Havre."

"Good God! Please tell me that you had nothing to do with *that* accident."

"Of course not. Raoul must have contacted some of his associates. It would have been easy enough to arrange. The other parents and Ronnie's grandmother were going to break the sad news when they met the girls at the railway station in Leeds and you can imagine the reaction when none of them got off the train."

"My mother must have come looking for me," said a small voice from the bed.

"Yes, *ma chérie*, of course she did." Jean-Claude was too choked with emotion to continue and looked helplessly at his father.

"I'm afraid she passed away, Daisy, later that same summer. Dr Simmonet was able to find out for us through his medical contacts in England. If that hadn't happened, we'd have come up with some way to let her know that you were safe."

Daisy took the news more calmly than Laura could ever have

imagined. "She missed Dad so much and always believed that they'd be together in heaven one day. If Mum was right, and she generally was, they'll both have watched over me all these years." She looked so certain of it, that Alain found the strength to continue.

"Well, your mother came over with Kate's parents and they stopped here for petrol. Telephone enquiries to the English and French police and even Interpol had got them nowhere and they were desperate. Your poor mother looked so fragile, Daisy, barely able to stand on her own two feet when she got out of the car, but she insisted on showing us the card she'd received from you with the village postmark on it. The Fairbairns hadn't had anything from Kate."

"But they must have done. I remember her writing cards and leaving them in the box in the office to be posted. Everyone did that, because the stamps were free."

"Given to Baltzinger by Jean-Claude's godmother?" asked Laura.

Alain nodded. "I suppose the cards were all read, posted from another area if they passed his scrutiny or simply destroyed. The youngsters who sent them would just have blamed the postal system for their failure to arrive."

"I suppose that could be true," agreed Daisy. "Kate would almost certainly have mentioned Raoul. Come to think of it, Mr and Mrs Tanner complained that Ronnie hadn't bothered to send a card to her grandmother, but perhaps she tried after all. She'd have had plenty to say and none of it complimentary."

Laura was puzzled. "And yet Mrs Dobson got a card from here."

"Yes," replied Alain, "but only because Daisy posted it herself in the village. She'd written that the living conditions were rather a disappointment, but she didn't care because she'd met someone very special. Jean-Claude nearly cracked when her mother asked if we had any idea who that might be, but he knew that we were being watched. Daisy was the weakest link in the chain, you see, and there was a very real danger that she might suffer the same fate as Doug. It was only because Valentin pleaded for her that his sister and the others grudgingly agreed to give her a chance."

"And so you imprisoned her in your home and forced your son to marry her?"

"No!" Jean-Claude was knuckling the tears away from his eyes. "That's not at all how it was. Papa, tell them what you said to me the night before the wedding."

Alain looked embarrassed. "Oh, I can't really remember."

"Well I can. You took me out into the garden and said, 'You're very young, son, and you must be absolutely sure that this girl is the one for you. If you have any doubts at all, tell me now and we'll find another way.' But I didn't have any doubts, did I, and I still love Daisy as much as I did then. Even more, probably. My only regret is that I've failed to give her the children we both so desperately wanted."

"Oh, my darling!" Their tears mingled as his wife reached out and clasped him to her. It was clear that they needed a private moment.

Alain's face was the picture of guilt as he stood with Laura on the landing. "Maybe it isn't too late," he whispered. "Jean-Pierre and I both thought it was for the best. The pills he's supplied for Daisy all these years haven't just been to make her periods less painful, you see. He got them from a colleague in England until they were made available here."

Laura was appalled. "How could you both play God with their marriage and risk Daisy's health?"

"She's been fine. The good doctor has monitored her very carefully and the pills don't seem to have done her any harm. She isn't quite forty yet and could still become pregnant if he took her off them now. It would seem like a miracle to her and Jean-Claude."

"Well, I can't allow you to manipulate her like that, whatever you do to your own son." Bursting back into the couple's room, Laura marched straight over to the bed and said, "Get up, Daisy! It's best that you come with me right now. There'll be things to sort out, but I'll soon have you back in Yorkshire where you belong."

The response shook her to the core. "Whatever gives you the right to decide?" Green eyes were glaring at her over Jean-Claude's broad shoulder. "It isn't the best for me and it certainly isn't what I want. My own mother's at peace, but do you think that Kate's or Ronnie's relatives would take any comfort after all these years from knowing what happened to them? And look at the harm it would do to these dear men who've been my world since I was seventeen? No. Daisy Dobson has gone for good. I'm Margot Binard, Jean-Claude's dotty wife with no memory of her past, and that's the way I'm going to stay. From choice, though. I'm no longer the weak link in the chain."

There was an ominous silence as three unsmiling faces studied Laura in a way that made her even more nervous than on her first night in the village.

"And I suppose *I* am?" she said at last.

"Yes," replied Alain simply.

"So where do we go from here? Would you take my word if I promised never to tell anyone about all this? It wouldn't bring back the dead and I'm certainly in no hurry to join them. Look, most of the village's secrets are so old and some so trivial compared to what has happened in other places that outsiders wouldn't care about them now anyway. There was widespread collaboration in all the occupied countries, even in our own Channel Islands, and the black market flourished everywhere too, but the world has moved on."

"Not for us and certainly not for Thérèse." Who still has an axe to grind, thought Laura, and in more ways than one. Her brain was working overtime. Where did Charlot go after he heard Daisy calling out to her in English? Evidently not in search of his uncle and cousin, so where was he? Rounding up a lynch mob? No, that was too far fetched, although he might well be regaling Thérèse with the information that Daisy had recovered her memory? If that were the case, though, surely something would have happened by now.

"Charlot was here earlier," she said cautiously. "You'd asked him to pick up my car. Then he saw me with Daisy and left in rather a hurry."

"I'm not surprised," said Jean-Claude, "He's been driving over to see a woman in Vaucresson every afternoon and I expect he wanted to make the most of the time before her poor husband came home."

How typical of Charlot that was, thought Laura. So full of his own grubby plans that the scene he'd witnessed earlier hadn't really registered. Well, that was something at least.

Daisy was smiling to herself as though she'd come to a decision. Pushing her husband aside and swinging her legs over the edge of the bed, she said in a much kinder voice, "Let's go downstairs and have a nice cup of tea while we discuss what's to be done."

Tea? The situation was becoming more surreal by the moment, but a lot of the tension went out of the atmosphere when they sat down round the kitchen table. Laura almost felt like part of the family as Daisy presided over the tea pot, Jean-Claude helped her to a piece of Victoria sponge and Alain passed the milk. All that was missing was the next generation. Any baby born to that household would be showered with love, but how would Daisy cope with the strains imposed by pregnancy and childbirth? They might well disturb her fragile equilibrium and bring back the shadows. What she needed was the support of an older woman in whom she could continue to confide, and who better than Laura herself? Just as there was something about her that Daisy had instinctively trusted, there was something about Daisy that brought out all childless Laura's protective instincts.

As she pondered, Alain cleared his throat and said, "Are you still determined to leave us today, Madame?"

"And what if I am? Should I expect a bullet through the head as I drive out of the village?" The question was a serious one and he treated it as such, yet his face softened a little.

"Certainly not from us and it doesn't look as though anyone else is aware of how much you've discovered. You've offered us your word not to cause any trouble and I believe you."

"So do I," said Jean-Claude, offering her a large and rather sticky hand to seal the bargain.

"But I'd much rather you didn't rush off." Alain was gazing at her in a speculative way that worried Laura. Was he working up to offering his own hand in a different way? Considering another loveless marriage as extra insurance? Laura's pride would never allow such a thing, even if she didn't jib at the idea of giving Thérèse another reason to kill her or, God forbid, becoming Charlot's aunt.

"Well," she said cautiously, "I was thinking of heading south to see what Matisse found so breathtaking about the coastline of the Côte d'Azur."

"But you'll keep in touch," pleaded Daisy, "and come back to see us before you return to England?"

"I promise."

"Before you go, I do have a favour to ask," said Alain. Laura braced herself. "Would you do me the honour..."

"Yes?"

"Of allowing me to take your Spitfire for a spin? I promise that I'll wear my new glasses."

As she drove past the barred sign at the outer limit of the village, Laura smiled to herself. She'd said a very fond farewell to Valentin when she picked up her belongings from the café and could picture a worse future for herself than selling up and moving to France. If she did, though, it would be on her own terms and to be with a man of her choosing.

THE END

About The Author

Born in Leeds, Maggie Cobbett ventured across the Pennines to study at the University of Manchester and then spent more years than she cares to remember teaching French, German and EFL in the UK and abroad. Now settled with her family and two ex-feral cats on the edge of the Yorkshire Dales, Maggie takes inspiration for her writing from her surroundings, travels, family history and her work as a television background artist.

Visit Maggie online at http://www.maggiecobbett.co.uk

OTHER BOOKS BY
MAGGIE COBBETT

ANYONE FOR MURDER?
A selection of murder mysteries to keep you
guessing until the very end

HAD WE BUT WORLD ENOUGH
Life in a new country sounds exciting, but will these
hopeful characters end up with more, or much less
than they bargained for?

SWINGS AND ROUNDABOUTS
In fiction, as in life, things rarely turn out
as we expect - for characters or readers

EASY MONEY FOR WRITERS AND
WANNABES
Your handy guide to writing fillers for
magazines and newspapers

ALL AVAILABLE IN PRINT
AND KINDLE EDITIONS

WWW.MAGGIECOBBETT.CO.UK

12935828R00226

Printed in Great Britain
by Amazon.co.uk, Ltd.,
Marston Gate.